D A R K

STORIES OF MADNESS, MURDER
AND THE SUPERNATURAL

DARK

STORIES OF MADNESS, MURDER AND THE SUPERNATURAL

EDITED BY CLINT WILLIS

Thunder's Mouth Press and
Balliett & Fitzgerald Inc.

New York

Adrenaline ™ and the Adrenaline™ logo are trademarks of
Balliett & Fitzgerald Inc. New York, NY.

An Adrenaline Book™

Published by
Thunder's Mouth Press
841 Broadway, 4th Floor
New York, NY 10003

and

Balliett & Fitzgerald Inc.
66 West Broadway, Suite 602
New York, NY 10007

Distributed by Publishers Group West

Book design: Sue Canavan

frontispiece photo: ©Annette Fournet/Corbis

Manufactured in the United States of America

ISBN: 1-56025-277-4

Library of Congress Cataloging-in-Publication Data

Dark : stories of madness, murder, and the supernatural / edited by
Clint Willis.
    p.cm.
"An adrenaline book"—T.p. verso.
Includes bibliograpical references.
ISBN 1-56025-277-4
1. Horror tales, American 2. Horror tales, English. 3. Supernatural—
Fiction. I. Willis Clint.

PS648.H6D332000
813'.0873808—dc21   00-044294

For Judy, because she is fearless.

c o n t e n t s

viii   **photographs**

ix   **introduction**

1   *Smee*
by A. M. Burrage

15   from *Asylum*
by Patrick McGrath

23   *They*
by Rudyard Kipling

47   from *The Haunting of Hill House*
by Shirley Jackson

69   from *The Wasp Factory*
by Iain Banks

79   *Home Burial*
by Robert Frost

85   *Seaton's Aunt*
by Walter de la Mare

119   *The Monkey's Paw*
by W. W. Jacobs

133   from *Tell My Horse*
by Zora Neale Hurston

151   *A Distant Episode*
by Paul Bowles

167   from *My Idea of Fun*
by Will Self

179   *The Cicerones*
by Robert Aickman

193   from *Communion: A True Story*
by Whitley Strieber

207   *The Yellow Wallpaper*
by Charlotte Perkins Gilman

227   from *The Shining*
by Stephen King

239   *The Cask of Amontillado*
by Edgar Allan Poe

249   *A Good Man Is Hard to Find*
by Flannery O'Connor

267   *The Beckoning Fair One*
by Oliver Onions

337   *They*
by Blue Balliett

345   *The Crown Derby Plate*
by Marjorie Bowen

359   *The Cafeteria*
by Isaac Bashevis Singer

377   **acknowledgments**

380   **bibliography**

p h o t o g r a p h s

1 Victorian Gothic English mansion
© Clay Perry/Corbis

15 Marsh
© Corbis

23 Hands
© Chris M. Rogers/PictureQuest

47 Haunted house
© Dan McCoy/PictureQuest

69 Boy with kite
© Richard Seagraves/Photonica

79 Family gravesite
© PUSH/Index Stock
Imagery/PictureQuest

85 Woman standing near gravestone
© Annette Fournet/Corbis

119 English cottage
© John Heseltine/Corbis

133 Voodoo ritual
© Morton Beebe, S.F./Corbis

151 Man in front of mud structure
© Earl & Nazima Kowall/Corbis

167 Abandoned warehouse
© Joe Sohm/PictureQuest

179 Cathedral
© MIT Collection/Corbis

193 Mysterious figure
© Walter Lopez/Corbis

207 Victorian-style bedroom
© Brian Harrison/Kudos; Elizabeth
Whiting & Associates/Corbis

227 Timberline lodge, Mount Hood
© Corbis

239 Catacombs
© Adam Woolfitt/PictureQuest

249 Misty country road
© Peter Essick/PictureQuest

267 Slum housing
© Hulton-Deutsch Collection/Corbis

337 New England house
© Philippa Lewis; Edifice/Corbis

345 Porcelain and utensils
© Picture Quest

359 Lone woman on New York's
Upper West Side
© Photofest/Icon Archives

introduction

As a young law student more than 50 years ago, my father rented a room in a house in New Orleans. The house stood on a corner, surrounded by trees; it was very quiet, with heavy shutters that stayed closed all day to keep the heat out. The room had a private entrance from the garden, and its own little bathroom.

My father heard voices murmering in the room at night. At first he took them for the voices of the two old women who owned the house and lived upstairs. But he (and later a friend) began to hear the voices when no one else was in the house. The voices always whispered or spoke quietly, as though not to disturb someone who might be resting or sleeping.

My father came to like the voices. He found them comforting, and they continued as long as he lived in the room. Some time later, he mentioned the voices to a niece of one of the old women. The niece explained that the room where my father had lived was known in her family as the dying room, where old or sick family members generally lived during their final illness or decline.

Other ghosts seem less harmless. My wife and I once rented from well-meaning friends an ancient house on Jamestown, Rhode Island. Our friends described the house to us as rustic. It was squalid. We arrived with our two very small children to find that a swarm of bees had taken up residence in the walls, which were crusty with dust and old cobwebs. The antique furniture was neglected and abused. No one had loved or lived in this house for many years. We decided we would make the best of it. We unpacked, and went shopping for cleaning supplies. When we returned to the house, I went upstairs. My attention fixed on a hook in the ceiling of a small room—the nursery?—off the largest bedroom. That did it, somehow. Without knowing why, we packed everything and everyone back into the car and set out to try to find a hotel room late on a Friday night in August at the Rhode Island seashore.

Ghosts don't always enter into the matter. I was more frightened at an almost empty campsite in Nova Scotia, some years later, where I'd pitched a tent for myself and my younger son. Two defeated-looking young men showed up near the end of the day. They looked us over. I was immediately afraid of them; I thought from their looks that they might want to hurt us—might even enjoy it. I told myself I was a fool, but my fear grew until I was almost sick with it. Another party—a family of five—stopped briefly at the campsite and asked me for directions. They lingered, and I took the opportunity to break camp and leave with them. I drove two hours through the night to another campground—one that overlooked the ocean and was crowded.

We like to visit the dark. We crack a door and peer inside; step across a threshold, move through rooms until we stand beneath a stairwell with a sense that sooner or later we'll be caught: Someone will show up or notice us; something will find us before we can find out what lives here. Still, we poke around and wonder what's upstairs or in the basement. And sometimes there is the sense that this is where we come from, that this dark place is our original and our ultimate home. The darkness we imagine or witness is familiar to us; we know it when we see it. We despise the wicked, we want to punish them, but they are our

kin: cousins, fathers, sisters, sons. As for the supernatural, what's that?
A whispering corpse is no stranger than the moon.

So what is darkness that we fear it? When you can't see things you
are as if floating; you're as if invisible yourself. Love—which is nothing
but our seeing and being seen—is absent. This absence is confusion
and desolation. It is for me the true turn of the screw; the thing that
scares me in the stories that scare me most. It takes real writers to do it:
writers like Shirley Jackson (*The Haunting of Hill House*), Patrick
McGrath (*Asylum*), Walter de la Mare ("Seaton's Aunt") or Paul Bowles
("A Distant Episode").

Some scary stories frighten us by reminding us that no one has yet
explained anything fundamental; that things may work according to
rules that are entirely alien to our beliefs (as in A.M. Burrage's
"Smee")—or else too close to some of them for comfort (as in Robert
Aikman's "The Cicerones").

But the very scariest stories—the ones that scare me, anyway—feature
malice, supernatural or otherwise. Here is just the merest taste of it from
Jackson's novel:

> I hate her, Eleanor thought, she sickens me; she is all
> washed and clean and wearing my red sweater.

We dread anyone who (or anything that) would harm us for gain
or—worse—for the pleasure of doing it. We know that such characters
are out there. The world routinely harms us for reasons we can't fathom,
but even tragedies don't frighten us all that much until we suspect or
identify evil intention at work. An unknowable or random universe
makes us uneasy at times, but the notion of evil is worse—it terrifies
us. It terrifies me. So does coldness where I expect (sometimes unreasonably) warmth. That is why I fear sharks, say: I (foolishly) dread being
eaten alive more than I fear most of my imagined versions of my
death.

I think we fear malice and coldness because we know them. They come from the darkness that we carry, a darkness we sometimes mistake for a refuge from pain. It is instead a place without love or light. Most of the stories in this book are about things that frighten all of us, including the wicked among us. The stories are about fears that drive us into hiding; the violence and the confusion that result; what happens when we hide from the light that illuminates the world for anyone willing to step into it.

Some scary books are hard to read. A book like Bret Easton Ellis' *American Psycho* upsets people because it tries to show us a person who cannot show himself apart from his darkness, which is in a sense the same as showing nothing. Patrick Bateman's cruelty in that book is almost inconceivable to us if we love anyone at all, because then we know that even a little courage brings us into the light, in reach of goodness, and teaches us to be yet more brave, which is to say more loving, less unkind. We are rightly terrified by someone who doesn't know anything about that—in the same way that we are afraid of the damned, who have nothing to lose and whose idea of love (what they sometimes call pleasure or fun) is to force us to join them in hell.

I imagine that we all have our versions of darkness, where some of us go when we are most afraid. We go there when we want a certain kind of power because we think it will protect us. The psychopathic killer and the witch who torture and manipulate their victims; the man who hits his wife; the bully who kicks a dog; all of them are for the moment lost as surely as an unloved child; their power has no power to protect them from their shame and fear; it has no power to connect.

It is frightening to realize that innocence is no shield from such cruelty and its worst consequences. The unloved child inhabits the dark and may grow into it. The same is true of any victim shamed by someone else's power; victims get frightened and angry, and then hide.

I carry in my head an old picture of a falling-down barn in the woods; it is black as pitch inside and never visited by anyone. I stayed there when I was most afraid of giving to life what it wanted from me: my presence.

The truth is this: We may be afraid of the dark, but sometimes the light scares us more.

—*Clint Willis*

Smee

by A. M. Burrage

Alfred McLelland Burrage (1889–1956) wrote more than 100 ghost stories, including several classics of the genre. "Smee" offers many of the pleasantly familiar elements of the old-fashioned English ghost story, as well as the genuine fright that such stories usually fail to deliver. Like Jackson in the story, you may in future avoid games of hide-and-seek played in the dark.

'No,' said Jackson, with a deprecatory smile, 'I'm sorry. I don't want to upset your game. I shan't be doing that because you'll have plenty without me. But I'm not playing any games of hide-and-seek.'

It was Christmas Eve, and we were a party of fourteen with just the proper leavening of youth. We had dined well; it was the season for childish games, and we were all in the mood for playing them—all, that is, except Jackson. When somebody suggested hide-and-seek there was rapturous and almost unanimous approval. His was the one dissentient voice.

It was not like Jackson to spoil sport or refuse to do as others wanted. Somebody asked him if he were feeling seedy.

'No,' he answered, 'I feel perfectly fit, thanks. But,' he added with a smile which softened without retracting the flat refusal, 'I'm not playing hide-and-seek.'

One of us asked him why not. He hesitated for some seconds before replying.

'I sometimes go and stay at a house where a girl was killed through playing hide-and-seek in the dark. She didn't know the house very well. There was a servants' staircase with a door to it. When she was pursued she opened the door and jumped into what she must have thought was one of the bedrooms—and she broke her neck at the bottom of the stairs.'

We all looked concerned, and Mrs Fernley said:

'How awful! And you were there when it happened?'

Jackson shook his head very gravely. 'No,' he said, 'but I was there when something else happened. Something worse.'

'I shouldn't have thought anything could be worse.'

'This was,' said Jackson, and shuddered visibly. 'Or so it seemed to me.'

I think he wanted to tell the story and was angling for encouragement. A few requests which may have seemed to him to lack urgency, he affected to ignore and went off at a tangent.

'I wonder if any of you have played a game called "Smee". It's a great improvement on the ordinary game of hide-and-seek. The name derives from the ungrammatical colloquialism, "It's me." You might care to play if you're going to play a game of that sort. Let me tell you the rules.

'Every player is presented with a sheet of paper. All the sheets are blank except one, on which is written "Smee". Nobody knows who is "Smee" except "Smee" himself—or herself, as the case may be. The lights are then turned out and "Smee" slips from the room and goes off to hide, and after an interval the other players go off in search, without knowing whom they are actually in search of. One player meeting another challenges with the word "Smee" and the other player, if not the one concerned, answers "Smee".

'The real "Smee" makes no answer when challenged, and the second player remains quietly by him. Presently they will be discovered by a third player, who, having challenged and received no answer, will link up with the first two. This goes on until all the players have formed a chain, and the last to join is marked down for a forfeit. It's a good noisy, romping game, and in a big house it often takes a long

time to complete the chain. You might care to try it; and I'll pay my forfeit and smoke one of Tim's excellent cigars here by the fire until you
get tired of it.'

I remarked that it sounded a good game and asked Jackson if he had
played it himself.

'Yes,' he answered; 'I played it in the house I was telling you about.'

'And *she* was there? The girl who broke—'

'No, no,' Mrs Fernley interrupted. 'He told us he wasn't there when
it happened.'

Jackson considered. 'I don't know if she was there or not. I'm afraid
she was. I know that there were thirteen of us and there ought only to
have been twelve. And I'll swear that I didn't know her name, or I think
I should have gone clean off my head when I heard that whisper in the
dark. No, you don't catch me playing that game, or any other like it,
any more. It spoiled my nerve quite a while, and I can't afford to take
long holidays. Besides, it saves a lot of trouble and inconvenience to
own up at once to being a coward.'

Tim Vouce, the best of hosts, smiled around at us, and in that smile
there was a meaning which is sometimes vulgarly expressed by the
slow closing of an eye. 'There's a story coming,' he announced.

'There's certainly a story of sorts,' said Jackson, 'but whether it's coming or not—' He paused and shrugged his shoulders.

'Well, you're going to pay a forfeit instead of playing?'

'Please. But have a heart and let me down lightly. It's not just a sheer
cussedness on my part.'

'Payment in advance,' said Tim, 'insures honesty and promotes good
feeling. You are therefore sentenced to tell the story here and now.'

And here follows Jackson's story, unrevised by me and passed on
without comment to a wider public:

Some of you, I know, have run across the Sangstons. Christopher
Sangston and his wife, I mean. They're distant connections of mine—
at least, Violet Sangston is. About eight years ago they bought a house
between the North and South Downs on the Surrey and Sussex bor-

der, and five years ago they invited me to come and spend Christmas with them.

It was a fairly old house—I couldn't say exactly of what period—and it certainly deserved the epithet 'rambling'. It wasn't a particularly big house, but the original architect, whoever he may have been, had not concerned himself with economising in space, and at first you could get lost in it quite easily.

Well, I went down for that Christmas, assured by Violet's letter that I knew most of my fellow-guests and that the two or three who might be strangers to me were all 'lambs'. Unfortunately, I'm one of the world's workers, and I couldn't get away until Christmas Eve, although the other members of the party had assembled on the preceding day. Even then I had to cut it rather fine to be there for dinner on my first night. They were all dressing when I arrived and I had to go straight to my room and waste no time. I may even have kept dinner waiting a bit, for I was last down, and it was announced within a minute of my entering the drawing-room. There was just time to say 'hullo' to everybody I knew, to be briefly introduced to the two or three I didn't know, and then I had to give my arm to Mrs Gorman.

I mention this as the reason why I didn't catch the name of a tall, dark, handsome girl I hadn't met before. Everything was rather hurried and I am always bad at catching people's names. She looked cold and clever and rather forbidding, the sort of girl who gives the impression of knowing all about men and the more she knows of them the less she likes them. I felt that I wasn't going to hit it off with this particular 'lamb' of Violet's, but she looked interesting all the same, and I wondered who she was. I didn't ask, because I was pretty sure of hearing somebody address her by name before very long.

Unluckily, though, I was a long way off her at table, and as Mrs Gorman was at the top of her form that night I soon forgot to worry about who she might be. Mrs Gorman is one of the most amusing women I know, an outrageous but quite innocent flirt, with a very sprightly wit which isn't always unkind. She can think half a dozen moves ahead in conversation just as an expert can in a game of chess.

We were soon sparring, or, rather, I was 'covering' against the ropes, and I quite forgot to ask her in an undertone the name of the cold, proud beauty. The lady on the other side of me was a stranger, or had been until a few minutes since, and I didn't think of seeking information in that quarter.

There was a round dozen of us, including the Sangstons themselves, and we were all young or trying to be. The Sangstons themselves were the oldest members of the party and their son Reggie, in his last year at Marlborough, must have been the youngest. When there was talk of playing games after dinner it was he who suggested 'Smee'. He told us how to play it just as I've described it to you.

His father chipped in as soon as we all understood what was going to be required of us. 'If there are any games of that sort going on in the house,' he said, 'for goodness' sake be careful of the back stairs on the first-floor landing. There's a door to them and I've often meant to take it down. In the dark anybody who doesn't know the house very well might think they were walking into a room. A girl actually did break her neck on those stairs about ten years ago when the Ainsties lived here.'

I asked how it happened.

'Oh,' said Sangston, 'there was a party here one Christmas time and they were playing hide-and-seek as you propose doing. This girl was one of the hiders. She heard somebody coming, ran along the passage to get away, and opened the door of what she thought was a bedroom, evidently with the intention of hiding behind it while her pursuer went past. Unfortunately it was the door leading to the back stairs, and that staircase is as straight and almost as steep as the shaft of a pit. She was dead when they picked her up.'

We all promised for our own sakes to be careful. Mrs Gorman said that she was sure nothing could happen to her, since she was insured by three different firms, and her next-of-kin was a brother whose consistent ill-luck was a byword in the family. You see, none of us had known the unfortunate girl, and as the tragedy was ten years old there was no need to pull long faces about it.

Well, we started the game almost immediately after dinner. The men allowed themselves only five minutes before joining the ladies, and then young Reggie Sangston went round and assured himself that the lights were out all over the house except in the servants' quarters and in the drawing-room where we were assembled. We then got busy with twelve sheets of paper which he twisted into pellets and shook up between his hands before passing them round. Eleven of them were blank, and 'Smee' was written on the twelfth. The person drawing the latter was the one who had to hide. I looked and saw that mine was a blank. A moment later out went the electric lights, and in the darkness I heard somebody get up and creep to the door.

After a minute or so somebody gave a signal and we made a rush for the door. I for one hadn't the least idea which of the party was 'Smee'. For five or ten minutes we were all rushing up and down passages and in and out rooms challenging one another and answering, 'Smee?—Smee!'

After a bit the alarums and excursions died down, and I guessed that 'Smee' was found. Eventually I found a chain of people all sitting still and holding their breath on some narrow stairs leading up to a row of attics. I hastily joined it, having challenged and been answered with silence, and presently two more stragglers arrived, each racing the other to avoid being last. Sangston was one of them, indeed it was he who was marked down for a forfeit, and after a little while he remarked in an undertone, 'I think we're all here now, aren't we?'

He struck a match, looked up the shaft of the staircase, and began to count. It wasn't hard, although we just about filled the staircase, for we were sitting each a step or two above the next, and all our heads were visible.

'. . . nine, ten, eleven, twelve—*thirteen*,' he concluded, and then laughed. 'Dash it all, that's one too many!'

The match had burned out and he struck another and began to count. He got as far as twelve, and then uttered an exclamation.

'There are thirteen people here!' he exclaimed. 'I haven't counted myself yet.'

'Oh, nonsense!' I laughed. 'You probably began with yourself, and now you want to count yourself twice.'

Out came his son's electric torch, giving a brighter and steadier light and we all began to count. Of course we numbered twelve.

Sangston laughed.

'Well,' he said, 'I could have sworn I counted thirteen twice.'

From halfway up the stairs came Violet Sangston's voice with a little nervous trill in it. 'I thought there was somebody sitting two steps above me. Have you moved up, Captain Ransome?'

Ransome said that he hadn't: he also said that he thought there was somebody sitting between Violet and himself. Just for a moment there was an uncomfortable Something in the air, a little cold ripple which touched us all. For that little moment it seemed to all of us, I think, that something odd and unpleasant had happened and was liable to happen again. Then we laughed at ourselves and at one another and were comfortable once more. There *were* only twelve of us, and there *could* only have been twelve of us, and there was no argument about it. Still laughing we trooped back to the drawing-room to begin again.

This time I was 'Smee', and Violet Sangston ran me to earth while I was still looking for a hiding-place. That round didn't last long, and we were a chain of twelve within two or three minutes. Afterwards there was a short interval. Violet wanted a wrap fetched for her, and her husband went up to get it from her room. He was no sooner gone than Reggie pulled me by the sleeve. I saw that he was looking pale and sick.

'Quick!' he whispered, 'while father's out of the way. Take me into the smoke room and give me a brandy or a whisky or something.'

Outside the room I asked him what was the matter, but he didn't answer at first, and I thought it better to dose him first and question him afterward. So I mixed him a pretty dark-complexioned brandy and soda which he drank at a gulp and then began to puff as if he had been running

'I've had rather a turn,' he said to me with a sheepish grin.

'What's the matter?'

'I don't know. You were "Smee" just now, weren't you? Well, of course I didn't know who "Smee" was, and while mother and the others ran into the west wing and found you, I turned east. There's a deep

clothes cupboard in my bedroom—I'd marked it down as a good place
to hide when it was my turn, and I had an idea that "Smee" might be
there. I opened the door in the dark, felt round, and touched somebody's hand. "Smee?" I whispered, and not getting any answer I
though I had found "Smee".'

'Well, I don't know how it was, but an odd creepy feeling came over
me, I can't describe it, but I felt that something was wrong. So I turned
on my electric torch and there was nobody there. Now, I swear I
touched a hand, and I was filling up the doorway of the cupboard at
the time, so nobody could get out and past me.' He puffed again. 'What
do you make of it?' he asked.

'You imagined that you had touched a hand,' I answered, naturally
enough.

He uttered a short laugh. 'Of course I knew you were going to say
that,' he said. 'I must have imagined it, mustn't I?' He paused and swallowed. 'I mean, it couldn't have been anything else *but* imagination,
could it?'

I assured him that it couldn't, meaning what I said, and he accepted
this, but rather with the philosophy of one who knows he is right but
doesn't expect to be believed. We returned together to the drawing-room
where, by that time, they were all waiting for us and ready to start again.

It may have been my imagination—although I'm almost sure it
wasn't—but it seemed to me that all enthusiasm for the game had suddenly melted like a white frost in strong sunlight. If anybody had suggested another game I'm sure we should all have been grateful and
abandoned 'Smee'. Only nobody did. Nobody seemed to like to. I for
one, and I can speak for some of the others too, was oppressed with the
feeling that there was something wrong. I couldn't have said what I
thought was wrong, indeed I didn't think about it at all, but somehow
all the sparkle had gone out of the fun, and hovering over my mind like
a shadow was the warning of some sixth sense which told me that there
was an influence in the house which was neither sane, sound nor
healthy. Why did I feel like that? Because Sangston had counted thirteen of us instead of twelve, and his son had thought he had touched

somebody in an empty cupboard. No, there was more in it than just that. One would have laughed at such things in the ordinary way, and it was just that feeling of something being wrong which stopped me from laughing.

Well, we started again, and when we went in pursuit of the unknown 'Smee', we were as noisy as ever, but it seemed to me that most of us were acting. Frankly, for no reason other than the one I've given you, we'd stopped enjoying the game. I had an instinct to hunt with the main pack, but after a few minutes, during which no 'Smee' had been found, my instinct to play winning games and be first if possible, set me searching on my own account. And on the first floor of the west wing following the wall which was actually the shell of the house, I blundered against a pair of human knees.

I put out my hand and touched a soft, heavy curtain. Then I knew where I was. There were tall, deeply-recessed windows with seats along the landing, and curtains over the recesses to the ground. Somebody was sitting in a corner of this window-seat behind the curtain. Aha, I had caught 'Smee'! So I drew the curtain aside, stepped in, and touched the bare arm of a woman.

It was a dark night outside, and, moreover, the window was not only curtained but a blind hung down to where the bottom panes joined up with the frame. Between the curtain and the window it was as dark as the plague of Egypt. I could not have seen my hand held six inches before my face, much less the woman sitting in the corner.

'Smee?' I whispered.

I had no answer. 'Smee' when challenged does not answer. So I sat down beside her, first in the field, to await the others. Then, having settled myself I leaned over to her and whispered:

'Who is it? What's your name, "Smee"?'

And out of the darkness beside me the whisper came back: 'Brenda Ford.'

I didn't know the name, but because I didn't know it I guessed at once who she was. The tall, pale, dark girl was the only person in the house I didn't know by name. Ergo my companion was the tall, pale, dark girl. It seemed rather intriguing to be there with her, shut in between a heavy curtain and a window, and I rather wondered whether she was enjoying the game we were all playing. Somehow she hadn't seemed to me to be one of the romping sort. I muttered one or two commonplace questions to her and had no answer.

'Smee' is a game of silence. 'Smee' and the person or persons who have found 'Smee' are supposed to keep quiet to make it hard for the others. But there was nobody else about, and it occurred to me that she was playing the game a little too much to the letter. I spoke again and got no answer, and then I began to be annoyed. She was of that cold, 'superior' type which affects to despise men; she didn't like me; and she was sheltering behind the rules of a game for children to be discourteous. Well, if she didn't like sitting there with me, I certainly didn't want to be sitting there with her! I half turned from her and began to hope that we should both be discovered without much more delay.

Having discovered that I didn't like being there alone with her, it was queer how soon I found myself hating it, and that for a reason very different from the one which had at first whetted my annoyance. The girl I had met for the first time before dinner, and seen diagonally across the table, had a sort of cold charm about her which had attracted while it had half angered me. For the girl who was with me, imprisoned in the opaque darkness between the curtain and the window, I felt no attraction at all. It was so very much the reverse that I should have wondered at myself if, after the first shock of the discovery that she had suddenly become repellent to me, I had had room in my mind for anything besides the consciousness that her close presence was an increasing horror to me.

It came upon me just as quickly as I've uttered the words. My flesh suddenly shrank from her as you see a strip of gelatine shrink and wither before the heat of a fire. That feeling of something being wrong had come back to me, but multiplied to an extent which turned foreboding into actual terror. I firmly believe that I should have got up and run if I had not felt that at my first movement she would have divined my intention and compelled me to stay, by some means of which I could not bear to think. The memory of having touched her bare arm made me wince and draw in my lips. I prayed that somebody else would come along soon.

My prayer was answered. Light footfalls sounded on the landing. Somebody on the other side of the curtain brushed again my knees. The curtain was drawn aside and a woman's hand, fumbling in the darkness, presently rested on my shoulder. 'Smee?' whispered a voice which I instantly recognised as Mrs Gorman's.

Of course she received no answer. She came and settled down beside me with a rustle, and I can't describe the sense of relief she brought me.

'It's Tony, isn't it?' she whispered.

'Yes,' I whispered back.

'You're not "Smee" are you?'

'No, she's on my other side.'

She reached a hand across me, and I heard one of her nails scratch the surface of a woman's silk gown.

'Hullo, "Smee"! How are you? *Who* are you? Oh, is it against the rules to talk? Never mind, Tony, we'll break the rules. Do you know, Tony, this game is beginning to irk me a little. I hope they're not going to run it to death by playing it all the evening. I'd like to play some game where we can all be together in the same room with a nice bright fire.'

'Same here,' I agreed fervently.

'Can't you suggest something when we go down? There's something rather uncanny in this particular amusement. I can't quite shed the delusion that there's somebody in this game who oughtn't to be in at all.'

That was just how I had been feeling, but I didn't say so. But for my part the worst of my qualms were now gone; the arrival of Mrs Gorman had dissipated them. We sat on talking, wondering from time to time when the rest of the party would arrive.

I don't know how long elapsed before we heard a clatter of feet on the landing and young Reggie's voice shouting, 'Hullo! Hullo, there! Anybody there?'

'Yes,' I answered.

'Mrs Gorman with you?'

'Yes.'

'Well, you're a nice pair! You've both forfeited. We've all been waiting for you for hours.'

'Why, you haven't found "Smee" yet,' I objected.

'*You* haven't, you mean. I happen to have been "Smee" myself.'

'But "Smee's" here with us,' I cried.

'Yes,' agreed Mrs Gorman.

The curtain was stripped aside and in a moment we were blinking
into the eye of Reggie's electric torch. I looked at Mrs Gorman and then
on my other side. Between me and the wall there was an empty space
on the window seat. I stood up at once and wished I hadn't, for I found
myself sick and dizzy.

'There *was* somebody there,' I maintained, 'because I touched her.'

'So did I,' said Mrs Gorman in a voice which had lost its steadiness.
'And I don't see how she could have got up and gone without our
knowing it.'

Reggie uttered a queer, shaken laugh. He, too, had had an unpleasant experience that evening. 'Somebody's been playing the goat,' he
remarked. 'Coming down?'

We were not very popular when we arrived in the drawing-room.
Reggie rather tactlessly gave it out that he had found us sitting on a
window-seat behind the curtain. I taxed the tall, dark girl with having
pretended to be 'Smee' and afterwards slipping away. She denied it.
After which we settled down and played other games. 'Smee' was done
with for the evening, and I for one was glad of it.

Some long while later, during an interval, Sangston told me, if I
wanted a drink, to go into the smoke room and help myself. I went,
and he presently followed me. I could see that he was rather peeved
with me, and the reason came out during the following minute or two.
It seemed that, in his opinion, if I must sit out and flirt with Mrs
Gorman—in circumstances which would have been considered highly
compromising in his young days—I needn't do it during a round game
and keep everybody waiting for us.

'But there was somebody else there,' I protested, 'somebody pretending to be "Smee". I believe it was that tall, dark girl, Miss Ford, although she denied it. She even whispered her name to me.'

Sangston stared at me and nearly dropped his glass.

'Miss *Who?*' he shouted.

'Brenda Ford—she told me her name was.'

Sangston put down his glass and laid a hand on my shoulder.

'Look here, old man,' he said, 'I don't mind a joke, but don't let it go too far. We don't want all the women in the house getting hysterical. Brenda Ford is the name of the girl who broke her neck on the stairs playing hide-and-seek here ten years ago.'

from Asylum
by Patrick McGrath

Patrick McGrath's (born 1950) fiction often features grotesque elements—rotting angels, tiny explorers, elderly hermaphrodites. Asylum is at once more realistic and more troubling in its vision of unadulterated unhappiness. Stella has an affair with a mental patient, damaging her marriage as well as her husband's prospects (he is a psychiatrist at the mental hospital).The couple move with their young son to a desolate corner of Wales, where matters do not improve.

One night they sat at supper and Charlie was agitated. He kept glancing at Max, and Stella guessed he wanted him to say something to her.

"Well, what is it?" she said eventually. "Why don't you tell me yourself?"

He cast a stricken look at Max, who sighed and dabbed at his lips with his napkin.

"Charlie's worried you've forgotten his class outing tomorrow."

"Are you still going to come?"

She stood up and went to the sink and put her plate on the draining board and leaned against the counter with her back to them. Through the window over the sink she could just see the sky to the west, lacy islands of cloud drifting into the sinking sun and a glow of the palest orange imaginable. A few seconds went by. She felt the blackness rising in her.

"Yes, I suppose so."

• • •

The bus came at half past nine. Charlie was pathetically grateful that his mother was going with him. She had had a bad night and in the morning regretted agreeing to this outing, but she didn't relish the prospect of staying by herself in the house. In better days, she thought, she would have asked Max to prescribe her something, after all there has to be some advantage to living with a psychiatrist, but then in better days she wouldn't have needed it. So she drank her coffee and smoked her cigarettes and Charlie packed his satchel, telling her about the pleasures awaiting them. She reflected on the child's ability to live in the present and be so seemingly unmarked by the unhappiness around him. There she sat, hollow-eyed and silent, the black hole in the heart of the family, the one responsible for destroying the joy of his childhood, and yet in the excitement of a day out together it was all forgotten, all that mattered was that he would board the bus with his mother, and the fact that she was a bitter, depressed woman who had shown him sparse tenderness or affection for weeks, this was forgotten.

They got on the bus and her heart sank as the eyes of two dozen Welsh schoolchildren and half a dozen adults watched them make their way down to the last empty seats at the back. Hugh Griffin, sitting by the driver, made friendly noises, but his was the only voice in that silent bus which did. Stella realized then that Charlie's unhappiness had locked him out of this community as effectively as hers had, and she felt a dull sense of confirmation, she felt she might have known, this is the nature of people, they unerringly select as their victim the one who most needs their warmth. They were outsiders, Charlie and she, and they sat quietly at the back of the bus, and slowly the murmuring of the adults resumed, the babble and cries of the children, as mother and son gazed out of the window at the foreign fields.

Cledwyn Heath was a barren tract of rolling upland and their bus labored as it climbed up out of the valley and onto the plateau. For miles around a desolate landscape of moss and bracken stretched in all directions with here and there a stunted tree hardy enough to sustain its bent and twisted outline against the wind. Deep fissures came into view, sudden gulleys that plunged away steeply from the road and formed steep pockets in which stagnant water pooled, these pools overhung with clumps of weeds and low trees in whose shadow the water looked black and thick and evil. Stella hated it, there was an atmosphere of violence about this lonely moor, and she was not the only one who sensed it, the rest of them fell silent and all that could be heard for a while was the wind. Eventually they pulled off the road and parked in a sheltered spot near some woods and as the children left the bus their voices rose again, and then Hugh Griffin was organizing them into groups and arranging where and when they would meet for lunch. Charlie and Stella were part of a group that was to follow a track around the eastern rim of the heath. Apparently they would come upon a prospect a clear sixty miles to the sea. They set off, mother and son bringing up the rear of the party, and another parent, a father who had hiked in the area, leading them.

Her feeling of unease deepened as she tramped along in her Wellington boots, her raincoat tightly belted and a head scarf knotted under her chin. The track was narrow and stony and the climb was steeper than it first appeared. There was low cloud overhead and the sky threatened rain. Already the others had disappeared from view, and they seemed now the only living creatures in this bleak place where hillocks and heather spread on all sides, rising and falling, and no structure, no tree even to break the empty vista of land and lowering sky. Charlie marched on ahead of Stella, his satchel bumping up and down on his back and his head moving from side to side so as to miss nothing, turning now and then to make sure his mother was keeping up, eager pleasure in his lonely little face. She felt the blackness rising in her again and wished she'd stayed at home, this was no place for her, these empty wastes, among unfriendly strangers, pushing against the harsh damp wind. By the time they reached the prospect of the sea she was struggling hard to keep going for there were forces at work in her mind that would have her sink to the ground with her arms over her head and never rise again. The father tried to talk to her but she had no conversation for him, she was beyond that.

They tramped on and eventually found themselves at the picnic site, a sheltered spot in the lee of a hill. On a low flat outcrop of rock Hugh Griffin and the others had begun to spread their sandwiches and drinks. The children were forming into small noisy, groups while the adults gathered around Hugh Griffin and poured hot tea from thermos flasks. There was laughter and shouting as a sudden gust of wind lifted a map from the rock and blew it away. Stella wandered a little way off by herself and a minute or two later was aware of Charlie beside her silently eating his sandwiches. He asked her if she was hungry and she shook her head. He asked her if she wanted to see what was on the other side of the hill and she said yes. Soon they were out of sight of the others. Charlie made his way down the steep slope to the pool at the bottom, where weeds grew thickly in the shallows. Stella followed him and settled herself on the ground some way back. She felt the first spots of rain. Charlie shouted that he thought there were newts. Stella let her head fall forward onto her knees and covered her face with her hands. This time it was very bad. Black waves swept through her. The ground seemed to be undulating beneath her. She lifted her head and the air was misted with a fine black dust like specks of graphite. It was starting to rain. She saw as though from a great distance and through a heavy scrim the dark pool, its surface running with little waves and splattered with raindrops, and Charlie splashing indistinctly among the dense weeds at the edge. She pulled out her cigarettes and lit one, cupping her hand around the lighter's flame. Charlie was trying to catch something in the shallows but it evaded him. She watched him mutely and passively and smoked her cigarette as he grabbed it, what-ever it was, and lost his balance. The air was dark and the rain was com-ing harder now and the awful undulation had almost stopped and she felt the creeping numbness that always came afterward. Charlie was in deeper water now, trying to scramble upright and flailing around and shouting, and something in his shouting brought her to her feet. She stood in the gusting wind and rain with her shoulders hunched up tight and watched him for a few moments. Then she turned her head to the side and brought the cigarette to her lips. The edges of her head scarf fluttered wildly about her face; the waves were almost gone. She turned back and dimly saw a head break the surface, and an arm claw the air, then go under again, and she turned aside and again brought the cigarette to her lips. With one hand she clutched her elbow as her arm rose straight and rigid to her mouth. She turned her head to the side and again brought the cigarette to her lips and inhaled, each movement tight, separate, and controlled.

She didn't see Hugh Griffin appear at the brow of the hill behind her. She didn't hear him shout as he saw her there, smoking her cigarette, turning her head away, then back, then away again, as an indistinct figure struggled in the water. She was aware of him only when he came bounding past her through the rain and went crashing into the water, still shouting.

It was all rather confused after that. Stella stood by while Hugh Griffin came splashing out with Charlie in his arms and laid him on the ground and tried to revive him. Then the others came running over the hill and she was forgotten in all the flurry of the children being got back to the bus, and the police being called, and so on, and one of the women gave her a cup of tea and put a rug around her shoulders, and she heard her say to someone that Mrs. Raphael was in shock, and eventually, after the bus had left, the police arrived, and when they got to the police station Max was there and after more cups of tea he drove her home and gave her a pill and she went to bed and slept.

She slept through the following day and when she came downstairs Mair told her Max was with the police and would be back at lunchtime. They sat in silence at the kitchen table. It was still raining.

"What a terrible thing," Mair said at last. "Terrible."

How would she know? Stella wondered. She hasn't any children. How would she know it was terrible if one of them drowned?

When Max came home Mair left. He sat down at the table and stared at her, simply stared at her. Then he said, in a tone of utter bafflement, "But why didn't you shout?"

She found this amusing: Max was asking her why she hadn't shouted.

"You didn't make a sound," he said, in the same astonished tone. "You didn't open your mouth."

Usually they want you to keep your mouth shut, but sometimes they want you to shout, and they expect you to know the difference. This was what amused her.

They

by Rudyard Kipling

Many readers know Kipling (1865–1936) for his patriotic poetry and children's stories. Edmund Wilson was among the first modern critics to appreciate his other fiction, which Wilson placed firmly in the context of Kipling's difficult personal life (poor eyesight; absentee parents; the loss of two children). Kipling wrote this story in 1904, five years after his daughter, aged six, died of pneumonia.

One view called me to another; one hill top to its fellow, half across the county, and since I could answer at no more trouble than the snapping forward of a lever, I let the county flow under my wheels. The orchid-studded flats of the East gave way to the thyme, ilex, and grey grass of the Downs; these again to the rich cornland and fig-trees of the lower coast, where you carry the beat of the tide on your left hand for fifteen level miles; and when at last I turned inland through a huddle of rounded hills and woods I had run myself clean out of my known marks. Beyond that precise hamlet which stands godmother to the capital of the United States, I found hidden villages where bees, the only things awake, boomed in eighty-foot lindens that overhung grey Norman churches; miraculous brooks diving under stone bridges built for heavier traffic than would ever vex them again; tithe-barns larger than their churches, and an old smithy that cried out aloud how it had once been a hall of the Knights of the Temple. Gipsies I found on a common where the gorse, bracken, and heath fought it out together up a mile of Roman road; and a little farther on I disturbed a red fox rolling dog-fashion in the naked sunlight.

As the wooded hills closed about me I stood up in the car to take the bearings of that great Down whose ringed head is a landmark for fifty miles across the low countries. I Judged that the lie of the country would bring me across some westward-running road that went to his feet, but I did not allow for the confusing veils of the woods. A quick turn plunged me first into a green cutting brim-full of liquid sunshine, next into a gloomy tunnel where last year's dead leaves whispered and scuffled about my tyres. The strong hazel stuff meeting overhead had not been cut for a couple of generations at least, nor had any axe helped the moss-cankered oak and beech to spring above them. Here the road changed frankly into carpeted ride on whose brown velvet spent primrose-clumps showed like jade, and a few sickly, white-stalked blue-bells nodded together. As the slope favoured I shut off the power and slid over the whirled leaves, expecting every moment to meet a keeper; but I only heard a jay, far off, arguing against the silence under the twilight of the trees.

Still the track descended. I was on the point of reversing and working my way back on the second speed ere I ended in some swamp, when I saw sunshine through the tangle ahead and lifted the brake.

It was down again at once. As the light beat across my face my forewheels took the turf of a great still lawn from which sprang horsemen ten feet high with levelled lances, monstrous peacocks, and sleek round-headed maids of honour—blue, black, and glistening—all of clipped yew. Across the lawn—the marshalled woods besieged it on three sides—stood an ancient house of lichened and weather-worn stone, with mullioned windows and roofs of rose-red tile. It was flanked by semi-circular walls, also rose-red, that closed the lawn on the fourth side, and at their feet a box hedge grew man-high. There were doves on the roof about the slim brick chimneys, and I caught a glimpse of an octagonal dove-house behind the screening wall.

Here, then, I stayed; a horseman's green spear laid at my breast; held by the exceeding beauty of that jewel in that setting.

'If I am not packed off for a trespasser, or if this knight does not ride a wallop at me,' thought I, 'Shakespeare and Queen Elizabeth at least must come out of that half-open garden door and ask me to tea.'

A child appeared at an upper window, and I thought the little thing waved a friendly hand. But it was to call a companion, for presently another bright head showed. Then I heard a laugh among the yew-peacocks, and turning to make sure (till then I had been watching the house only) I saw the silver of a fountain behind a hedge thrown up against the sun. The doves on the roof cooed to the cooing water; but between the two notes I caught the utterly happy chuckle of a child absorbed in some light mischief.

The garden door—heavy oak sunk deep in the thickness of the wall—opened further: a woman in a big garden hat set her foot slowly on the time-hollowed stone step and as slowly walked across the turf. I was forming some apology when she lifted up her head and I saw that she was blind.

'I heard you,' she said. 'Isn't that a motor car?'

'I'm afraid I've made a mistake in my road. I should have turned off up above—I never dreamed —' I began.

'But I'm very glad. Fancy a motor car coming into the garden! It will be such a treat—' She turned and made as though looking about her. 'You—you haven't seen anyone, have you—perhaps?'

'No one to speak to, but the children seemed interested at a distance.'

'Which?'

'I saw a couple up at the window just now, and I think I heard a little chap in the grounds.'

'Oh, lucky you!' she cried, and her face brightened. 'I hear them, of course, but that's all. You've seen them and heard them?'

'Yes,' I answered. 'And if I know anything of children, one of them's having a beautiful time by the fountain yonder. Escaped, I should imagine.'

'You're fond of children?'

I gave her one or two reasons why I did not altogether hate them.

'Of course, of course,' she said. 'Then you understand. Then you won't think it foolish if I ask you to take your car through the gardens, once or twice—quite slowly. I'm sure they'd like to see it. They see so little, poor things. One tries to make their life pleasant, but—' she threw out her hands towards the woods. 'We're so out of the world here.'

'That will be splendid,' I said. 'But I can't cut up your grass.'

She faced to the right. 'Wait a minute,' she said. 'We're at the South gate, aren't we? Behind those peacocks there's a flagged path. We call it the Peacocks' Walk. You can't see it from here, they tell me, but if you squeeze along by the edge of the wood you can turn at the first peacock and get on to the flags.'

It was sacrilege to wake that dreaming house-front with the clatter of machinery, but I swung the car to clear the turf, brushed along the edge of the wood and turned in on the broad stone path where the fountain-basin lay like one star-sapphire.

'May I come too?' she cried. 'No, please don't help me. They'll like it better if they see me.'

She felt her way lightly to the front of the car, and with one foot on the step she called: 'Children, oh, children! Look and see what's going to happen!'

The voice would have drawn lost souls from the Pit, for the yearning that underlay its sweetness, and I was not surprised to hear an answering shout behind the yews. It must have been the child by the fountain, but he fled at our approach, leaving a little toy boat in the water. I saw the glint of his blue blouse among the still horsemen.

Very disposedly we paraded the length of the walk and at her request backed again. This time the child had got the better of his panic, but stood far off and doubting.

'The little fellow's watching us,' I said. 'I wonder if he'd like a ride.'

'They're very shy still. Very shy. But, oh, lucky you to be able to see them! Let's listen.'

I stopped the machine at once, and the humid stillness, heavy with the scent of box, cloaked us deep. Shears I could hear where some gardener was clipping; a mumble of bees and broken voices that might have been the doves.

'Oh, unkind!' she said weariedly.

'Perhaps they're only shy of the motor. The little maid at the window looks tremendously interested.'

'Yes?' She raised her head. 'It was wrong of me to say that. They are really fond of me. It's the only thing that makes life worth living— when they're fond of you, isn't it ? I daren't think what the place would be without them. By the way, is it beautiful?'

'I think it is the most beautiful place I have ever seen.'

'So they all tell me. I can feel it, of course, but that isn't quite the same thing.'

'Then have you never—?' I began, but stopped abashed.

'Not since I can remember. It happened when I was only a few months old, they tell me. And yet I must remember something, else how could I dream about colours. I see light in my dreams, and colours, but I never see *them*. I only hear them just as I do when I'm awake.'

'It's difficult to see faces in dreams. Some people can, but most of us haven't the gift,' I went on, looking up at the window where the child stood all but hidden.

'I've heard that too,' she said. 'And they tell me that one never sees a dead person's face in a dream. Is that true?'

'I believe it is—now I come to think of it.'

'But how is it with yourself—yourself?' The blind eyes turned towards me.

'I have never seen the faces of my dead in any dream,' I answered.

'Then it must be as bad as being blind.'

The sun had dipped behind the woods and the long shades were possessing the insolent horsemen one by one. I saw the light die from the top of a glossy-leaved lance and all the brave hard green turned to soft black. The house, accepting another day at end, as it had accepted an hundred thousand gone, seemed to settle deeper into its rest among the shadows.

'Have you ever wanted to?' she said after the silence.

'Very much sometimes,' I replied. The child had left the window as the shadows closed upon it.

'Ah! So've I, but I don't suppose it's allowed . . . . Where d'you live?'

'Quite the other side of the county—sixty miles and more, and I must be going back. I've come without my big lamp.'

'But it's not dark yet. I can feel it.'

'I'm afraid it will be by the time I get home. Could you lend me someone to set me on my road at first? I've utterly lost myself.'

'I'll send Madden with you to the cross-roads. We are so out of the world, I don't wonder you were lost! I'll guide you round to the front of the house; but you will go slowly, won't you, till you're out of the grounds? It isn't foolish, do you think?'

'I promise you I'll go like this,' I said, and let the car start herself down the flagged path.

We skirted the left wing of the house, whose elaborately cast lead guttering alone was worth a day's journey; passed under a great rose-grown gate in the red wall, and so round to the high front of the house which in beauty and stateliness as much excelled the back as that all others I had seen.

'Is it so very beautiful?' she said wistfully when she heard my raptures. 'And you like the lead-figures too? There's the old azalea garden behind. They say that this place must have been made for children. Will you help me out, please? I should like to come with you as far as the cross-roads, but I mustn't leave them. Is that you, Madden? I want you to show this gentleman the way to the cross-roads. He has lost his way—but he has seen them.'

A butler appeared noiselessly at the miracle of old oak that must be called the front door, and slipped aside to put on his hat. She stood looking at me with open blue eyes in which no sight lay, and I saw for the first time that she was beautiful.

'Remember,' she said quietly, 'if you are fond of them you will come again,' and disappeared within the house.

The butler in the car said nothing till we were nearly at the lodge gates, where catching a glimpse of a blue blouse in a shrubbery I swerved amply lest the devil that leads little boys to play should drag me into child-murder.

'Excuse me,' he asked of a sudden, 'but why did you do that, Sir?'

'The child yonder.'

'Our young gentleman in blue?'

'Of course.'

'He runs about a good deal. Did you see him by the fountain, Sir?'

'Oh, yes, several times. Do we turn here?'

'Yes, Sir. And did you 'appen to see them upstairs too?'

'At the upper window? Yes.'

'Was that before the mistress came out to speak to you, Sir?'

'A little before that. Why d'you want to know?'

He paused a little. 'Only to make sure that—that they had seen the car, Sir, because with children running about, though I'm sure you're driving particularly careful, there might be an accident. That was all, Sir. Here are the cross-roads. You can't miss your way from now on. Thank you, Sir, but that isn't *our* custom, not with—'

'I beg your pardon,' I said, and thrust away the British silver.

'Oh, it's quite right with the rest of 'em as a rule. Good-bye, Sir.'

He retired into the armour-plated conning tower of his caste and walked away. Evidently a butler solicitous for the honour of his house, and interested, probably through a maid, in the nursery.

Once beyond the signposts at the cross-roads I looked back, but the crumpled hills interlaced so jealously that I could not see where the house had lain. When I asked its name at a cottage along the road, the fat woman who sold sweetmeats there gave me to understand that people with motor cars had small right to live—much less to 'go about talking like carriage folk'. They were not a pleasant-mannered community.

When I retraced my route on the map that evening I was little wiser. Hawkin's Old Farm appeared to be the Survey title of the place, and the old County Gazetteer, generally so ample, did not allude to it. The big house of those parts was Hodnington Hall, Georgian with early Victorian embellishments, as an atrocious steel engraving attested. I

carried my difficulty to a neighbour—a deep-rooted tree of that soil—
and he gave me a name of a family which conveyed no meaning.

A month or so later—I went again, or it may have been that my car
took the road of her own volition. She over-ran the fruitless Downs,
threaded every turn of the maze of lanes below the hills, drew through
the high-walled woods, impenetrable in their full leaf, came out at the
cross-roads where the butler had left me, and a little farther on developed an internal trouble which forced me to turn her in on a grass
way-waste that cut into a summer-silent hazel wood. So far as I could
make sure by the sun and a six-inch Ordnance map, this should be the
road flank of that wood which I had first explored from the heights
above. I made a mighty serious business of my repairs and a glittering
shop of my repair kit, spanners, pump, and the like, which I spread out
orderly upon a rug. It was a trap to catch all childhood, for on such a
day, I argued, the children would not be far off. When I paused in my
work I listened, but the wood was so full of the noises of summer
(though the birds had mated) that I could not at first distinguish these
from the tread of small cautious feet stealing across the dead leaves. I
rang my bell in an alluring manner, but the feet fled, and I repented,
for to a child a sudden noise is very real terror. I must have been at
work half an hour when I heard in the wood the voice of the blind
woman crying: 'Children, oh children! Where are you?' and the stillness made slow to close on the perfection of that cry. She came towards
me, half feeling her way between the tree boles, and though a child it
seemed clung to her skirt, it swerved into the leafage like a rabbit as she
drew nearer.

'Is that you?' she said, 'from the other side of the county?'

'Yes, it's me from the other side of the county.'

'Then why didn't you come through the upper woods? They were
there just now.'

'They were here a few minutes ago. I expect they knew my car had
broken down, and came to see the fun.'

'Nothing serious, I hope? How do cars break down?'

'In fifty different ways. Only mine has chosen the fifty-first.'

She laughed merrily at the tiny joke, cooed with delicious laughter, and pushed her hat back.

'Let me hear,' she said.

'Wait a moment,' I cried, 'and I'll get you a cushion.'

She set her foot on the rug all covered with spare parts, and stooped over it eagerly. 'What delightful things!' The hands through which she saw glanced in the chequered sunlight. 'A box here—another box! Why you've arranged them like playing shop!'

'I confess now that I put it out to attract them. I don't need half those things really.'

'How nice of you! I heard your bell in the upper wood. You say they were here before that?'

'I'm sure of it. Why are they so shy? That little fellow in blue who was with you just now ought to have got over his fright. He's been watching me like a Red Indian.'

'It must have been your bell,' she said. 'I heard one of them go past me in trouble when I was coming down. They're shy—so shy even with me.' She turned her face over her shoulder and cried again: 'Children, oh, children! Look and see!'

'They must have gone off together on their own affairs,' I suggested, for there was a murmur behind us of lowered voices broken by the sudden squeaking giggles of childhood. I returned to my tinkerings and she learned forward, her chin on her hand, listening interestedly.

'How many are they?' I said at last. The work was finished, but I saw no reason to go.

Her forehead puckered a little in thought. 'I don't quite know,' she said simply. 'Sometimes more—sometimes less. They come and stay with me because I love them, you see.'

'That must be very jolly,' I said, replacing a drawer, and as I spoke I heard the inanity of my answer.

'You—you aren't laughing at me,' she cried. 'I—I haven't any of my own. I never married. People laugh at me sometimes about them because—because—'

'Because they're savages,' I returned. 'It's nothing to fret for. That sort laugh at everything that isn't in their own fat lives.'

'I don't know. How should I? I only don't like being laughed at about *them*. It hurts; and when one can't see . . . . I don't want to seem silly,' her chin quivered like a child's as she spoke, 'but we blindies have only one skin, I think. Everything outside hits straight at our souls. It's different with you. You've such good defences in your eyes—looking out—before anyone can really pain you in your soul. People forget that with us.'

I was silent reviewing that inexhaustible matter—the more than inherited (since it is also carefully taught) brutality of the Christian peoples, beside which the mere heathendom of the West Coast nigger is clean and restrained. It led me a long distance into myself.

'Don't do that!' she said of a sudden, putting her hands before her eyes.

'What?'

She made a gesture with her hand.

'That! It's—it's all purple and black. Don't! That colour hurts.'

'But, how in the world do you know about colours?' I exclaimed, for here was a revelation indeed.

'Colours as colours?' she asked.

'No. *Those* Colours which you saw just now.'

'You know as well as I do,' she laughed, 'else you wouldn't have asked that question. They aren't in the world at all. They're in *you*—when you went so angry.'

'D'you mean a dull purplish patch, like port wine mixed with ink?' I said.

'I've never seen ink or port wine, but the colours aren't mixed. They are separate—all separate.'

'Do you mean black streaks and jags across the purple?'

She nodded. 'Yes—if they are like this,' and zig-zagged her finger again, 'but it's more red than purple—that bad colour.'

'And what are the colours at the top of the—whatever you see?'

Slowly she leaned forward and traced on the rug the figure of the Egg itself.

'I see them so,' she said, pointing with a grass stem, 'white, green, yellow, red, purple, and when people are angry or bad, black across the red—as you were just now.'

'Who told you anything about it—in the beginning?' I demanded.

'About the colours? No one. I used to ask what colours were when I was little—in table-covers and curtains and carpets, you see—because some colours hurt me and some made me happy. People told me; and when I got older that was how I saw people.' Again she traced the outline of the Egg which it is given to very few of us to see.

'All by yourself?' I repeated.

'All by myself. There wasn't anyone else. I only found out afterwards that other people did not see the Colours.'

She leaned against the tree-bole plaiting and unplaiting chance-plucked grass stems. The children in the wood had drawn nearer. I could see them with the tail of my eye frolicking like squirrels.

'Now I am sure you will never laugh at me,' she went on after a long silence. 'Nor at *them*.'

'Goodness! No!' I cried, jolted out of my train of thought. 'A man who laughs at a child—unless the child is laughing too—is a heathen!'

'I didn't mean that, of course. You'd never laugh *at* children, but I thought—I used to think—that perhaps you might laugh about *them*. So now I beg your pardon . . . . What are you going to laugh at?'

I had made no sound, but she knew.

'At the notion of your begging my pardon. If you had done your duty as a pillar of the State and a landed proprietress you ought to have summoned me for trespass when I barged through your woods the other day. It was disgraceful of me—inexcusable.'

She looked at me, her head against the tree trunk—long and steadfastly—this woman who could see the naked soul.

'How curious,' she half whispered. 'How very curious.'

'Why, what have I done?'

'You don't understand . . . and yet you understood about the Colours. Don't you understand?'

She spoke with a passion that nothing had justified, and I faced her bewilderedly as she rose. The children had gathered themselves in a roundel behind a bramble bush. One sleek head bent over something smaller, and the set of the little shoulders told me that fingers were on lips. They, too, had some child's tremendous secret. I alone was hopelessly astray there in the broad sunlight.

'No,' I said, and shook my head as though the dead eyes could note. 'Whatever it is, I don't understand yet. Perhaps I shall later—if you'll let me come again.'

'You will come again,' she answered. 'You will surely come again and walk in the wood.'

'Perhaps the children will know me well enough by that time to let me play with them—as a favour. You know what children are like.'

'It isn't a matter of favour but of right,' she replied, and while I wondered what she meant, a dishevelled woman plunged round the bend of the road, loose-haired, purple, almost lowing with agony as she ran. It was my rude, fat friend of the sweetmeat shop. The blind woman heard and stepped forward. 'What is it, Mrs Madehurst?' she asked.

The woman flung her apron over her head and literally grovelled in the dust, crying that her grandchild was sick to death, that the local doctor was away fishing, that Jenny the mother was at her wits' end, and so forth, with repetitions and bellowings.

'Where's the next nearest doctor?' I asked between paroxysms.

'Madden will tell you. Go round to the house and take him with you. I'll attend to this. Be quick!' She half supported the fat woman into the shade. In two minutes I was blowing all the horns of Jericho under the front of the House Beautiful, and Madden, in the pantry, rose to the crisis like a butler and a man.

A quarter of an hour at illegal speeds caught us a doctor five miles away. Within the half-hour we had decanted him, much interested in motors, at the door of the sweetmeat shop, and drew up the road to await the verdict.

'Useful things cars,' said Madden, all man and no butler. 'If I'd had one when mine took sick she wouldn't have died.'

'How was it?' I asked.

'Croup. Mrs Madden was away. No one knew what to do. I drove eight miles in a tax cart for the doctor. She was choked when we came back. This car 'd ha' saved her. She'd have been close on ten now.'

'I'm sorry,' I said. 'I thought you were rather fond of children from what you told me going to the cross-roads the other day.'

'Have you seen 'em again, Sir—this mornin'?'

'Yes, but they're well broke to cars. I couldn't get any of them within twenty yards of it.'

He looked at me carefully as a scout considers a stranger—not as a menial should lift his eyes to his divinely appointed superior.

'I wonder why,' he said just above the breath that he drew.

We waited on. A light wind from the sea wandered up and down the long lines of the woods, and the wayside grasses, whitened already with summer dust, rose and bowed in sallow waves.

A woman, wiping the suds off her arms, came out of the cottage next the sweetmeat shop.

'I've be'n listenin' in de back-yard,' she said cheerily. 'He says Arthur's unaccountable bad. Did ye hear him shruck just now? Unaccountable bad. I reckon t'will come Jenny's turn to walk in de wood nex' week along, Mr Madden.'

'Excuse me, Sir, but your lap-robe is slipping,' said Madden deferentially. The woman started, dropped a curtsey, and hurried away.

'What does she mean by "walking in the wood"?' I asked.

'It must be some saying they use hereabouts. I'm from Norfolk myself,' said Madden. 'They're an independent lot in this county. She took you for a chauffeur, Sir.'

I saw the Doctor come out of the cottage followed by a draggle-tailed wench who clung to his arm as though he could make treaty for her with Death. 'Dat sort,' she wailed—'dey're just as much to us dat has 'em as if dey was lawful born. Just as much—just as much! An' God he'd be just as pleased if you saved 'un, Doctor. Don't take it from me. Miss Florence will tell ye de very same. Don't leave 'im, doctor!'

'I know, I know,' said the man; 'but he'll be quiet for a while now. We'll get the nurse and the medicine as fast as we can.' He signalled me

to come forward with the car, and I strove not to be privy to what followed; but I saw the girl's face, blotched and frozen with grief, and I felt
the hand without a ring clutching at my knees when we moved away.

The Doctor was a man of some humour, for I remember he
claimed my car under the Oath of Æsculapius, and used it and me
without mercy. First we convoyed Mrs Madehurst and the blind
woman to wait by the sick bed till the nurse should come. Next we
invaded a neat county town for prescriptions (the Doctor said the
trouble was cerebro-spinal meningitis), and when the County
Institute, banked and flanked with scared market cattle, reported
itself out of nurses for the moment we literally flung ourselves loose
upon the county. We conferred with the owners of great houses—
magnates at the ends of overarching avenues whose big-boned wom-
enfolk strode away from their tea-tables to listen to the imperious
Doctor. At last a white-haired lady sitting under a cedar of Lebanon
and surrounded by a court of magnificent Borzois—all hostile to
motors—gave the Doctor, who received them as from a princess,
written orders which we bore many miles at top speed, through a park,
to a French nunnery, where we took over in exchange a pallid-faced
and trembling Sister. She knelt at the bottom of the tonneau telling her
beads without pause till, by short cuts of the Doctor's invention, we
had her to the sweetmeat shop once more. It was a long afternoon
crowded with mad episodes that rose and dissolved like the dust of our
wheels; cross-sections of remote and incomprehensible lives through
which we raced at right angles; and I went home in the dusk, wearied
out, to dream of the clashing horns of cattle; round-eyed nuns walking
in a garden of graves; pleasant tea-parties beneath shaded trees; the
carbolic-scented, grey-painted corridors of the County Institute; the
steps of shy children in the wood, and the hands that clung to my
knees as the motor began to move.

I had intended to return in a day or two, but it pleased Fate to hold me
from that side of the county, on many pretexts, till the elder and the
wild rose had fruited. There came at last a brilliant day, swept clear

from the south-west, that brought the hills within hand's reach—a day
of unstable airs and high filmy clouds. Through no merit of my own I
was free, and set the car for the third time on that known road. As I
reached the crest of the Downs I felt the soft air change, saw it glaze
under the sun; and, looking down at the sea, in that instant beheld the
blue of the Channel turn through polished silver and dulled steel to
dingy pewter. A laden collier hugging the coast steered outward for
deeper water, and, across copper-coloured haze, I saw sails rise one by
one on the anchored fishing-fleet. In a deep dene behind me an eddy
of sudden wind drummed through sheltered oaks, and spun aloft the
first dry sample of autumn leaves. When I reached the beach road the
sea-fog fumed over the brickfields, and the tide was telling all the groins
of the gale beyond Ushant. In less than an hour summer England vanished in chill grey. We were again the shut island of the North, all the
ships of the world bellowing at our perilous gates; and between their
outcries ran the piping of bewildered gulls. My cap dripped moisture,
the folds of the rug held it in pools or sluiced it away in runnels, and
the salt-rime stuck to my lips.

Inland the smell of autumn loaded the thickened fog among the
trees, and the drip became a continuous shower. Yet the late flowers—
mallow of the wayside, scabious of the field, and dahlia of the
garden—showed gay in the mist, and beyond the sea's breath there
was little sign of decay in the leaf. Yet in the villages the house doors
were all open, and bare-legged, bare-headed children sat at ease on
the damp doorsteps to shout 'pip-pip' at the stranger.

I made bold to call at the sweetmeat shop, where Mrs Madehurst
met me with a fat woman's hospitable tears. Jenny's child, she said,
had died two days after the nun had come. It was, she felt, best out of
the way, even though insurance offices, for reasons which she did not
pretend to follow, would not willingly insure such stray lives. 'Not but
what Jenny didn't tend to Arthur as though he'd come all proper at de
end of de first year—like Jenny herself.' Thanks to Miss Florence, the
child had been buried with a pomp which, in Mrs Madehurst's opinion, more than covered the small irregularity of its birth. She described

the coffin, within and without, the glass hearse, and the evergreen lining of the grave.'

'But how's the mother?' I asked.

'Jenny? Oh, she'll get over it. I've felt dat way with one or two o' my own. She'll get over. She's walkin' in de wood now.'

'In this weather?'

Mrs Madehurst looked at me with narrowed eyes across the counter.

'I dunno but it opens de 'eart like. Yes, it opens de 'eart. Dat's where losin' and bearin' comes so alike in de long run, we do say.'

Now the wisdom of the old wives is greater than that of all the Fathers, and this last oracle sent me thinking so extendedly as I went up the road, that I nearly ran over a woman and a child at the wooded corner by the lodge gates of the House Beautiful.

'Awful weather!' I cried, as I slowed dead for the turn.

'Not so bad,' she answered placidly out of the fog. 'Mine's used to 'un. You'll find yours indoors, I reckon.'

Indoors, Madden received me with professional courtesy, and kind inquiries for the health of the motor, which he would put under cover.

I waited in a still, nut-brown hall, pleasant with late flowers and warmed with a delicious wood fire—a place of good influence and great peace. (Men and women may sometimes, after great effort, achieve a creditable lie; but the house, which is their temple, cannot say anything save the truth of those who have lived in it.) A child's cart and a doll lay on the black-and-white floor, where a rug had been kicked back. I felt that the children had only just hurried away—to hide themselves, most like—in the many turns of the great adzed staircase that climbed statelily out of the hall, or to crouch at gaze behind the lions and roses of the carven gallery above. Then I heard her voice above me, singing as the blind sing—from the soul:—

In the pleasant orchard-closes.

And all my early summer came back at the call.

In the pleasant orchard-closes,
God bless all our gains say we—
But may God bless all our losses,
Better suits with our degree.

She dropped the marring fifth line, and repeated—

Better suits with our degree!

I saw her lean over the gallery, her linked hands white as pearl against the oak.

'Is that you—from the other side of the county?' she called.

'Yes, me—from the other side of the county,' I answered, laughing.

'What a long time before you had to come here again,' She ran down the stairs, one hand lightly touching the broad rail. 'It's two months and four days. Summer's gone!'

'I meant to come before, but Fate prevented.'

'I knew it. Please do something to that fire. They won't let me play with it, but I can feel it's behaving badly. Hit it!'

I looked on either side of the deep fireplace, and found but a half-charred hedge-stake with which I punched a black log flame.

'It never goes out, day or night,' she said, as though explaining. 'In case anyone comes in with cold toes, you see.'

'It's even lovelier inside than it was out,' I murmured. The red light poured itself along the age-polished dusky panels till the Tudor roses and lions of the gallery took colour and motion. An old eagle-topped convex mirror gathered the picture into its mysterious heart, distorting afresh the distorted shadows, and curving the gallery lines into the curves of a ship. The day was shutting down in half a gale as the fog turned to stringy scud. Through the uncurtained mullions of the broad window I could see valiant horsemen of the lawn rear and recover against the wind that taunted them with legions of dead leaves.

'Yes, it must be beautiful,' she said. 'Would you like to go over it? There's still light enough upstairs.'

I followed her up the unflinching, wagon-wide staircase to the gallery whence opened the thin fluted Elizabethan doors.

'Feel how they put the latch low down for the sake of the children.' She swung a light door inward.

'By the way, where are they?' I asked. 'I haven't even heard them to-day.'

She did not answer at once. Then, 'I can only hear them,' she replied softly. 'This is one of their rooms—everything ready, you see.'

She pointed into a heavily-timbered room. There were little low gate tables and children's chairs. A doll's house, its hooked front half open, faced a great dappled rocking-horse, from whose padded saddle it was but a child's scramble to the broad window-seat overlooking the lawn. A toy gun lay in a corner beside a gilt wooden cannon.

'Surely they've only just gone,' I whispered. In the failing light a door creaked cautiously. I heard the rustle of a frock and the patter of feet—quick feet through a room beyond.

'I heard that,' she cried triumphantly. 'Did you? Children, oh, children! Where are you?'

The voice filled the walls that held it lovingly to the last perfect note, but there came no answering shout such as I had heard in the garden. We hurried on from room to oak-floored room; up a step here, down three steps there; among a maze of passages; always mocked by our quarry. One might as well have tried to work an unstopped warren with a single ferret. There were bolt-holes innumerable—recesses in walls, embrasures of deep slitten windows now darkened, whence they could start up behind us; and abandoned fireplaces, six feet deep in the masonry, as well as the tangle of communicating doors. Above all, they had the twilight for their helper in our game. I had caught one or two joyous chuckles of evasion, and once or twice had seen the silhouette of a child's frock against some darkening window at the end of a passage; but we returned empty-handed to the gallery, just as a middle-aged woman was setting a lamp in its niche.

'No, I haven't seen her either this evening, Miss Florence,' I heard her say, 'but that Turpin he says he wants to see you about his shed.'

'Oh, Mr Turpin must want to see me very badly. Tell him to come to the hall, Mrs Madden.'

I looked down into the hall whose only light was the dulled fire, and deep in the shadow I saw them at last. They must have slipped down while we were in the passages, and now thought themselves perfectly hidden behind an old gilt leather screen. By child's law, my fruitless chase was as good as an introduction, but since I had taken so much trouble I resolved to force them to come forward later by the simple trick, which children detest, of pretending not to notice them. They lay close, in a little huddle, no more than shadows except when a quick flame betrayed an outline.

'And now we'll have some tea,' she said. 'I believe I ought to have offered it you at first, but one doesn't arrive at manners somehow when one lives alone and is considered—h'm—peculiar.' Then with very pretty scorn, 'Would you like a lamp to see to eat by?'

'The firelight's much pleasanter, I think.' We descended into that delicious gloom and Madden brought tea.

I took my chair in the direction of the screen ready to surprise or be surprised as the game should go, and at her permission, since a hearth is always sacred, bent forward to play with the fire.

'Where do you get these beautiful short faggots from?' I asked idly. 'Why, they are tallies!'

'Of course,' she said. 'As I can't read or write I'm driven back on the early English tally for my accounts. Give me one and I'll tell you what it meant.'

I passed her an unburned hazel-tally, about a foot long, and she ran her thumb down the nicks.

'This is the milk-record for the home farm for the month of April last year, in gallons,' said she. 'I don't know what I should have done without tallies. An old forester of mine taught me the system. It's out of date now for everyone else; but my tenants respect it. One of them's coming now to see me. Oh, it doesn't matter. He has no business here out of office hours. He's a greedy, ignorant man—very greedy or—he wouldn't come here after dark.'

'Have you much land then?'

'Only a couple of hundred acres in hand, thank goodness. The other six hundred are nearly all let to folk who knew my folk before me, but this Turpin is quite a new man—and a highway robber.'

'But are you sure I shan't be—?'

'Certainly not. You have the right. He hasn't any children.'

'Ah, the children!' I said, and slid my low chair back till it nearly touched the screen that hid them. 'I wonder whether they'll come out for me.'

There was a murmur of voices—Madden's and a deeper note—at the low, dark side door, and a ginger-headed, canvas-gaitered giant of the unmistakable tenant-farmer type stumbled or was pushed in.

'Come to the fire, Mr Turpin,' she said.

'If—if you please, Miss, I'll—I'll be quite as well by the door.' He clung to the latch as he spoke like a frightened child. Of a sudden I realised that he was in the grip of some almost overpowering fear.

'Well?'

'About that new shed for the young stock—that was all. These first autumn storms settin' in . . . but I'll come again, Miss.' His teeth did not chatter much more than the door latch.

'I think not,' she answered levelly. 'The new shed—m'm. What did my agent write you on the 15th?'

'I—fancied p'raps that if I came to see you—ma—man to man like, Miss. But —'

His eyes rolled into every corner of the room wide with horror. He half opened the door through which he had entered, but I noticed it shut again—from without and firmly.

'He wrote what I told him,' she went on. 'You are overstocked already. Dunnett's Farm never carried more than fifty bullocks—even in Mr Wright's time. And *he* used cake. You've sixty-seven and you don't cake. You've broken the lease in that respect. You're dragging the heart out of the farm.'

'I'm—I'm getting some minerals—superphosphates—next week. I've as good as ordered a truck-load already. I'll go down to the station tomorrow about 'em. Then I can come and see you man to man like,

Miss, in the daylight . . . . That gentleman's not going away, is he?' He almost shrieked.

I had only slid the chair a little farther back, reaching behind me to tap on the leather of the screen, but he jumped like a rat.

'No. Please attend to me, Mr Turpin.' She turned in her chair and faced him with his back to the door. It was an old and sordid little piece of scheming that she forced from him—his plea for the new cowshed at his landlady's expense, that he might with the covered manure pay his next year's rent out of the valuation after, as she made clear, he had bled the enriched pastures to the bone. I could not but admire the intensity of his greed, when I saw him out-facing for its sake whatever terror it was that ran wet on his forehead.

I ceased to tap the leather—was, indeed, calculating the cost of the shed—when I felt my relaxed hand taken and turned softly between the soft hands of a child. So at last I had triumphed. In a moment I would turn and acquaint myself with those quick-footed wanderers . . . .

The little brushing kiss fell in the centre of my palm—as a gift on which the fingers were, once, expected to close: as the all-faithful half-reproachful signal of a waiting child not used to neglect even when grown-ups were busiest—a fragment of the mute code devised very long ago.

Then I knew. And it was as though I had known from the first day when I looked across the lawn at the high window.

I heard the door shut. The woman turned to me in silence, and I felt that she knew.

What time passed after this I cannot say. I was roused by the fall of a log, and mechanically rose to put it back. Then I returned to my place in the chair very close to the screen.

'Now you understand,' she whispered, across the packed shadows.

'Yes, I understand—now. Thank you.'

'I—I only hear them.' She bowed her head in her hands. 'I have no right, you know—no other right. I have neither borne nor lost—neither borne nor lost!'

'Be very glad then,' said I, for my soul was torn open within me.

'Forgive me!'

She was still, and I went back to my sorrow and my joy.

'It was because I loved them so,' she said at last, brokenly. '*That* was why it was, even from the first—even before I knew that they—they were all I should ever have. And I loved them so!'

She stretched out her arms to the shadows and the shadows within the shadow.

'They came because I loved them—because I needed them. I—I must have made them come. Was that wrong, think you?'

'No—no.'

'I—I grant you that the toys and—and all that sort of thing were nonsense, but—but I used to so hate empty rooms myself when I was little.' She pointed to the gallery. 'And the passages all empty . . . . And how could I ever bear the garden door shut? Suppose—'

'Don't! For pity's sake, don't!' I cried. The twilight had brought a cold rain with gusty squalls that plucked at the leaded windows.

'And the same thing with keeping the fire in all night. *I* don't think it so foolish—do you?'

I looked at the broad brick hearth, saw, through tears I believe, that there was no unpassable iron on or near it, and bowed my head.

'I did all that and lots of other things—just to make believe. Then they came. I heard them, but I didn't know that they were not mine by right till Mrs Madden told me—'

'The butler's wife? What?'

'One of them—I heard—she saw. And knew. Hers! *Not* for me. I didn't know at first. Perhaps I was jealous. Afterwards, I began to understand that it was only because I loved them, not because— . . . Oh, you *must* bear or lose,' she said piteously. 'There is no other way— and yet they love me. They must! Don't they?'

There was no sound in the room except the lapping voices of the fire, but we two listened intently, and she at least took comfort from what she heard. She recovered herself and half rose. I sat still in my chair by the screen.

'Don't think me a wretch to whine about myself like this, but—but I'm all in the dark, you know, and *you* can see.'

In truth I could see, and my vision confirmed me in my resolve, though that was like the very parting of spirit and flesh. Yet a little longer I would stay since it was the last time.

'You think it is wrong, then?' she cried sharply, though I had said nothing.

'Not for you. A thousand times no. For you it is right . . . . I am grateful to you beyond words. For me it would be wrong. For me only . . . .'

'Why?' she said, but passed her hand before her face as she had done at our second meeting in the wood. 'Oh, I see,' she went on simply as a child. 'For you it would be wrong.' Then with a little indrawn laugh, 'and, d'you remember, I called you lucky—once—at first. You who must never come here again!'

She left me to sit a little longer by the screen, and I heard the sound of her feet die out along the gallery above.

from The Haunting of Hill House
by Shirley Jackson

The premise of Shirley Jackson's (1919–1965) creepiest work (and that's saying a lot) sounds almost goofy now: A researcher invites several people to stay in a supposedly haunted house, where he plans to study their reactions to whatever unfolds. But there's nothing goofy about what happens to the visitors, who include a lonely and somewhat bitter young woman named Eleanor. Evil does not overpower her. It seduces her—which is at once more interesting and much more unsettling to watch.

Looking at herself in the mirror, with the bright morning sunlight freshening even the blue room of Hill House, Eleanor thought, It is my second morning in Hill House, and I am unbelievably happy. Journeys end in lovers meeting; I have spent an all but sleepless night, I have told lies and made a fool of myself, and the very air tastes like wine. I have been frightened half out of my foolish wits, but I have somehow earned this joy; I have been waiting for it for so long. Abandoning a lifelong belief that to name happiness is to dissipate it, she smiled at herself in the mirror and told herself silently, You are happy, Eleanor, you have finally been given a part of your measure of happiness. Looking away from her own face in the mirror, she thought blindly, Journeys end in lovers meeting, lovers meeting.

"Luke?" It was Theodora, calling outside in the hall. "You carried off one of my stockings last night, and you are a thieving cad, and I hope Mrs. Dudley can hear me."

Eleanor could hear Luke, faintly, answering; he protested that a gentleman had a right to keep the favors bestowed upon him by a lady, and he was absolutely certain that Mrs. Dudley could hear every word.

"Eleanor?" Now Theodora pounded on the connecting door. "Are you awake? May I come in?"

"Come, of course," Eleanor said, looking at her own face in the mirror. You deserve it, she told herself, you have spent your life earning it. Theodora opened the door and said happily, "How pretty you look this morning, my Nell. This curious life agrees with you."

Eleanor smiled at her; the life clearly agreed with Theodora too.

"We ought by rights to be walking around with dark circles under our eyes and a look of wild despair," Theodora said, putting an arm around Eleanor and looking into the mirror beside her, "and look at us—two blooming, fresh young lovelies."

"I'm thirty-four years old," Eleanor said, and wondered what obscure defiance made her add two years.

"And you look about fourteen," Theodora said. "Come along; we've earned our breakfast."

Laughing, they raced down the great staircase and found their way through the game room and into the dining room. "Good morning," Luke said brightly. "And how did everyone sleep?"

"Delightfully, thank you," Eleanor said. "Like a baby."

"There may have been a little noise," Theodora said, "but one has to expect that in these old houses. Doctor, what do we do this morning?"

"Hm?" said the doctor, looking up. He alone looked tired, but his eyes were lighted with the same brightness they found, all, in one another; it is excitement, Eleanor thought; we are all enjoying ourselves.

"Ballechin House," the doctor said, savoring his words. "Borley Rectory. Glamis Castle. It is incredible to find oneself experiencing it, absolutely incredible. I could *not* have believed it. I begin to understand, dimly, the remote delight of your true medium. I think I shall have the marmalade, if you would be so kind. Thank you. My wife will never believe me. Food has a new flavor—do you find it so?"

"It isn't just that Mrs. Dudley has surpassed herself, then; I was wondering," Luke said.

"I've been trying to remember," Eleanor said. "About last night, I mean. I can remember *knowing* that I was frightened, but I can't imagine actually *being* frightened—"

"I remember the cold," Theodora said, and shivered.

"I think it's because it was so unreal by any pattern of thought I'm used to; I mean, it just didn't make *sense*." Eleanor stopped and laughed, embarrassed.

"I agree," Luke said. "I found myself this morning *telling* myself what had happened last night; the reverse of a bad dream, as a matter of fact, where you keep telling yourself that it *didn't* really happen."

"I thought it was exciting," Theodora said.

The doctor lifted a warning finger. "It is still perfectly possible that it is all caused by subterranean waters."

"Then more houses ought to be built over secret springs," Theodora said.

The doctor frowned. "This excitement troubles me," he said. "It is intoxicating, certainly, but might it not also be dangerous? An effect of the atmosphere of Hill House? The first sign that we have—as it were—fallen under a spell?"

"Then I will be an enchanted princess," Theodora said.

"And yet," Luke said, "if last night is a true measure of Hill House, we are not going to have much trouble; we were frightened, certainly, and found the experience unpleasant while it was going on, and yet I cannot remember that I felt in any *physical* danger; even Theodora telling that whatever was outside her door was coming to eat her did not really sound—"

"I know what she meant," Eleanor said, "because I thought it was exactly the right word. The sense was that it wanted to consume us, take us into itself, make us a part of the house, maybe—oh, dear. I thought I knew what I was saying, but I'm doing it very badly."

"No physical danger exists," the doctor said positively. "No ghost in all the long histories of ghosts has ever hurt anyone physically. The only damage done is by the victim to himself. One cannot even say that the ghost attacks the mind, because the mind, the conscious, thinking mind, is invulnerable; in all our conscious minds, as we sit here talking, there is not one iota of belief in ghosts. Not one of us, even after last night, can say the word 'ghost' without a little involuntary smile. No, the menace of the supernatural is that it attacks where modern minds are weakest, where we have abandoned our protective armor of superstition and have no substitute defense. Not one of us thinks rationally that what ran through the garden last night was a ghost, and what knocked on the door was a ghost, and yet there was certainly *something* going on in Hill House last night, and the mind's instinctive refuge— self-doubt—is eliminated. We cannot say, 'It was my imagination,' because three other people were there too."

"I could say," Eleanor put in, smiling, "'All three of you are in my imagination; none of this is real.'"

"If I thought you could really believe that," the doctor said gravely, "I would turn you out of Hill House this morning. You would be venturing far too close to the state of mind which would welcome the perils of Hill House with a kind of sisterly embrace."

"He means he would think you were batty, Nell dear."

"Well," Eleanor said, "I expect I would be. If I had to take sides with Hill House against the rest of you, I would expect you to send me away." Why me, she wondered, why me? Am I the public conscience? Expected always to say in cold words what the rest of them are too arrogant to recognize? Am I supposed to be the weakest, weaker than Theodora? Of all of us, she thought, I am surely the one least likely to turn against the others.

"Poltergeists are another thing altogether," the doctor said, his eyes resting briefly on Eleanor. "They deal entirely with the physical world; they throw stones, they move objects, they smash dishes; Mrs. Foyster at Borley Rectory was a long-suffering woman, but she finally lost her temper entirely when her best teapot was hurled through the window. Poltergeists, however, are rock-bottom on the supernatural social scale; they are destructive, but mindless and will-less; they are merely undirected force. Do you recall," he asked with a little smile, "Oscar Wilde's lovely story, 'The Canterville Ghost'?"

"The American twins who routed the fine old English ghost," Theodora said.

"Exactly. I have always liked the notion that the American twins were actually a poltergeist phenomenon; certainly poltergeists can over-shadow any more interesting manifestation. Bad ghosts drive out good." And he patted his hands happily. "They drive out everything else, too," he added. "There is a manor in Scotland, infested with pol-tergeists, where as many as seventeen spontaneous fires have broken out in one day; poltergeists like to turn people out of bed violently by tipping the bed end over end, and I remember the case of a minister who was forced to leave his home because he was tormented, day after day, by a poltergeist who hurled at his head hymn books stolen from a rival church."

Suddenly, without reason, laughter trembled inside Eleanor; she wanted to run to the head of the table and hug the doctor, she wanted to reel, chanting, across the stretches of the lawn, she wanted to sing and to shout and to fling her arms and move in great emphatic, pos-sessing circles around the rooms of Hill House; I am here, I am here, she thought. She shut her eyes quickly in delight and then said demurely to the doctor, "And what do we do today?"

"You're still like a pack of children," the doctor said, smiling too. "Always asking me what to do today. Can't you amuse yourselves with your toys? Or with each other? *I* have work to do."

"All I *really* want to do"—and Theodora giggled—"is slide down that banister." The excited gaiety had caught her as it had Eleanor.

"Hide and seek," Luke said.

"Try not to wander around alone too much," the doctor said. "I can't think of a good reason why not, but it does seem sensible."

"Because there are bears in the woods," Theodora said.

"And tigers in the attic," Eleanor said.

"And an old witch in the tower, and a dragon in the drawing room."

"I am quite serious," the doctor said, laughing.

"It's ten o'clock. I clear—"

"Good morning, Mrs. Dudley," the doctor said, and Eleanor and Theodora and Luke leaned back and laughed helplessly.

"I clear at ten o'clock."

"We won't keep you long. About fifteen minutes, please, and then you can clear the table."

"I clear breakfast at ten o'clock. I set on lunch at one. Dinner I set on at six. It's ten o'clock."

"Mrs. Dudley," the doctor began sternly, and then, noticing Luke's face tight with silent laughter, lifted his napkin to cover his eyes, and gave in. "You may clear the table, Mrs. Dudley," the doctor said brokenly.

Happily, the sound of their laughter echoing along the halls of Hill House and carrying to the marble group in the drawing room and the nursery upstairs and the odd little top to the tower, they made their way down the passage to their parlor and fell, still laughing, into chairs. "We must not make fun of Mrs. Dudley," the doctor said and leaned forward, his face in his hands and his shoulders shaking.

They laughed for a long time, speaking now and then in half-phrases, trying to tell one another something, pointing at one another wildly, and their laughter rocked Hill House until, weak and aching, they lay back, spent, and regarded one another. "Now—" the doctor began, and was stopped by a little giggling burst from Theodora.

"Now," the doctor said again, more severely, and they were quiet. "I want more coffee," he said, appealing. "Don't we all?"

"You mean go right in there and ask Mrs. Dudley? Eleanor asked.

"Walk right up to her when it isn't one o'clock or six o'clock and just *ask* her for some coffee?" Theodora demanded.

"Roughly, yes," the doctor said. "Luke, my boy, I have observed that you are already something of a favorite with Mrs. Dudley—"

"And how," Luke inquired with amazement, "did you ever manage to observe anything so unlikely? Mrs. Dudley regards me with the same particular loathing she gives a dish not properly on its shelf; in Mrs. Dudley's eyes—"

"You are, after all, the heir to the house," the doctor said coaxingly.

"Mrs. Dudley must feel for you as an old family retainer feels for the young master."

"In Mrs. Dudley's eyes I am something lower than a dropped fork. I beg of you, if you are contemplating asking the old fool for something, send Theo, or our charming Nell. *They* are not afraid—"

"Nope," Theodora said. "You can't send a helpless female to face down Mrs. Dudley. Nell and I are here to be protected, not to man the battlements for you cowards."

"The doctor—"

"Nonsense," the doctor said heartily. "You certainly wouldn't think of asking *me*, an older man; anyway, you *know* she adores you."

"Insolent graybeard," Luke said. "Sacrificing me for a cup of coffee. Do not be surprised, and I say it darkly, do not be surprised if you lose your Luke in this cause; perhaps Mrs. Dudley has not yet had her own mid-morning snack, and she is perfectly capable of a *filet de Luke à la meunière*, or perhaps *dieppoise*, depending upon her mood; if I do not return"—and he shook his finger warningly under the doctor's nose—"I entreat you to regard your lunch with the gravest suspicion." Bowing extravagantly, as befitted one off to slay a giant, he closed the door behind him.

"Lovely Luke." Theodora stretched luxuriously.

"Lovely Hill House," Eleanor said. "Theo, there is a kind of little summerhouse in the side garden, all overgrown; I noticed it yesterday. Can we explore it this morning?"

"Delighted," Theodora said. "I would not like to leave one inch of Hill House uncherished. Anyway, it's too nice a day to stay inside."

"We'll ask Luke to come too," Eleanor said. "And you, Doctor?

"My notes—" the doctor began, and then stopped as the door opened so suddenly that in Eleanor's mind was only the thought that Luke had not dared face Mrs. Dudley after all, but had stood, waiting, pressed against the door; then, looking at his white face and hearing the doctor say with fury, "I broke my own first rule; I sent him alone," she found herself only asking urgently, "Luke? Luke?"

"It's all right." Luke even smiled. "But, come into the long hallway."

Chilled by his face and his voice and his smile, they got up silently and followed him through the doorway into the dark long hallway which led back to the front hall. "Here," Luke said, and a little winding shiver of sickness went down Eleanor's back when she saw that he was holding a lighted match up to the wall.

"It's—writing?" Eleanor asked, pressing closer to see.

"Writing," Luke said. "I didn't even notice it until I was coming back. Mrs. Dudley said no," he added, his voice tight.

"My flash." The doctor took his flashlight from his pocket, and under its light, as he moved slowly from one end of the hall to the other, the letters stood out clearly. "Chalk," the doctor said, stepping forward to touch a letter with the tip of his finger. "Written in chalk."

The writing was large and straggling and ought to have looked, Eleanor thought, as though it had been scribbled by bad boys on a fence. Instead, it was incredibly real, going in broken lines over the thick paneling of the hallway. From one end of the hallway to the other the letters went, almost too large to read, even when she stood back against the opposite wall.

"Can you read it?" Luke asked softly, and the doctor, moving his flashlight, read slowly: HELP ELEANOR COME HOME.

"No." And Eleanor felt the words stop in her throat; she had seen her name as the doctor read it. It is me, she thought. It is my name standing out there so clearly; I should not be on the walls of this house. "Wipe it off, *please*," she said, and felt Theodora's arm go around her shoulders. "It's *crazy*," Eleanor said, bewildered.

"Crazy is the word, all right," Theodora said strongly. "Come back inside, Nell, and sit down. Luke will get something and wipe it off."

"But it's *crazy*," Eleanor said, hanging back to see her name on the wall. "*Why—?*"

Firmly the doctor put her through the door into the little parlor and closed it; Luke had already attacked the message with his handkerchief. "Now you listen to me," the doctor said to Eleanor. "Just because your name—"

"That's it," Eleanor said, staring at him. "It knows my name, doesn't it? It knows *my* name."

"Shut up, will you?" Theodora shook her violently. "It could have said any of us; it knows *all* our names."

"Did you write it?" Eleanor turned to Theodora. "Please tell me—I won't be angry or anything, just so I can know that—maybe it was only a joke? To frighten me?" She looked appealingly at the doctor.

"You know that none of us wrote it," the doctor said.

Luke came in, wiping his hands on his handkerchief, and Eleanor turned hopefully. "Luke'" she said, "you wrote it, didn't you? When you went out?"

Luke stared, and then came to sit on the arm of her chair. "Listen," he said, "you want me to go writing your name everywhere? Carving your initials on trees? Writing 'Eleanor, Eleanor' on little scraps of paper?" He gave her hair a soft little pull. "I've got more sense," he said. "Behave yourself."

"Then why me?" Eleanor said, looking from one of them to another; I am outside, she thought madly, I am the one chosen, and she said quickly, beggingly, "Did I do something to attract attention, more than anyone else?"

"No more than usual, dear," Theodora said. She was standing by the fireplace, leaning on the mantel and tapping her fingers, and when she spoke she looked at Eleanor with a bright smile. "Maybe you wrote it yourself."

Angry, Eleanor almost shouted. "You think I *want* to see my name scribbled all over this foul house? You think *I* like the idea that I'm the center of attention? I'm not the spoiled baby, after all—I don't like being singled out—"

"Asking for help, did you notice?" Theodora said lightly. "Perhaps the spirit of the poor little companion has found a means of communication at last. Maybe she was only waiting for some drab, timid—"

"Maybe it was only addressed to me because no possible appeal for help could get through that iron selfishness of yours; maybe I might have more sympathy and understanding in one minute than—"

"And maybe, of course, you wrote it to yourself," Theodora said again.

After the manner of men who see women quarreling, the doctor and

Luke had withdrawn, standing tight together in miserable silence; now, at last, Luke moved and spoke. "That's enough, Eleanor," he said, unbelievably, and Eleanor whirled around, stamping. "How dare you?" she said, gasping. "How *dare* you?"

And the doctor laughed, then, and she stared at him and then at Luke, who was smiling and watching her. What is wrong with me? she thought. Then—but they think Theodora did it on purpose, made me mad so I wouldn't be frightened; how shameful to be maneuvered that way. She covered her face and sat down in her chair.

"Nell, dear," Theodora said, "I *am* sorry."

I must say something, Eleanor told herself; I must show them that I am a good sport, after all; a good sport; let them think that I am ashamed of myself. "*I'm* sorry," she said. "I was frightened."

"Of course you were," the doctor said, and Eleanor thought, How simple he is, how transparent; he believes every silly thing he has ever heard. He thinks, even, that Theodora shocked me out of hysteria. She smiled at him and thought, Now I am back in the fold.

"I really thought you were going to start shrieking," Theodora said, coming to kneel by Eleanor's chair. "*I* would have, in your place. But we can't afford to have you break up, you know."

We can't afford to have anyone but Theodora in the center of the stage, Eleanor thought; if Eleanor is going to be the outsider, she is going to be it all alone. She reached out and patted Theodora's head and said, "Thanks. I guess I was kind of shaky for a minute."

"I wondered if you two were going to come to blows," Luke said, "until I realized what Theodora was doing."

Smiling down into Theodora's bright, happy eyes, Eleanor thought, But that isn't what Theodora was doing at all.

Time passed lazily at Hill House. Eleanor and Theodora, the doctor and Luke, alert against terror, wrapped around by the rich hills and securely set into the warm, dark luxuries of the house, were permitted a quiet day and a quiet night—enough, perhaps, to dull them a little. They took their meals together, and Mrs. Dudley's cooking stayed perfect. They talked together and played chess; the doctor finished *Pamela* and began on *Sir Charles Grandison*. A compelling need for occasional privacy led them to spend some hours alone in their separate rooms, without disturbance. Theodora and Eleanor and Luke explored the tangled thicket behind the house and found the little summerhouse, while the doctor sat on the wide lawn, writing, within sight and hearing. They found a walled-in rose garden, grown over with weeds, and a vegetable garden tenderly nourished by the Dudleys. They spoke often of arranging their picnic by the brook. There were wild strawberries near the summerhouse, and Theodora and Eleanor and Luke brought back a handkerchief full and lay on the lawn near the doctor, eating them, staining their hands and their mouths; like children, the doctor told them, looking up with amusement from his notes. Each of them had written—carelessly, and with little attention to detail—an account of what they thought they had seen and heard so far in Hill House, and the doctor had put the papers away in his portfolio. The next morning—their third morning in Hill House—the doctor, aided by Luke, had spent a loving and maddening hour on the floor of the upstairs hall, trying, with chalk and measuring tape, to determine the precise dimensions of the cold spot, while Eleanor and Theodora sat cross-legged on the hall floor, noting down the doctor's measurements and playing tic-tac-toe. The doctor was considerably hampered in his work by the fact that, his hands repeatedly chilled by the extreme cold, he could not hold either the chalk or the tape for more than a minute at a time. Luke, inside the nursery doorway, could hold one end of the tape until his hand came into the cold spot, and then his fingers lost strength and relaxed helplessly. A thermometer, dropped into the center of the cold spot, refused to register any change at all, but continued doggedly maintaining that the temperature there was the same as the temperature down the rest of the hall, causing the doctor to fume wildly against the statisticians of Borley Rectory, who had caught an eleven-degree drop. When he had defined the cold spot as well as he could, and noted his results in his notebook, he brought them downstairs for lunch and issued a general challenge to them, to meet him at croquet in the cool of the afternoon.

"It seems foolish," he explained, "to spend a morning as glorious as this has been looking at a frigid place on a floor. We must plan to spend more time outside"—and was mildly surprised when they laughed.

"Is there still a world somewhere?" Eleanor asked wonderingly. Mrs. Dudley had made them a peach shortcake, and she looked down at her plate and said, "I am sure Mrs. Dudley goes somewhere else at night, and she brings back heavy cream each morning, and Dudley comes up with groceries every afternoon, but as far as I can remember there is no other place than this."

"We are on a desert island," Luke said.

"I can't picture any world but Hill House," Eleanor said.

"Perhaps," Theodora said, "we should make notches on a stick, or pile pebbles in a heap, one each day, so we will know how long we have been marooned."

"How pleasant not to have any word from outside." Luke helped himself to an enormous heap of whipped cream. "No letters, no newspapers; anything might be happening."

"Unfortunately—" the doctor said, and then stopped. "I beg your pardon," he went on. "I meant only to say that word *will* be reaching us from outside, and of course it is not unfortunate at all. Mrs. Montague—my wife, that is—will be here on Saturday."

"But when is Saturday?" Luke asked. "Delighted to see Mrs. Montague, of course."

"Day after tomorrow." The doctor thought. "Yes," he said after a minute, "I believe that the day after tomorrow is Saturday. We will know it is Saturday, of course," he told them with a little twinkle, "because Mrs. Montague will be here."

"I hope she is not holding high hopes of things going bump in the night," Theodora said. "Hill House has fallen far short of its original promise, I think. Or perhaps Mrs. Montague will be greeted with a volley of psychic experiences."

"Mrs. Montague," the doctor said, "will be perfectly ready to receive them."

"I wonder," Theodora said to Eleanor as they left the lunch table under Mrs. Dudley's watchful eye, "why everything *has* been so quiet. I think this waiting is nerve-racking, almost worse than having something happen."

"It's not us doing the waiting," Eleanor said. "It's the house. I think it's biding its time."

"Waiting until we feel secure, maybe, and then it will pounce."

"I wonder how long it can wait." Eleanor shivered and started up the great staircase. "I am almost tempted to write a letter to my sister. You know—'Having a perfectly *splendid* time here in jolly old Hill House . . . .'"

"'You really must plan to bring the whole family next summer,'" Theodora went on. "'We sleep under blankets every night . . .'"

"'The air is so bracing, particularly in the upstairs hall . . . .' "

"'You go around all the time just glad to be alive . . . .'"

"'There's something going on every minute . . . .'"

"'Civilization seems so far away . . . .'"

Eleanor laughed. She was ahead of Theodora, at the top of the stairs. The dark hallway was a little lightened this afternoon, because they had left the nursery door open and the sunlight came through the windows by the tower and touched the doctor's measuring tape and chalk on the floor. The light reflected from the stained-glass window on the stair landing and made shattered fragments of blue and orange and green on the dark wood of the hall. "I'm going to sleep," she said. "I've never been so lazy in my life."

"I'm going to lie on my bed and dream about streetcars," Theodora said.

It had become Eleanor's habit to hesitate in the doorway of her room, glancing around quickly before she went inside; she told herself that this was because the room was so exceedingly blue and always took a moment to get used to. When she came inside she went across to open the window, which she always found closed; today she was halfway across the room before she heard Theodora's door slam back, and Theodora's smothered "Eleanor!" Moving quickly, Eleanor ran into the hall and to Theodora's doorway, to stop, aghast, looking over Theodora's shoulder. "What *is* it?" she whispered.

"What does it *look* like?" Theodora's voice rose crazily. "What does it *look* like, you fool?"

And I won't forgive her *that*, either, Eleanor thought concretely through her bewilderment. "It looks like paint," she said hesitantly. "Except"—realizing—"except the smell is awful."

"It's blood," Theodora said with finality. She clung to the door, swaying as the door moved, staring. "Blood," she said. "All over. Do you see it? "

"Of course I see it. And it's not *all* over. Stop making such a fuss." Although, she thought conscientiously, Theodora was making very little of a fuss, actually. One of these times, she thought, one of us *is* going to put her head back and really howl, and I hope it won't be me, because I'm trying to guard against it; it *will* be Theodora who . . . And then, cold, she asked, "Is that more writing on the wall?"—and heard Theodora's wild laugh, and thought, Maybe it will be me, after all, and I can't afford to. I must be steady, and she closed her eyes and found herself saying silently, O stay and hear, your true love's coming, that can sing both high and low. Trip no further, pretty sweeting; journeys end in lovers meeting . . .

"Yes indeed, dear," Theodora said. "I don't know how you managed it."

Every wise man's son doth know. "Be sensible," Eleanor said. "Call Luke. And the doctor."

"Why?" Theodora asked. "Wasn't it to be just a little private surprise for me? A secret just for the two of us?" Then, pulling away from Eleanor, who tried to hold her from going farther into the room, she ran to the great wardrobe and threw open the door and, cruelly, began to cry. "My clothes," she said. "My clothes."

Steadily Eleanor turned and went to the top of the stairs. "Luke," she called, leaning over the banisters. "Doctor." Her voice was not loud, and she had tried to keep it level, but she heard the doctor's book drop to the floor and then the pounding of feet as he and Luke ran for the stairs. She watched them, seeing their apprehensive faces, wondering at the uneasiness which lay so close below the surface in all of them, so that each of them seemed always waiting for a cry for help from one of the others; intelligence and understanding are really no protection at all, she thought "It's Theo," she said as they came to the top of the stairs. "She's hysterical. Someone—something—has gotten red paint in her room, and she's crying over her clothes." Now I could not have put it more fairly than that, she thought, turning to follow them. Could I have put it more fairly than that? she asked herself, and found that she was smiling.

Theodora was still sobbing wildly in her room and kicking at the wardrobe door, in a tantrum that might have been laughable if she had not been holding her yellow shirt, matted and stained; her other clothes had been torn from the hangers and lay trampled and disordered on the wardrobe floor, all of them smeared and reddened. "What is it?" Luke asked the doctor, and the doctor, shaking his head, said, "I would swear that it was blood, and yet to get so much blood one would almost have to . . ." and then was abruptly quiet.

All of them stood in silence for a moment and looked at HELP ELEANOR COME HOME ELEANOR written in shaky red letters on the wallpaper over Theodora's bed.

This time I am ready, Eleanor told herself, and said, "You'd better get her out of here; bring her into my room."

"My clothes are ruined," Theodora said to the doctor. "Do you see my clothes?"

The smell was atrocious, and the writing on the wall had dripped and splattered. There was a line of drops from the wall to the wardrobe—perhaps what had first turned Theodora's attention that way—and a great irregular stain on the green rug. "It's disgusting," Eleanor said. "Please get Theo into my room."

Luke and the doctor between them persuaded Theodora through the bathroom and into Eleanor's room, and Eleanor, looking at the red paint (It must be paint, she told herself; it's simply *got* to be paint; what else *could* it be?), said aloud, "But *why?*"—and stared up at the writing on the wall. Here lies one, she thought gracefully, whose name was writ in blood; is it possible that I am not quite coherent at this moment?

"Is she all right?" she asked, turning as the doctor came back into the room.

"She will be in a few minutes. We'll have to move her in with you for a while, I should think; I can't imagine her wanting to sleep in *here* again." The doctor smiled a little wanly. "It will be a long time, I think, before she opens another door by herself."

"I suppose she'll have to wear my clothes."

"I suppose she will, if you don't mind." The doctor looked at her curiously. "This message troubles you less than the other?"

"It's too silly," Eleanor said, trying to understand her own feelings. "I've been standing here looking at it and just wondering *why*. I mean, it's like a joke that didn't come off; I was supposed to be *much* more frightened than this, I think, and I'm not because it's simply *too* horrible to be real. And I keep remembering Theo putting red polish . . ." She giggled, and the doctor looked at her sharply, but she went on, "It might as *well* be paint, don't you see?" I can't stop talking, she thought; what do *I* have to explain in all this? "Maybe I can't take it seriously," she said, "after the sight of Theo screaming over her poor clothes and accusing me of writing my name all over her wall. Maybe I'm getting used to her blaming me for everything."

"Nobody's blaming you for anything," the doctor said, and Eleanor felt that she had been reproved.

"I hope my clothes will be good enough for her," she said tartly.

The doctor turned, looking around the room; he touched one finger gingerly to the letters on the wall and moved Theodora's yellow shirt with his foot. "Later," he said absently. "Tomorrow, perhaps." He glanced at Eleanor and smiled. "I can make an exact sketch of this," he said.

"I can help you," Eleanor said. "It makes me sick, but it doesn't frighten me."

"Yes," the doctor said. "I think we'd better close up the room for now, however; we don't want Theodora blundering in here again. Then later, at my leisure, I can study it. Also," he said with a flash of amusement, "I would not like to have Mrs. Dudley coming in here to straighten up."

Eleanor watched silently while he locked the hall door from inside the room, and then they went through the bathroom and he locked the connecting door into Theodora's green room. "I'll see about moving in another bed," he said, and then, with some awkwardness, "You've kept your head well, Eleanor; it's a help to me."

"I told you, it makes me sick but it doesn't frighten me," she said, pleased, and turned to Theodora. Theodora was lying on Eleanor's bed, and Eleanor saw with a queasy turn that Theodora had gotten red on her hands and it was rubbing off onto Eleanor's pillow. "Look," she said harshly, coming over to Theodora, you'll have to wear my clothes until you get new ones, or until we get the others cleaned."

"Cleaned?" Theodora rolled convulsively on the bed and pressed her stained hands against her eyes. "*Cleaned?*"

"For heaven's sake," Eleanor said, "let me wash you off." She thought, without trying to find a reason, that she had never felt such uncontrollable loathing for any person before, and she went into the bathroom and soaked a towel and came back to scrub roughly at Theodora's hands and face. "You're filthy with the stuff," she said, hating to touch Theodora.

Suddenly Theodora smiled at her. "I don't really think you did it," she said, and Eleanor turned to see that Luke was behind her, looking down at them. "What a fool I am," Theodora said to him, and Luke laughed.

"You will be a delight in Nell's red sweater," he said.

She is wicked, Eleanor thought, beastly and soiled and dirty. She took the towel into the bathroom and left it to soak in cold water; when she came out Luke was saying, ". . .another bed in here; you girls are going to share a room from now on."

"Share a room and share our clothes," Theodora said. "We're going to be practically twins."

"Cousins," Eleanor said, but no one heard her.

"It was the custom, rigidly adhered to," Luke said, turning the brandy in his glass, "for the public executioner, before a quartering, to outline his knife strokes in chalk upon the belly of his victim—for fear of a slip, you understand."

I would like to hit her with a stick, Eleanor thought, looking down on Theodora's head beside her chair; I would like to batter her with rocks.

"An exquisite refinement, exquisite. Because of course the chalk strokes would have been almost unbearable, excruciating, if the victim were ticklish."

I hate her, Eleanor thought, she sickens me; she is all washed and clean and wearing my red sweater.

"When the death was by hanging in chains, however, the executioner . . ."

"Nell?" Theodora looked up at her and smiled. "I really am sorry, you know," she said.

I would like to watch her dying, Eleanor thought, and smiled back and said, "Don't be silly."

"Among the Sufis there is a teaching that the universe has never been created and consequently cannot be destroyed. I have spent the afternoon," Luke announced gravely, "browsing in our little library."

The doctor sighed. "No chess tonight, I think," he said to Luke, and Luke nodded. "It has been an exhausting day," the doctor said, "and I think you ladies should retire early."

"Not until I am well dulled with brandy," Theodora said firmly.

"Fear," the doctor said, "is the relinquishment of logic, the *willing* relinquishing of reasonable patterns. We yield to it or we fight it, but we cannot meet it halfway."

"I was wondering earlier," Eleanor said, feeling she had somehow an apology to make to all of them. "I thought I was altogether calm, and yet now I know I was terribly afraid." She frowned, puzzled, and they waited for her to go on. "When I *am* afraid, I can see perfectly the sensible, beautiful not-afraid side of the world, I can see chairs and tables and windows staying the same, not affected in the least, and I can see things like the careful woven texture of the carpet, not even moving.

But when I am afraid I no longer exist in any relation to these things. I suppose because things are *not* afraid."

"I think we are only afraid of ourselves," the doctor said slowly.

"No," Luke said. "Of seeing ourselves clearly and without disguise."

"Of knowing what we really want," Theodora said. She pressed her cheek against Eleanor's hand and Eleanor, hating the touch of her, took her hand away quickly.

"I am always afraid of being alone," Eleanor said, and wondered, Am *I* talking like this? Am I saying something I will regret bitterly tomorrow? Am I making more guilt for myself? "Those letters spelled out *my* name, and none of you know what that feels like—it's so *familiar*." And she gestured to them, almost in appeal. "Try to *see*," she said. "It's my own dear name, and it belongs to me, and something is using it and writing it and calling me with it and my own *name* . . ." She stopped and said, looking from one of them to another, even down onto Theodora's face looking up at her, "Look. There's only one of me, and it's all I've got. I *hate* seeing myself dissolve and slip and separate so that I'm living in one half, my mind, and I see the other half of me helpless and frantic and driven and I can't stop it, but I know I'm not really going to be hurt and yet time is so long and even a second goes on and on and I could stand any of it if I could only surrender—"

"*Surrender?*" said the doctor sharply, and Eleanor stared.

"Surrender?" Luke repeated.

"I don't know," Eleanor said, perplexed. I was just talking along, she told herself, I was saying something—what was I just saying?

"She has done this before," Luke said to the doctor.

"I know," said the doctor gravely, and Eleanor could feel them all looking at her. "I'm sorry," she said. "Did I make a fool of myself? It's probably because I'm tired."

"Not at all," the doctor said, still grave. "Drink your brandy."

"Brandy?" And Eleanor looked down, realizing that she held a brandy glass. "What did I *say*?" she asked them.

Theodora chuckled. "Drink," she said, "You need it, my Nell."

Obediently Eleanor sipped at her brandy, feeling clearly its sharp burn, and then said to the doctor, "I must have said something silly, from the way you're all staring at me."

The doctor laughed. "Stop trying to be the center of attention."

"Vanity," Luke said serenely,

"Have to be in the limelight," Theodora said, and they smiled fondly, all looking at Eleanor.

Sitting up in the two beds beside each other, Eleanor and Theodora reached out between and held hands tight; the room was brutally cold and thickly dark. From the room next door, the room which until that morning had been Theodora's, came the steady low sound of a voice babbling, too low for words to be understood, too steady for disbelief. Holding hands so hard that each of them could feel the other's bones, Eleanor and Theodora listened, and the low, steady sound went on and on, the voice lifting sometimes for an emphasis on a mumbled word, falling sometimes to a breath, going on and on. Then, without warning, there was a little laugh, the small gurgling laugh that broke through the babbling, and rose as it laughed, on up and up the scale, and then broke off suddenly in a little painful gasp, and the voice went on.

Theodora's grasp loosened, and tightened, and Eleanor, lulled for a minute by the sounds, started and looked across to where Theodora ought to be in the darkness, and then thought, screamingly, Why is it dark? *Why is it dark?* She rolled and clutched Theodora's hand with both of hers, and tried to speak and could not, and held on, blindly, and frozen, trying to stand her mind on its feet, trying to reason again. We left the light on, she told herself, so why is it dark? Theodora, she tried to whisper, and her mouth could not move; Theodora, she tried to ask, why is it dark? and the voice went on, babbling, low and steady, a little liquid gloating sound. She thought she might be able to distinguish words if she lay perfectly still, if she lay perfectly still, and listened, and listened and heard the voice going on and on, never ceasing, and she hung desperately to Theodora's hand and felt an answering weight on her own hand.

Then the little gurgling laugh came again, and the rising mad sound of it drowned out the voice, and then suddenly absolute silence. Eleanor took a breath, wondering if she could speak now, and then she heard a little soft cry which broke her heart, a little infinitely sad cry, a little sweet moan of wild sadness. It is a *child*, she thought with disbelief, a child is crying somewhere, and then, upon that thought, came the wild shrieking voice she had never heard before and yet knew she had heard always in her nightmares. "Go away!" it screamed. "Go away, go away, don't hurt me," and, after, sobbing, "Please don't hurt me. Please let me go home," and then the little sad crying again.

I can't stand it, Eleanor thought concretely. This is monstrous, this is cruel, they have been hurting a child and I won't let anyone hurt a child, and the babbling went on, low and steady, on and on and on, the voice rising a little and falling a little, going on and on.

Now, Eleanor thought, perceiving that she was lying sideways on the bed in the black darkness, holding with both hands to Theodora's hand, holding so tight she could feel the fine bones of Theodora's fingers, now, I will not endure this. They think to scare me. Well, they have. I am scared, but more than that, I am a person, I am human, I am a walking reasoning humorous human being and I will take a lot from this lunatic filthy house but I will not go along with hurting a child, no, I will not; I will by God get my mouth to open right now and I will yell I will I will yell "STOP IT," she shouted, and the lights were on the way they had left them and Theodora was sitting up in bed, startled and disheveled.

"What?" Theodora was saying. "What, Nell? What?"

"God God," Eleanor said, flinging herself out of bed and across the room to stand shuddering in a corner, "God God—whose hand was I holding?"

from The Wasp Factory
by Iain Banks

English novelist Iain Banks' (born 1954) first book caused a sensation when it was published in 1984. The protagonist is Frank, a teenager who lives with his ex-hippie father on a Scottish island. Frank has been told that the family's sheepdog castrated him at a tender age. He keeps up his spirits by killing other children (his younger brother and two small cousins) and by engaging in elaborate murders of insects and small animals. Still, Frank is polite, and he tells a good story.

I killed little Esmerelda because I felt I owed it to myself and to the world in general. I had, after all, accounted for two male children and thus done womankind something of a statistical favour. If I really had the courage of my convictions, I reasoned, I ought to redress the balance at least slightly. My cousin was simply the easiest and most obvious target.

Again, I bore her no personal ill-will. Children aren't real people, in the sense that they are not small males and females but a separate species which will (probably) grow into one or the other in due time. Younger children in particular, before the insidious and evil influence of society and their parents have properly got to them, are sexlessly open and hence perfectly likeable. I did like Esmerelda (even if I thought her name was a bit soppy) and played with her a lot when she came to stay. She was the daughter of Harmsworth and Morag Stove, my half-uncle and half-aunt by my father's first marriage; they were the couple who had looked after Eric between the ages of three and five. They

would come over from Belfast to stay with us in the summers sometimes; my father used to get on well with Harmsworth, and because I
looked after Esmerelda they could have a nice relaxing holiday here. I
think Mrs Stove was a little worried about trusting her daughter to me
that particular summer, as it was the one after I'd struck young Paul
down in his prime, but at nine years of age I was an obviously happy
and well-adjusted child, responsible and well-spoken and, when it was
mentioned, demonstrably sad about my younger brother's demise. I
am convinced that only my genuinely clear conscience let me convince the adults around me that I was totally innocent. I even carried
out a double-bluff of appearing slightly guilty *for the wrong reasons*, so
that adults told me I shouldn't blame myself because I hadn't been
able to warn Paul in time. I was brilliant.

I had decided I would try to murder Esmerelda before she and her
parents even arrived for their holiday. Eric was away on a school cruise,
so there would only be me and her. It would be risky, so soon after
Paul's death, but I had to do something to even up the balance. I could
feel it in my guts, in my bones; I *had* to. It was like an itch, something
I had no way of resisting, like when I walk along a pavement in
Porteneil and I accidentally scuff one heel on a paving stone. I *have* to
scuff the other foot as well, with as near as possible the same weight,
to feel good again. The same if I brush one arm against a wall or a
lamp-post; I must brush the other one as well, soon, or at the very least
scratch it with the other hand. In a whole range of ways like that I try
to keep balanced, though I have no idea why. It is simply something
that must be done; and, in the same way, I had to get rid of *some*
woman, tip the scales back in the other direction.

I had taken to making kites that year. It was 1973, I suppose. I used
many things to make them: cane and dowelling and metal coathang-
ers and aluminium tent-poles, and paper and plastic sheeting and
dustbin bags and sheets and string and nylon rope and twine and all
sorts of little straps and buckles and bits of cord and elastic bands and
strips of wire and pins and screws and nails and pieces cannibalised
from model yachts and various toys. I made a hand winch with a dou-

ble handle and a ratchet and room for half a kilometre of twine on the drum; I made different types of tails for the kites that needed them, and dozens of kites large and small, some stunters. I kept them in the shed and eventually had to put the bikes outside under a tarpaulin when the collection got too large.

That summer I took Esmerelda kiting quite a lot. I let her play with a small, single-string kite while I used a stunter. I would send it swooping over and under hers, or dive it down to the sands while I stood on a dune cliff, pulling the kite down to nick tall towers of sand I'd built, then pulling up again, the kite trailing a spray of sand through the air from the collapsing tower. Although it took a while and I crashed a couple of times, once I even knocked a dam down with a kite. I swooped it so that on each pass it caught the top of the dam wall with one corner, gradually producing a nick in the sand barrier which the water was able to flow through, quickly going on to overwhelm the whole dam and the sand-house village beneath.

Then one day I was standing there on a dune top, straining against the pull of the wind in the kite, gripping and hauling and sensing and adjusting and twisting, when one of those twists became like a strangle around Esmerelda's neck, and the idea was there. Use the kites.

I thought about it calmly, still standing there as though nothing had passed through my mind but the continual computation guiding the kite, and I thought it seemed reasonable. As I thought about it, the notion took its own shape, blossoming, as it were, and escalating into what I finally conceived as my cousin's nemesis. I grinned then, I recall, and brought the stunter down fast and acute across the weeds and the water, the sand and the surf, scudding it in across the wind to jerk and zoom just before it hit the girl herself where she sat on the dune top holding and spasmodically jerking the string she held in her hand, connected to the sky. She turned, smiled and shrieked then, squinting in the summer light. I laughed, too, controlling the thing in the skies above and the thing in the brain beneath, equally well.

I built a big kite.

It was so big it didn't even fit inside the shed. I made it from old aluminium tent-poles, some of which I had found in the attic a long time previously and some I had got from the town dump. The fabric, at first, was black plastic bags, but later became tent fabric, also from the attic.

I used heavy orange nylon fishing-line for the string, wound round a specially made drum for the winch, which I had strengthed and fit-ted with a chest-brace. The kite had a tail of twisted magazine pages— *Guns and Ammo*, which I got regularly at the time. I painted the head of a dog on the canvas in red paint because I had yet to learn I was not a Canis. My father had told me years before that I was born under the starsign of the Dog because Sirius was overhead at the time. Anyway, that was just a symbol.

I went out very early one morning, just after the sun came up and long before anybody else woke. I went to the shed, got the kite, walked a way along the dunes and assembled it, battered a tent-peg into the ground, tied the nylon to it, then flew the kite on a short string for a while. I sweated and strained with it, even in quite a light wind, and my hands grew warm despite the heavy-duty welding-gloves I had on. I decided the kite would do, and brought it in.

That afternoon, while the same wind, now freshened, still blew across the island and off into the North Sea, Esmerelda and I went out as usual, and stopped off at the shed to pick up the dismantled kite. She helped me carry it far along the dunes, dutifully clutching the lines and winch to her flat little chest and clicking the ratchet on the drum, until we reached a point well out of sight from the house. It was a tall dune head stuck nodding towards distant Norway or Denmark, grass like hair swept over the brow and pointing.

Esmerelda searched for flowers while I constructed the kite with an appropriately solemn slowness. She talked to the flowers, I recall, as though trying to persuade them to show themselves and be collected, broken and bunched. The wind blew her blonde hair in front of her face as she walked, squatted, crawled and talked, and I assembled.

Finally the kite was finished, fully made up and lying like a col-lapsed tent on the grass, green on green. The wind coursed over it and flapped it—little whip noises that stirred it and made it seem alive, the dog-face scowling. I sorted the orange nylon lines out and did some tying, untangling line from line, knot from knot.

I called Esmerelda over. She had a fistful of tiny flowers, and made me wait patiently while she described them all, making up her own names when she forgot or had never learned the real ones. I accepted the daisy she gave me graciously and put it in the buttonhole of my jacket's left breast pocket. I told her that I had finished constructing the new kite, and that she could help me test it in the wind. She was excited, wanting to hold the strings. I told her she might get a chance, though of course I would have the ultimate control. She wanted to hold the flowers as well, and I told her that might just be possible.

Esmerelda ooh'd and ah'd over the size of the kite and the fierce doggy painted on it. The kite lay on the wind-ruffled grass like an impatient manta, rippling. I found the main control lines and gave them to Esmerelda, showing her how to hold them, and where. I had made loops to go over her wrists, I told her, so that she wouldn't lose her grip. She struck her hands through the braided nylon, holding one line tight and grasping the posy of bright flowers and the second line with her other hand. I got my part of the control lines together and carried them in a loop round to the kite. Esmerelda jumped up and down and told me to hurry up and make the kite fly. I took a last look round, then only had to kick the top edge of the kite up a little for it to take the wind and lift. I ran back behind my cousin while the slack between her and the rapidly ascending kite was taken up.

The kite blew into the sky like something wild, hoisting its tail with a noise like tearing cardboard. It shook itself and cracked in the air. It sliced its tail and flexed its hollow bones. I came up behind Esmerelda and held the lines just behind her little freckled elbows, waiting for the tug. The lines came taut, and it came. I had to dig my heels in to stay steady. I bumped into Esmerelda and made her squeal. She had let the lines go when the first brutal snap had straightened the nylon, and stood glancing back at me and staring up into the sky as I fought to control the power in the skies above us. She still clutched the flowers, and my tuggings on the lines moved her arms like a marionette, guided by the loops. The winch rested against my chest, a little slack between it and my hands. Esmerelda looked round one last time at me, giggling, and I laughed back. Then I let the lines go.

The winch hit her in the small of the back and she yelped. Then she was dragged off her feet as the lines pulled her and the loops tightened round her wrists. I staggered back, partly to make it look good on the offchance there was somebody watching and partly because letting go of the winch had put me off balance. I fell to the ground as Esmerelda left it forever. The kite just kept snapping and flapping and flapping and snapping and it hauled the girl off the earth and into the air, winch and all. I lay on my back and watched it for a second, then got up and ran after her as fast as I could, again just because I knew I couldn't catch her. She was screaming and waggling her legs for all she was worth, but the cruel loops of nylon had her about the wrists, the kite was in the jaws of the wind, and she was already well out of reach even if I had wanted to catch her.

I ran and ran, jumping off a dune and rolling down its seaward face, watching the tiny struggling figure being hoisted farther and farther into the sky as the kite swept her away. I could just barely hear her yells and shouts, a thin wailing carried on the wind. She sailed over the sands and the rocks and out towards the sea, me running, exhilarated, underneath, watching the stuck winch bob under her kicking feet. Her dress billowed out around her.

She went higher and higher and I kept running, outpaced now by the wind and the kite. I ran through the ripple-puddles at the margins of the sea, then into it, up to my knees. Just then something, at first seemingly solid, then separating and dissociating, fell from her. At first I though she had pissed herself, then I saw flowers tumble out of the sky and hit the water ahead of me like some strange rain. I waded out over the shallows until I came to them, and gathered the ones I could, looking up from my harvest as Esmerelda and kite struck out for the North Sea. It did cross my mind that she might actually get across the damn thing and hit land before the wind dropped, but I reckoned that even if that happened I had done my best, and honour was satisfied.

I watched her get smaller and smaller, then turned and headed for shore.

I knew that three deaths in my immediate vicinity within four years *had* to look suspicious, and I had already planned my reaction carefully. I didn't run straight home to the house, but went back up into the dunes and sat down there, holding the flowers. I sang songs to myself, made up stories, got hungry, rolled around in the sand a bit, rubbed a little of it into my eyes and generally tried to psyche myself up into something that might look like a terrible state for a wee boy to be in. I was still sitting there in the early evening, staring out to sea when a young forestry worker from the town found me.

He was one of the search party drummed up by Diggs after my father and relations missed us and couldn't find us and called the police. The young man came over the tops of the dunes, whistling and casually whacking clumps of reed and grass with a stick.

I didn't take any notice of him. I kept staring and shivering and clutching the flowers. My father and Diggs came along after the young man passed word along the line of people beating their way along the dunes, but I didn't take any notice of those two, either. Eventually there were dozens of people clustered around me, looking at me, asking me questions, scratching their heads, looking at their watches and gazing about. I didn't take any notice of them. They formed their line again and started searching for Esmerelda while I was carried back to the house. They offered me soup I was desperate for but took no notice of, asked me questions I answered with a catatonic silence and a stare. My uncle and aunt shook me, their faces red and eyes wet, but I took no notice of them. Eventually my father took me to my room, undressed me and put me to bed.

Somebody stayed in my room all night and, whether it was my father, Diggs or anybody else, I kept them and me awake all night by lying quiet for a while, feigning sleep, then screaming with all my might and falling out of bed to thrash about on the floor. Each time I was picked up, cuddled and put back to bed. Each time I pretended to go to sleep again and went crazy after a few minutes. If any of them talked to me, I just lay shaking in the bed staring at them, soundless and deaf.

I kept that up until dawn, when the search party returned, Esmerelda-less, then I let myself go to sleep.

It took me a week to recover, and it was one of the best weeks of my life. Eric came back from his school cruise and I started to talk a little after he arrived; just nonsense at first, then later disjointed hints at what had happened, always followed by screaming and catatonia.

Sometime around the middle of the week, Dr MacLennan was allowed to see me for a while, after Diggs overruled my father's refusal to have me medically inspected by anybody else but him. Even so, he stayed in the room, glowering and suspicious, making sure that the examination was kept within certain limits; I was glad he didn't let the doctor look all over me, and I responded by becoming a little more lucid.

By the end of the week I was still having the occasional fake nightmare, I would suddenly go very quiet and shivery every now and again, but I was eating more or less normally and could answer most questions quite happily. Talking about Esmerelda, and what had happened to her, still brought on mini-fits and screams and total withdrawal for a while, but after long and patient questioning by my father and Diggs I let them know what I wanted them to think had happened—a big kite; Esmerelda becoming entangled in the lines; me trying to help her and the winch slipping out of my fingers; desperate running; then a blank.

I explained that I was afraid I was jinxed, that I brought death and destruction upon all those near me, and also that I was afraid I might get sent to prison because people would think I had murdered Esmerelda. I wept and I hugged my father and I even hugged Diggs, smelling his hard-blue uniform fabric as I did so and almost feeling him melt and believe me. I asked him to go to the shed and take all my kites away and burn them, which he duly did, in a hollow now called Kite Pyre Dell. I was sorry about the kites, and I knew that I'd have to give up flying them for good to keep the act looking realistic, but it was worth it. Esmerelda never did show up; nobody saw her after me, as far as Diggs' enquiries of trawlers and drillingrigs and so on could show.

So I got to even up the score and have a wonderful, if demanding, week of full acting. The flowers that I had still been clutching when they carried me back to the house had been prised from my fingers and left in a plastic bag on top of the fridge. I discovered them there, shrivelled and dead, forgotten and unnoticed, two weeks later. I took them for the shrine in the loft one night, and have them to this day, little brown twists of dried plant like old Sellotape, stuck in a little glass bottle. I wonder sometimes where my cousin ended up; at the bottom of the sea, or washed on to some craggy and deserted shore, or blown on to a high mountain face, to be eaten by gulls or eagles . . . .

I would like to think that she died still being floated by the giant kite, that she went round the world and rose higher as she died of starvation and dehydration and so grew less weighty still, to become, eventually, a tiny skeleton riding the jetstreams of the planet; a sort of Flying Dutchwoman. But I doubt that such a romantic vision really matches the truth.

Home Burial
by Robert Frost

Some readers find this Robert Frost (1874–1963) poem more sad than frightening. But sadness often keeps its distance from another person's loss. Come closer, and suddenly you are afraid.

He saw her from the bottom of the stairs
Before she saw him. She was starting down,
Looking back over her shoulder at some fear.
She took a doubtful step and then undid it
To raise herself and look again. He spoke
Advancing toward her: "What is it you see
From up there always—for I want to know."
She turned and sank upon her skirts at that,
And her face changed from terrified to dull.
He said to gain time: "What is it you see,"
Mounting until she cowered under him.
"I will find out now—you must tell me, dear."
She, in her place, refused him any help
With the least stiffening of her neck and silence.
She let him look, sure that he wouldn't see,

Blind creature; and a while he didn't see.
But at last he murmured, "Oh," and again, "Oh."

"What is it—what?" she said.

                                        "Just that I see."

"You don't," she challenged. "Tell me what it is."

"The wonder is I didn't see at once.
I never noticed it from here before.
I must be wonted to it—that's the reason.
The little graveyard where my people are!
So small the window frames the whole of it.
Not so much larger than a bedroom, is it?
There are three stones of slate and one of marble,
Broad-shouldered little slabs there in the sunlight
On the sidehill. We haven't to mind *those*.
But I understand: it is not the stones,
But the child's mound—"

                            "Don't, don't, don't, don't," she cried.

She withdrew shrinking from beneath his arm
That rested on the banister, and slid downstairs;
And turned on him with such a daunting look,
He said twice over before he knew himself:
"Can't a man speak of his own child he's lost?"

"Not you! Oh, where's my hat? Oh, I don't need it!
I must get out of here. I must get air.
I don't know rightly whether any man can."

"Amy! Don't go to someone else this time.
Listen to me. I won't come down the stairs."
He sat and fixed his chin between his fists.
"There's something I should like to ask you, dear."

"You don't know how to ask it."

"Help me, then."

Her fingers moved the latch for all reply.
"My words are nearly always an offence.
I don't know how to speak of anything
So as to please you. But I might be taught,
I should suppose. I can't say I see how.
A man must partly give up being a man
With women-folk. We could have some arrangement
By which I'd bind myself to keep hands off
Anything special you're a-mind to name.
Though I don't like such things 'twixt those that love.
Two that don't love can't live together without them.
But two that do can't live together with them."
She moved the latch a little. "Don't—don't go.
Don't carry it to someone else this time.
Tell me about it if it's something human.
Let me into your grief. I'm not so much
Unlike other folks as your standing there
Apart would make me out. Give me my chance.
I do think, though, you overdo it a little.
What was it brought you up to think it the thing
To take your mother-loss of a first child
So inconsolably—in the face of love.
You'd think his memory might be satisfied—"

"There you go sneering now!"

                                                          "I'm not, I'm not!
You make me angry. I'll come down to you.
God, what a woman! And it's come to this,
A man can't speak of his own child that's dead."

"You can't because you don't know how.
If you had any feelings, you that dug
With your own hand—how could you?—his little grave;
I saw you from that very window there,
Making the gravel leap and leap in air,
Leap up, like that, like that, and land so lightly
And roll back down the mound beside the hole.
I thought, Who is that man? I didn't know you.
And I crept down the stairs and up the stairs
To look again, and still your spade kept lifting.
Then you came in. I heard your rumbling voice
Out in the kitchen, and I don't know why,
But I went near to see with my own eyes.
You could sit there with the stains on your shoes
Of the fresh earth from your own baby's grave
And talk about your everyday concerns.
You had stood the spade up against the wall
Outside there in the entry, for I saw it."

"I shall laugh the worst laugh I ever laughed.
I'm cursed. God, if I don't believe I'm cursed."

"I can repeat the very words you were saying.
'Three foggy mornings and one rainy day
Will rot the best birch fence a man can build.'
Think of it, talk like that at such a time!
What had how long it takes a birch to rot
To do with what was in the darkened parlour?

You *couldn't* care! The nearest friends can go
With anyone to death, comes so far short
They might as well not try to go at all.
No, from the time when one is sick to death,
One is alone, and he dies more alone.
Friends make pretence of following to the grave,
But before one is in it, their minds are turned
And making the best of their way back to life
And living people, and things they understand.
But the world's evil. I won't have grief so
If I can change it. Oh, I won't, I won't!"

"There, you have said it all and you feel better.
You won't go now. You're crying. Close the door.
The heart's gone out of it: why keep it up?
Amy! There's someone coming down the road!"

"*You*—oh, you think the talk is all. I must go—
Somewhere out of this house. How can I make you—"

"If—you—do!" She was opening the door wider.
"Where do you mean to go? First tell me that.
I'll follow and bring you back by force. I *will!*—"

Seaton's Aunt
by Walter de la Mare

Walter de la Mare (1873–1953), who is buried in St. Paul's Cathedral in London, wrote scores of somewhat gloomy stories, novels and poems. His literary output included many works for children, but this isn't one of them. It is, however, a story about a child—one who suffers from malice beyond easy understanding.

I had heard rumours of Seaton's Aunt long before I actually encountered her. Seaton, in the hush of confidence, or at any little show of toleration on our part, would remark, "My aunt," or "My old aunt, you know," as if his relative might be a kind of cement to an *entente cordiale*.

He had an unusual quantity of pocket-money; or, at any rate, it was bestowed on him in unusually large amounts; and he spent it freely, though none of us would have described him as an "awfully generous chap." "Hullo, Seaton," we would say, "the old Begum?" At the beginning of term, too, he used to bring back surprising and exotic dainties in a box with a trick padlock that accompanied him from his first appearance at Gummidge's in a billy-cock hat to the rather abrupt conclusion of his schooldays.

From a boy's point of view he looked distastefully foreign, with his yellow skin, and slow chocolate-coloured eyes, and lean weak figure. Merely for his looks he was treated by most of us true-blue Englishmen with condescension, hostility, or contempt. We used to call him "Pongo," but without any much better excuse for the nickname than his skin. He was, that is, in one sense of the term what he assuredly was not in the other sense—a sport.

Seaton and I, as I may say, were never in any sense intimate at school; our orbits only intersected in class. I kept deliberately aloof from him. I felt vaguely he was a sneak, and remained quite unmollified by advances on his side, which, in a boy's barbarous fashion, unless it suited me to be magnanimous, I haughtily ignored.

We were both of us quick-footed, and at Prisoner's Base used occasionally to bide together. And so I best remember Seaton—his narrow watchful face in the dusk of a summer evening; his peculiar crouch, and his inarticulate whisperings and mumblings. Otherwise he played all games slackly and limply; used to stand and feed at his locker with a crony or two until his "tuck" gave out; or waste his money on some outlandish fancy or other. He bought, for instance, a silver bangle, which he wore above his left elbow, until some of the fellows showed their masterly contempt of the practice by dropping it nearly red-hot down his back.

It needed, therefore, a rather peculiar taste, a rather rare kind of schoolboy courage and indifference to criticism, to be much associated with him. And I had neither the taste nor, perhaps, the courage. None the less, he did make advances, and on one memorable occasion went to the length of bestowing on me a whole pot of some outlandish mulberry-coloured jelly that had been duplicated in his term's supplies. In the exuberance of my gratitude I promised to spend the next half-term holiday with him at his aunt's house.

I had clean forgotten my promise when, two or three days before the holiday, he came up and triumphantly reminded me of it.

"Well, to tell you the honest truth, Seaton, old chap——" I began graciously; but he cut me short.

"My aunt expects you," he said; "she is very glad you are coming. She's sure to be quite decent to *you*, Withers."

I looked at him in sheer astonishment; the emphasis was so

uncalled for. It seemed to suggest an aunt not hitherto hinted at, and a friendly feeling on Seaton's side that was far more disconcerting than welcome.

We reached his home partly by train, partly by a lift in an empty farm-cart, and partly by walking. It was a whole-day holiday, and we were to sleep the night; he lent me extraordinary night-gear, I remember. The village street was unusually wide, and was fed from a green by two converging roads, with an inn, and a high green sign at the corner. About a hundred yards down the street was a chemist's shop—a Mr. Tanner's. We descended the two steps into his dusky and odorous interior to buy, I remember, some rat poison. A little beyond the chemist's was the forge. You then walked along a very narrow path, under a fairly high wall, nodding here and there with weeds and tufts of grass, and so came to the iron garden-gates, and saw the high, flat house behind its huge sycamore. A coach-house stood on the left of the house, and on the right a gate led into a kind of rambling orchard. The lawn lay away over to the left again, and at the bottom (for the whole garden sloped gently to a sluggish and rushy pond-like stream) was a meadow.

We arrived at noon, and entered the gates out of the hot dust beneath the glitter of the dark-curtained windows. Seaton led me at once through the little garden-gate to show me his tadpole pond, swarming with what (being myself not in the least interested in low life) I considered the most horrible creatures—of all shapes, consistencies and sizes, but with whom Seaton seemed to be on the most intimate of terms. I can see his absorbed face now as he sat on his heels and fished the slimy things out in his sallow palms. Wearying at last of these pets, we loitered about awhile in an aimless fashion. Seaton seemed to be listening, or at any rate waiting, for something to happen or for someone to come. But nothing did happen and no one came.

That was just like Seaton. Anyhow, the first view I got of his aunt was when, at the summons of a distant gong, we turned from the garden, very hungry and thirsty, to go into luncheon. We were approaching the house when Seaton suddenly came to a standstill. Indeed, I have always had the impression that he plucked at my sleeve. Something, at least, seemed to catch me back, as it were, as he cried, "Look out, there she is!"

She was standing at an upper window which opened wide on a hinge, and at first sight she looked an excessively tall and overwhelming figure. This, however, was mainly because the window reached all but to the floor of the bedroom. She was in reality rather an undersized woman, in spite of her long face and big bead. She must have stood, I think, unusually still, with eyes fixed on us, though this impression may be due to Seaton's sudden warning and to my consciousness of the cautious and subdued air that had fallen on him at sight of her. I know that, without the least reason in the world, I felt a kind of guiltiness, as if I had been "caught." There was a silvery star pattern sprinkled on her black silk dress, and even from the ground I could see the immense coils of her hair and the rings on her left hand which was held fingering the small jet buttons of her bodice. She watched our united advance without stirring, until, imperceptibly, her eyes raised and lost themselves in the distance, so that it was out of an assumed reverie that she appeared suddenly to awaken to our presence beneath her when we drew close to the house.

"So this is your friend Mr. Smithers, I suppose?" she said, bobbing to me.

"Withers, aunt," said Seaton.

"It's much the same," she said, with eyes fixed on me. "Come in, Mr. Withers, and bring him along with you."

She continued to gaze at me—at least, I think she did so. I know that the fixity of her scrutiny and her ironical "Mr." made me feel peculiarly uncomfortable. None the less she was extremely kind and attentive to me, though, no doubt, her kindness and attention showed up more vividly against her complete neglect of Seaton. Only one remark that I have any recollection of she made to him: "When I look on my nephew, Mr. Smithers, I realise that dust we are, and dust shall become. You are hot, dirty, and incorrigible, Arthur."

She sat at the head of the table, Seaton at the foot, and I, before a wide waste of damask tablecloth, between them. It was an old and rather close dining-room, with windows thrown wide to the green garden and a wonderful cascade of fading roses. Miss Seaton's great chair faced this window, so that its rose-reflected light shone full on her yellowish face, and on just such chocolate eyes as my schoolfellow's, except that hers were more than half-covered by unusually long and heavy lids.

There she sat, steadily eating, with those sluggish eyes fixed for the most part on my face; above them stood the deep-lined fork between her eyebrows; and above that the wide expanse of a remarkable brow beneath its strange steep bank of hair. The lunch was copious, and consisted, I remember, of all such dishes as are generally considered too rich and too good for the schoolboy digestion—lobster mayonnaise, cold game sausages, an immense veal and ham pie farced with eggs, truffles, and numberless delicious flavours; besides kickshaws, creams, and sweetmeats. We even had wine, a half-glass of old darkish sherry each.

Miss Seaton enjoyed and indulged an enormous appetite. Her example and a natural schoolboy voracity soon overcame my nervousness of her, even to the extent of allowing me to enjoy to the best of my bent so rare a spread. Seaton was singularly modest; the greater part of his meal consisted of almonds and raisins, which he nibbled surreptitiously and as if he found difficulty in swallowing them.

I don't mean that Miss Seaton "conversed" with me. She merely scattered trenchant remarks and now and then twinkled a baited question over my head. But her face was like a dense and involved accompaniment to her talk. She presently dropped the "Mr.," to my intense relief, and called me now Withers, or Wither, now Smithers, and even once towards, the close of the meal distinctly Johnson, though how on earth my name suggested it, or whose face mine had reanimated in memory, I cannot conceive.

"And is Arthur a good boy at school, Mr. Wither?" was one of her many questions. "Does he please his masters? Is he first in his class? What does the reverend Dr. Gummidge think of him, eh?"

I knew she was jeering at him, but her face was adamant against the least flicker of sarcasm or facetiousness. I gazed fixedly at a blushing crescent of lobster.

"I think you're eighth, aren't you, Seaton?"

Seaton moved his small pupils towards his aunt. But she continued to gaze with a kind of concentrated detachment at me

"Arthur will never make a brilliant scholar, I fear," she said lifting a dextrously-burdened fork to her wide mouth . . . .

After luncheon she proceeded me up to my bedroom. It was a jolly little bedroom, with a brass fender and rugs and a polished floor, on which it was possible, I afterwards found, to play "snowshoes." Over the washstand was a little black-framed water-colour drawing, depicting a large eye with an extremely fishlike intensity in the spark of light on the dark pupil; and in "illuminated" lettering beneath was printed very minutely, "Thou God, Seest ME," followed by a long looped monogram, "S.S.," in the corner. The other pictures were all of the sea: brigs on blue water; a schooner overtopping chalk cliffs; a rocky island of prodigious steepness, with two tiny sailors dragging a monstrous boat up a shelf of beach.

"This is the room, Withers, my brother William died in when a boy. Admire the view!"

I looked out of the window across the tree-tops. It was a day hot with sunshine over the green fields, and the cattle were standing swishing their tails in the shallow water. But the view at the moment was only exaggeratedly vivid because I was horribly dreading that she would presently enquire after my luggage, and I had not brought even a toothbrush. I need have had no fear. Hers was not that highly-civilised type of mind that is stuffed with sharp, material details. Nor could her ample presence be described as in the least motherly.

"I would never consent to question a schoolfellow behind my nephew's back," she said, standing in the middle of the room, "but tell me, Smithers, why is Arthur so unpopular? You, I understand, are his only close friend." She stood in a dazzle of sun, and out of it her eyes regarded me with such leaden penetration beneath their thick lids that I doubt if my face concealed the least thought from her. "But there,

there," she added very suavely, stooping her head a little, "don't trouble to answer me. I never extort an answer. Boys are queer fish. Brains might perhaps have suggested his washing his hands before luncheon; but—not my choice, Smithers. God forbid! And now, perhaps, you would like to go into the garden again. I cannot actually see from here, but I should not be surprised if Arthur is now skulking behind that hedge."

He was. I saw his head come out and take a rapid glance at the windows.

"Join him, Mr. Smithers; we shall meet again, I hope, at the tea-table. The afternoon I spend in retirement."

Whether or not, Seaton and I had not been long engaged with the aid of two green switches in riding round and round a lumbering old grey horse we found in the meadow, before a rather bunched-up figure appeared, walking along the field-path on the other side of the water, with a magenta parasol studiously lowered in our direction throughout our slow progress, as if that were the magnetic needle and we the fixed Pole. Seaton at once lost all nerve in his riding. At the next lurch of the old mare's heels he toppled over in the grass, and I slid off the sleek broad back to join him where he stood, rubbing his shoulder and sourly watching the rather pompous figure till it was out of sight.

"Was that your aunt, Seaton?" I enquired; but not till then.

He nodded.

"Why didn't she take any notice of us, then?"

"She never does."

"Why not?"

"Oh, she knows all right, without; that's the dam awful part of it." Seaton was about the only fellow at Gummidge's who ever had the ostentation to use bad language. He had suffered for it too. But it wasn't, I think, bravado. I believe he really felt certain things more intensely than most of the other fellows, and they were generally things that fortunate and average people do not feel at all—the peculiar quality, for instance, of the British schoolboy's imagination.

"I tell you, Withers," he went on moodily, slinking across the meadow with his hands covered up in his pockets, "she sees everything. And what she doesn't see she knows without."

"But how?" I said, not because I was much interested, but because the afternoon was so hot and tiresome and purposeless, and it seemed more of a bore to remain silent. Seaton turned gloomily and spoke in a very low voice.

"Don't appear to be talking of her, if you wouldn't mind. It's— because she's in league with the devil." He nodded his head and stooped to pick up a round flat pebble. "I tell you," he said, still stooping, "you fellows don't realise what it is. I know I'm a bit close and all that. But so would you be if you had that old hag listening to every thought you think."

I looked at him, then turned and surveyed one by one the windows of the house.

"Where's your *pater?*" I said awkwardly.

"Dead, ages and ages ago, and my mother too. She's not my aunt by right."

"What is she, then?"

"I mean she's not my mother's sister, because my grandmother married twice; and she's one of the first lot. I don't know what you call her, anyhow she's not my real aunt."

"'She gives you plenty of pocket-money."

Seaton looked steadfastly at me out of his flat eyes. "She can't give me what's mine. When I come of age half the whole lot will be mine; and what's more"—he turned his back on the house—"I'll make her hand over every blessed shilling of it."

I put my hands in my pockets and stared at Seaton; "Is it much?"

He nodded.

"Who told you?" He got suddenly very angry; a darkish red came into his cheeks, his eyes glistened, but he made no answer, and we loitered listlessly about the garden until it was time for tea . . . .

Seaton's aunt was wearing an extraordinary kind of lace jacket when we sidled sheepishly into the drawing-room together. She greeted me with a heavy and protracted smile, and bade me bring a chair close to the little table.

"I hope Arthur has made you feel at home," she said, as she handed me my cup in her crooked hand. "He don't talk much to me; but then I'm an old woman. You must come again, Wither, and draw him out of his shell. You old snail!" She wagged her head at Seaton, who sat munching cake and watching her intently.

"And we must correspond, perhaps." She nearly shut her eyes at me. "You must write and tell me everything behind the creature's back." I confess I found her rather disquieting company. The evening drew on. Lamps were brought in by a man with a nondescript face and very quiet footsteps. Seaton was told to bring out the chess-men. And we played a game, she and I, with her big chin thrust over the board at every move as she gloated over the pieces and occasionally croaked "Check!"—after which she would sit back inscrutably staring at me. But the game was never finished. She simply hemmed me defencelessly in with a cloud of men that held me impotent, and yet one and all refused to administer to my poor flustered old king a merciful *coup de grâce*.

"There," she said as the clock struck ten—"a drawn game, Withers. We are very evenly matched. A very creditable defence, Withers. You know your room. There's supper on a tray in the dining-room. Don't let the creature over-eat himself. The gong will sound three-quarters of an hour *before* a punctual breakfast." She held out her cheek to Seaton, and he kissed it with obvious perfunctoriness. With me she shook hands.

"An excellent game," she said cordially, "but my memory is poor, and"—she swept the pieces helterskelter into the box—"the result will never be known." She raised her great head far back. "Eh?"

It was a kind of challenge, and I could only murmur: "Oh, I was absolutely in a hole, you know!" when she burst out laughing and waved us both out of the room.

Seaton and I stood and ate our supper, with one candlestick to light us, in a corner of the dining-room. "Well, and how would you like it?" he said very softly, after cautiously poking his head round the doorway.

"Like what?"

"Being spied on—every blessed thing you do and think?"

"I shouldn't like it at all," I said, "if she does."

"And yet you let her smash you up at chess!"

"I didn't let her!" I said, indignantly.

"Well, you funked it, then."

"And I didn't funk it either," I said; "she's so jolly clever with her knights." Seaton stared fixedly at the candle. "You wait, that's all," he said slowly. And we went upstairs to bed.

I had not been long in bed, I think, when I was cautiously awakened by a touch on my shoulder. And there was Seaton's face in the candle-light—and his eyes looking into mine.

"What's up?" I said, rising quickly to my elbow.

"Don't scurry," he whispered, "or she'll hear. I'm sorry for waking you, but I didn't think you'd be asleep so soon."

"Why, what's the time, then?" Seaton wore, what was then rather unusual, a night-suit, and he hauled his big silver watch out of the pocket in his jacket.

"It's a quarter to twelve. I never get to sleep before twelve—not here."

"What do you do, then?"

"Oh, I read and listen."

"Listen?"

Seaton stared into his candle-flame as if he were listening even then. "You can't guess what it is. All you read in ghost stories, that's all rot. You can't see much, Withers, but you know all the same."

"Know what?"

"Why, that they're there."

"Who's there?" I asked fretfully, glancing at the door.

"Why, in the house. It swarms with 'em. Just you stand still and listen outside my bedroom door in the middle of the night. I have, dozens of times; they're all over the place."

"Look here, Seaton," I said, "you asked me to come here, and I didn't mind chucking up a leave just to oblige you, and because I'd promised; but don't get talking a lot of rot, that's all, or you'll know the difference when we get back."

"Don't fret," he said coldly, turning away. "I shan't be at school long. And what's more, you're here now, and there isn't anybody else to talk to. I'll chance the other."

"Look here, Seaton," I said, "you may think you're going to scare me with a lot of stuff about voices and all that. But I'll just thank you to clear out; and you may please yourself about pottering about all night."

He made no answer; he was standing by the dressing-table looking across his candle into the looking-glass; he turned and stared slowly round the walls.

"Even this room's nothing more than a coffin. I suppose she told you—'It's exactly the same as when my brother William died'—trust her for that! And good luck to him, say I. Look at that." He raised his candle close to the little water-colour I have mentioned. "There's hundreds of eyes like that in this house; and even if God does see you, He takes precious good care you don't see Him. And it's just the same with them. I tell you what, Withers, I'm getting sick of all this. I shan't stand it much longer."

The house was silent within and without, and even in the yellowish radiance of the candle a faint silver showed through the open window on my blind. I slipped off the bedclothes, wide awake, and sat irresolutely on the bedside.

"I know you're only guying me," I said angrily, "but why is the house full of—what you say? Why do you hear—what you *do* hear? Tell me that, you silly fool!"

Seaton sat down on a chair and rested his candlestick on his knee. He blinked at me calmly. "She brings them," he said, with lifted eyebrows.

"Who? Your aunt?"

He nodded.

"How?"

"I told you," he answered pettishly. "She's in league. You don't know. She as good as killed my mother; I know that. But it's not only her by a long chalk. She just sucks you dry. I know. And that's what she'll do for me; because I'm like her—like my mother, I mean. She simply hates to see me alive. I wouldn't be like that old she-wolf for a million pounds.

And so"—he broke off, with a comprehensive wave of his candlestick—"they're always here. Ah, my boy, wait till she's dead! She'll hear something then, I can tell you. It's all very well now, but wait till then! I wouldn't be in her shoes when she has to clear out—for something. Don't you go and believe I care for ghosts, or whatever you like to call them. We're all in the same box. We're all under her thumb."

He was looking almost nonchalantly at the ceiling at the moment, when I saw his face change, saw his eyes suddenly drop like shot birds and fix themselves on the cranny of the door he had just left ajar. Even from where I sat I could see his colour change; he went greenish. He crouched without stirring, simply fixed. And I, scarcely daring to breathe, sat with creeping skin, simply watching him. His hands relaxed, and he gave a kind of sigh.

"Was that one?" I whispered, with a timid show of jauntiness. He looked round, opened his mouth, and nodded. "What?" I said. He jerked his thumb with meaningful eyes, and I knew that he meant that his aunt had been there listening at our door cranny

"Look here, Seaton," I said once more, wriggling to my feet. "You may think I'm a jolly noodle; just as you please. But your aunt has been civil to me and all that, and I don't believe a word you say about her, that's all, and never did. Every fellow's a bit off his pluck at night, and you may think it a fine sport to try your rubbish on me. I heard your aunt come upstairs before I fell asleep. And I'll bet you a level tanner she's in bed now. What's more, you can keep your blessed ghosts to yourself. It's a guilty conscience, I should think."

Seaton looked at me curiously, without answering for a moment. "I'm not a liar, Withers; but I'm not going to quarrel either. You're the only chap I care a button for; or, at any rate, you're the only chap that's ever come here; and it's something to tell a fellow what you feel. I don't care a fig for fifty thousand ghosts, although I swear on my solemn oath that I know they're here. But she"—he turned deliberately—"you laid a tanner she's in bed, Withers; well, I know different. She's never in bed much of the night, and I'll prove it, too, just to show you I'm not such a nolly as you think I am. Come on!"

"Come on where?"

"Why, to see."

I hesitated. He opened a large cupboard and took out a small dark dressing-gown and a kind of shawl-jacket. He threw the jacket on the bed and put on the gown. His dusky face was colourless, and I could see by the way he fumbled at the sleeves he was shivering. But it was no good showing the white feather now. So I threw the tasselled shawl over my shoulders and, leaving our candle brightly burning on the chair, we went out together and stood in the corridor.

"Now then, listen!" Seaton whispered.

We stood leaning over the staircase. It was like leaning over a well, so still and chill the air was all around us. But presently, as I suppose happens in most old houses, began to echo and answer in my ears a medley of infinite small stirrings and whisperings. Now out of the distance an old timber would relax its fibres, or a scurry die away behind the perishing wainscoat. But amid and behind such sounds as these I seemed to begin to be conscious, as it were, of the lightest of footfalls, sounds as faint as the vanishing remembrance of voices in a dream. Seaton was all in obscurity except his face; out of that his eyes gleamed darkly, watching me. "You'd hear, too, in time, my fine soldier," he muttered. "Come on!"

He descended the stairs, slipping his lean fingers lightly along the balusters. He turned to the right at the loop, and I followed him barefooted along a thickly-carpeted corridor. At the end stood a door ajar. And from here we very stealthily and in complete blackness ascended five narrow stairs. Seaton, with immense caution, slowly pushed open a door, and we stood together looking into a great pool of duskiness, out of which, lit by the feeble clearness of a night-light, rose a vast bed. A heap of clothes lay on the floor; beside them two slippers dozed, with noses each to each, two yards apart. Somewhere a little clock ticked huskily. There was a rather close smell of lavender and *eau de cologne*, mingled with the fragrance of ancient sachets, soap, and drugs. Yet it was a scent even more peculiarly commingled than that.

And the bed! I stared warily in; it was mounded gigantically, and it was empty.

Seaton turned a vague pale face, all shadows: "What did I say?" he muttered. "Who's—who's the fool now, I say? How are we going to get back without meeting her, I say? Answer me that! Oh, I wish to goodness you hadn't come here, Withers."

He stood visibly shivering in his skimpy gown, and could hardly speak for his teeth chattering. And very distinctly, in the hush that followed his whisper, I heard approaching a faint unhurried voluminous rustle. Seaton clutched my arm, dragged me to the right across the room to a large cupboard, and drew the door close to on us. And presently, as with bursting lungs I peeped out into the long, low, curtained bedroom, waddled in that wonderful great head and body. I can see her now, all patched and lined with shadow, her tied-up hair (she must have had enormous quantities of it for so old a woman), her heavy lids above those flat, slow, vigilant eyes. She just passed across my ken in the vague dusk; but the bed was out of sight.

We waited on and on, listening to the clock's muffled ticking. Not the ghost of a sound rose up from the great bed. Either she lay archly listening or slept a sleep serener than an infant's. And when, it seemed, we had been hours in hiding and were cramped, chilled, and half suffocated, we crept out on all fours, with terror knocking at our ribs, and so down the five narrow stairs and back to the little candle-lit blue-and-gold bedroom.

Once there, Seaton gave in. He sat livid on a chair with closed eyes.

"Here," I said shaking his arm, "I'm going to bed; I've had enough of this foolery; I'm going to bed." His lips quivered, but he made no answer. I poured out some water into my basin and, with that cold pictured azure eye fixed on us, bespattered Seaton's sallow face and forehead and dabbled his hair. He presently sighed and opened fish-like eyes.

"Come on!" I said. "Don't get shamming, there's a good chap. Get on my back if you like, and I'll carry you into your bedroom."

He waved me away and stood up. So, with my candle in one hand, I took him under the arm and walked him along according to his direction down the corridor. His was a much dingier room than mine, and lit-tered with boxes, paper, cages, and clothes. I huddled him into bed and turned to go. And suddenly—I can hardly explain it now—a kind of cold and deadly terror swept over me. I almost ran out of the room, with eyes fixed rigidly in front of me, blew out my candle, and buried my head under the bedclothes.

When I awoke, roused not by a gong, but by a long-continued tap-ping at my door, sunlight was raying in on cornice and bedpost, and birds were singing in the garden. I got up, ashamed of the night's folly, dressed quickly, and went downstairs. The breakfast-room was sweet with flowers and fruit and honey. Seaton's aunt was standing in the gar-den beside the open French windows, feeding a great flutter of birds. I watched her for a moment, unseen. Her face, was set in a deep reverie beneath the shadow of a big loose sun-hat. It was deeply lined, crooked, and, in a way I can't describe, fixedly vacant and strange, I coughed, and she turned at once with a prodigious smile to enquire how I had slept. And in that mysterious way by which we learn each other's secret thoughts without a sentence spoken I knew that she had followed every word and movement of the night before, and was tri-umphing over my affected innocence and ridiculing my friendly and too easy advances.

We returned to school, Seaton and I, lavishly laden, and by rail all the way. I made no reference to the obscure talk we had had, and resolutely refused to meet his eyes or to take up the hints he let fall. I was relieved—and yet I was sorry—to be going back, and strode on as fast as I could from the station, with Seaton almost trotting at my heels. But he insisted on buying more fruit and sweets—my share of which I accepted with a very bad grace. It was uncomfortably like a bribe; and, after all, I had no quarrel with his rum old aunt, and hadn't really believed half the stuff he had told me.

I saw as little of him as I could after that. He never referred to our visit or resumed his confidences, though in class I would sometimes catch his eyes fixed on mine, full of a mute understanding, which I easily affected not to understand. He left Gummidge's rather abruptly, though I never heard of anything to his discredit. And I did not see him or have any news of him again till by chance we met one summer afternoon in the Strand.

He was dressed rather oddly in a coat too large for him and a bright silky tie. But we instantly recognised one another under the awning of a cheap jeweler's shop. He immediately attached himself to me and dragged me off, not too cheerfully, to lunch with him at an Italian restaurant near by. He chattered about our old school, which he remembered only with dislike and disgust; told me cold-bloodedly of the disastrous fate of one or two of the old fellows who had been among his chief tormentors; insisted on an expensive wine and the whole gamut of the foreign menu; and finally informed me, with a good deal of niggling, that he had come up to town to buy an engagement-ring.

And of course: "How is your aunt?" I enquired at last.

He seemed to have been awaiting the question. It fell like a stone into a deep pool, so many expressions flitted across his long un-English face.

"She's aged a good deal," he said softly, and broke off.

"She's been very decent," he continued presently after, and paused again. "In a way." He eyed me fleetingly. "I dare say you heard that—she—that is, that we—had lost a good deal of money."

"No," I said.

"Oh, yes!" said Seaton, and paused again.

And somehow, poor fellow, I knew in the clink and clatter of glass and voices that he had lied to me; that he did not possess, and never had possessed, a penny beyond what his aunt had squandered on his too ample allowance of pocket-money.

"And the ghosts?" I enquired quizzically.

He grew instantly solemn, and, though it may have been my fancy, slightly yellowed. But "You are making game of me, Withers," was all he said.

He asked for my address, and I rather reluctantly gave him my card.

"Look here, Withers," he said, as we stood together in the sunlight on the kerb, saying good-bye, "here I am, and—and it's all very well. I'm not perhaps as fanciful as I was. But you are practically the only friend I have on earth—except Alice . . . And there—to make a clean breast of it, I'm not sure my aunt cares much about my getting married. She doesn't say so, of course. You know her well enough for that." He looked sidelong at the rattling gaudy traffic.

"What I was going to say is this: Would you mind coming down? You needn't stay the night unless you please, though, of course, you know you would be awfully welcome. But I should like you to meet my—to meet Alice; and then, perhaps, you might tell me your honest opinion of—of the other too."

I vaguely demurred. He pressed me. And we parted with a half promise that I would come. He waved his ball-topped cane at me and ran off in his long jacket after a 'bus.

A letter arrived soon after, in his small weak handwriting, giving me full particulars regarding route and trains. And without the least curiosity, even, perhaps, with some little annoyance that chance should have thrown us together again, I accepted his invitation and arrived one hazy midday at his out-of-the-way station to find him sitting on a low seat under a clump of double hollyhocks, awaiting me.

His face looked absent and singularly listless; but he seemed, none the less, pleased to see me.

We walked up the village street, past the little dingy apothecary's and the empty forge, and, as on my first visit, skirted the house together, and, instead of entering by the front door, made our way down the green path into the garden at the back. A pale haze of cloud muffled the sun; the garden lay in a grey shimmer—its old trees, its snap-dragoned faintly glittering walls. But now there was an air of slovenliness where before all had been neat and methodical. In a patch of shallowly-dug soil stood a worn-down spade leaning against a tree. There was an old broken wheelbarrow. The roses had run to leaf and briar; the fruit-trees were unpruned. The goddess of neglect brooded in secret.

"You ain't much of a gardener, Seaton," I said, with a sigh of ease.

"I think, do you know, I like it best like this," said Seaton. "We haven't any man now, of course. Can't afford it." He stood staring at his little dark square of freshly-turned earth. "And it always seems to me, " he went on ruminatingly, "that, after all we are nothing better than interlopers on the earth, disfiguring and staining wherever we go. I know its shocking blasphemy to say so, but then it's different here, you see. We are further away."

"To tell you the truth, Seaton, I *don't* quite see," I said; "but it isn't a new philosophy, is it? Anyhow, it's a precious beastly one."

"It's only what I think," he replied, with all his odd old stubborn meekness.

We wandered on together, talking little, and still with that expression of uneasy vigilance on Seaton's face. He pulled out his watch as we stood gazing idly over the green meadows and the dark motionless bulrushes.

"I think, perhaps, it's nearly time for lunch," he said. "Would you like to come in?"

We turned and walked slowly towards the house, across whose windows I confess my own eyes, too, went restlessly wandering in search of its rather disconcerting inmate. There was a pathetic look of draggledness, of want of means and care, rust and overgrowth and faded paint. Seaton's aunt, a little to my relief, did not share our meal. Seaton carved the cold meat, and dispatched a heaped-up plate by an elderly servant for his aunt's private consumption. We talked little and in half-suppressed tones, and sipped a bottle of Madeira which Seaton had rather heedfully fetched out of the great mahogany sideboard.

I played him a dull and effortless game of chess, yawning between the moves he himself made almost at haphazard, and with attention elsewhere engaged. About five o'clock came the sound of a distant ring, and Seaton jumped up, overturning the board, and so ending a game that else might have fatuously continued to this day. He effusively excused himself, and after some little while returned with a slim, dark, rather sallow girl of about nineteen, in a white gown and hat, to whom I was presented with some little nervousness as his "dear old friend and schoolfellow."

We talked on in the pale afternoon light, still, as it seemed to me, and even in spite of a real effort to be clear and gay, in a half-suppressed, lack-lustre fashion. We all seemed, if it were not my fancy, to me expectant, to be rather anxiously awaiting an arrival, the appearance of someone who all but filled our collective consciousness. Seaton talked least of all, and in a restless interjectory way, as he continually fidgeted from chair to chair. At last be proposed a stroll in the garden before the sun should have quite gone down.

Alice walked between us. Her hair and eyes were conspicuously dark against the whiteness of her gown. She carried herself not ungracefully, and yet without the least movement of her arms and body, and answered us both without turning her head. There was a curious provocative reserve in that impassive and rather long face, a half-unconscious strength of character.

And yet somehow I knew—I believe we all knew—that this walk, this discussion of their future plans was a futility. I had nothing to base such a cynicism on, except only a vague sense of oppression, the foreboding remembrance of the inert invincible power in the background, to whom optimistic plans and lovemaking and youth are as chaff and thistle-down. We came back silent, in the last light. Seaton's aunt was there—under an old brass lamp. Her hair was as barbarously massed and curled as ever. Her eyelids, I think, hung even a little heavier in age over their slow-moving inscrutable pupils. We filed in softly out of the evening, and I made my bow.

"In this short interval, Mr. Withers," she remarked amiably, "you have put off youth, put on the man. Dear me, how sad it is to see the young days vanishing! Sit down. My nephew tells me you met by chance—or act of Providence, shall we call it?—and in my beloved Strand! You, I understand, are to be best man—yes, best man, or am I divulging secrets?" She surveyed Arthur and Alice with overwhelming graciousness. They sat apart on two low chairs and smiled in return.

"And Arthur—how do you think Arthur is looking?"

"I think he looks very much in need of a change," I said deliberately.

"A change! Indeed?" She all but shut her eyes at me and with an exaggerated sentimentality shook her head. "My dear Mr. Withers! Are we not *all* in need of a change in this fleeting, fleeting world?" She mused over the remark like a connoisseur. "And you," she continued, turning abruptly to Alice, "I hope you pointed out to Mr. Withers all my pretty bits?"

"We walked round the garden," said Alice, looking out of the window. "It's a very beautiful evening."

"*Is* it?" said the old lady, starting up violently. "Then on this very beautiful evening we will go in to supper. Mr. Withers, your arm; Arthur, bring your bride."

I can scarcely describe with what curious ruminations I led the way into the faded, heavy-aired dining-room, with this indefinable old creature leaning weightily on my arm—the large flat bracelet on the yellow-laced wrist. She fumed a little, breathed rather heavily, as if with an effort of mind rather than of body; for she had grown much stouter and yet little more proportionate. And to talk into that great white face, so close to mine, was a queer experience in the dim light of the corridor, and even in the twinkling crystal of the candles. She was naïve—appallingly naïve; she was sudden and superficial; she was even arch; and all these in the brief, rather puffy passage from one room to the other, with these two tongue-tied children bringing up the rear. The meal was tremendous. I have never seen such a monstrous salad. But the dishes were greasy and over-spiced, and were indifferently cooked. One thing only was quite unchanged—my hostess's appetite was as Gargantuan as ever. The old solid candelabra that lighted us stood before her high-backed chair. Seaton sat a little removed, with his plate almost in darkness.

And throughout this prodigious meal his aunt talked, mainly to me, mainly at Seaton, with an occasional satirical courtesy to Alice and muttered explosions of directions to the servant. She had aged, and yet, if it be not nonsense to say so, seemed no older. I suppose to the Pyramids a decade is but as the rustling down of a handful of dust. And she reminded me of some such unshakable prehistoricism. She certainly was an amazing talker—racy, extravagant, with a delivery that was perfectly overwhelming. As for Seaton—her flashes of silence were for him. On her enormous volubility would suddenly fall a hush: acid sarcasm would be left implied; and she would sit softly moving her great head, with eyes fixed full in a dreamy smile; but with her whole attention, one could see, slowly, joyously absorbing his mute discomfiture.

She confided in us her views on a theme vaguely occupying at the moment, I suppose, all our minds. "We have barbarous institutions, and so must put up, I suppose, with a never-ending procession of fools—of fools *ad infinitum*. Marriage, Mr. Withers, was instituted in the privacy of a garden; *sub rosa*, as it were. Civilization flaunts it in the glare of day. The dull marry the poor; the rich the effete; and so our New Jerusalem is peopled with naturals, plain and coloured, at either end. I detest folly; I detest still more (if I must be frank, dear Arthur), mere cleverness. Mankind has simply become a tailless host of unin-stinctive animals. We should never have taken to Evolution, Mr. Withers. 'Natural Selection!'—little gods and fishes!—the deaf for the dumb. We should have used our brains—intellectual pride, the ecclesi-astics call it. And by brains I mean—what do I mean, Alice?—I mean, my dear child"—and she laid two gross fingers on Alice's narrow sleeve—"I mean courage. Consider it, Arthur. I read that the scientific world is once more beginning to be afraid of spiritual agencies. Spiritual agencies that tap, and actually float, bless their hearts! I think just one more of those mulberries—thank you.

"They talk about 'blind Love,'" she ran inconsequently on as she helped herself, with eyes roving on the dish, "but why blind? I think, do you know, from weeping over its rickets. After all, it is we plain women that triumph, Mr. Withers, beyond the mockery of time. Alice, now! Fleeting, fleeting is youth, my child. What's that you were con-fiding to your plate, Arthur? Satirical boy. He laughs at his old aunt: nay, but thou didst laugh. He detests all sentiment. He whispers the most acid asides. Come, my love, we will leave these cynics; we will go and commiserate with each other on our sex. The choice of two evils, Mr. Smithers!" I opened the door, and she swept out as if borne on a torrent of unintelligible indignation; and Arthur and I were left in the clear four-flamed light alone.

For a while we sat in silence. He shook his head at my cigarette-case, and I lit a cigarette. Presently he fidgeted in his chair and poked his head forward into the light. He paused to rise and shut again the shut door.

"How long will you be?" he said, standing by the table.

I laughed.

"Oh, it's not that!" he said, in some confusion. "Of course, I like to be with her. But it's not that. The truth is, Withers, I don't care about leaving her too long with my aunt."

I hesitated. He looked at me questioningly.

"Look here, Seaton," I said, "you know well enough that I don't want to interfere in your affairs, or to offer advice where it is not wanted. But don't you think perhaps you may not treat your aunt quite in the right way? As one gets old, you know, a little give and take. I have an old godmother, or something. She talks, too . . . . A little allowance: it does no harm. But hang it all, I'm no talker."

He sat down with his hands in his pockets and still with his eyes fixed almost incredulously on mine. "How?" he said.

"Well, my dear fellow, if I'm any judge—mind, I don't say that I am—but I can't help thinking she thinks you don't care for her; and perhaps takes your silence for—for bad temper. She has been very decent to you, hasn't she?"

"'Decent?' My God!" said Seaton.

I smoked on in silence; but he continued to look at me with that peculiar concentration I remembered of old.

"I don't think, perhaps, Withers," he began presently, "I don't think you quite understand. Perhaps you are not quite our kind. You always did, just like the other fellows, guy me at school. You laughed at me that night you came to stay here—about the voices and all that. But I don't mind being laughed at—because I know."

"Know what?" It was the same old system of dull question and evasive answer.

"I mean I know that what we see and hear is only the smallest fraction of what is. I know she lives quite out of this. She *talks* to you; but it's all make-believe. It's all a 'parlour game.' She's not really with you; only pitting her outside wits against yours and enjoying the fooling. She's living on inside on what you're rotten without. That's what it is— a cannibal feast. She's a spider. It doesn't much matter what you call it. It means the same kind of thing. I tell you, Withers, she hates me; and you can scarcely dream what that hatred means. I used to think I had an inkling of the reason. It's oceans deeper than that. It just lies behind: herself against myself. Why, after all, how much do we really understand of anything? We don't even know our own histories, and not a tenth, not a tenth of the reasons. What has life been to me?—nothing but a trap. And when one is set free, it only begins again. I thought you might understand; but you are on a different level: that's all."

"What on earth are you talking about?" I said contemptuously, in spite of myself.

"I mean what I say," he said gutturally. "All this outside's only make-believe—but there! what's the good of talking? So far as this is concerned I'm as good as done. You wait."

Seaton blew out three of the candles, and, leaving the vacant room in semi-darkness, we groped our way along the corridor to the drawing-room. There a full moon stood shining in at the long garden windows. Alice sat stooping at the door, with her hands clasped, looking out, alone.

"Where is she?" Seaton asked in a low tone.

Alice looked up; their eyes met in a kind of instantaneous understanding, and the door immediately afterwards opened behind us.

"*Such* a moon!" said a voice that, once heard, remained unforgettably on the ear. "A night for lovers Mr. Withers, if ever there was one. Get a shawl, my dear Arthur, and take Alice for a little promenade. I dare say we old cronies will manage to keep awake. Hasten, hasten, Romeo! My poor, poor Alice, how laggard a lover!"

Seaton returned with a shawl. They drifted out into the moonlight. My companion gazed after them till they were out of hearing, turned to me gravely, and suddenly twisted her white face into such a convulsion of contemptuous amusement that I could only stare blankly in reply.

"Dear innocent children!" she said, with inimitable unctuousness. "Well, well, Mr. Withers, we poor seasoned old creatures must move with the times. Do you sing?"

I scouted the idea.

"Then you must listen to my playing. Chess"—she clasped her forehead with both cramped hands—"chess is now completely beyond my poor wits."

She sat down at the piano and ran her fingers in a flourish over the keys. "What shall it be? How shall we capture them, those passionate hearts? That first fine careless rapture? Poetry itself." She gazed softly into the garden a moment, and presently, with a shake of her body, began to play the opening bars of Beethoven's "Moonlight Sonata." The piano was old and woolly. She played without music. The lamplight was rather dim. The moonbeams from the window lay across the keys. Her head was in shadow. And whether it was simply due to her personality or to some really occult skill in her playing I cannot say: I only know that she gravely and deliberately set herself to satirise the beautiful music. It brooded on the air, disillusioned, charged with mockery and bitterness. I stood at the window; far down the path I could see the white figure glimmering in that pool of colourless light. A few faint stars shone, and still that amazing woman behind me dragged out of the unwilling keys her wonderful grotesquerie of youth, and love, and beauty. It came to an end. I knew the player was watching me. "Please, please, go on!" I murmured, without turning. "Please go on playing, Miss Seaton."

No answer was returned to my rather fluttering sarcasm, but I knew in some indefinite way that I was being acutely scrutinised, when suddenly there followed a procession of quiet, plaintive chords which broke at last softly into the hymn, "A Few More Years Shall Roll."

I confess it held me spellbound. There is a wistful, strained, plangent pathos in the tune; but beneath those masterly old hands it cried softly and bitterly the solitude and desperate estrangement of the world. Arthur and his lady-love vanished from my thoughts. No one could put into a rather hackneyed old hymn-tune such an appeal who had never known the meaning of the words. Their meaning, anyhow, isn't commonplace.

I turned very cautiously and glanced at the musician. She was leaning forward a little over the keys, so that at the approach of my cautious glance she had but to turn her face into the thin flood of moonlight for every feature to become distinctly visible. And so, with the tune abruptly terminated, we steadfastly regarded one another, and she broke into a chuckle of laughter.

"Not quite so seasoned as I supposed, Mr. Withers. I see you are a real lover of music. To me it is too painful. It evokes too much thought . . . ."

I could scarcely see her little glittering eyes under their penthouse lids.

"And now," she broke off crisply, "tell me, as a man of the world, what do you think of my new niece?"

I was not a man of the world, nor was I much flattered in my stiff and dullish way of looking at things by being called one; and I could answer her without the least hesitation.

"I don't think, Miss Seaton, I'm much of a judge of character. She's very charming."

"A brunette?"

"I think I prefer dark women."

"And why? Consider, Mr. Withers; dark hair, dark eyes, dark cloud, dark night, dark vision, dark death, dark grave, dark DARK!"

Perhaps the climax would have rather thrilled Seaton, but I was too thick-skinned. "I don't know much about all that," I answered rather pompously. "Broad daylight's difficult enough for most of us."

"Ah," she said, with a sly inward burst of satirical laughter.

"And I suppose," I went on, perhaps a little nettled, "it isn't the actual darkness one admires, it's the contrast of the skin, and the colour of the eyes, and—and their shining. Just as," I went blundering on, too late to turn back, "just as you only see the stars in the dark. It would be a long day without any evening. As for death and the grave,

I don't suppose we shall much notice that." Arthur and his sweetheart were slowly returning along the dewy path. "I believe in making the best of things."

"How very interesting!" came the smooth answer. "I see you are a philosopher, Mr. Withers. H'm! 'As for death and the grave, I don't suppose we shall much notice that.' Very interesting . . . . And I'm sure," she added in a particularly suave voice, "I profoundly hope so." She rose slowly from her stool. "You will take pity on me again, I hope. You and I would get on famously—kindred spirits—elective affinities. And, of course, now that my nephew's going to leave us, now that his affections are centred on another, I shall be a very lonely old woman . . . . Shall I not, Arthur?"

Seaton blinked stupidly. "I didn't hear what you said, Aunt."

"I was telling our old friend, Arthur, that when you are gone I shall be a very lonely old woman."

"Oh, I don't think so," he said in a strange voice.

"He means, Mr. Withers, he means, my dear child," she said, sweeping her eyes over Alice, "he means that I shall have memory for company—heavenly memory—the ghosts of other days. Sentimental boy! And did you enjoy our music, Alice? Did I really stir that youthful heart? . . . O,O,O," continued the horrible old creature, "you billers and cooers, I have been listening to such flatteries, such confessions! Beware, beware, Arthur, there's many a slip." She rolled her little eyes at me, she shrugged her shoulders at Alice, and gazed an instant stonily into her nephew's face,

I held out my hand. "Good night, good night!" she cried. "He that fights and runs away. Ah, good night, Mr. Withers; come again soon!" She thrust out her cheek at Alice, and we all three filed slowly out of the room.

Black shadow darkened the porch and half the spreading sycamore. We walked without speaking up the dusty village street. Here and there a crimson window glowed. At the fork of the high road I said good-bye. But I had taken hardly more than a dozen paces when a sudden impulse seized me.

"Seaton!" I called.

He turned in the moonlight.

"You have my address; if by any chance, you know, you should care to spend a week or two in town between this and the—the Day, we should be delighted to see you."

"Thank you, Withers, thank you," he said in a low voice.

"I dare say"—I waved my stick gallantly to Alice—"I dare say you will be doing some shopping; we could all meet," I added laughing.

"Thank you, thank you, Withers—immensely," he repeated.

And so we parted.

But they were out of the jog-trot of my prosaic life. And being of a stolid and incurious nature, I left Seaton and his marriage, and even his aunt, to themselves in my memory, and scarcely gave a thought to them until one day I was walking up the Strand again, and passed the flashing gloaming of the covered-in jeweller's shop where I had accidentally encountered my old schoolfellow in the summer. It was one of those still close autumnal days after a rainy night. I cannot say why, but a vivid recollection returned to my mind of our meeting and of how suppressed Seaton had seemed, and of how vainly he had endeavoured to appear assured and eager. He must be married by now, and had doubtless returned from his honeymoon. And I had clean forgotten my manners, had sent not a word of congratulation, nor—as I might very well have done, and as I knew he would have been immensely pleased at my doing—the ghost of a wedding-present.

On the other hand, I pleaded with myself, I had had no invitation. I paused at the corner of Trafalgar Square, and at the bidding of one of those caprices that seize occasionally on even an unimaginative mind, I suddenly ran after a green 'bus that was passing, and found myself bound on a visit I had not in the least foreseen.

The colours of autumn were over the village when I arrived. A beautiful late afternoon sunlight bathed thatch and meadow. But it was close and hot. A child, two dogs, a very old woman with a heavy basket I encountered. One or two incurious tradesmen looked idly up as I passed by. It was all so rural and so still, my whimsical impulse had so much flagged, that for a while I hesitated to venture under the shadow of the sycamore-tree to enquire after the happy pair. I deliberately passed by the faint-blue gates and continued my walk under the high green and tufted wall. Hollyhocks had attained their topmost bud and seeded in the little cottage gardens beyond; the Michaelmas daisies were in flower; a sweet warm aromatic smell of fading leaves was in the air. Beyond the cottages lay a field where cattle were grazing, and beyond that I came to a little churchyard. Then the road wound on, pathless and houseless among gorse and bracken. I turned impatiently and walked quickly back to the house and rang the bell.

The rather colourless elderly woman who answered my enquiry informed me that Miss Seaton was at home, as if only taciturnity forbade her adding, "But she doesn't want to see *you*."

"Might I, do you think, have Mr. Arthur's address?" I said.

She looked at me with quiet astonishment, as if waiting for an explanation. Not the faintest of smiles came into her thin face.

"I will tell Miss Seaton," she said after a pause. "Please walk in."

She showed me into the dingy undusted drawing-room, filled with evening sunshine and with the green-dyed light that penetrated the leaves overhanging the long French windows. I sat down and waited on and on, occasionally aware of a creaking footfall overhead. At last the door opened a little, and the great face I had once known peered round at me. For it was enormously changed; mainly, I think, because the old eyes had rather suddenly failed, and so a kind of stillness and darkness lay over its calm and wrinkled pallor.

"Who is it?" she asked.

I explained myself and told her the occasion of my visit.

She came in and shut the door carefully after her and, though the fumbling was scarcely perceptible, groped her way to a chair. She had on an old dressing-gown, like a cassock, of a patterned cinnamon colour.

"What is it you want?" she said, seating herself and lifting her blank face to mine.

"Might I just have Arthur's address?" I said deferentially. "I am so sorry to have disturbed you."

"H'm. You have come to see my nephew?"

"Not necessarily to see him, only to hear how he is, and, of course, Mrs. Seaton, too. I am afraid my silence must have, appeared . . ."

"He hasn't noticed your silence," croaked the old voice out of the great mask; "besides, there isn't any Mrs. Seaton."

"Ah, then," I answered, after a momentary pause, "I have not seemed so black as I painted myself! And how is Miss Outram?"

"She's gone into Yorkshire," answered Seaton's aunt.

"And Arthur too?"

She did not reply, but simply sat blinking at me with lifted chin, as if listening, but certainly not for what I might have to say. I began to feel rather at a loss.

"You were no close friend of my nephew's, Mr. Smithers?" she said presently.

"No," I answered, welcoming the cue, "and yet, do you know, Miss Seaton, he is one of the very few of my old schoolfellows I have come across in the last few years, and I suppose as one gets older one begins to value old associations . . ." My voice seemed to trail off into a vacuum. "I thought Miss Outram," I hastily began again, "a particularly charming girl. I hope they are both quite well."

Still the old face solemnly blinked at me in silence.

"You must find it very lonely, Miss Seaton, with Arthur away?"

"I was never lonely in my life," she said sourly. "I don't look to flesh and blood for my company. When you've got to be my age, Mr. Smithers (which God forbid), you'll find life a very different affair from what you seem to think it is now. You won't seek company then, I'll be bound. It's thrust on you." Her face edged round into the clear green light, and her eyes groped, as it were, over my vacant, disconcerted face. "I dare say, now," she said, composing her mouth, "I dare say my nephew told you a good many tarradiddles in his time. Oh, yes, a good many, eh? He was always a liar. What, now, did he say of me? Tell me, now." She leant forward as far as she could, trembling, with an ingratiating smile.

"I think he is rather superstitious," I said coldly, "but, honestly, I have a very poor memory, Miss Seaton."

"Why?" she said. "*I* haven't."

"The engagement hasn't been broken off, I hope."

"Well, between you and me," she said, shrinking up and with an immensely confidential grimace, "it has."

"I'm sure I'm very sorry to hear it. And where is Arthur?"

"Eh?"

"Where is Arthur?"

We faced each other mutely among the dead old bygone furniture. Past all my scrutiny was that large, flat, grey, cryptic countenance. And then, suddenly, our eyes for the first time really met. In some indescribable way out of that thick-lidded obscurity a far small something stooped and looked out at me for a mere instant of time that seemed of almost intolerable protraction. Involuntarily I blinked and shook my head She muttered something with great rapidity, but quite inarticularly; rose and hobbled to the door. I thought I heard, mingled in broken mutterings, something about tea.

"Please, please, don't trouble," I began, but could say no more, for the door was already shut between us. I stood and looked out on the long-neglected garden. I could just see the bright greenness of Seaton's old tadpole pond. I wandered about the room. Dusk began to gather, the last birds in that dense shadowiness of trees had ceased to sing. And not a sound was to be heard in the house. I waited on and on, vainly speculating. I even attempted to ring the bell; but the wire was broken, and only jangled loosely at my efforts.

I hesitated, unwilling to call or to venture out, and yet more unwilling to linger on, waiting for a tea that promised to be an exceedingly comfortless supper. And as darkness drew down, a feeling of the utmost unease and disquietude came over me. All my talks with Seaton returned on me with a suddenly enriched meaning. I recalled again his face as we had stood hanging over the staircase, listening in the small hours to the inexplicable stirrings of the night. There were no candles in the room; every minute the autumnal darkness deepened. I cautiously opened the door and listened, and with some little dismay withdrew, for I was uncertain of my way out. I even tried the garden, but was confronted under a veritable thicket of foliage by a padlocked gate. It would be a little too ignominious to be caught scaling a friend's garden fence!

Cautiously returning into the still and musty drawing-room, I took out my watch, and gave the incredible old woman ten minutes in which to reappear. And when that tedious ten minutes had ticked by I could scarcely distinguish its hands. I determined to wait no longer, drew open the door, and, trusting to my sense of direction, groped my way through the corridor that I vaguely remembered led to the front of the house.

I mounted three or four stairs, and, lifting a heavy curtain, found myself facing the starry fanlight of the porch. From here I glanced into the gloom of the dining-room. My fingers were on the latch of the outer door when I heard a faint stirring in the darkness above the hall. I looked up and became conscious of, rather than saw, the huddled old figure looking down on me.

There was an immense hushed pause. Then, "Arthur, Arthur," whispered in inexpressibly peevish, rasping voice, "is that you? Is that you, Arthur?"

I can scarcely say why, but the question horribly startled me. No conceivable answer occurred to me. With head craned back, hand clenched on my umbrella, I continued to stare up into the gloom, in this fatuous confrontation.

"Oh, oh"; the voice croaked. "It is you, is it? *That* disgusting man! . . . Go away out. Go away out."

Hesitating no longer, I caught open the door and, slamming it behind me, ran out into the garden, under the gigantic old sycamore, and so out at the open gate.

I found myself half up the village street before I stopped running. The local butcher was sitting in his shop reading a piece of newspaper by the light of a small oil-lamp. I crossed the road and enquired the way to the station. And after he had with minute and needless care directed me, I asked casually if Mr. Arthur Seaton still lived with his aunt at the big house just beyond the village. He poked his head in at the little parlour door.

"Here's a gentleman enquiring after young Mr. Seaton, Millie," he said. "He's dead, ain't he?"

"Why, yes, bless you," replied a cheerful voice from within. "Dead and buried these three months or more—young Mr. Seaton. And just before he was to be married, don't you remember, Bob?"

I saw a fair young woman's face peer over the muslin of the little door at me.

"Thank you," I replied, "then I go straight on?"

"That's it, sir; past the pond; bear up the hill a bit to the left, and then there's the station lights before your eyes."

We looked intelligently into each other's faces in the beam of the smoky lamp. But not one of the many questions in my mind could I put into words.

And again I paused irresolutely a few paces further on. It was not fancy, merely a foolish apprehension of what the raw-boned butcher might "think" that prevented my going back to see if I could find Seaton's grave in the benighted churchyard. There was precious little use in pottering about in the muddy dark, merely to discover where he was buried. And yet I felt a little uneasy. My rather horrible thought was that, so far as I was concerned—one of his extremely few friends—he had never been much better than "buried" in my mind.

The Monkey's Paw

by W.W. Jacobs

William Wymark Jacobs (1863–1943) in his
own time was best known as a humorist. The
critic and novelist G.K. Chesterton favorably
compared Jacobs' stories to the work of Dickens
and Kipling. Chesterton added that Jacobs'
supernatural stories "rise out of terror into
awe." This masterpiece of horror, combining as
it does elements of grief and wickedness, lives
up to that billing. It's not at all funny.

Without, the night was cold and wet, but in the small parlor of Laburnam Villa the blinds were drawn and the fire burned brightly. Father and son were at chess, the former, who possessed ideas about the game involving radical changes, putting his king into such sharp and unnecessary perils that it even provoked comment from the white-haired old lady knitting placidly by the fire.

"Hark at the wind," said Mr. White, who, having seen a fatal mistake after it was too late, was amiably desirous of preventing his son from seeing it.

"I'm listening," said the latter, grimly surveying the board as he stretched out his hand. "Check."

"I should hardly think that he'd come to-night," said his father, with his hand poised over the board.

"Mate," replied the son.

"That's the worst of living so far out," bawled Mr. White, with sudden and unlooked-for violence; "of all the beastly, slushy, out-of-the-way places to live in, this is the worst. Pathway's a bog, and the road's a torrent. I don't know what people are thinking about. I suppose because only two houses in the road are let, they think it doesn't matter."

"Never mind, dear," said his wife, soothingly; "perhaps you'll win the next one."

Mr. White looked up sharply, just in time to intercept a knowing glance between mother and son. The words died away on his lips, and he hid a guilty grin in his thin gray beard.

"There he is," said Herbert White, as the gate banged to loudly and heavy footsteps came toward the door.

The old man rose with hospitable haste, and opening the door, was heard condoling with the new arrival. The new arrival also condoled with himself, so that Mrs. White said, "Tut, tut!" and coughed gently as her husband entered the room, followed by a tall, burly man, beady of eye and rubicund of visage.

"Sergeant-Major Morris," he said, introducing him.

The sergeant-major shook hands, and taking the proffered seat by the fire, watched contentedly while his host got out whisky and tumblers and stood a small copper kettle on the fire.

At the third glass his eyes got brighter, and he began to talk, the little family circle regarding with eager interest this visitor from distant parts, as he squared his broad shoulders in the chair and spoke of wild scenes and doughty deeds, of wars and plagues and strange peoples.

"Twenty-one years of it," said Mr. White, nodding at his wife and son. "When he went away he was a slip of a youth in the warehouse. Now look at him."

"He don't look to have taken much harm," said Mrs. White, politely.

"I'd like to go to India myself," said the old man, "just to look round a bit, you know."

"Better where you are," said the sergeant-major, shaking his head. He put down the empty glass, and sighing softly, shook it again.

"I should like to see those old temples and fakirs and jugglers," said the old man. "What was that you started telling me the other day about a monkey's paw or something, Morris?"

"Nothing," said the soldier hastily. "Leastways nothing worth hearing."

"Monkey's paw?" said Mrs. White, curiously.

"Well, it's just a bit of what you might call magic, perhaps," said the sergeant-major off-handedly.

His three listeners leaned forward eagerly. The visitor absent-mindedly put his empty glass to his lips and then set it down again. His host filled it for him.

"To look at," said the sergeant-major, fumbling in his pocket, "it's just an ordinary little paw, dried to a mummy."

He took something out of his pocket and proffered it. Mrs. White drew back with a grimace, but her son, taking it, examined it curiously.

"And what is there special about it?" inquired Mr. White as he took it from his son, and having examined it, placed it upon the table.

"It had a spell put on it by an old fakir," said the sergeant-major, "a very holy man. He wanted to show that fate ruled people's lives, and that those who interfered with it did so to their sorrow. He put a spell on it so that three separate men could each have three wishes from it."

His manner was so impressive that his hearers were conscious that their light laughter jarred somewhat.

"Well, why don't you have three, sir?" said Herbert White cleverly.

The soldier regarded him in the way that middle age is wont to regard presumptuous youth. "I have," he said quietly, and his blotchy face whitened.

"And did you really have the three wishes granted?" asked Mrs. White.

"I did," said the sergeant-major, and his glass tapped against his strong teeth.

"And has anybody else wished?" persisted the old lady.

"The first man had his three wishes. Yes," was the reply; "I don't know what the first two were, but the third was for death. That's how I got the paw."

His tones were so grave that a hush fell upon the group.

"If you've had your three wishes, it's no good to you now, then, Morris," said the old man at last. "What do you keep it for?"

The soldier shook his head. "Fancy, I suppose," he said slowly. "I did have some idea of selling it, but I don't think I will. It has caused enough mischief already. Besides, people won't buy. They think it's a fairy tale; some of them, and those who do think anything of it want to try it first and pay me afterward."

"If you could have another three wishes," said the old man, eyeing him keenly, "would you have them?"

"I don't know," said the other. "I don't know."

He took the paw, and dangling it between his forefinger and thumb, suddenly threw it upon the fire. White, with a slight cry, stooped down and snatched it off.

"Better let it burn," said the soldier solemnly.

"If you don't want it, Morris," said the other, "give it to me."

"I won't," said his friend doggedly. "I threw it on the fire. If you keep it, don't blame me for what happens. Pitch it on the fire again like a sensible man."

The other shook his head and examined his new possession closely. "How do you do it?" he inquired.

"Hold it up in your right hand and wish aloud," said the sergeant-major, "but I warn you of the consequences."

"Sounds like the *Arabian Nights,*" said Mrs. White, as she rose and began to set the supper. "Don't you think you might wish for four pairs of hands for me?"

Her husband drew the talisman from his pocket, and then all three burst into laughter as the sergeant-major, with a look of alarm on his face, caught him by the arm.

"If you must wish," he said gruffly, "wish for something sensible."

Mr. White dropped it back in his pocket, and placing chairs, motioned his friend to the table. In the business of supper the talisman was partly forgotten, and afterward the three sat listening in an enthralled fashion to a second installment of the soldier's adventures in India.

"If the tale about the monkey's paw is not more truthful than those he has been telling us," said Herbert, as the door closed behind their guest, just in time for him to catch the last train, "we shan't make much out of it."

"Did you give him anything for it, father?" inquired Mrs. White, regarding her husband closely.

"A trifle," said he, coloring slightly. "He didn't want it, but I made him take it. And he pressed me again to throw it away."

"Likely," said Herbert, with pretended horror. "Why, we're going to be rich, and famous and happy. Wish to be an emperor, father, to begin with; then you can't be henpecked."

He darted round the table, pursued by the maligned Mrs. White armed with an antimacassar.

Mr. White took the paw from his pocket and eyed it dubiously. "I don't know what to wish for, and that's a fact," he said slowly. "It seems to me I've got all I want."

"If you only cleared the house, you'd be quite happy wouldn't you?" said Herbert, with his hand on his shoulder. "Well, wish for two hundred pounds, then; that'll just do it."

His father, smiling shamefacedly at his own credulity, held up the talisman, as his son, with a solemn face, somewhat marred by a wink at his mother, sat down at the piano and struck a few impressive chords.

"I wish for two hundred pounds," said the old man distinctly.

A fine crash from the piano greeted the words, interrupted by a shuddering cry from the old man. His wife and son ran toward him.

"It moved," he cried, with a glance of disgust at the object as it lay on the floor. "As I wished, it twisted in my hand like a snake."

"Well, I don't see the money," said his son as he picked it up and placed it on the table, "and I bet I never shall."

"It must have been your fancy, father," said his wife, regarding him anxiously.

He shook his head. "Never mind, though; there's no harm done, but it gave me a shock all the same."

They sat down by the fire again while the two men finished their pipes. Outside, the wind was higher than ever, and the old man started nervously at the sound of a door banging upstairs. A silence unusual and depressing settled upon all three, which lasted until the old couple rose to retire for the night.

"I expect you'll find the cash tied up in a big bag in the middle of your bed," said Herbert, as he bade them good night, "and something horrible squatting up on top of the wardrobe watching you as you pocket your ill-gotten gains."

He sat alone in the darkness, gazing at the dying fire, and seeing faces in it. The last face was so horrible and so simian that he gazed at it in amazement. It got so vivid that, with a little uneasy laugh, he felt on the table for a glass containing a little water to throw over it. His hand grasped the monkey's paw, and with a little shiver he wiped his hand on his coat and went up to bed.

In the brightness of the wintry sun next morning as it streamed over the breakfast table he laughed at his fears. There was an air of prosaic wholesomeness about the room which it had lacked on the previous night, and the dirty, shriveled little paw was pitched on the sideboard with a carelessness which betokened no great belief in its virtues.

"I suppose all old soldiers are the same," said Mrs. White. "The idea of our listening to such nonsense! How could wishes be granted in these days? And if they could, how could two hundred pounds hurt you, father?"

"Might drop on his head from the sky," said the frivolous Herbert.

"Morris said the things happened so naturally," said his father, "that you might if you so wished attribute it to coincidence."

"Well, don't break into the money before I come back," said Herbert as he rose from the table. "I'm afraid it'll turn you into a mean, avaricious man, and we shall have to disown you."

His mother laughed, and following him to the door, watched him down the road; and returning to the breakfast table, was very happy at the expense of her husband's credulity. All of which did not prevent her from scurrying to the door at the postman's knock, nor prevent her from referring somewhat shortly to retired sergeant-majors of bibulous habits when she found that the post brought a tailor's bill.

"Herbert will have some more of his funny remarks, I expect, when he comes home," she said, as they sat at dinner.

"I dare say," said Mrs. White, pouring himself out some beer; "but for all that, the thing moved in my hand; that I'll swear to."

"You thought it did," said the old lady soothingly.

"I say it did," replied the other. "There was no thought about it; I had just——What's the matter?"

His wife made no reply. She was watching the mysterious movements of a man outside, who, peering in an undecided fashion at the house, appeared to be trying to make up his mind to enter. In mental connection with the two hundred pounds, she noticed that the stranger was well dressed, and wore a silk hat of glossy newness. Three times he paused at the gate, and then walked on again. The fourth time he stood with his hand upon it, and then with sudden resolution flung it open and walked up the path. Mrs. White at the same moment placed her hands behind her, and hurriedly unfastening the strings of her apron, put that useful article of apparel beneath the cushion of her chair.

She brought the stranger, who seemed ill at ease, into the room. He gazed at her furtively, and listened in a preoccupied fashion as the old lady apologized for the appearance of the room, and her husband's coat, a garment which he usually reserved for the garden. She then waited as patiently as her sex would permit, for him to broach his business, but he was at first strangely silent.

"I—was asked to call," he said at last, and stooped and picked a piece of cotton from his trousers. "I come from Maw and Meggins."

The old lady started. "Is anything the matter?" she asked breathlessly. "Has anything happened to Herbert? What is it? What is it?"

Her husband interposed. "There, there, mother," he said hastily. "Sit down, and don't jump to conclusions. You've not brought bad news, I'm sure, sir; " and he eyed the other wistfully.

"I'm sorry——" began the visitor.

"Is he hurt?" demanded the mother wildly.

The visitor bowed in assent. "Badly hurt," he said quietly, "but he is not in any pain."

"Oh, thank God!" I said the old woman, clasping her hands. "Thank God for that! Thank——"

She broke off suddenly as the sinister meaning of the assurance dawned upon her and she saw the awful confirmation of her fears in the other's averted face. She caught her breath, and turning to her slower-witted husband, laid her trembling old hand upon his. There was a long silence.

"He was caught in the machinery," said the visitor at length in a low voice.

"Caught in the machinery," repeated Mr. White, in a dazed fashion, "yes."

He sat staring blankly out at the window, and taking his wife's hand between his own, pressed it as he had been wont to do in their old courting-days nearly forty years before.

"He was the only one left to us," he said, turning gently to the visitor. "It is hard."

The other coughed, and rising, walked slowly to the window. "The firm wished me to convey their sincere sympathy with you in your great loss," he said, without looking round. "I beg that you will understand I am only their servant and merely obeying orders."

There was no reply; the old woman's face was white, her eyes staring, and her breath inaudible; on the husband's face was a look such as his friend the sergeant-major might have carried into his first action.

"I was to say that Maw and Meggins disclaim all responsibility," continued the other. "They admit no liability at all, but in consideration of your son's services, they wish to present you with a certain sum as compensation."

Mr. White dropped his wife's hand, and rising to his feet, gazed with a look of horror at his visitor. His dry lips shaped the words, How much?"

"Two hundred pounds," was the answer.

Unconscious of his wife's shriek, the old man smiled faintly, put out his hands like a sightless man, and dropped, a senseless heap, to the floor.

In the huge new cemetery, some two miles distant, the old people buried their dead, and came back to a house steeped in shadow and silence. It was all over so quickly that at first they could hardly realize it, and remained in a state of expectation as though of something else to happen—something else which was to lighten this load, too heavy for old hearts to bear.

But the days passed, and expectation gave place to resignation—the hopeless resignation of the old, sometimes miscalled apathy. Sometimes they hardly exchanged a word, for now they had nothing to talk about, and their days were long to weariness.

It was about a week after that the old man, waking suddenly in the night, stretched out his hand and found himself alone. The room was in darkness, and the sound of subdued weeping came from the window. He raised himself in bed and listened.

"Come back," he said tenderly. "You will be cold."

"It is colder for my son," said the old woman, and wept afresh.

The sound of her sobs died away on his ears. The bed was warm, and his eyes heavy with sleep. He dozed fitfully, and then slept until a sudden wild cry from his wife awoke him with a start.

"The paw!" she cried wildly. "The monkey's paw!"

He started up in alarm. "Where? Where is it? What's the matter?"

She came stumbling across the room toward him. "I want it," she said quietly. "You've not destroyed it?"

"It's in the parlor, on the bracket," he replied, marvelling. "Why?"

She cried and laughed together, and bending over, kissed his cheek.

"I only just thought of it," she said hysterically. "Why didn't I think of it before? Why didn't *you* think of it?"

"Think of what?" he questioned.

"The other two wishes," she replied rapidly. "We've only had one."

"Was not that enough?" he demanded fiercely.

"No," she cried triumphantly; "we'll have one more. Go down and get it quickly, and wish our boy alive again."

The man sat up in bed and flung the bedclothes from his quaking limbs. "Good God, you are mad!" he cried, aghast.

"Get it," she panted; "get it quickly, and wish——Oh, my boy, my boy!"

Her husband struck a match and lit the candle. "Get back to bed," he said unsteadily. "You don't know what you are saying."

"We had the first wish granted," said the old woman feverishly; "why not the second?"

"A coincidence," stammered the old man.

"Go and get it and wish," cried his wife, quivering with excitement.

The old man turned and regarded her, and his voice shook. "He has been dead ten days, and besides he—I would not tell you else, but—I could only recognize him by his clothing. If he was too terrible for you to see then, how now?"

"Bring him back," cried the old woman, and dragged him toward the door. "Do you think I fear the child I have nursed?"

He went down in the darkness, and felt his way to the parlor, and then to the mantelpiece. The talisman was in its place, and a horrible fear that the unspoken wish might bring his mutilated son before him ere he could escape from the room seized upon him, and he caught his breath as he found that he had lost the direction of the door. His brow cold with sweat, he felt his way round the table, and groped along the wall until he found himself in the small passage with the unwholesome thing in his hand.

Even his wife's face seemed changed as he entered the room. It was white and expectant, and to his fears seemed to have an unnatural look upon it. He was afraid of her.

"*Wish!*" she cried, in a strong voice.

"It is foolish and wicked," he faltered.

"*Wish!*" repeated his wife.

He raised his hand. "I wish my son alive again."

The talisman fell to the floor, and he regarded it fearfully. Then he sank trembling into a chair as the old woman, with burning eyes, walked to the window and raised the blind.

He sat until he was chilled with the cold, glancing occasionally at the figure of the old woman peering through the window. The candle-end, which had burned below the rim of the china candlestick, was throwing pulsating shadows on the ceiling and walls, until, with a flicker larger than the rest, it expired. The old man, with an unspeakable sense of relief at the failure of the talisman, crept back to his bed, and a minute or two afterward the old woman came silently and apathetically beside him.

Neither spoke, but lay silently listening to the ticking of the clock. A stair creaked, and a squeaky mouse scurried noisily through the wall. The darkness was oppressive, and after lying for some time screwing up his courage, he took the box of matches, and striking one, went downstairs for a candle.

At the foot of the stairs the match went out, and he paused to strike another; and at the same moment a knock, so quiet and stealthy as to be scarcely audible, sounded on the front door.

The matches fell from his hand and spilled in the passage. He stood motionless: his breath suspended until the knock was repeated. Then he turned and fled swiftly back to his room, and closed the door behind him. A third knock sounded through the house.

"What's that?" cried the old woman, starting up,

"A rat," said the old man in shaking tones, "a rat. It passed me on the stairs."

His wife sat up in bed listening. A loud knock resounded through the house.

"It's Herbert!" she screamed. "It's Herbert!"

She ran to the door, but her husband was before her, and catching her by the arm, held her tightly.

"What are you going to do?" he whispered hoarsely.

"It's my boy; it's Herbert!" she cried, struggling mechanically. "I forgot it was two miles away. What are you holding me for? Let go. I must open the door."

"For God's sake don't let it in," cried the old man, trembling.

"You're afraid of your own son," she cried, struggling. "Let me go. I'm coming, Herbert; I'm coming."

There was another knock, and another. The old woman with a sudden wrench broke free and ran from the room. Her husband followed to the landing, and called after her appealingly as she hurried downstairs. He heard the chain rattle back and the bottom bolt drawn slowly and stiffly from the socket. Then the old woman's voice, strained and panting.

"The bolt," she cried loudly. "Come down. I can't reach it."

But her husband was on his hands and knees groping wildly on the floor in search of the paw. If he could only find it before the thing outside got in. A perfect fusillade of knocks reverberated through the house, and he heard the scraping of a chair as his wife put it down in the passage against the door. He heard the creaking of the bolt as it came slowly back, and at the same moment he found the monkey's paw, and frantically breathed his third and last wish.

The knocking ceased suddenly, although the echoes of it were still in the house. He heard the chair drawn back, and the door opened. A cold wind rushed up the staircase, and a long loud wail of disappointment and misery from his wife gave him courage to run down to her side, and then to the gate beyond. The street lamp flickering opposite shone on a quiet and deserted road.

from Tell My Horse
by Zora Neale Hurston

134

Novelist, folklorist and anthropologist Zora Neale Hurston (1891–1960) was an important part of the Harlem Renaissance. Her 1938 anthropological work Tell My Horse included this chillingly matter-of-fact discussion of Haiti's Zombie problem.

What is the whole truth and nothing else but the truth about Zombies? I do not know, but I know that I saw the broken remnant, relic, or refuse of Felicia Felix-Mentor in a hospital yard.

Here in the shadow of the Empire State Building, death and the graveyard are final. It is such a positive end that we use it as a measure of nothingness and eternity. We have the quick and the dead. But in Haiti there is the quick, the dead, and then there are Zombies.

This is the way Zombies are spoken of: They are the bodies without souls. The living dead. Once they were dead, and after that they were called back to life again.

No one can stay in Haiti long without hearing Zombies mentioned in one way or another, and the fear of this thing and all that it means seeps over the country like a ground current of cold air. This fear is real and deep. It is more like a group of fears. For there is the outspoken fear among the peasants of the work of Zombies. Sit in the market place and pass a day with the market women and notice how often some vendeuse cries out that a Zombie with its invisible hand has filched her money, or her goods. Or the accusation is made that a Zombie has been set upon her or some one of her family to work a piece of evil. Big Zombies who come in the night to do malice are talked about. Also the little girl Zombies who are sent out by their owners in the dark dawn to sell little packets of roasted coffee. Before sun up their cries of "Cafe grille" can be heard from dark places in the streets and one can only see them if one calls out for the seller to come with her goods. Then the little dead one makes herself visible and mounts the steps.

The upper class Haitians fear too, but they do not talk about it so openly as do the poor. But to them also it is a horrible possibility. Think of the fiendishness of the thing. It is not good for a person who has lived all his life surrounded by a degree of fastidious culture, loved to his last breath by family and friends, to contemplate the probability of his resurrected body being dragged from the vault—the best that love and means could provide, and set to toiling ceaselessly in the banana fields, working like a beast, unclothed like a beast, and like a brute crouching in some foul den in the few hours allowed for rest and food. From an educated, intelligent being to an unthinking, unknowing beast. Then there is the helplessness of the situation. Family and friends cannot rescue the victim because they do not know. They think the loved one is sleeping peacefully in his grave. They may motor past the plantation where the Zombie who was once dear to them is held captive often and again and its soulless eyes may have fallen upon them without thought or recognition. It is not to be wondered at that now and then when the rumor spreads that a Zombie has been found and recognized, that angry crowds gather and threaten violence to the persons alleged to be responsible for the crime.

Yet in spite of this obvious fear and the preparations that I found being made to safeguard the bodies of the dead against this possibility I was told by numerous upper class Haitians that the whole thing was a myth. They pointed out that the common people were superstitious, and that the talk of Zombies had no more basis in fact than the European belief in the Werewolf.

But I had the good fortune to learn of several celebrated cases in the past and then in addition, I had the rare opportunity to see and touch an authentic case. I listened to the broken noises in its throat, and then, I did what no one else had ever done, I photographed it. If I had not experienced all of this in the strong sunlight of a hospital yard, I might have come away from Haiti interested but doubtful. But I saw this case of Felicia Felix-Mentor which was vouched for by the highest authority. So I know that there are Zombies in Haiti. People have been called back from the dead.

Now, why have these dead folk not been allowed to remain in their graves? There are several answers to this question, according to the case.

A was awakened because somebody required his body as a beast of burden. In his natural state he could never have been hired to work with his hands, so he was made into a Zombie because they wanted his services as a laborer. B was summoned to labor also but he is reduced to the level of a beast as an act of revenge. C was the culmination of "ba' Moun" ceremony and pledge. That is, he was given as a sacrifice to pay off a debt to a spirit for benefits received.

I asked how the victims were chosen and many told me that any corpse not too old to work would do. The Bocor watched the cemetery and went back and took suitable bodies. Others said no, that the Bocor and his associates knew exactly who was going to be resurrected even before they died. They knew this because they themselves brought about the "death."

Maybe a plantation owner has come to the Bocor to "buy" some laborers, or perhaps an enemy wants the utmost in revenge. He makes an agreement with the Bocor to do the work. After the proper ceremony, the Bocor in his most powerful and dreaded aspect mounts a horse with his face toward the horse's tail and rides after dark to the house of the victim. There he places his lips to the crack of the door and sucks out the soul of the victim and rides off in all speed. Soon the victim falls ill, usually beginning with a headache, and in a few hours is dead. The Bocor, not being a member of the family is naturally not invited to the funeral. But he is there in the cemetery. He has spied on everything from a distance. He is in the cemetery but does not approach the party. He never even faces it directly, but takes in everything out of the corner of his eye. At midnight he will return for his victim.

Everybody agrees that the Bocor is there at the tomb at midnight with the soul of the dead one. But some contend that he has it in a bottle all labelled. Others say no, that he has it in his bare hand. That is the only disagreement. The tomb is opened by the associates and Bocor enters the tomb, calls the name of the victim. He *must* answer because the Bocor has the soul there in his hand. The dead man answers by lifting his head and the moment he does this, the Bocor passes the soul under his nose for a brief second and chains his wrists. Then he beats the victim on the head to awaken him further. Then he leads him forth and the tomb is closed again as if it never had been disturbed.

The victim is surrounded by the associates and the march to the hounfort (voodoo temple and its surroundings) begins. He is hustled along in the middle of the crowd. Thus he is screened from prying eyes to a great degree and also in his half-waking state he is unable to orientate himself. But the victim is not carried directly to the hounfort. First he is carried past the house where he lived. *This* is always done. *Must* be. If the victim were not taken past his former house, later on he would recognize it and return. But once he is taken past, it is gone from his consciousness forever. It is as if it never existed for him. He is then taken to the hounfort and given a drop of a liquid, the formula for which is most secret. After that the victim is a Zombie. He will work ferociously and tirelessly without consciousness of his surroundings and conditions and without memory of his former state. He can never speak again, unless he is given salt. "We have examples of a man who gave salt to a demon by mistake and he come man again and can write the name of the man who gave him to the loa," Jean Nichols told me and added that of course the family of the victim went straight to a Bocor and "gave" the man who had "given" their son.

Now this "Ba Moun" (give man) ceremony is a thing much talked about in Haiti. It is the old European belief in selling one's self to the devil but with Haitian variations. In Europe the man gives himself at the end of a certain period. Over in Haiti he gives others and only gives himself when no more acceptable victims can be found. But he cannot give strangers. It must be a real sacrifice. He must give members of his own family or most intimate friends. Each year the sacrifice must be renewed and there is no avoiding the payments. There are tales of men giving every member of the family, even his wife after nieces, nephews, sons and daughters were gone. Then at last he must go himself. There are lurid tales of the last days of men who have gained wealth and power thru "Give man."

The wife of one man found him sitting apart from the family weeping. When she demanded to know the trouble, he told her that he had been called to go, but she was not to worry because he had put everything in order. He was crying because he had loved her very much and it was hard to leave her. She pointed out that he was not sick and of course it was ridiculous for him to talk of death. Then with his head in her lap he told her about the "services" he had made to obtain the advantages he had had in order to surround her with increasing comforts. Finally she was the only person left that he could offer but that he would gladly die himself rather than offer her as a sacrifice. He told her of watching the day of the vow come and go while his heart grew heavier with every passing hour. The second night of the contract lapsed and he heard the beasts stirring in their little box. The third night which was the one just past, a huge and a terrible beast had emerged in the room. If he could go to the Bocor that same day with a victim, he still could go another year at least. But he had no one to offer except his wife and he had no desire to live without her. He took an affectionate farewell of her, shut himself in his own room and continued to weep. Two days later he was dead.

Another man received the summons late one night. Bosu Tricorne, the terrible three-horned god had appeared in his room and made him know that he must go. Bosu Tricorne bore a summons from Baron

Cimiterre, the lord of the cemetery. He sprang from his bed in terror and woke up his family by his fear noises. He had to be restrained from hurling himself out of the window. And all the time he was shouting of the things he had done to gain success. Naming the people he had given. The family in great embarrassment dragged him away from the window and tried to confine him in a room where his shouts could not be heard by the neighbors. That failing, they sent him off to a private room in a hospital where he spent two days confessing before he died. There are many, many tales like that in the mouths of the people.

There is the story of one man of great courage who, coming to the end of his sacrifices, feeling that he had received what he bargained for, went two days ahead and gave himself up to the spirit to die. But the spirit so admired his courage that he gave him back all of the years he had bargained to take.

Why do men allegedly make such bargains with the spirits who have such terrible power to reward and punish?

When a man is ambitious and sees no way to get there, he becomes desperate. When he has nothing and wants prosperity he goes to a houngan and says, "I have nothing and I am disposed to do anything to have money."

The houngan replies, "He who does not search, does not find."

"I have come to you because I wish to search," the man replies.

"Well, then," the houngan says, "we are going to make a ceremony, and the loa are going to talk with you."

The houngan and the man go into the hounfort. He goes to a small altar and makes the symbol with ashes and gunpowder (indicating that it is a Petro invocation), pours the libation and begins to sing with the Asson and then asks the seeker, "What loa you want me to call for you?"

The man makes his choice. Then the houngan begins in earnest to summon the loa wanted. No one knows what he says because he is talking "langage" that is language, a way of denoting the African patter used by all houngans for special occasions. The syllables are his very own, that is something that cannot be taught. It must come to the priest from the loa. He calls many gods. Then the big jars under the table that contain spirits of houngans long dead begin to groan. These spirits in jars have been at the bottom of the water for a long time. The loa was not taken from their heads at death and so they did not go away from the earth but went to the bottom of the water to stay until they got tired and demanded to be taken out. All houngans have one or more of these spirit jars in the hounfort. Some have many. The groaning of the jars gets louder as the houngan keeps calling. Finally one jar speaks distinctly, "Pourquoi, ou derange' moi?" (Why do you disturb me?) The houngan signals the man to answer the loa. So he states his case.

"Papa, loa, ou mem, qui connais toute baggaye ou mem qui chef te de l'eau, moi derange' ou pour mande' ou servir moi." (Papa, loa, yourself, who knows all things, you yourself who is master of waters, I disturb you to ask you to serve me.)

The Voice: Ma connais ca ou besoin. Mais, ou dispose pour servir moi aussi? (I know what you want, but are you disposed to serve me also?)

The Man: Yes, command me what you want.

Voice: I am going to give you all that you want, but you must make all things that I want. Write your name in your own blood and put the paper in the jar.

The houngan still chanting pricks the man's finger so sharply that he cries out. The blood flows and the supplicant dips a pen in it and writes his name and puts the paper in the jar. The houngan opens a bottle of rum and pours some in the jar. There is the gurgling sound of drinking.

The Voice: And now I am good (I do good) for you. Now I tell you what you must do. You must give me someone that you love. Today you are going into your house and stay until tomorrow. On the eighth day you are returning here with something of the man that you are going to give me. Come also with some money in gold. The voice ceases. The houngan finishes presently after repeating everything that the Voice from the jar has said and dismisses the man. He goes away and returns on the day appointed and the houngan calls up the loa again.

The Voice: Are you prepared for me?

The Man: Yes.

The Voice: Have you done all that I told you?

The Man: Yes.

The Voice (to houngan): Go out. (To man) Give me the gold money. (The man gives it.)

The Voice: Now, you belong to me and I can do with you as I wish. If I want you in the cemetery I can put you there.

The Man: Yes, I know you have all power with me. I put myself in your care because I want prosperity.

The Voice: That I will give you. Look under the table. You will find a little box. In this box there are little beasts. Take this little box and put it in your pocket. Every eighth day you must put in it five hosts (Communion wafers). *Never forget to give the hosts.* Now, go to your house and put the little box in a big box. Treat it as if it were your son. It is now your son. Every midnight open the box and let the beasts out. At four o'clock he will return and cry to come in and you will open for him and close the box again. And every time you give the beasts the communion, immediately after, you will receive large sums of money. Each year on this date you will come to me with another man that you wish to give me. Also you must bring the box with the beasts. If you do not come, the third night after the date, the beasts in the box will become great huge animals and execute my will upon you for your failure to keep your vow. If you are very sick on that day that the offering falls due say to your best friend that he must bring the offering box for you. Also you must send the name of the person you intend to give me as pay for working for you and he must sign a new contract with me for you.

All is finished between the Voice and the man. The houngan re-enters and sends the man away with assurance that he will commence the work at once. Alone he makes ceremony to call the soul of the person who is to be sacrificed. No one would be permitted to see that. When the work in the hounfort is finished, then speeds the rider on the horse. The rider who faces backwards on the horse, who will soon place his lips to the crack of the victim's door and draw his soul away. Then will follow the funeral and after that the midnight awakening. And the march to the hounfort for the drop of liquid that will make him a Zombie, one of the living dead.

Some maintain that a real and true priest of Voodoo, the houngan, has nothing to do with such practices. That it is the bocor and priests of the devil—worshipping cults who do these things. But it is not always easy to tell just who is a houngan and who is a bocor. Often the two offices occupy the same man at different times. There is no doubt that some houngans hold secret ceremonies which their usual following know nothing of. It would be necessary to investigate every houngan and bocor in Haiti rigidly over a period of years to determine who was purely houngan and who was purely Bocor. There is certainly some overlapping in certain cases. A well known houngan of Leogane, who has become a very wealthy man by his profession is spoken of as a bocor more often than as a houngan. There are others in the same category that I could name. Soon after I arrived in Haiti a young woman who was on friendly terms with me said, "You know, you should not go around alone picking acquaintances with these houngans. You are liable to get involved in something that is not good. You must have someone to guide you." I laughed it off at the time, but months later I began to see what she was hinting at.

What is involved in the "give man" and making of Zombies is a question that cannot be answered anywhere with legal proof. Many names are called. Most frequently mentioned in this respect is the Man of Trou Forban. That legendary character who lives in the hole in the mountain near St. Marc. He who has enchanted caves full of coffee and sugar plantations. The entrance to this cave or this series of caves is said to be closed by a huge rock that is lifted by a glance from the master. The Marines are said to have blown up this great rock with dynamite at one time, but the next morning it was there whole and in place again. When the master of Trou Forban walks, the whole earth trembles. There are tales of the master and his wife, who is reputed to be a greater Bocor than he. She does not live with him at Trou Forban. She is said to have a great hounfort of her own on the mountain called Tapion near Petit Gouave. She is such a great houngan that she is honored by Agoue' te Royo, Maitre l'eau, and walks the waters with the same ease that others walk the earth. But she rides in boats whenever it suits her fancy. One time she took a sailboat to go up the coast near St. Marc to visit her husband, Vixama. She appeared to be an ordinary peasant woman and the captain paid her no especial attention until they arrived on the coast below Trou Forban. Then she revealed herself and expressed her great satisfaction with the voyage. She felt that the captain had been extremely kind and courteous, so she went to call her husband to come down to the sea to meet him. Realizing now who she was, the captain was afraid and made ready to sail away before she could return from the long trip up the mountain. But she had mounted to the trou very quickly and returned with Vixama to find the captain and his crew poling the boat away from the shore in the wildest terror. The wind was against them and they could not sail away. Mme. Vixama smiled at their fright and hurled two grains of corn which she held in her hand, on to the deck of the boat and they immediately turned into golden coin. The captain was more afraid and hastily brushed them into the sea. They sailed south all during the night, much relieved that they had broken all connections with Vixama and his wife. But at first light the next morning he found four gold coins of the same denomination as the two that he had refused the day before. Then he knew that the woman of Vixama had passed the night on board and had given them a good voyage as well—the four gold coins were worth twenty dollars each.

There are endless tales of the feats of the occupant of this hole high up on this inaccessible mountain. But in fact it has yet to be proved that anyone has ever laid eyes on him. He is like the goddess in the volcano of Hawaii, and Vulcan in Mt. Vesuvius. It is true that men, taking advantage of the legend and the credulous nature of the people, have set up business in the mountain to their profit. The name of this Man of Trou Forban is known by few and rarely spoken by those who know it. This whispered name is Vixama, which in itself means invisible spirit. He who sits with a hive of honey-bees in his long flowing beard. It is he who is reputed to be the greatest buyer of souls. His contact man is reputed to be Mardi Progres. But we hear too much about the practice around Archahaie and other places to credit Trou Forban as the headquarters. Some much more accessible places than the mountain top is the answer. And some much more substantial being than the invisible Vixama.

If embalming were customary, it would remove the possibility of Zombies from the minds of the people. But since it is not done, many families take precaution against the body being disturbed.

Some set up a watch in the cemetery for thirty-six hours after the burial. There could be no revival after that. Some families have the bodies cut open, insuring real death. Many peasants put a knife in the right hand of the corpse and flex the arm in such a way that it will deal a blow with the knife to whoever disturbs it for the first day or so. But the most popular defense is to poison the body. Many of the doctors have especially long hypodermic needles for injecting a dose of poison into the heart, and sometimes into other parts of the body as well.

A case reported from Port du Paix proves the necessity of this. In Haiti if a person dies whose parents are still alive, the mother does not follow the body to the grave unless it is an only child. Neither does she wear mourning in the regular sense. She wears that coarse material known as "gris-blanc." The next day after the burial, however, she goes to the grave to say her private farewell.

In the following case everything had seemed irregular. The girl's sudden illness and quick death. Then, too, her body stayed warm. So the family was persuaded that her death was unnatural and that some further use was to be made of her body after burial. They were urged to have it secretly poisoned before it was interred. This was done and the funeral went off in routine manner.

The next day like Mary going to the tomb of Jesus, the mother made her way to the cemetery to breathe those last syllables that mothers do over their dead, and like Mary she found the stones rolled away. The tomb was open and the body lifted out of the coffin. It had not been moved because it was so obviously poisoned. But the ghouls had not troubled themselves to rearrange things as they were.

Testimony regarding Zombies with names and dates come from all parts of Haiti. I shall cite a few without using actual names to avoid embarrassing the families of the victims.

In the year 1898 at Cap Haitian a woman had one son who was well educated but rather petted and spoiled. There was some trouble about a girl. He refused to accept responsibility and when his mother was approached by a member of the girl's family she refused to give any sort of satisfaction. Two weeks later the boy died rather suddenly and was buried. Several Sundays later the mother went to church and after she went wandering around the town—just walking aimlessly in her grief, she found herself walking along Bord Mer. She saw some laborers loading ox carts with bags of coffee and was astonished to see her son among these silent workers who were being driven to work with ever increasing speed by the foreman. She saw her son see her without any sign of recognition. She rushed up to him screaming out his name. He regarded her without recognition and without sound. By this time the foreman tore her loose from the boy and drove her away. She went to get help, but it was a long time and when she returned she could not find him. The foreman denied that there had ever been anyone of that description around. She never saw him again, though she haunted the water front and coffee warehouses until she died.

A white protestant Missionary Minister told me that he had a young man convert to his flock who was a highly intelligent fellow and a clever musician. He went to a dance and fell dead on the floor. The missionary conducted the funeral and saw the young man placed in the tomb and the tomb closed. A few weeks later another white minister of another protestant denomination came to him and said, "I had occasion to visit the jail and who do you suppose I saw there? It was C. R."

"But it is not possible. C. R. is dead. I saw him buried with my own eyes."

"Well, you just go down to the prison and see for yourself. He is there for nobody knows I saw him. After I had talked with a prisoner I went there to see, I passed along the line of cells and saw him crouching like some wild beast in one of the cells. I hurried here to tell you about it."

The former pastor of C.R. hurried to the prison and made some excuse to visit in the cell block. And there was his late convert, just as he had been told. This happened in Port-au-Prince.

Then there was the case of P., also a young man. He died and was buried. The day of the funeral passed and the mother being so stricken some friends remained overnight in the house with her and her daughter. It seems that the sister of the dead boy was more wakeful than the rest. Late in the night she heard the subdued chanting, the sound of blows in the street approaching the house and looked out of the window. At the moment she did so, she heard the voice of her brother crying out: "Mama! mama! Sauvez moi!" (Save me!) She screamed and aroused the house and others of the inside looked out and saw the procession and heard the cry. But such is the terror inspired by these ghouls, that no one, not even the mother or sister dared go out to attempt a rescue. The procession moved on out of sight. And in the morning the young girl was found to be insane.

But the most famous Zombie case of all Haiti is the case of Marie M. It was back in October 1909 that this beautiful young daughter of a prominent family died and was buried. Everything appeared normal and people generally forgot about the beautiful girl who had died in the very bloom of her youth. Five years passed.

Then one day a group of girls from the same school which Marie had attended went for a walk with one of the Sisters who conducted the school. As they passed a house one of the girls screamed and said that she had seen Marie M. The Sister tried to convince her she was mistaken. But others had seen her too. The news swept over Port-au-Prince like wild fire. The house was surrounded, but the owner refused to let anyone enter without the proper legal steps. The father of the supposedly dead girl was urged to take out a warrant and have the house searched. This he refused to do at once. Finally he was forced to do so by the pressure of public opinion. By that time the owner had left secretly. There was no one nor nothing in the house. The sullen action of the father caused many to accuse him of complicity in the case. Some accused her uncle and others her god father. And some accused all three. The public clamored for her grave to be opened for inspection. Finally this was done. A skeleton was in the coffin but it was too long for the box. Also the clothes that the girl had been buried in were not upon the corpse. They were neatly folded beside the skeleton that had strangely outgrown its coffin.

It is said that the reason she was in the house where she was seen was that the houngan who had held her had died. His wife wanted to be rid of the Zombies that he had collected. She went to a priest about it and he told her these people must be liberated. Restitution must be made as far as possible. So the widow of the houngan had turned over Marie M. among others to this officer of the church and it was while they were wondering what steps to take in the matter that she was seen by her school mates. Later dressed in habit of a nun she was smuggled off to France where she was seen later in a Convent by her brother. It was the most notorious case in all Haiti and people still talk about it whenever Zombies are mentioned.

In the course of a conversation on November 8, 1936, Dr. Rulx Leon, Director-General of the Service d'Hygiene told me that a Zombie had been found on the road and was now at the hospital at Gonaives. I had his permission to make an investigation of the matter. He gave me letters to the officers of the hospital. On the following Sunday I went up to Gonaives and spent the day. The Chief of staff of the hospital was very kind and helped me in every way that he could. We found the Zombie in the hospital yard. They had just set her dinner before her but she was not eating. She hovered against the fence in a sort of defensive position. The moment that she sensed our approach, she broke off a limb of a shrub and began to use it to dust and clean the ground and the fence and the table which bore her food. She huddled the cloth about her head more closely and showed every sign of fear and expectation of abuse and violence. The two doctors with me made kindly noises and tried to reassure her. She seemed to hear nothing. Just kept on trying to hide herself. The doctor uncovered her head for a moment but she promptly clapped her arms and hands over it to shut out the things she dreaded.

I said to the doctor that I had permission of Dr. Leon to take some pictures and he helped me to go about it. I took her first in the position that she assumed herself whenever left alone. That is cringing against the wall with the cloth hiding her face and head. Then in other positions. Finally the doctor forcibly uncovered her and held her so that I could take her face. And the sight was dreadful. That blank face with the dead eyes. The eyelids were white all around the eyes as if they had been burned with acid. It was pronounced enough to come out in the picture. There was nothing that you could say to her or get from her except by looking at her, and the sight of this wreckage was too much to endure for long. We went to a more cheerful part of the hospital and sat down to talk. We discussed at great length the theories of how Zombies come to be. It was concluded that it is not a case of awakening the dead, but a matter of the semblance of death induced by some drug known to a few. Some secret probably brought from Africa and handed down from generation to generation. These men know the effect of the drug and the antidote. It is evident that it destroys that part of the brain which governs speech and will power. The victims can move and act but cannot formulate thought. The two doctors expressed their desire to gain this secret, but they realize the impossibility of doing so. These secret societies are secret. They will die before they will tell. They cited instances. I said I was willing to try. Dr. Legros said that perhaps I would find myself involved in something so terrible, something from which I could not extricate myself alive and that I would curse the day that I had entered upon my search. Then we came back to the case in hand, and Dr. Legros and Dr. Belfong told me her story.

Her name is Felicia Felix-Mentor. She was a native of Ennery and she and her husband kept a little grocery. She had one child, a boy. In 1907 she took suddenly ill and died and was buried. There were the records to show. The years passed. The husband married again and advanced himself in life. The little boy became a man. People had forgotten all about the wife and mother who had died so long ago.

Then one day in October 1936 someone saw a naked woman on the road and reported it to the Garde d'Haiti. Then this same woman turned up on a farm and said, "This is the farm of my father. I used to live here." The tenants tried to drive her away. Finally the boss was sent for and he came and recognized her as his sister who had died and been buried twenty-nine years before. She was in such wretched condition that the authorities were called in and she was sent to the hospital. Her husband was sent for to confirm the identification, but he refused. He was embarrassed by the matter as he was now a minor official and wanted nothing to do with the affair at all. But President Vincent and Dr. Leon were in the neighborhood at the time and he was forced to come. He did so and reluctantly made the identification of this woman as his former wife.

How did this woman, supposedly dead for twenty-nine years come to be wandering naked on a road? Nobody will tell who knows. The secret is with some bocor dead or alive. Sometimes a missionary converts one of these bocors and he gives up all his paraphernalia to the church and frees his captives if he has any. They are not freed publicly, you understand, as that would bring down the vengeance of the community upon his head. These creatures, unable to tell anything—for almost always they have lost the power of speech forever, are found wandering about. Sometimes the bocor dies and his widow refuses their responsibility for various reasons. Then again they are set free. Neither of these happenings is common.

But Zombies are wanted for more uses besides field work. They are reputedly used as sneak thieves. The market women cry out continually that little Zombies are stealing their change and goods. Their invisible hands are believed to provide well for their owners. But I have heard of still another service performed by Zombies. It is in the story that follows:

A certain matron of Port-au-Prince had five daughters and her niece also living with her. Suddenly she began to marry them off one after the other in rapid succession. They were attractive girls but there were numerous girls who were more attractive whose parents could not find desirable husbands for. People began to marvel at the miracle. When madame was asked directly how she did it, she always answered by saying, "filles ce'marchandies peressables" (Girls are perishable goods, it is necessary to get them off hand quickly). That told nobody anything, but they kept on wondering just the same.

Then one morning a woman well acquainted with the madame of the marrying daughters got up to go to the lazy people's mass. This is celebrated at 4:00 a.m. and is called the lazy people's mass because it is not necessary to dress properly to attend it. It is held mostly for the servants anyway. So people who want to go to mass and want no bother, get up and go and come back home and go to sleep again.

This woman's clock had stopped so she guessed at the hour and got up at 2:00 a.m. instead of 3:00 a.m. and hurried to St. Anne's to the mass. She hurried up the high steps expecting to find the service about to begin. Instead she found an empty church except for the vestibule. In the vestibule she found two little girls dressed for first communion and with lighted candles in their hands kneeling on the floor. The whole thing was too out of place and distorted and for a while the woman just stared. Then she found her tongue and asked, "What are you two little girls doing here at such an hour and why are you dressed for first communion?"

She got no answer as she asked again, "Who are you anyway? You must go home. You cannot remain here like this."

Then one of the little figures in white turned its dead eyes on her and said, "We are here at the orders of Madame M. P., and we shall not be able to depart until all of her daughters are married."

At this the woman screamed and fled.

It is told that before the year was out all of the girls in the family had married. But already four of them had been divorced. For it is said that nothing gotten through "give man" is permanent.

Ah Bo Bo!

A Distant Episode

by Paul Bowles

This story by novelist and short-story writer Paul Bowles (1910–1999) isn't easy to like, in part because it's so hard to forget. The story reeks of inhumanity: the falling away of the things that make us capable of taking pleasure or doing a kindness; the fragility of our comfort, our senses, our connections.

The September sunsets were at their reddest the week the Professor decided to visit Aïn Tadouirt, which is in the warm country. He came down out of the high, flat region in the evening by bus, with two small overnight bags full of maps, sun lotions and medicines. Ten years ago he had been in the village for three days; long enough, however, to establish a fairly firm friendship with the café-keeper, who had written him several times during the first year after his visit, if never since. "Hassan Ramani," the Professor said over and over, as the bus bumped downward through ever warmer layers of air. Now facing the flaming sky in the west, and now facing the sharp mountains, the car followed the dusty trail down the canyons into air which began to smell of other things besides the endless ozone of the heights: orange blossoms, pepper, sun-baked excrement, burning olive oil, rotten fruit. He closed his eyes happily and lived for an instant in a purely olfactory world. The distant past returned—what part of it, he could not decide.

The chauffeur, whose seat the Professor shared, spoke to him without taking his eyes from the road. *"Vous êtes géologue?"*

"A geologist? Ah, no! I'm a linguist."

"There are no languages here. Only dialects."

"Exactly. I'm making a survey of variations on Moghrebi."

The chauffeur was scornful. "Keep on going south," he said. "You'll find some languages you never heard of before."

As they drove through the town gate, the usual swarm of urchins rose up out of the dust and ran screaming beside the bus. The Professor folded his dark glasses, put them in his pocket; and as soon as the vehicle had come to a standstill he jumped out, pushing his way through the indignant boys who clutched at his luggage in vain, and walked quickly into the Grand Hotel Saharien. Out of its eight rooms there were two available—one facing the market and the other, a smaller and cheaper one, giving onto a tiny yard full of refuse and barrels, where two gazelles wandered about. He took the smaller room, and pouring the entire pitcher of water into the tin basin, began to wash the grit from his face and ears. The afterglow was nearly gone from the sky, and the pinkness in objects was disappearing, almost as he watched. He lit the carbide lamp and winced at its odor.

After dinner the Professor walked slowly through the streets to Hassan Ramani's café, whose back room hung hazardously out above the river. The entrance was very low, and he had to bend down slightly to get in. A man was tending the fire. There was one guest sipping tea. The *qaouaji* tried to make him take a seat at the other table in the front room, but the Professor walked airily ahead into the back room and sat down. The moon was shining through the reed latticework and there was not a sound outside but the occasional distant bark of a dog. He changed tables so he could see the river. It was dry, but there was a pool here and there that reflected the bright night sky. The *qaouaji* came in and wiped off the table.

"Does this café still belong to Hassan Ramani?" he asked him in the Moghrebi he had taken four years to learn.

The man replied in bad French: "He is deceased."

"Deceased?" repeated the Professor, without noticing the absurdity of the word. "Really? When?"

"I don't know," said the *qaouaji*. "One tea?"

"Yes. But I don't understand . . ."

The man was already out of the room, fanning the fire. The Professor sat still, feeling lonely, and arguing with himself that to do so was ridiculous. Soon the *qaouaji* returned with the tea. He paid him and gave him an enormous tip, for which he received a grave bow.

"Tell me," he said, as the other started away. "Can one still get those little boxes made from camel udders?"

The man looked angry. "Sometimes the Reguibat bring in those things. We do not buy them here." Then insolently, in Arabic: "And why a camel-udder box?"

"Because I like them," retorted the Professor. And then because he was feeling a little exalted, he added, "I like them so much I want to make a collection of them, and I will pay you ten francs for every one you can get me."

"*Khamstache*," said the *qaouaji*, opening his left hand rapidly three times in succession.

"Never. Ten."

"Not possible. But wait until later and come with me. You can give me what you like. And you will get camel-udder boxes if there are any."

He went out into the front room, leaving the Professor to drink his tea and listen to the growing chorus of dogs that barked and howled as the moon rose higher into the sky. A group of customers came into the front room and sat talking for an hour or so. When they had left, the *qaouaji* put out the fire and stood in the doorway putting on his burnous. "Come," he said.

Outside in the street there was very little movement. The booths were all closed and the only light came from the moon. An occasional pedestrian passed, and grunted a brief greeting to the *qaouaji*.

"Everyone knows you," said the Professor, to cut the silence between them.

"Yes. "

"I wish everyone knew me," said the Professor, before he realized how infantile such a remark must sound.

"*No* one knows you," said his companion gruffly.

They had come to the other side of the town, on the promontory above the desert, and through a great rift in the wall the Professor saw the white endlessness, broken in the foreground by dark spots of oasis. They walked through the opening and followed a winding road between rocks, downward toward the nearest small forest of palms. The Professor thought: "He may cut my throat. But his café—he would surely be found out."

"Is it far?" he asked, casually.

"Are you tired?" countered the *qaouaji*.

"They are expecting me back at the Hotel Saharien," he lied.

"You can't be there and here," said the *qaouaji*.

The Professor laughed. He wondered if it sounded uneasy to the other.

"Have you owned Ramani's café long?"

"I work there for a friend." The reply made the Professor more unhappy than he had imagined it would.

"Oh. Will you work tomorrow?"

"That is impossible to say."

The Professor stumbled on a stone, and fell, scraping his hand. The *qaouaji* said: "Be careful."

The sweet black odor of rotten meat hung in the air suddenly.

"Agh!" said the Professor, choking. "What is it?"

The *qaouaji* had covered his face with his burnous and did not answer. Soon the stench had been left behind. They were on flat ground. Ahead the path was bordered on each side by a high mud wall. There was no breeze and the palms were quite still, but behind the walls was the sound of running water. Also, the odor of human excrement was almost constant as they walked between the walls.

The Professor waited until he thought it seemed logical for him to ask with a certain degree of annoyance: "But where are we going?"

"Soon," said the guide, pausing to gather some stones in the ditch.

"Pick up some stones," he advised. "Here are bad dogs."

"Where?" asked the Professor, but he stooped and got three large ones with pointed edges.

They continued very quietly. The walls came to an end and the bright desert lay ahead. Nearby was a ruined marabout, with its tiny dome only half standing, and the front wall entirely destroyed. Behind it were clumps of stunted, useless palms. A dog came running crazily toward them on three legs. Not until it got quite close did the Professor hear its steady low growl. The *qaouaji* let fly a large stone at it, striking it square in the muzzle. There was a strange snapping of jaws and the dog ran sideways in another direction, falling blindly against rocks and scrambling haphazardly about like an injured insect.

Turning off the road, they walked across the earth strewn with sharp stones, past the little ruin, through the trees, until they came to a place where the ground dropped abruptly away in front of them.

"It looks like a quarry," said the Professor, resorting to French for the word "quarry," whose Arabic equivalent he could not call to mind at the moment. The *qaouaji* did not answer. Instead he stood still and turned his head, as if listening. And indeed, from somewhere down below, but very far below, came the faint sound of a low flute. The *qaouaji* nodded his head slowly several times. Then he said: "The path begins here. You can see it well all the way. The rock is white and the moon is strong. So you can see well. I am going back now and sleep. It is late. You can give me what you like."

Standing there at the edge of the abyss which at each moment looked deeper, with the dark face of the *qaouaji* framed in its moonlit burnous close to his own face, the Professor asked himself exactly what he felt. Indignation, curiosity, fear, perhaps, but most of all relief and the hope that this was not a trick, the hope that the *qaouaji* would really leave him alone and turn back without him.

He stepped back a little from the edge, and fumbled in his pocket for a loose note, because he did not want to show his wallet. Fortunately there was a fifty-franc bill there, which he took out and handed to the man. He knew the *qaouaji* was pleased, and so he paid no attention when he heard him saying: "It is not enough. I have to walk a long way home and there are dogs. . . . "

"Thank you and good night," said the Professor, sitting down with his legs drawn up under him, and lighting a cigarette. He felt almost happy.

"Give me only one cigarette," pleaded the man.

"Of course," he said, a bit curtly, and he held up the pack.

The *qaouaji* squatted close beside him. His face was not pleasant to see. "What is it?" thought the Professor, terrified again, as he held out his lighted cigarette toward him.

The man's eyes were almost closed. It was the most obvious registering of concentrated scheming the Professor had ever seen. When the second cigarette was burning, he ventured to say to the still-squatting Arab: "What are you thinking about?"

The other drew on his cigarette deliberately, and seemed about to speak. Then his expression changed to one of satisfaction, but he did not speak. A cool wind had risen in the air, and the Professor shivered. The sound of the flute came up from the depths below at intervals, sometimes mingled with the scraping of nearby palm fronds one against the other. "These people are not primitives," the Professor found himself saying in his mind.

"Good," said the *qaouaji*, rising slowly. "Keep your money. Fifty francs is enough. It is an honor." Then he went back into French: "*Ti n'as qu'à discendre, to' droit.*" He spat, chuckled (or was the Professor hysterical?), and strode away quickly.

The Professor was in a state of nerves. He lit another cigarette, and found his lips moving automatically. They were saying: "Is this a situation or a predicament? This is ridiculous." He sat very still for several minutes, waiting for a sense of reality to come to him. He stretched out on the hard, cold ground and looked up at the moon. It was almost like looking straight at the sun. If he shifted his gaze a little at a time, he could make a string of weaker moons across the sky. "Incredible," he whispered. Then he sat up quickly and looked about. There was no guarantee that the *qaouaji* really had gone back to town. He got to his feet and looked over the edge of the precipice. In the moonlight the bottom seemed miles away. And there was nothing to give it scale; not a tree, not a house, not a person. . . . He listened for the flute, and heard only the wind going by his ears. A sudden violent desire to run back to the road seized him, and he turned and looked in the direction the *qaouaji* had taken. At the same time he felt softly of his wallet in his breast pocket. Then he spat over the edge of the cliff. Then he made water over it, and listened intently, like a child. This gave him the impetus to start down the path into the abyss. Curiously enough, he was not dizzy. But prudently he kept from peering to his right, over the edge. It was a steady and steep downward climb. The monotony of it put him into a frame of mind not unlike that which had been induced by the bus ride. He was murmuring "Hassan Ramani" again, repeatedly and in rhythm. He stopped, furious with himself for the sinister overtones the name now suggested to him. He decided he was exhausted from the trip. "And the walk," he added.

He was now well down the gigantic cliff, but the moon, being directly overhead, gave as much light as ever. Only the wind was left behind, above, to wander among the trees, to blow through the dusty streets of Aïn Tadouirt, into the hall of the Grand Hotel Saharien, and under the door of his little room.

It occurred to him that he ought to ask himself why he was doing this irrational thing, but he was intelligent enough to know that since he was doing it, it was not so important to probe for explanations at that moment.

Suddenly the earth was flat beneath his feet. He had reached the bottom sooner than he expected. He stepped ahead distrustfully still, as if he expected another treacherous drop. It was so hard to know in this uniform, dim brightness. Before he knew what had happened the dog was upon him, a heavy mass of fur trying to push him backwards, a sharp nail rubbing down his chest, a straining of muscles against him to get the teeth into his neck. The Professor thought: "I refuse to die this way." The dog fell back; it looked like an Eskimo dog. As it sprang again, he called out, very loud: "Ay!" It fell against him, there was a confusion of sensations and a pain somewhere. There was also the sound of voices very near to him, and he could not understand what they were saying. Something cold and metallic was pushed brutally against his spine as the dog still hung for a second by his teeth from a mass of clothing and perhaps flesh. The Professor knew it was a gun, and he raised his hands, shouting in Moghrebi: "Take away the dog!" But the gun merely pushed him forward, and since the dog, once it was back on the ground, did not leap again, he took a step ahead. The gun kept pushing: he kept taking steps. Again he heard voices, but the person directly behind him said nothing. People seemed to be running about; it sounded that way, at least. For his eyes, he discovered, were still shut tight against the dog's attack. He opened them. A group of men was advancing toward him. They were dressed in the black clothes of the Reguibat. "The Reguiba is a cloud across the face of the sun." "When the Reguiba appears the righteous man turns away." In how many shops and marketplaces he had heard these maxims uttered banteringly among friends. Never to a Reguiba, to be sure, for these men do not frequent towns. They send a representative in disguise, to arrange with shady elements there for the disposal of captured goods. "An opportunity," he thought quickly, "of testing the accuracy of such statements." He did not doubt for a moment that the adventure would prove to be a kind of warning against such foolishness on his part—a warning which in retrospect would be half sinister, half farcical.

Two snarling dogs came running from behind the oncoming men and threw themselves at his legs. He was scandalized to note that no one paid any attention to this breach of etiquette. The gun pushed him harder as he tried to sidestep the animals' noisy assault. Again he cried: "The dogs! Take them away!" The gun shoved him forward with great force and he fell, almost at the feet of the crowd of men facing him. The dogs were wrenching at his hands and arms. A boot kicked them aside, yelping, and then with increased vigor it kicked the Professor in the hip. Then came a chorus of kicks from different sides, and he was rolled violently about on the earth for a while. During this time he was conscious of hands reaching into his pockets and removing everything from them. He tried to say: "You have all my money; stop kicking me!"

But his bruised facial muscles would not work; he felt himself pouting, and that was all. Someone dealt him a terrific blow on the head, and he thought: "Now at least I shall lose consciousness, thank Heaven." Still he went on being aware of the guttural voices he could not understand, and of being bound tightly about the ankles and chest. Then there was black silence that opened like a wound from time to time, to let in the soft, deep notes of the flute playing the same succession of notes again and again. Suddenly he felt excruciating pain everywhere— pain and cold. "So I have been unconscious, after all," he thought. In spite of that, the present seemed only like a direct continuation of what had gone before.

It was growing faintly light, There were camels near where he was lying; he could hear their gurgling and their heavy breathing. He could not bring himself to attempt opening his eyes, just in case it should turn out to be impossible. However, when he heard someone approaching, he found that he had no difficulty in seeing.

The man looked at him dispassionately in the gray morning light. With one hand he pinched together the Professor's nostrils. When the Professor opened his mouth to breathe, the man swiftly seized his tongue and pulled on it with all his might. The Professor was gagging and catching his breath; he did not see what was happening. He could not distinguish the pain of the brutal yanking from that of the sharp knife. Then there was an endless choking and spitting that went on automatically, as though he were scarcely a part of it. The word "operation" kept going through his mind; it calmed his terror somewhat as he sank back into darkness.

The caravan left sometime toward midmorning. The Professor, not unconscious, but in a state of utter stupor, still gagging and drooling blood, was dumped doubled-up into a sack and tied at one side of a camel. The lower end of the enormous amphitheater contained a natural gate in the rocks. The camels, swift *mehara*, were lightly laden on this trip. They passed through single file, and slowly mounted the gentle slope that led up into the beginning of the desert. That night, at a stop behind some low hills, the men took him out, still in a state which permitted no thought, and over the dusty rags that remained of his clothing they fastened a series of curious belts made of the bottoms of tin cans strung together. One after another of these bright girdles was wired about his torso, his arms and legs, even across his face, until he was entirely within a suit of armor that covered him with its circular metal scales. There was a good deal of merriment during this decking-out of the Professor. One man brought out a flute and a younger one (did a not ungraceful caricature of an Ouled Naïl executing a cane dance. The Professor was no longer conscious; to be exact, he existed in the middle of the movements made by these other men. When they had finished dressing him the way they wished him to look, they stuffed some food under the tin bangles banging over his face. Even though he chewed mechanically, most of it eventually fell out onto the ground. They put him back into the sack and left him there.

Two days later they arrived at one of their own encampments. There were women and children here in the tents, and the men had to drive away the snarling dogs they had left there to guard them. When they emptied the Professor out of his sack, there were screams of fright, and it took several hours to convince the last woman that he was harmless, although there had been no doubt from the start that he was a valuable possession. After a few days they began to move on again, taking everything with them, and traveling only at night as the terrain grew warmer.

Even when all his wounds had healed and he felt no more pain, the Professor did not begin to think again; he ate and defecated, and he danced when he was bidden, a senseless hopping up and down that delighted the children, principally because of the wonderful jangling racket it made. And he generally slept through the heat of the day, in among the camels.

Wending its way southeast, the caravan avoided all stationary civilization. In a few weeks they reached a new plateau, wholly wild and with a sparse vegetation. Here they pitched camp and remained, while the *mehara* were turned loose to graze. Everyone was happy here; the weather was cooler and there was a well only a few hours away on a seldom-frequented trail. It was here they conceived the idea of taking the Professor to Fogara and selling him to the Touareg.

It was a full year before they carried out this project. By this time the Professor was much better trained. He could do a handspring, make a series of fearful growling noises which had, nevertheless, a certain element of humor; and when the Reguibat removed the tin from his face they discovered he could grimace admirably while he danced. They also taught him a few basic obscene gestures which never failed to elicit delighted shrieks from the women. He was now brought forth only after especially abundant meals, when there was music and festivity. He easily fell in with their sense of ritual, and evolved an elementary sort of "program" to present when he was called for: dancing, rolling on the ground, imitating certain animals, and finally rushing toward the group in feigned anger, to see the resultant confusion and hilarity.

When three of the men set out for Fogara with him, they took four *mehara* with them, and he rode astride his quite naturally. No precautions were taken to guard him, save that he was kept among them, one man always staying at the rear of the party. They came within sight of the walls at dawn, and they waited among the rocks all day. At dusk the youngest started out, and in three hours he returned with a friend who carried a stout cane. They tried to put the Professor through his routine then and there, but the man from Fogara was in a hurry to get back to town, so they all set out on the *mehara*.

In the town they went directly to the villager's home, where they had coffee in the courtyard sitting among the camels. Here the Professor went into his act again, and this time there was prolonged merriment and much rubbing together of hands. An agreement was reached, a sum of money paid, and the Reguibat withdrew, leaving the Professor in the house of the man with the cane, who did not delay in locking him into a tiny enclosure off the courtyard.

The next day was an important one in the Professor's life, for it was then that pain began to stir again in his being. A group of men came to the house, among whom was a venerable gentleman, better clothed than those others who spent their time flattering him, setting fervent kisses upon his hands and the edges of his garments. This person made a point of going into classical Arabic from time to time, to impress the others, who had not learned a word of the Koran. Thus his conversation would run more or less as follows: "Perhaps at In Salah. The French there are stupid. Celestial vengeance is approaching. Let us not hasten it. Praise the highest and cast thine anathema against idols. With paint on his face. In case the police wish to look close." The others listened and agreed, nodding their heads slowly and solemnly. And the Professor in his stall beside them listened, too. That is, he was *conscious* of the sound of the old man's Arabic. The words penetrated for the first time in many months. Noises, then: "Celestial vengeance is approaching." Then: "It is an honor. Fifty francs is enough. Keep your money. Good." And the *qaouaji* squatting near him at the edge of the precipice. Then "anathema against idols" and more gibberish. He turned over panting on the sand and forgot about it. But the pain had begun. It operated in a kind of delirium, because he had begun to enter into consciousness again. When the man opened the door and prodded him with his cane, he cried out in a rage, and everyone laughed.

They got him onto his feet, but he would not dance. He stood before them, staring at the ground, stubbornly refusing to move. The owner was furious, and so annoyed by the laughter of the others that he felt obliged to send them away, saying that he would await a more propitious time for exhibiting his property, because he dared not show his anger before the elder. However, when they had left he dealt the Professor a violent blow on the shoulder with his cane, called him various obscene things, and went out into the street, slamming the gate behind him. He walked straight to the street of the Ouled Naïl, because he was sure of finding the Reguibat there among the girls, spending the money. And there in a tent he found one of them still abed, while an Ouled Naïl washed the tea glasses. He walked in and almost decapitated the man before the latter had even attempted to sit up. Then he threw his razor on the bed and ran out.

The Ouled Naïl saw the blood, screamed, ran out of her tent into the next, and soon emerged from that with four girls who rushed together into the coffeehouse and told the *qaouaji* who had killed the Reguiba. It was only a matter of an hour before the French military police had caught him at a friend's house, and dragged him off to the barracks. That night the Professor had nothing to eat, and the next afternoon, in the slow sharpening of his consciousness caused by increasing hunger, he walked aimlessly about the courtyard and the rooms that gave onto it. There was no one. In one room a calendar hung on the wall. The Professor watched nervously, like a dog watching a fly in front of its nose. On the white paper were black objects that made sounds in his head. He heard them: "*Grande Epicerie du Sahel. Juin. Lundi, Mardi, Mercredi . . . .*"

The tiny ink marks of which a symphony consists may have been made long ago, but when they are fulfilled in sound they become imminent and mighty. So a kind of music of feeling began to play in the Professor's head, increasing in volume as he looked at the mud wall, and he had the feeling that He was performing what had been written for him long ago. He felt like weeping; he felt like roaring through the little house, upsetting and smashing the few breakable objects. His emotion got no further than this one overwhelming desire. So, bellowing as loud as he could, he attacked the house and its belongings. Then he attacked the door into the street, which resisted for a while and finally broke. He climbed through the opening made by the boards be had ripped apart, and still bellowing and shaking his arms in the air to make as loud a jangling is possible, he began to gallop along the quiet street toward the gateway of the town. A few people looked at him with great curiosity. As he passed the garage, the last building before the high mud archway that framed the desert beyond, a French soldier saw him. "*Tiens,*" he said to himself," a holy maniac."

Again it was sunset time. The Professor ran beneath the arched gate, turned his face toward the red sky, and began to trot along the Piste d'In Salah, straight into the setting sun. Behind him, from the garage, the soldier took a potshot at him for good luck. The bullet whistled dangerously near the Professor's head, and his yelling rose into an indignant lament as he waved his arms more wildly, and hopped high into the air at every few steps, in an access of terror.

The soldier watched a while, smiling, as the cavorting figure grew smaller in the oncoming evening darkness, and the rattling of the tin became a part of the great silence out there beyond the gate. The wall of the garage as he leaned against it still gave forth heat, left there by the sun, but even then the lunar chill was growing in the air.

from My Idea of Fun
by Will Self

Former heroin addict Will Self (born 1961) has made black humor a specialty. Still, My Idea of Fun isn't everyone's. Protagonist Ian Wharton gets his jollies killing and mutilating people and animals, and consorts with shadowy characters whose provenance is at best uncertain. Here he finds himself in a setting that is hard to place.

Dreamless sleep. No sensation even of having slept. Sleep simply as a gap, an absence. Sleep so blank and black that it shatters the cycle of the eight thousand moments that make up the waking mind. Hume spoke of consciousness as analogous to inertia, transmitted from moment to moment as force is transferred from one billiard ball to the next. In this instance a white-gloved hand of more than average size had come down to seize the pink.

Ian woke up and knew this before he opened his eyes. Then he opened them and found himself back in the Land of Children's Jokes. Pinky stood like some mutant Bonnard in the wash of lilac and lemon light that fell from the tall unshuttered sash windows. He was eating a Barratt's sherbert dip, using the stick of liquorice that plugged the cylindrical paper packet to dig out the yellow powder. He sucked the stick then plunged it back in and each time he drew it out more of the dusty stuff adhered. Pinky was eating the sherbert dip with great concentration and attention to detail but quite clearly he wasn't enjoying it. It was a task for him, to be carried out with diligence and application; nonetheless he had noticed Ian waking up.

'Are you with us, dearie?' said the gloriously nude man, and turned to confront Ian with his stubby cock and Tartar's-hat muff of white pubic hair.

Ian kept silent. The last time he visited the Land of Children's Jokes he had an awful time. The key to refusing entry into the delusion—or so he imagined—was not to manifest any kind of lucidity. That had been his downfall before, so he resolved to stay silent.

But then something moved in the corner of the room. It was too dark there to make out colour, or even shape, but something moved and abruptly.

'What's that!' cried Ian involuntarily, lifting himself up on his elbows. It was too late. Although the whatever-it-was had stopped moving he still found himself embodied, centre stage in the awful land.

'I see you are with us again, dearie, now that the cat has left off your tongue.' Pinky was welcoming enough, if guarded. He turned back to face the window and went on with his thrusting of liquorice stick into sherbert pond. Ian took a look around the room.

It had changed. It was recognisably the room in which Pinky and the thin man had entertained him before—there were the same high sash windows and there was the same fungal smell. The bed was also the same—huge with curling prows for the foot and headboards. It was even set in the same position, at right-angles to the window. But everything else was different.

The fungus was all gone. The button mushrooms that had clustered in fairy rings on the damp carpets had been dusted up. The giant toadstools and fly agarics that served as tables and chairs had been uprooted and removed. The enormous puff balls, which Ian remembered as being fully six feet across, had been rolled out from the corners of the room and disposed of. Indeed, now that Ian looked more closely, he could see that the room hardly had corners any more to speak of. He had the impression that the room's space had been translated into a vacancy within a far larger structure, some kind of barn, perhaps, or giant warehousing unit. The prevailing colours of the land were now slurry-greys and dried dirt-browns. The air had a sharp tang of high octane and there were lumps of formless detritus scattered around on the carpet.

'What is this place?' asked Ian aloud. 'And why am I here?'

Pinky turned from the window and came and sat on the bed beside him. He went on eating the sherbert dip. On his face brown liquorice stains and plashes of yellow powder had combined, making it look like he'd been subjected to an attack with some new and vile kind of chemical weapon. He regarded Ian with an open but searching expression, not unlike that of a provincial bank manager. 'I cannot say why you are here.' He spoke softly. 'This is not something that can be said. That whereof we cannot speak, thereof we must remain silent.'

'Wittgenstein,' said Ian—it was one of the few quotations he knew.

Pinky flew into a rage. 'It wasn't! It wasn't! The frigging little pansified bitch!' He shook with anger, his ample bosoms swinging from side to side. 'He stole everything, absolutely everything. All my best lines, all my best gags!' He was like a child having a tantrum, a tantrum that departed as suddenly as it had arrived.

'I'm sorry,' said Ian, 'I had no idea it was your line.'

'No, no, it's my fault, I overreacted. I'm sorry, things haven't been going too well with the worm recently and you know how little sympathy I get from *him*.'

Ian glanced around quickly, Pinky had given such emphasis to the 'him' that he assumed the thin man was about to burst forth, twirling his cane and chanting his mantric 'Cha, cha, *cha!*' but there was no sign of him. 'What's the problem with the worm?' Ian asked. By way of answering Pinky opened his mouth wide and indicated that Ian should look inside. He bent forward. In the red-ribbed recesses of Pinky's gullet he caught a glimpse of something with an alien's head. It was white and diffidently questing. 'Is that it—is that the worm?'

'Oh yes,' said Pinky. 'He won't have anything to do with chocolate now and he won't deign to come out of my bum any more either. It has to be my mouth and sherbert fountains are his preferred tipple. I can't begin to tell you how much I hate the things, they make me feel quite quite nauseous.'

'What's your name?' Ian broke in, keen to change the subject.

'Pinky,' said Pinky.

'I knew that,' said Ian and then, 'What is this place, Pinky?'

'This,' said Pinky, getting up and turning a full circle with his flabby arms outstretched, 'is the Land of Children's Jokes.' His Hottentot buttocks hung behind him like a sack. 'And your host for this evening is—' The thing in the corner that had stirred before moved again. 'The one and only man in the Laud of Children's Jokes with a spade in his head. Yes, Ian, with a spade actually in his head. Will you put your hands together, please, and give a big welcome to—Doug!'

Without quite knowing why Ian found himself applauding. His cold hands banged flatly against one another and the split-second echo bounced off the metal walls with a tuning fork's whine. The thing in the corner shifted again, resolving itself into a shape that then took on extension and colour, until it finally became the figure of a man. The man stepped forward—he was in the middle of his middle years and conventionally dressed in a worn but still serviceable single-breasted pin-stripe suit. He was taller than average and slim with sandy hair cut *en brosse*, his features were symmetrical and fine, his countenance pleasing. Ian found him instantly reassuring.

'I'm Doug,' said the man, still standing in the shadows. 'I've come to give you a look-see around the Land of Children's Jokes, if that's all right with you?'

'Um, well, err—absolutely.' Ian struggled to find the words.

'Good, good, but before we set out I need to—how can I put it, let me think—' There was a long and considered pause, clearly Doug wasn't the sort of man to rush into anything. Ian felt relaxed just being in his presence, it was such a contrast to Pinky. So much so that he wasn't surprised when he looked round and saw that Pinky had gone, taking his sherbert fountain with him.

'I need to familiarise you with my condition,' Doug said at last.

'What exactly do you mean?' Ian was bemused. Doug stepped back further into the shadows and Ian could make out one arm going up to fidget in the sandy hair.

'You heard what my colleague said?'

'Oh, you mean about the spade in your head.'

'Exactly. It's not pretty but there it is and we have to get on with things. It's just that one's first sight of it can be a little disturbing.' With this he stepped right forward into the wash of light from the high sash windows.

He really did have a spade in his head, a large garden spade. It was the kind with a blond-wood varnished shaft, a two-tone metal blade and a galvanised rubber handle. This was the part of the spade that was furthest from the ground, for the thing had obviously been plunged into the top of Doug's head vertically, as if some sadistic gardener had stood on his shoulders and started digging. The spade's blade ran perpendicular to Doug's forehead like a surreal coxcomb or hair-parting device. Surrounding the point of entry there was about an inch of corrupted flesh, a ditch and dyke of purpled pus, garnished with matted hair and what might have been brain.

Ian gagged and then, sprawling over the side of the great bed, vomited on to the carpet.

'I am sorry,' said Doug, who had by now moved right up to the foot of the bed, where he stood playing with his watch chain, 'but there's very little that I can do to lessen the impact of the thing. It's useless trying to warn people or explain to them what they're about to see.'

Ian couldn't look at him, he looked at the carpet instead and said, 'Impact would have to be the operative word.'

'Quite so,' said Doug. And suddenly Ian found that he could look at the man with the spade in his head, that it hardly bothered him at all.

'Are you feeling a little better now?' Doug was solicitous. He had the old-world charm Ian associated with British civil servants of the pre-war period. His mien was compounded of concern, probity and duty, more or less in equal parts. There was also something peculiarly affecting about the waxy patina of his sticky-out ears. 'You're so right to remark on my use of the word "impact". You know, I hope I may speak frankly to you, Mr Wharton, for without a certain frankness what is the point of conversation? You see I find this image—' he gestured towards the implement buried in his cranium—' to be almost integral to any understanding of the modern world. Metal into flesh—the impact of metal on flesh. Isn't that the whole of progress in a nutshell—a spade in the head? I only have to contemplate the world to feel it entering into me as steelily and as surely as this spade bisects my skull. Do you follow me?'

'Why yes,' said Ian. 'I suppose I do.'

'I'm dreadfully sorry to bang on about it like this—you must think me a frightful bore but it's so rare that I get the opportunity to talk to anyone.'

'What about Pinky?' said Ian with a creeping sense of *déjà entendu.*

'Oh my dear boy, he's far too tied up in his own problems to have any concern for mine. Somehow that's the way that things tend to be here. Come now, get up and I'll take you for a bit of a tour—you'd like that, wouldn't you?'

Doug gave Ian his smooth hand and assisted him to stand. Throwing off the covers, swinging his legs sideways and then standing up, these actions brought Ian still further into the reality of the Land of Children's Jokes. He found himself upright, fully dressed, next to the man with the spade in his head, within the bounds of the fan of light that spread out from the windows across the lumpy floor. Still holding him by the hand, Doug led him away into the dark.

Doug wouldn't let go of Ian's hand. He pulled him gently but firmly into the crepuscular hinterland of the giant shed, if that's what it was. From somewhere in the distance Ian could hear faint noises that might have been cries but they were too indistinct to make out.

'I ought to warn you,' Doug threw over his shoulder, 'we're going to see some things that may disturb you.' Ian grinned to himself, he was beginning to get the hang of the Land of Children's Jokes.

At that moment there was a squeal in a dark corner some twenty yards off to their right. Ian jumped. 'What's that!'

'The first of them, I suppose, come on, we'd better take a look.' The man with the spade in his head pulled a torch from his pocket and, using its pencil beam tentatively, guided them through the maze of rubbish that littered the floor.

They rounded a low bank, which as far as Ian could make out was composed of tumbleweeds of swarf, dripping with oil and frosted with sawdust. Behind it there was a bloody baby. Doug's torch gave the baby's head a weak yellow halo. It was around nine months old, wearing a terry-towelling Babygro and sitting solidly on its broad-nappied base. Its chin, its hands, its Babygro, even the beaten floor beneath it, were all covered in blood. Something glinted in the baby's tender pink paw, something bright which travelled towards its budding mouth.

'Jesus!' cried Ian. 'That baby's got a razor blade!' But immediately he saw the stupidity of saying it, for scattered at the baby's feet were ten or fifteen more razor blades, all within easy reach. While they watched the baby raised the blade to its mouth, opened wide and inserted it vertically. The baby's blue eyes twinkled merrily at Ian as it bit down on the blade, which straight away sliced through lip and gum at top and bottom. Ian could see the layers of flesh and tissue all the way to the bone; he screamed weakly and Doug squeezed his hand as if to reassure. Thick plashes of blood gave the baby a red bib, but it continued to sit upright and was even happily burbling.

'What's red,' Doug asked, 'and sits in the corner?'

Up above them some sort of dawn had begun to break. In the vaulting of the high ceiling Ian could descry rhubarb girders bursting from a piecrust of concrete. 'Come on.' Doug tugged at his hand. 'There's someone else who wants to meet you.'

They walked for what seemed like hours through the echoing space, sometimes crossing wide expanses of concrete, other times crouching to make their way through twisting tunnels lined with chipboard, or Formica. Everywhere there was evidence of failed industry. Defunct machinery lay about, dusty and rusty. Bolts, brackets, angle irons and other unidentifiable hunks of metal were scattered on the floor; a floor that changed from concrete to beaten earth and in places disappeared altogether underneath a foot or more of water.

The Land of Children's Jokes was locked in the bony embrace of winter, the limitless building must have central unheating, Ian reflected miserably. It was also awkward walking hand-in-hand with Doug, who often had to proceed with extreme caution in order to avoid knocking the spade in his head. Eventually they came to a tunnel that was different to all the others. This one was tiled. It was, Ian realised as they splashed through a footbath, set in its slippery floor, the sort of tunnel you go through on your way from the changing rooms to a public swimming pool.

He was right. When they emerged they were standing at the side of a swimming pool, an old-fashioned thirties' pool with magnolia tiling everywhere, a couple of tiers of wooden seats for spectators and green water lapping at its sides. Doug said, 'I have to go on a bit and check that everything has been prepared. If you don't mind I'd be obliged if you'd wait here for a while.' Before Ian could object, or remonstrate with him in any way he was gone, back through the footbath.

Ian sat down in one of the seats. This, he thought to himself, is no dream. It's too cold, for a start, never mind its terrible lucidity. There was a splash and an explosion of breath from the pool—there was something, or someone in it. Ian rushed down to the edge and peered in. Nothing. The greenish surface of the water lapped towards him and then away from him again. But then he saw something move, right down towards the deep end where the gently sloping bottom suddenly took a dive. It looked like a piece of statuary, a bust or torso of some kind, although not quite the right shape; and anyway, Ian observed, a trail of tiny air-bubbles linked it to the surface.

It lurched, then shot up from the bottom of the pool in a shroud of air and water—whoosh! Ian recoiled, it was bobbing in the open air, the torso of a man, quite a small man with collar-length dark hair. The armless and legless man wriggled his torso feverishly to remain upright in the water, his breath came out in hard 'paffs'.

Ian was a little blasé by now. 'You must be Bob,' he said.

'Aye—that's me,' replied the quadra-amputee, still jerking spasmodically. He had a pronounced Strathclyde accent. His limbs had been chopped off right at the joins, shoulder and groin. Ian could see distinct ovals of recently grafted skin framed by the empty legs of his blue swimming trunks. For some reason the most revolting thing about Bob was this, that he had troubled to clothe his bottom half; the empty legs of his trunks stretched down from his groin, under his perineum and up his arse cleft at the back, framing the scar tissue with shocking clarity in spite of the ultramarine wavering.

Bob had managed to stabilise himself. He was sufficiently buoyant to prevent the water from coming above his nipples and he was now keeping himself upright with nice twitches of his hips and buttocks. Ian examined him more closely. He had the sharp features of a Gorbals hard man and the razor scars to go with them—thin blue capillaries radiated across his face from his nose. His narrow hairless chest—and indeed the rest of his body from what Ian could see of it—was packed with taut muscle under a pale freckled skin.

'Did yer mother never teach you that it's rude to stare like that at the disabled?' Bob snapped.

'Oh God, I'm sorry, I'm a bit disoriented, you see. I've no idea either how I got here or what the hell it's all about.'

'You can be forgiven for that,' said Bob, mellowing. 'I dinna' ken anyone who rightly knows how he came here.' He moved his head around to indicate the place they found themselves in. It was an amazingly expressive gesture, as if his neck were an arm and his face a hand he could talk with. 'Ahm from Scotty land—originally like.'

'Oh,' said Ian.

'D'ye ken it?'

'Well, I went when I was a child, to Edinburgh on a school trip.'

'Edinburgh! Pshaw! Edinburgh! Thass no more Scotty Land than the bloody Tyne, man.'

'Where are you from?' asked Ian, sort of knowing that this was the right thing to do.

'Glasgie, man, Glasgie, not that that's necessarily yer real Scotty land, ahm not claiming that because anyone from north of the Gramps always says that they're the real Scotties and I can see their point.' Bob finished this speech by arching his pale body right out of the water like some hideous Rainbow trout, then he plunged his head down into the pool, so that his foreshortened rear end shot up in the air. The arch was followed by another and then another. Ian watched dumbfounded as the amputee propelled himself the length of the pool by exercising this limbless butterfly stroke.

Bob reached the shallows and regained his equilibrium in the far corner of the pool, his narrow shoulders jammed up against the rails of the ladder. There was a splashing from the footbath—Ian turned and saw Doug emerging spadefirst.

'About bloody time!' hooted Bob.

'I'm sorry?' said Doug, urbane as ever.

'You leave the bloody man in my pool without so much as by your leave—what kind of manners are those then?'

'It was only for a couple of minutes—'

'Dinne give me that crap, many mickles make a muckle; and you can tell his fucking nibs from me, that ahm no afraid of him neither. There's little else he can do to hurt me, now is there?'

'I'm sorry if I offended you,' said Ian. He couldn't say why but he rather liked Bob. There was something truly admirable about the way the spunky Scot had overcome his terrifying disability.

'Oh dinna you worry, lad, I was jus' letting off some blather. You run along now; and as the medieval knights used to say to one another on parting, "Be-sieging you!" Ahahaha! Hahah'ha!'

And it was this cackling laughter that followed Ian as he splashed his way back through the footbath behind Doug.

The Cicerones
by Robert Aickman

The work of Robert Fordyce Aickman (1913–1981) often shows up in ghost story collections. But traditional ghost stories usually include some sort of explanation of the spirits' motives. Aikman's ghosts aren't all traditional, and he isn't always around to clear up the mystery, which thus tends to linger, in a way that is pleasant and unpleasant.

John Trant entered the Cathedral of St Bavon at almost exactly 11.30.

An unexpected week's holiday having come his way, he was spending it in Belgium, because Belgium was near and it was late in the season, and because he had never been there. Trant, who was unmarried (though one day he intended to marry), was travelling alone, but he seldom felt lonely at such times because he believed that his solitude was optional and regarded it rather as freedom. He was thirty-two and saw himself as quite ordinary, except perhaps in this very matter of travel, which he thought he took more seriously and systematically than most. The hour at which he entered the Cathedral was important, because he had been inconvenienced in other towns by the irritating continental habit of shutting tourist buildings between 12.00 and 2.00, even big churches. In fact, he had been in two minds as to whether to visit the Cathedral at all with so little time in hand. One could not even count upon the full half-hour, because the driving out of visitors usually began well before the moment of actual closure. It was a still morning, very still but overcast. Men were beginning to wait, one might say, for the year finally to die.

The thing that struck Trant most as he entered the vast building was how silent it seemed to be within; how empty. Other Belgian cathedrals had contained twenty or thirty scattered people praying, or anyway kneeling; priests importantly on the move, followed by acolytes; and, of course, Americans. There had always been dingy bustle, ritual action, and neck-craning. Here there seemed to be no one; other, doubtless, than the people in the tombs. Trant again wondered whether the informed did not know that it was already too late to go in.

He leant against a column at the west end of the nave as he always did, and read the history of the cathedral in his Blue Guide. He chose this position in order that when he came to the next section to be perused, the architectual summary, he could look about him to the best advantage. He usually found, none the less, that he soon had to move if he were to follow what the guide book had to say, as the architecture of few cathedrals can be apprehended, even in outline, by a newcomer from a single point. So it was now: Trant found that he was losing the thread, and decided he would have to take up the guide book's trail. Before doing so, he looked around him for a moment. The Cathedral seemed still to be quite empty. It was odd, but a very pleasant change.

Trant set out along the south aisle of the nave, holding the guide book like a breviary. 'Carved oak pulpit,' said the guide book, 'with marble figures, all by Laurent Delvaux.' Trant had observed it vaguely from afar, but as, looking up from the book, he began consciously to think about it, he saw something extraordinary. Surely there was a figure in the pulpit, not standing erect, but slumped forward over the preacher's cushion? Trant could see the top of a small, bald head with a deep fringe, almost a halo, of white hair; and, on each side, widespread arms, with floppy hands. Not that it appeared to be a priest: the figure was wearing neither white nor black, but on the contrary, bright colours, several of them. Though considerably unnerved, Trant went forward, passed the next column, in the arcade between the nave and the aisle, and looked again, through the next bay. He saw at once that there was nothing: at least there was only a litter of minor vestments and scripts in coloured bindings.

Trant heard a laugh. He turned. Behind him stood a slender, brown-haired young man in a grey suit.

'Excuse me,' said the young man. 'I saw it myself so don't be frightened.' He spoke quite clearly, but had a vague foreign accent.

'It was terrifying,' said Trant. 'Out of this world.'

'Yes. Out of this world, as you say. Did you notice the hair?'

'I did indeed.' The young man had picked on the very detail which had perturbed Trant the most. 'What did you make of it?'

'Holy, holy, holy,' said the young man in his foreign accent; then smiled and sauntered off westwards. Trant was *almost* sure that this was what he had said. The hair of the illusory figure in the pulpit had, at the time, reminded Trant of the way in which nimbuses are shown in certain old paintings; with wide bars or strips of light linking an outer misty ring with the sacred head. The figure's white hair had seemed to project in just such spikes.

Trant pulled himself together and reached the south transept, hung high with hatchments. He sought out 'Christ among the Doctors', 'The masterpiece of Frans Pourbus the Elder', the guide book remarked, and set himself to identifying the famous people said to be depicted in it, including the Duke of Alva, Vigilius ab Ayatta, and even the Emperor Charles V himself.

In the adjoining chapel, 'The Martyrdom of St Barbara' by De Crayer proved to be covered with a cloth, another irritating continental habit, as Trant had previously discovered. As there seemed to be no one about, Trant lifted a corner of the cloth, which was brown and dusty, like so many things in Belgian cathedrals, and peered beneath. It was difficult to make out very much, especially as the light was so poor.

'Let me help,' said a transatlantic voice at Trant's back. 'Let me take it right off, and then you'll see something, believe me.'

Again it was a young man, but this time a red-haired cheerful looking youth in a green windcheater.

The youth not only removed the cloth, but turned on an electric light.

'Thank you,' said Trant.

'Now have a good look.'

Trant looked. It was an extremely horrible scene.

'Oh, boy.' Trant had no desire to look any longer. 'Thank you all the same,' he said, apologizing for his repulsion.

'What a circus those old saints were,' commented the transatlantic youth, as he replaced the worn cloth.

'I suppose they received their reward in heaven,' suggested Trant.

'You bet they did,' said the youth, with a fervour that Trant couldn't quite fathom. He turned off the light. 'Be seeing you.'

'I expect so,' said Trant smiling.

The youth said no more, but put his hands in his pockets, and departed whistling towards the south door. Trant himself would not have cared to whistle so loudly in a foreign church.

As all the world knows, the most important work of art in the Cathedral of St Bavon is the 'Adoration' by the mysterious van Eyck or van Eycks, singular or plural. Nowadays the picture is hung in a small, curtained-off chapel leading from the south choir ambulatory; and most strangers must pay to see it. When Trant reached the chapel, he saw the notice at the door, but, hearing nothing, as elsewhere, supposed the place to be empty. Resenting mildly the demand for a fee, as Protestants do, he took the initiative and gently lifted the dark red curtain.

The chapel, though still silent, was not empty at all. On the contrary, it was so full that Trant could have gone no further inside, even had he dared.

There were two kinds of people in the chapel. In front were several rows of men in black. They knelt shoulder to shoulder, heads dropped, hip-bone against hip-bone, in what Trant took to be silent worship. Behind them, packed in even more tightly, was a group, even a small crowd, of funny old Belgian women, fat, ugly, sexless, and bossy, such as Trant had often seen in other places both devotional and secular. The old women were not kneeling but sitting. All the same, they seemed eerily rapt. Strangest of all was their motionless silence. Trant had seen such groups everywhere in Belgium, but never, never silent, very far from it. Not a single one of this present group seemed even to be aware that he was there: something equally unusual with a people so given to curiosity.

And in this odd setting not the least strange thing was the famous picture itself, with its enigmatic monsters, sibyls, and walking allegories, and its curiously bright, other-world colours: a totality doubtless interpretable in terms of Freud, but, all the same, as dense as an oriental carpet, and older than Adam and Eve, who stand beside. Trant found the picture all too cognate to the disconcerting devotees.

He let fall the curtain and went on his way, distinctly upset.

Two chapels further around, he came upon the 'Virgin Glorified' by Liemakere. Here a choir-boy in a red cassock was polishing the crucifix on the altar. Already, he had thin black hair and a grey, watchful face.

'Onze lieve Vrouw,' said the choir-boy, explaining the picture to Trant.

'Yes,' said Trant. 'Thank you.'

It occurred to him that polishing was odd work for a choir-boy. Perhaps this was not a choir-boy at all, but some other kind of young servitor. The idea of being shortly ejected from the building returned to Trant's mind. He looked at his watch. It had stopped. It still showed 11.28.

Trant shook the watch against his ear, but there were no recovering ticks. He saw that the polishing boy (he was at work on the pierced feet) wore a watch also, on a narrow black strap. Trant gesticulated again. The boy shook his head more violently. Trant could not decide whether the boy's own watch was broken, or whether, conceivably, he thought that Trant was trying to take it from him. Then, all in seconds, it struck Trant that, whatever else there was about the boy he certainly did not appear alarmed. Far from it. He seemed as aloof as if he were already a priest, and to be refusing to tell Trant the time on principle; almost implying, as priests presume to do, that he was refusing for the other's good. Trant departed from the chapel containing Liemakere's masterpiece rather quickly.

How much time had he left?

In the next chapel was Rubens's vast altarpiece of St Bavon distributing all his goods among the poor.

In the next was the terrifying 'Martyrdom of Saint Livinus' by Seghers.

After one more chapel, Trant had reached the junction of the north transept and the choir. The choir was surrounded by a heavy and impenetrable screen of black marble, like a cage for the imperial lions. The guide book recommended the four tombs of past bishops which were said to be inside; but Trant, peering through the stone bars, could hardly see even outlines. He shifted from end to end of the choir steps seeking a viewpoint where the light might be better. It was useless. In the end, he tried the handle of the choir gate. The gate had given every appearance of being locked, but in fact it opened at once when Trant made the attempt. He tiptoed into the dark enclosure and thought he had better shut the gate behind him. He was not sure that he was going to see very much of the four tombs even now; but there they were, huge boxes flanking the high altar, like dens for the lions.

He stood at the steps of the altar itself, leaning across the marble rails, the final barricade, trying to read one of the Latin inscriptions. In such an exercise Trant made it a matter of principle not lightly to admit defeat. He craned his neck and screwed up his eyes until he was half-dazed; capturing the antique words one at a time, and trying to construe them. The matter of the cathedral shutting withdrew temporarily to the back of his mind. Then something horrible seemed to happen; or rather two things, one after the other. Trant thought, first, that the stone panel he was staring at so hard, seemed somehow to move; and then that a hand had appeared round one upper corner of it. It seemed to Trant a curiously small hand.

Trant decided, almost calmly, to see it out. There must obviously be an explanation, and anything like flight would make him look ridiculous, as well as leaving the mystery unsolved. An explanation there was; the stone opened further, and from within emerged a small, fair-haired child.

'Hullo,' said the child, looking at Trant across the black marble barrier and smiling.

'Hullo,' said Trant. 'You speak very good English.'

'I *am* English,' said the child. It was wearing a dark brown garment open at the neck, and dark brown trousers, but Trant could not quite decide whether it was a boy or a girl. From the escapade a boy seemed likelier, but there was something about the child which was more like a girl, Trant thought.

'Should you have been in there?'

'I always go in.'

'Aren't you afraid?'

'No one could be afraid of Bishop Triest. He gave us those candlesticks.' The child pointed to four copper objects; which seemed to Trant to offer no particular confirmation of the child's logic.

'Would *you* like to go in?' enquired the child politely.

'No, thank you,' said Trant.

'Then I'll just shut up.' The child heaved the big stone slab into place. It was a feat of strength all the more remarkable in that Trant noticed that the child seemed to limp.

'Do you live here?' asked Trant.

'Yes,' said the child, and, child-like, said no more.

It limped forward, climbed the altar rail, and stood beside Trant, looking up at him. Trant found it difficult to assess how old it was.

'Would you like to see one of the other bishops?'

'No thank you,' said Trant.

'I think you ought to see a bishop,' said the child quite gravely.

'I'd rather not,' said Trant smiling.

'There may not be another chance.'

'I expect not,' said Trant, still smiling. He felt it was best to converse with the child at its own level, and make no attempt at adult standards of flat questioning and conventionalized reference.

'Then I'll take you to the crypt,' said the child.

The crypt was the concluding item in the guide book. Entered from just by the north-western corner of the choir, it was, like the 'Adoration', a specialty, involving payment. Trant had rather assumed that he would not get round to it.

'Shall I have time?' he asked, looking instinctively at his stopped watch, still showing 11.28.

'Yes,' said the child, as before.

The child limped ahead, opened the choir-gate, and held it for Trant, his inscriptions unread, to pass through. The child closed the gate, and led the way to the crypt entry, looking over its shoulder to see that Trant was following. In the rather better light outside the choir, Trant saw that its hair was a wonderful mass of silky gold; its face almost white, with the promise of fine bones; its lips unusually full and red.

'This is called the crossing,' said the child informatively. Trant knew that the term was sometimes applied to the intersection of nave and transepts.

'Or the narthex, I believe,' he said, plunging in order to show who was the grown-up.

The child, not unnaturally, looked merely puzzled.

There was still no one else visible in the cathedral.

They began to descend the crypt stairs, the child holding on to the iron handrail, because of its infirmity. There was a table at the top, obviously for the collection of the fee, but deserted. Trant did not feel called upon to comment.

In the crypt, slightly to his surprise, many of the lights were on. Probably the custodian had forgotten to turn them off when he or she had hurried forth to eat.

The guide book described the crypt as 'large', but it was much larger than Trant had expected. The stairs entered it at one corner, and columns seemed to stretch away like trees into the distance. They were built in stones of different colours, maroon, purple, green, grey, gold; and they often bore remains of painting as well, which also spread over areas of the vaulted stone roof and weighty walls. In the soft patchy light, the place was mysterious and beautiful; and all the more so because the whole area could not be seen simultaneously. With the tide of centuries the stone-paved floor had become rolling and uneven, but agreeably so. There were occasional showcases and objects on pedestals, and there was a gentle perfume of incense. As Trant entered, all was silence. He even felt for a moment that there was something queer about the silence; that only sounds of another realm moved in it, and that the noises of this world, of his own arrival for example, were in a different dimension and irrelevant. He stood, a little awed, and listened for a moment to the nothingness.

The child stood too, or rather rested against a pillar. It was smiling again, though very slightly. Perhaps it smiled like this all the time, as if always happy.

Trant thought more than ever that it might be a girl. By this time it was rather absurd not to be sure, but by this time it was more than before difficult to ask.

'Bishop Triest's clothes,' said the child, pointing. They were heavy vestments, hanging, enormously embroidered, in a glass cabinet.

'Saint Livinus's ornament,' said the child, and crossed itself. Trant did not know quite what to make of the ornament.

'Animals,' said the child. It was an early book of natural history, written by a monk, and even the opened page showed some very strange ones.

The child was now beginning positively to dart about in its eagerness, pointing out item after item.

'Shrine of Saint Marcarius,' said the child, not crossing itself, presumably because the relic was absent.

'Abbot Hughenois's clothes.' They were vestments again, and very much like Triest's vestments, Trant thought.

'What's that?' asked Trant, taking the initiative and pointing. Right on the other side of the crypt, as it seemed, and now visible to Trant for the first time through the forest of soft coloured columns, was something which appeared to be winking and gleaming with light.

'That's at the end,' replied the child. 'You'll be there soon.'

Soon indeed, at this hour, thought Trant: if in fact we're not thrown out first.

'Via Dolorosa,' said the child, pointing to a picture. It was a gruesome scene, painted very realistically, as if the artist had been a bystander at the time; and it was followed by another which was even more gruesome and at least equally realistic.

'Calvary,' explained the child.

They rounded a corner with a stone wall on the left, the forest of columns on the right. The two parts of a diptych came into view, of which Trant had before seen only the discoloured reverse.

'The blessed and the lost,' said the child, indicating, superfluously, which was which.

Trant thought that the pictures and frescoes were becoming more and more morbid, but supposed that this feeling was probably the result of their cumulative impact. In any case, there could not be much more.

But there were still many things to be seen. In due course they came to a group of pictures hanging together.

'The sacrifice of three blessed martyrs,' said the child. Each of the martyrs had died in a different way: by roasting on a very elaborate gridiron; by disembowelling; and by some process involving a huge wheel. The paintings, unlike some of the others, were extraordinarily well preserved. The third of the martyrs was a young woman. She had been martyred naked and was of great and still living beauty. Next to her hung a further small picture, showing a saint carrying his own skin. Among the columns to the right, was an enormous black cross. At a little distance, the impaled figure looked lifelike in the extreme.

The child was still skipping in front, making so light of its disability that Trant could not but be touched. They turned another corner. At the end of the ambulatory ahead was the gleaming, flashing object that Trant had noticed from the other side of the crypt. The child almost ran on, ignoring the intervening sights, and stood by the object, waiting for Trant to catch up. The child's head was sunk, but Trant could see that it was looking at him from under its fair, silky eyelashes.

This time the child said nothing, and Trant could only stare.

The object was a very elaborate, jewelled reliquary of the renaissance. It was presumably the jewels which had seemed to give off the flashing lights, because Trant could see no lights now. At the centre of the reliquary was a transparent vertical tube or cylinder. It was only about an inch high, and probably made of crystal. Just visible inside it was a short black thread, almost like the mercury in a minute thermometer; and at the bottom of the tube was, Trant noticed, a marked discoloration.

The child was still standing in the same odd position; now glancing sideways at Trant, now glancing away. It was perhaps smiling a little more broadly, but its head was sunk so low that Trant could not really see. Its whole posture and behaviour suggested that there was something about the reliquary which Trant should be able to see for himself. It was almost as if the child were timing him, to see how long he took.

Time, thought Trant, yet again; and now with a start. The reliquary was so fascinating that he had managed somehow almost to forget about time. He looked away and along the final ambulatory, which ran to the foot of the staircase by which he had descended. While he had been examining the reliquary, someone else had appeared in the crypt. A man stood in the centre of the passage, a short distance from Trant. Or not exactly a man: it was, Trant realized, the acolyte in the red cassock, the boy who had been polishing the brass feet. Trant had no doubt that he had come to hurry him out.

Trant bustled off, full of unreasonable guilt, without even properly thanking his child guide. But when he reached the boy in the cassock, the boy silently stretched out his arms to their full length and seemed, on the contrary, to bar his passage.

It was rather absurd; and especially as one could so readily turn right and weave a way out through the Gothic columns.

Trant, in fact, turned his head in that direction, simply upon instinct. But, in the bay to his right, stood the youth from across the Atlantic in the green windcheater. He had the strangest of expressions (unlike the boy in the cassock, who seemed the same dull peasant as before); and as soon as Trant caught his eye, he too raised his arms to their full extent, as the boy had done.

There was still one more free bay. Trant retreated a step or two, but then saw among the shadows within (which seemed to be deepening) the man in the grey suit with the vague foreign accent. His arms were going up even as Trant sighted him, but when their eyes met (though Trant could not see his face very well) he did something the others had not done. He laughed.

And in the entrance to the other ambulatory, through which Trant had just come and down which the child had almost run, bravely casting aside its affliction, stood that same child, now gazing upwards again, and indeed looking quite radiant, as it spread its arms almost as a bird taking flight.

Trant heard the great clock of the cathedral strike twelve. In the crypt, the tone of the bell was lost: there was little more to be distinguished than twelve great thuds, almost as if cannon were being discharged. The twelve strokes of the hour took a surprisingly long time to complete.

In the meantime, and just beside the reliquary, a small door had opened, in the very angle of the crypt. Above it was a small but exquisite and well preserved alabaster keystone showing a soul being dragged away on a hook by a demon. Trant had hardly noticed the door before, as people commonly overlook the working details of a place which is on show, the same details that those who work the place look to first.

In the door, quite filling it, was the man Trant believed himself to have seen in the pulpit soon after he had first entered the great building. The man looked bigger now, but there were the same bald head, the same resigned hands, the same multicoloured garments. It was undoubtedly the very person, but in some way enlarged or magnified; and the curious fringe of hair seemed more luminous than ever.

'You must leave now,' said the man kindly but firmly. 'Follow me.'

The four figures encircling Trant began to shut in on him until their extended finger-tips were almost touching.

His questions went quite unanswered, his protests quite unheard; especially after everyone started singing.

from Communion: A True Story
by Whitley Strieber

Whitley Strieber (born 1945) has written six books about encounters with aliens. This passage comes from the first of them, which purports to describe Strieber's 1985 experience as a victim of alien abduction. The experience sounds extremely uncomfortable—and his account of it is more convincing than one might wish.

December 26, 1985

My wife and I own a log cabin in a secluded corner of upstate New York. It is in this cabin that our primary experiences have taken place. I will deal first with what I remember of December 26, 1985, and then with what was subsequently jogged into memory concerning October 4, 1985. Until I sought help, I remembered only that there was a strange disturbance on October 4. An interviewer asked if I could recall any other unusual experiences in my past. The night of October 4 had also been one of turmoil, but it took discussions with the other people who had been in the cabin at the time to help me reconstruct it.

This part of my narrative, covering December 26, is derived from journal material I had written before undergoing any hypnosis or even discussing my situation with anybody.

When I was alone, this is what it was like.

Our cabin is very hidden and quiet, part of a small group of cabins scattered across an area served by a private dirt road, which itself branches off a little-used country road that leads to an old town that isn't even mentioned on many maps. We spend more than half of our time at the cabin, because I do most of my work there. We also have an apartment in New York City.

Ours is a very sedate life. We don't go out much, we rarely drink more than wine, and neither of us has ever used drugs. From 1977 until 1983 I wrote imaginative thrillers, but in recent years I had been concentrating on much more serious fiction about peace and the environment, books that were firmly grounded in fact. Thus, at this time in my life, I wasn't even working on horror stories, and at no time had I ever been in danger of being deluded by them.

We were having a lovely Christmas at the cabin in late December 1985. On Christmas Eve there was snow, which continued for two more days. My son had discovered to his delight that the snow would fall in perfect crystalline flakes on his gloves if he stood still with his hands out.

On December 26 we spent a happy morning breaking in his new sled, then went cross-country skiing in the afternoon. For supper we had leftover Christmas goose, cranberry sauce, and cold sweet potatoes. We drank seltzer with fresh lime in it. After our son went to bed, Anne and I sat quietly together listening to some music and reading.

At about eight-thirty I turned on the burglar alarm, which covers every accessible window and all the doors. For no reason then apparent, I had developed an unusual habit the previous fall. As secretly as ever I made a tour of the house, peering in closets and even looking under the guest-room bed for hidden intruders. I did this immediately after setting the alarm. By ten o'clock we were in bed, and by eleven both of us were asleep.

The night of the twenty-sixth was cold and cloudy. There were perhaps eight inches of snow on the ground, and it was still falling lightly.

I do not recall any dreams or disturbances at all. There was apparently a large unknown object seen in the immediate vicinity at approximately this time of month, but a report of it would not be published for another week. Even when I read that report, though, I did not relate it in any way to my experience. Why should I? The report attributed the sightings to a practical joke. Only much later, when I researched it myself, did I discover how inaccurate that report was.

I have never seen an unidentified flying object. I thought that the whole subject had been explained by science. It took me a couple of months to establish the connection between what had happened to me and possible nonhuman visitors, so unlikely did such a connection seem.

In the middle of the night of December 26—I do not know the exact time—I abruptly found myself awake. And I knew why: I heard a peculiar whooshing, swirling noise coming from the living room downstairs. This was no random creak, no settling of the house, but a sound as if a large number of people were moving rapidly around in the room.

I listened carefully. The noise just didn't make sense. I sat up in bed, shocked and very curious. There was an edge of fear. The night was dead still, windless. My eyes went straight to the burglar-alarm panel beside the bed. The system was armed and working perfectly. Not a covered window or door was opened, and nobody had entered—at least according to the row of glowing lights.

What I did next may seem peculiar. I settled back in bed. For some reason the extreme strangeness of what I was hearing did not rouse me to action. Over the course of this narrative this sort of inappropriate response will be repeated many times. If something is strange enough, the reaction is very different from what one would think. The mind seems to tune it out as if by some sort of instinct.

No sooner had I settled back than I noticed that one of the double doors leading into our bedroom was moving closed. As they close outward, this meant that the opening was getting smaller, concealing whatever was behind that door. I sat up again. My mind was sharp. I was not asleep, nor in a hypnopompic state between sleep and waking. I wish to be clear that I felt, at that moment, wide awake and in full possession of all my faculties. I could easily have gotten up and read a book or listened to the radio or gone for a midnight walk in the snow.

I could not imagine what could be going on, and I got very uneasy.

My heart started beating harder. I wasn't settled back anymore; I was sitting up, a question just forming in my mind. What could be moving the door?

Then I saw edging around it a compact figure. It was so distinct and yet so completely, impossibly astonishing that at first I could not understand it at all. I simply sat there staring, too stunned to move.

Months and months later, I discovered that another person who has had the visitor experience first encountered it through the medium of this same peculiar figure rushing toward her in exactly the way that this one now rushed toward me.

Before I narrate those next few seconds, though, I would like to give an exact description of how the figure looked to me. First, I will describe the physical conditions under which I was seeing it. The room was dim but not dark. The burglar-alarm panel alone emitted enough light for me to see. In addition, there was snow on the ground and that added some ambient light. Had it been a person peeking into the room, I could have made out his or her features clearly.

This figure was too small to be a person, unless a child. I have measured the approximate distance that the top of the head was from the ground, based on my memory of the figure's position in the doorway, and I believe that it was roughly three and a half feet tall, altogether smaller and lighter than my son.

I could see perhaps a third of the figure, the part that was bending around the door so that it could see me. It had a smooth, rounded hat on, with an odd, sharp rim that jutted out easily four inches on the side I could see. Below this was a vague area. I could not see the face, or perhaps I would not see it. A few moments later, when it was close to the bed, I saw two dark holes for eyes and a black downturning line of a mouth that later became an O.

From shoulder to midriff was the visible third of a square plate etched with concentric circles. This plate stretched from just below the chin to the waist area. At the time I thought it looked like some sort of breastplate, or even an armored vest. Beneath it was a rectangular appliance of the same type, which covered the lower waist to just above the knees. The angle at which the individual was leaning was such that the lower legs were hidden behind the door.

I was quite shocked, but what I was seeing was so strange I had to assume that it was a dream. Maybe this is why I continued to sit in bed, taking no action. Or perhaps my mind was already under some sort of control.

In any case, I sat there frightened but unable or unwilling to deal with what I was observing. My mind explained my vision to me: Despite my full wakefulness, it must be a hypnopompic hallucination. Such phenomena sometimes occur as one drifts between waking and sleep. I assumed that some minor disturbance had awakened me and I was experiencing such an illusion, and never mind the fact that I felt fully awake.

Because of its isolation, the house not only had a burglar alarm but contained a shotgun, which was not far from the bed at the time. Was that why the thing behind the door was wearing a shield, if that was indeed what it was? I have subsequently wondered if an earlier reconnaissance of the house might not have taken place and revealed the presence of the weapon?

The previous July we'd had an experience that should be reported here. I was reading at about half past eleven at night, when I distinctly heard footsteps—normal, human-sounding footsteps—move stealthily down our front porch to the area where I had just had a motion-sensitive light installed. The peculiar thing about these footsteps was that they came from the pool area and moved toward the road, the opposite of the direction that they would have come if it was a prowler from the road. At the time, I thought to myself that I would take the gun and go downstairs if the light came on.

No sooner had I thought that than it did. I dashed downstairs but saw nobody even though the light was still on. As it was attached to a fifteen-second timer, I found this startling. I had gotten out onto the porch in no more than ten seconds, and there was no place for an intruder to hide between the house and the road, not in that short time.

A careful investigation, shotgun in hand, uncovered nothing. I had been certain that I would see whomever it was running off. At the time I even entertained the notion that they must have jumped onto the roof, but there was nobody there.

Subsequently the light never worked right, although it was in good order earlier that very evening. In September I took the bulbs out. Later in the fall the unit was replaced.

The next thing I knew, the figure came rushing into the room. I recall only blackness after that, for an unknown period of time. I don't remember falling asleep or lying awake. What I do remember is far, far more disturbing. My next conscious recollection is of being in motion. I was naked, with my arms and legs extended, as if I had been frozen in mid-leap. I was moving out of the room. There was no physical sensation at all, not of being touched, not of being warm or cold. I could feel myself as a shape and a mass, but not in terms of sensation. It was as if I had become profoundly paralyzed. Although I wanted desperately to move, I could not.

Because of my state of apparent paralysis, I am afraid that I cannot report that I was floating along on some magical pallet or a flying carpet. It could easily be that I was being carried. In any case, I was at this point in a state of panic. Gone was any fleeting thought of dream or hallucination. Something was hideously wrong, so wrong that my mind went blank. I couldn't think. Even if I had been able to make a sound, which I doubt, I couldn't try.

I must have blacked out again, because I have no further memories of being moved. The next thing I knew, I was sitting in a small sort of depression in the woods. It was quite dark, and frozen creeper was pressing tightly around me. I remember being startled that there was no snow on the gray earth.

I sat with my legs partly bent and my hands in my lap. Although I cannot recall this in any detail, I may have been leaning against something. I was still absent sensation. Across the depression to my left there was a small individual whom I could see only out of the corner of my eye. This person was wearing a gray-tan body suit and sitting on the ground with knees drawn up and hands clasped around them.

There were two dark eyeholes and a round mouth hole. I had the impression of a face mask.

I felt that I was under the exact and detailed control of whomever had me. I could not move my head, or my hands, or any part of my body save for my eyes. Despite this, I was not tied.

Immediately on my right was another figure, this one completely invisible except for an occasional flash of movement. This person was working busily at something that seemed to have to do with the right side of my head. It wore dark-blue coveralls and was extremely fast.

The depression appeared to be no more than four feet in diameter, but my eyes were not functioning normally—maybe for no other reason than that I wasn't wearing my glasses. (I am mildly nearsighted.) While the presence of others remains vague in my mind, the individual to my left made a clear impression. I do not know why, but I had the distinct feeling that this was a woman, and so I shall refer to her in the feminine.

She was as small as the others, and appeared almost bored or indifferent. I also felt that she was explaining something to me, but I cannot remember what it was.

I then saw branches moving past my face, then a sweep of treetops. I looked down, and below me the whole tall forest was corkscrewing slowly to the right. There was no chance to question how in the world I had gotten above the trees. I only saw and recorded. Then a gray floor obscured my vision, slipping below my feet like an iris closing.

The next thing I knew, I was sitting in a messy round room. My impression is that at this point I was actually being cradled by these people, as if they were aware of what was about to transpire. Movement to this totally unfamiliar environment, so suddenly and under these extremely unusual conditions, stripped away whatever reserves of collectedness I still possessed. While I had up until that point been able to retain a degree of control of my attention, this now left me and I became entirely given over to extreme dread. The fear was so powerful that it seemed to make my personality completely evaporate. This was not a theoretical or even a mental experience, but something profoundly physical.

"Whitley" ceased to exist. What was left was a body in a state of raw fear so great that it swept about me like a thick, suffocating curtain, turning paralysis into a condition that seemed dose to death. I do not think that my ordinary humanity survived the transition to this little room. I died, and a wild animal appeared in my place. Not everything was gone, though. What remained, although small, nevertheless was occupied with an essential task of verification. I was looking around as best I could, recording what I saw.

The small, circular chamber had a domed, grayish-tan ceiling with ribs appearing at intervals of about a foot. I had an impression that it was messy, a living space. Across the room to my right some clothing was thrown on the floor. As a matter of fact, the thought even crossed my mind that the place was actually dirty. It was close and confining for me. The whole scale of it was small, tight, and enclosed. I seem to remember that the room was stuffy and the air quite dry, so it could be that the numbness of panic was wearing off.

Tiny people were now moving around me at great speed. Their quickness was disturbing, and in a curious way ugly. I had the thought that I was being taken away, and remembered my family. An acute, gnawing feeling of being in a trap overcame me. It was a truly awful sensation, accompanied as it was by the sense that I was absolutely helpless in the hands of these strange creatures.

Despite my extreme terror, I was aware of my surroundings. I know that I was seated on a bench, leaning against a wall. The predominant colors were tan and gray. The bench was the same color as the walls, and was rimmed by a lip of dark brown. From the clarity of my memory of these rather muted colors, I surmise that the room was lit, although I did not see the source of the fight.

There was something quite beautiful, I think, having to do with a lens in the ceiling, but I can remember little about it. Perhaps there was a lens at the point of the ceiling, through which some colorful scene could be observed.

There is no way to be certain of how long I remained in this room. It seemed to be a stay of no more than a few minutes or even seconds.

It may have been longer, though, because I had time to look around me and note numerous details. While I had before been totally paralyzed, I was now able to move at least my eyes and possibly my head.

I was so scared that my memories are indistinct and covered by amnesia. Even as I write this, I am aware that a great deal more happened. I just can't get to it. This might be terror amnesia, or drugs, or hypnosis, or even doses of all three. There is one drug, tetradotoxin, which could approximate such a state. In small doses it causes external anesthesia. Larger doses bring about the "out of the body" sensation occasionally reported by victims of visitor abduction. Greater quantities can cause the appearance of death—even the brain ceases detectable function.

This rare drug is the core of the zombie poison of Haiti, and little is known about why it works as it does. It is also the notorious "fugu" poison of Japan, found in the tissues of a blowfish, which is an esteemed if deadly aphrodisiac.

My surroundings were so unfamiliar in every detail and my surprise was so great that I simply faded away, in the sense that my ability to direct myself was lost, mentally as well as physically. Not only was I physically anesthetized (although no longer so much paralyzed as totally limp), I was in a mental state that separated me from myself so completely that I had no way to filter my emotions or most immediate reactions, nor could my personality initiate anything. I was reduced to raw biological response. It was as if my forebrain had been separated from the rest of my system, and all that remained was a primitive creature, in effect the ape out of which we evolved long ago.

I was not, however, in the ape. I was in my forebrain, locked away from the rest of myself. My mind had become a prison.

One being was on my right, another on my left. Within my field of vision a great deal of rushing about commenced again. The next thing I knew, I was being shown a tiny gray box with a sliding lid. There was a curved lip at one end of this box, to make it easy to push it open. It was being held by a thin, graceful person whose appearance was not distinct. Was this the female again? I'm not sure. It almost seems, as I remember, that something had been done to my eyes to affect my ability to concentrate my vision. Glances around the room were quite detailed in recollection, but any attempts to steady my vision and view a particular being resulted in blurring. It would be interesting to know if this was an induced effect or something caused by my own fear of what I was seeing.

My memory of the one that came before me next is of a tiny, squat person, crouching as if huddled over something. He had been given the box and now slid it open, revealing an extremely shiny, hair-thin needle mounted on a black surface. This needle glittered when I saw it out of the corner of my eye, but was practically invisible straight on.

I became aware—I think I was told—that they proposed to insert this into my brain.

If I had been afraid before, I now became quite simply crazed with terror. I argued with them. "This place is filthy," I remember saying. Then, "You'll ruin a beautiful mind." I could imagine my family awakening in the morning and finding me a vegetable. A great sadness overtook me. I do not recall screaming, but evidently I was doing so, because I remember the next exchange quite clearly.

One of them, I think it was the one I had identified earlier as the woman, said, "What can we do to help you stop screaming?" This voice was remarkable. It was definitely aural, that is to say, I heard it rather than sensed it. It had a subtly electronic tone to it, the accents flat and startlingly Midwestern.

My reply was unexpected. I heard myself say, "You could let me smell you." I was embarrassed; that is not a normal request, and it bothered me. But it made a great deal of sense, as I have afterward realized.

The one to my right replied, "Oh, OK, I can do that," in a similar voice, speaking very rapidly, and held his hand against my face, cradling my head with his other hand. The odor was distinct, and gave me exactly what I needed, an anchor in reality. It remained the most convincing aspect of the whole memory, because that odor was completely indistinguishable from a real one. It did not seem in any way a dream experience or a hallucination. I remembered it as an actual smell.

There was a slight scent of cardboard to it, as if the sleeve of the coverall that was partly pressed against my face were made of some substance like paper. The hand itself had a faint but distinctly organic sourness in its odor. It was not a human smell, but it was unmistakably the smell of something alive. There was a subtle overtone that seemed a little like cinnamon.

The next thing I knew, there was a bang and a flash, and I realized that they had performed the proposed operation on my head. I felt like weeping and I recall sinking down into a cradle of tiny arms.

At this point, I had some feeling, and enough muscle tone had returned to enable me to slide my feet along the floor in an effort to avoid falling all the way. Then I was lifted up and seemed suddenly to be in another room, or perhaps I simply saw my present surroundings differently. It appeared to be a small operating theater. I was in the center of it on a table, and three tiers of benches were populated with a few huddled figures, some with round, as opposed to slanted, eyes.

I was aware that I had seen four different types of figures. The first was the small robotlike being that had led the way into my bedroom. He was followed by a large group of short, stocky ones in the dark-blue coveralls. These had wide faces, appearing either dark gray or dark blue in that light, with glittering deep-set eyes, pug noses, and broad, somewhat human mouths. Inside the room, I encountered two types of creature that did not look at all human. The most provocative of these was about five feet tall, very slender and delicate, with extremely prominent and mesmerizing black slanted eyes. This being had an almost vestigial mouth and nose. The huddled figures in the theater were somewhat smaller, with similarly shaped heads but round, black eyes like large buttons.

Throughout the whole experience, the stocky ones were always present. They were apparently responsible for moving and controlling me, and I had the distinct impression that they were a sort of "good army." Why good I do not know.

I do not remember what, if anything, happened in the operating theater. My memories of movement from place to place are the hardest to recall because it was then that I felt the most helpless. My fear

would rise when they touched me. Their hands were soft, even soothing, but there were so many of them that it felt a little as if I were being
passed along by rows of insects. It was very distressing.

Soon I was in more intimate surroundings once again. There were
clothes strewn about, and two of the stocky ones drew my legs apart.
The next thing I knew I was being shown an enormous and extremely
ugly object, gray and scaly, with a sort of network of wires on the end.
It was at least a foot long, narrow, and triangular in structure. They
inserted this thing into my rectum. It seemed to swarm into me as if it
had a life of its own. Apparently its purpose was to take samples, possibly of fecal matter, but at the time I had the impression that I was
being raped, and for the first time I felt anger.

Only when the thing was withdrawn did I see that it was a mechani-
cal device. The individual holding it pointed to the wire cage on the tip
and seemed to warn me about something. But what? I never found out.

Events once again started moving very quickly.

One of them took my right hand and made an incision on my forefinger. There was no pain at all. Abruptly, my memories end. There isn't
even blackness, just morning.

I had no further recollection of the incident.

The Yellow Wallpaper

by Charlotte Perkins Gilman

Readers of this story won't be surprised to learn that Charlotte Perkins Gilman (1860–1935) was an early feminist. But her politics don't entirely explain the impact of "The Yellow Wallpaper," a frightening story which also manages to be terribly sad. Its residue includes a lingering sense that these things happen all the time.

It is very seldom that mere ordinary people like John and myself secure ancestral halls for the summer.

A colonial mansion, a hereditary estate, I would say a haunted house, and reach the height of romantic felicity—but that would be asking too much of fate!

Still I will proudly declare that there is something queer about it.

Else, why should it be let so cheaply? And why have stood so long untenanted?

John laughs at me, of course, but one expects that in man. John is practical in the extreme. He has no patience with faith, an intense horror of superstition, and he scoffs openly at any talk of things not to be felt and seen and put down in figures.

John is a physician, and *perhaps*—(I would not say it to a living soul, of course, but this is dead paper and a great relief to my mind)—*perhaps* that is one reason I do not get well faster.

You see he does not believe I am sick! And what can one do?

If a physician of high standing, and one's own husband, assures friends and relatives that there is really nothing the matter with one but temporary nervous depression—a slight hysterical tendency—what is one to do?

My brother is also a physician, and also of high standing, and he says the same thing.

So I take phosphates or phosphites—whichever it is—and tonics, and journeys, and air, and exercise, and am absolutely forbidden to "work" until I am well again.

Personally, I disagree with their ideas.

Personally, I believe that congenial work, with excitement and change, would do me good.

But what is one to do?

I did write for a while in spite of them; but it *does* exhaust me a good deal—having to be so sly about it, or else meet with heavy opposition.

I sometimes fancy that in my condition if I had less opposition and more society and stimulus—but John says the very worst thing I can do is to think about my condition, and I confess it always makes me feel bad.

So I will let it alone and talk about the house.

The most beautiful place! It is quite alone, standing well back from the road, quite three miles from the village. It makes me think of English places that you read about, for there are hedges and walls and gates that lock, and lots of separate little houses for the gardeners and people.

There is a *delicious* garden! I never saw such a garden—large and shady, full of box-bordered paths, and lined with long grape-covered arbors with seats under them.

There were greenhouses, too, but they are all broken now.

There was some legal trouble, I believe, something about the heirs and co-heirs; anyhow, the place has been empty for years.

That spoils my ghostliness, I am afraid, but I don't care—there is something strange about the house—I can feel it.

I even said so to John one moonlight evening, but he said what I felt was a draught, and shut the window.

I get unreasonably angry with John sometimes. I'm sure I never used to be so sensitive. I think it is due to this nervous condition.

But John says if I feel so I shall neglect proper self-control; so I take pains to control myself—before him, at least, and that makes me very tired.

I don't like our room a bit. I wanted one downstairs that opened on the piazza and had roses all over the window, and such pretty old-fashioned chintz hangings! But John would not hear of it.

He said there was only one window and not room for two beds, and no near room for him if he took another.

He is very careful and loving, and hardly lets me stir without special direction.

I have a schedule prescription for each hour in the day; he takes all care from me, and so I feel basely ungrateful not to value it more.

He said we came here solely on my account; that I was to have perfect rest and all the air I could get. "Your exercise depends on your strength, my dear," said he, "and your food somewhat on your appetite; but air you can absorb all the time." So we took the nursery at the top of the house.

It is a big, airy room, the whole floor nearly, with windows that look all ways, and air and sunshine galore. It was nursery first and then play-room and gymnasium, I should judge; for the windows are barred for little children, and there are rings and things in the walls.

The paint and paper look as if a boys' school had used it. It is stripped off—the paper—in great patches all around the head of my bed, about as far as I can reach, and in a great place on the other side of the room low down. I never saw a worse paper in my life.

One of those sprawling flamboyant patterns committing every artistic sin.

It is dull enough to confuse the eye in following, pronounced enough constantly to irritate and provoke study, and when you follow the lame uncertain curves for a little distance they suddenly commit suicide—plunge off at outrageous angles, destroy themselves in unheard of contradictions.

The color is repellent, almost revolting; a smouldering unclean yellow, strangely faded by the slow-turning sunlight.

It is a dull yet lurid orange in some places, a sickly sulphur tint in others.

No wonder the children hated it! I should hate it myself if I had to live in this room long.

There comes John, and I must put this away—he hates to have me write a word.

We have been here two weeks, and I haven't felt like writing before, since that first day.

I am sitting by the window now, up in this atrocious nursery, and there is nothing to hinder my writing as much as I please, save lack of strength.

John is away all day, and even some nights when his cases are serious.

I am glad my case is not serious!

But these nervous troubles are dreadfully depressing.

John does not know how much I really suffer. He knows there is no *reason* to suffer, and that satisfies him.

Of course it is only nervousness. It does weigh on me so not to do my duty in any way!

I meant to be such a help to John, such a real rest and comfort, here I am a comparative burden already!

Nobody would believe what an effort it is to do what little I am able—to dress and entertain, and order things.

It is fortunate Mary is so good with the baby. Such a dear baby!

And yet I *cannot* be with him, it makes me so nervous.

I suppose John never was nervous in his life. He laughs at me so about this wallpaper!

At first he meant to repaper the room, but afterwards he said that I was letting it get the better of me, and that nothing was worse for a nervous patient than to give way to such fancies.

He said that after the wallpaper was changed it would be the heavy bedstead, and then the barred windows, and then that gate at the head of the stairs, and so on.

"You know the place is doing you good," he said, "and really, dear, I don't care to renovate the house just for a three months' rental. "

"Then do let us go downstairs," I said, "there are such pretty rooms there."

Then he took me in his arms and called me a blessed little goose, and said he would go down cellar, if I wished, and have it whitewashed into the bargain.

But he is right enough about the beds and windows and things.

It is an airy and comfortable room as any one need wish, and, of course, I would not be so silly as to make him uncomfortable just for a whim.

I'm really getting quite fond of the big room, all but that horrid paper.

Out of one window I can see the garden, those mysterious deep-shaded arbors, the riotous old-fashioned flowers, and bushes and gnarly trees.

Out of another I get a lovely view of the bay and a little private wharf belonging to the estate. There is a beautiful shaded lane that runs down there from the house. I always fancy I see people walking in these numerous paths and arbors, but John has cautioned me not to give way to fancy in the least. He says that with my imaginative power and habit of story-making, a nervous weakness like mine is sure to lead to all manner of excited fancies, and that I ought to use my will and good sense to check the tendency. So I try.

I think sometimes that if I were only well enough to write a little it would relieve the press of ideas and rest me.

But I find I get pretty tired when I try.

It is so discouraging not to have any advice and companionship about my work. When I get really well, John says we will ask Cousin Henry and Julia down for a long visit; but he says he would as soon put fireworks in my pillowcase as to let me have those stimulating people about now.

I wish I could get well faster.

But I must not think about that. This paper looks to me as if it *knew* what a vicious influence it had!

There is a recurrent spot where the pattern lolls like a broken neck and two bulbous eyes stare at you upside down.

I get positively angry with the impertinence of it and the everlast-ingness. Up and down and sideways they crawl, and those absurd, unblinking eyes are everywhere. There is one place where two breadths didn't match, and the eyes go all up and down the line, one a little higher than the other.

I never saw so much expression in an inanimate thing before, and we all know how much expression they have! I used to lie awake as a child and get more entertainment and terror out of blank walls and plain furniture than most children could find in a toy-store.

I remember what a kindly wink the knobs of our big, old bureau used to have, and there was one chair that always seemed like a strong friend.

I used to feel that if any of the other things looked too fierce I could always hop into that chair and be safe.

The furniture in this room is no worse than inharmonious, however, for we had to bring it all from downstairs. I suppose when this was used as a playroom they had to take the nursery things out, and no wonder! I never saw such ravages as the children have made here.

The wallpaper, as I said before, is torn off in spots, and it sticketh closer than a brother—they must have had perseverance as well as hatred.

Then the floor is scratched and gouged and splintered, the plaster itself is dug out here and there, and this great heavy bed which is all we found in the room, looks as if it had been through the wars.

But I don't mind it a bit—only the paper.

There comes John's sister. Such a dear girl as she is, and so careful of me! I must not let her find me writing.

She is a perfect and enthusiastic housekeeper, and hopes for no bet-ter profession. I verily believe she thinks it is the writing which made me sick!

But I can write when she is out, and see her a long way off from these windows.

There is one that commands the road, a lovely shaded winding road, and one that just looks off over the country. A lovely country, too, full of great elms and velvet meadows.

This wallpaper has a kind of sub-pattern in a different shade, a particularly irritating one, for you can only see it in certain lights, and not clearly then.

But in the places where it isn't faded and where the sun is just so—I can see a strange, provoking, formless sort of figure, that seems to skulk about behind that silly and conspicuous front design.

There's sister on the stairs!

Well, the Fourth of July is over! The people are all gone and I am tired out. John thought it might do me good to see a little company, so we just had mother and Nellie and the children down for a week.

Of course I didn't do a thing. Jennie sees to everything now.

But it tired me all the same.

John says if I don't pick up faster he shall send me to Weir Mitchell in the fall.

But I don't want to go there at all. I had a friend who was in his hands once, and she says he is just like John and my brother, only more so!

Besides, it is such an undertaking to go so far.

I don't feel as if it was worth while to turn my hand over for anything, and I'm getting dreadfully fretful and querulous.

I cry at nothing, and cry most of the time.

Of course I don't when John is here, or anybody else, but when I am alone.

And I am alone a good deal just now. John is kept in town very often by serious cases, and Jennie is good and lets me alone when I want her to.

So I walk a little in the garden or down that lovely lane, sit on the porch under the roses, and lie down up here a good deal.

I'm getting really fond of the room in spite of the wallpaper. Perhaps *because* of the wallpaper.

It dwells in my mind so!

I lie here on this great immovable bed—it is nailed down, I believe—and follow that pattern about by the hour. It is as good as gymnastics, I assure you. I start, we'll say, at the bottom, down in the corner over there where it has not been touched, and I determine for the thousandth time that I *will* follow that pointless pattern to some sort of a conclusion.

I know a little of the principle of design, and I know this thing was not arranged on any laws of radiation, or alternation, or repetition, or symmetry, or anything else that I ever heard of.

It is repeated, of course, by the breadths, but not otherwise.

Looked at in one way each breadth stands alone, the bloated curves and flourishes—a kind of "debased Romanesque" with delirium tremens—go waddling up and down in isolated columns of fatuity.

But, on the other hand, they connect diagonally, and the sprawling outlines run off in great slanting waves of optic horror, like a lot of wallowing sea-weeds in full chase.

The whole thing goes horizontally, too, at least it seems so, and I exhaust myself trying to distinguish the order of its going in that direction.

They have used a horizontal breadth for a frieze, and that adds wonderfully to the confusion.

There is one end of the room where it is almost intact, and there, when the crosslights fade and the low sun shines directly upon it, I can almost fancy radiation after all,—the interminable grotesques seem to form around a common centre and rush off in headlong plunges of equal distraction.

It makes me tired to follow it. I will take a nap I guess.

I don't know why I should write this.

I don't want to.

I don't feel able.

And I know John would think it absurd. But I *must* say what I feel and think in some way—it is such a relief!

But the effort is getting to be greater than the relief.

Half the time now I am awfully lazy, and lie down ever so much.

John says I mustn't lose my strength, and has me take cod liver oil and lots of tonics and things, to say nothing of ale and wine and rare meat.

Dear John! He loves me very dearly, and hates to have me sick. I tried to have a real earnest reasonable talk with him the other day, and tell him how I wish he would let me go and make a visit to Cousin Henry and Julia.

But he said I wasn't able to go, nor able to stand it after I got there; and I did not make out a very good case for myself, for I was crying before I had finished.

It is getting to be a great effort for me to think straight. Just this nervous weakness I suppose.

And dear John gathered me up in his arms, and just carried me upstairs and laid me on the bed, and sat by me and read to me till it tired my head.

He said I was his darling and his comfort and all he had, and that I must take care of myself for his sake, and keep well.

He says no one but myself can help me out of it, that I must use my will and self-control and not let any silly fancies run away with me.

There's one comfort, the baby is well and happy, and does not have to occupy this nursery with the horrid wallpaper.

If we had not used it, that blessed child would have! What a fortunate escape! Why, I wouldn't have a child of mine, an impressionable little thing, live in such a room for worlds.

I never thought of it before, but it is lucky that John kept me here after all, I can stand it so much easier than a baby, you see.

Of course I never mention it to them any more—I am too wise—but I keep watch for it all the same.

There are things in that paper that nobody knows but me, or ever will.

Behind that outside pattern the dim shapes get clearer every day.

It is always the same shape, only very numerous.

And it is like a woman stooping down and creeping about behind that pattern. I don't like it a bit. I wonder—I begin to think—I wish John would take me away from here!

It is so hard to talk with John about my case, because he is so wise, and because he loves me so.

But I tried it last night.

It was moonlight. The moon shines in all around just as the sun does.

I hate to see it sometimes, it creeps so slowly, and always comes in by one window or another.

John was asleep and I hated to waken him, so I kept still and watched the moonlight on that undulating wallpaper till I felt creepy.

The faint figure behind seemed to shake the pattern, just as if she wanted to get out.

I got up softly and went to feel and see if the paper *did* move, and when I came back John was awake.

"What is it, little girl?" he said. "Don't go walking about like that— you'll get cold."

I thought it was a good time to talk so I told him that I really was not gaining here, and that I wished he would take me away.

"Why darling!" said he, "our lease will be up in three weeks, and I can't see how to leave before.

"The repairs are not done at home, and I cannot possibly leave town just now. Of course if you were in any danger, I could and would, but you really are better, dear, whether you can see it or not. I am a doctor, dear, and I know. You are gaining flesh and color, your appetite is better, I feel really much easier about you."

"I don't weigh a bit more," said I, "nor as much; and my appetite may be better in the evening when you are here, but it is worse in the morning when you are away!"

"Bless her little heart!" said he with a big hug, "she shall be as sick as she pleases! But now let's improve the shining hours by going to sleep, and talk about it in the morning!"

"And you won't go away?" I asked gloomily.

"Why, how can I, dear? It is only three weeks more and then we will take a nice little trip of a few days while Jennie is getting the house ready. Really, dear, you are better!"

"Better in body perhaps—" I began, and stopped short, for he sat up straight and looked at me with such a stern, reproachful look that I could not say another word.

"My darling," said he, "I beg of you, for my sake and for our child's sake, as well as for your own, that you will never for one instant let that idea enter your mind! There is nothing so dangerous, so fascinating, to a temperament like yours. It is a false and foolish fancy. Can you not trust me as a physician when I tell you so?"

So of course I said no more on that score, and we went to sleep before long. He thought I was asleep first, but I wasn't, and lay there for hours trying to decide whether that front pattern and the back pattern really did move together or separately.

On a pattern like this, by daylight, there is a lack of sequence, a defiance of law, that is a constant irritant to a normal mind.

The color is hideous enough, and unreliable enough, and infuriating enough, but the pattern is torturing.

You think you have mastered it, but just as you get well underway in following, it turns a back-somersault and there you are. It slaps you in the face, knocks you down, and tramples upon you. It is like a bad dream.

The outside pattern is a florid arabesque, reminding one of a fungus. If you can imagine a toadstool in joints, an interminable string of toadstools, budding and sprouting in endless convolutions—why, that is something like it.

That is, sometimes!

There is one marked peculiarity about this paper, a thing nobody seems to notice but myself, and that is that it changes as the light changes.

When the sun shoots in through the east window—I always watch for that first, long, straight ray—it changes so quickly that I never can quite believe it.

That is why I watch it always.

By moonlight—the moon shines in all night when there is a moon—I wouldn't know it was the same paper.

At night in any kind of light, in twilight, candlelight, lamplight, and worst of all by moonlight, it becomes bars! The outside pattern I mean, and the woman behind it is as plain as can be.

I didn't realize for a long time what the thing was that showed behind, that dim sub-pattern, but now I am quite sure it is a woman.

By daylight she is subdued, quiet. I fancy it is the pattern that keeps her so still. It is so puzzling. It keeps me quiet by the hour.

I lie down ever so much now. John says it is good for me, and to sleep all I can.

Indeed he started the habit by making me lie down for an hour after each meal.

It is a very bad habit I am convinced, for you see I don't sleep.

And that cultivates deceit, for I don't tell them I'm awake—O, no!

The fact is I am getting a little afraid of John.

He seems very queer sometimes, and even Jennie has an inexplicable look.

It strikes me occasionally, just as a scientific hypothesis, that perhaps it is the paper!

I have watched John when he did not know I was looking, and come into the room suddenly on the most innocent excuses, and I've caught him several times *looking at the paper!* And Jennie too. I caught Jennie with her hand on it once.

She didn't know I was in the room, and when I asked her in a quiet, a very quiet voice, with the most restrained manner possible, what she was doing with the paper—she turned around as if she had been caught stealing, and looked quite angry—asked me why I should frighten her so!

Then she said that the paper stained everything it touched, that she had found yellow smooches on all my clothes and John's, and she wished we would be more careful!

Did not that sound innocent? But I know she was studying that pattern, and I am determined that nobody shall find it out but myself!

Life is very much more exciting now than it used to be. You see I have something more to expect, to look forward to, to watch. I really do eat better, and am more quiet than I was.

John is so pleased to see me improve! He laughed a little the other day, and said I seemed to be flourishing in spite of my wallpaper.

I turned it off with a laugh. I had no intention of telling him it was *because* of the wallpaper—he would make fun of me. He might even want to take me away.

I don't want to leave now until I have found it out. There is a week more, and I think that will be enough.

I'm feeling ever so much better! I don't sleep much at night, for it is so interesting to watch developments; but I sleep a good deal in the daytime.

In the daytime it is tiresome and perplexing.

There are always new shoots on the fungus, and new shades of yellow all over it. I cannot keep count of them, though I have tried conscientiously.

It is the strangest yellow, that wallpaper! It makes me think of all the yellow things I ever saw—not beautiful ones like buttercups, but old foul, bad yellow things.

But there is something else about that paper—the smell! I noticed it the moment we came into the room, but with so much air and sun it was not bad. Now we have had a week of fog and rain, and whether the windows are open or not, the smell is here.

It creeps all over the house.

I find it hovering in the dining-room, skulking in the parlor, hiding in the hall, lying in wait for me on the stairs.

It gets into my hair.

Even when I go to ride, if I turn my head suddenly and surprise it—there is that smell!

Such a peculiar odor, too! I have spent hours in trying to analyze it, to find what it smelled like.

It is not bad—at first, and very gentle, but quite the subtlest, most enduring odor I ever met.

In this damp weather it is awful, I wake up in the night and find it hanging over me.

It used to disturb me at first. I thought seriously of burning the house—to reach the smell.

But now I am used to it. The only thing I can think of that it is like is the *color* of the paper! A yellow smell.

There is a very funny mark on this wall, low down, near the mopboard. A streak that runs round the room. It goes behind every piece of furniture, except the bed, a long, straight, even *smooch*, as if it had been rubbed over and over.

I wonder how it was done and who did it, and what they did it for. Round and round and round—round and round and round—it makes me dizzy!

I really have discovered something at last.

Through watching so much at night, when it changes so, I have finally found out.

The front pattern *does* move—and no wonder! The woman behind shakes it!

Sometimes I think there are a great many women behind, and sometimes only one, and she crawls around fast, and her crawling shakes it all over.

Then in the very bright spots she keeps still, and in the very shady spots she just takes hold of the bars and shakes them hard.

And she is all the time trying to climb through. But nobody could climb through that pattern—it strangles so; I think that is why it has so many heads.

They get through, and then the pattern strangles them off and turns them upside down, and makes their eyes white!

If those heads were covered or taken off it would not be half so bad.

I think that woman gets out in the daytime!

And I'll tell you why—privately—I've seen her!

I can see her out of every one of my windows!

It is the same woman, I know, for she is always creeping, and most women do not creep by daylight.

I see her in that long shaded lane, creeping up and down. I see her in those dark grape arbors, creeping all around the garden.

I see her on that long road under the trees, creeping along, and when a carriage comes she hides under the blackberry vines.

I don't blame her a bit. It must be very humiliating to be caught creeping by daylight!

I always lock the door when I creep by daylight. I can't do it at night, for I know John would suspect something at once.

And John is so queer now, that I don't want to irritate him. I wish he would take another room! Besides, I don't want anybody to get that woman out at night but myself.

I often wonder if I could see her out of all the windows at once.

But, turn as fast as I can, I can only see out of one at one time.

And though I always see her, she *may* be able to creep faster than I can turn!

I have watched her sometimes away off in the open country, creeping as fast as a cloud shadow in a high wind.

If only that top pattern could be gotten off from the under one! I mean to try it, little by little.

I have found out another funny thing, but I shan't tell it this time! It does not do to trust people too much.

There are only two more days to get this paper off, and I believe John is beginning to notice. I don't like the look in his eyes.

And I heard him ask Jennie a lot of professional questions about me. She had a very good report to give.

She said I slept a good deal in the daytime.

John knows I don't sleep very well at night, for all I'm so quiet!

He asked me all sorts of questions, too, and pretended to be very loving and kind.

As if I couldn't see through him!

Still, I don't wonder he acts so, sleeping under this paper for three months.

It only interests me, but I feel sure John and Jennie are secretly affected by it.

Hurrah! This is the last day, but it is enough. John is to stay in town over night, and won't be out until this evening.

Jennie wanted to sleep with me—the sly thing! but I told her I should undoubtedly rest better for a night all alone.

That was clever, for really I wasn't alone a bit! As soon as it was moonlight and that poor thing began to crawl and shake the pattern, I got up and ran to help her.

I pulled and she shook, I shook and she pulled, and before morning we had peeled off yards of that paper.

A strip about as high as my head and half around the room.

And then when the sun came and that awful pattern began to laugh at me, I declared I would finish it to-day!

We go away to-morrow, and they are moving all my furniture down again to leave things as they were before.

Jennie looked at the wall in amazement, but I told her merrily that I did it out of pure spite at the vicious thing.

She laughed and said she wouldn't mind doing it herself, but I must not get tired.

How she betrayed herself that time!

But I am here, and no person touches this paper but Me—not *alive*!

She tried to get me out of the room—it was too patent! But I said it was so quiet and empty and clean now that I believed I would lie down again and sleep all I could; and not to wake me even for dinner—I would call when I woke.

So now she is gone, and the servants are gone, and the things are gone, and there is nothing left but that great bedstead nailed down, with the canvas mattress we found on it.

We shall sleep downstairs to-night, and take the boat home to-morrow.

I quite enjoy the room, now it is bare again.

How those children did tear about here!

This bedstead is fairly gnawed!

But I must get to work.

I have locked the door and thrown the key down into the front path.

I don't want to go out, and I don't want to have anybody come in, till John comes.

I want to astonish him.

I've got a rope up here that even Jennie did not find. If that woman does get out, and tries to get away, I can tie her!

But I forgot I could not reach far without anything to stand on!

This bed will *not* move!

I tried to lift and push it until I was lame, and then I got so angry I bit off a little piece at one corner—but it hurt my teeth.

Then I peeled off all the paper I could reach standing on the floor. It sticks horribly and the pattern just enjoys it! All those strangled heads and bulbous eyes and waddling fungus growths just shriek with derision!

I am getting angry enough to do something desperate. To jump out of the window would be admirable exercise, but the bars are too strong even to try.

Besides I wouldn't do it. Of course not. I know well enough that a step like that is improper and might be misconstrued.

I don't like to *look* out of the windows even—there are so many of those creeping women, and they creep so fast.

I wonder if they all come out of that wallpaper as I did?

But I am securely fastened now by my well-hidden rope—you don't get *me* out in the road there!

I suppose I shall have to get back behind the pattern when it comes night, and that is hard!

It is so pleasant to be out in this great room and creep around as I please!

I don't want to go outside. I won't, even if Jennie asks me to.

For outside you have to creep on the ground, and everything is green instead of yellow.

But here I can creep smoothly on the floor, and my shoulder just fits in that long smooch around the wall, so I cannot lose my way.

Why there's John at the door!

It is no use, young man, you can't open it!

How he does call and pound!

Now he's crying for an axe.

It would be a shame to break down that beautiful door!

"John dear!" said I in the gentlest voice, "the key is down by the front steps, under a plantain leaf!"

That silenced him for a few moments.

Then he said, very quietly indeed, "Open the door, my darling!"

"I can't," said. I. "The key is down by the front door under a plantain leaf!"

And then I said it again, several times, very gently and slowly, and said it so often that he had to go and see, and he got it of course, and came in. He stopped short by the door.

"What is the matter?" he cried. "For God's sake, what are you doing!"

I kept on creeping just the same, but I looked at him over my shoulder.

"I've got out at last," said I, "in spite of you and Jane. And I've pulled off most of the paper, so you can't put me back!"

Now why should that man have fainted? But he did, and right across my path by the wall, so that I had to creep over him every time!

from The Shining
by Stephen King

Stephen King (born 1947) in 1977 published the ultimate novel of cabin fever (Stanley Kubrick's movie version came three years later). Jack Torrance, winter caretaker of an isolated and extremely haunted mountain resort, decides to polish off his only (human) company: his wife and young son. Wendy manages to lock her homicidal mate in the kitchen pantry—but at this point, Jack's hard to discourage.

Wendy Torrance stood indecisive in the middle of the bedroom, looking at her son, who had fallen fast asleep.

Half an hour ago the sounds had ceased. All of them, all at once. The elevator, the party, the sound of room doors opening and closing. Instead of easing her mind it made the tension that had been building in her even worse; it was like a malefic hush before the storm's final brutal push. But Danny had dozed off almost at once; first into a light, twitching doze, and in the last ten minutes or so a heavier sleep. Even looking directly at him she could barely see the slow rise and fall of his narrow chest.

She wondered when he had last gotten a full night's sleep, one without tormenting dreams or long periods of dark wakefulness, listening to revels that had only become audible—and visible—to her in the last couple of days, as the Overlook's grip on the three of them tightened.

(Real psychic phenomena or group hypnosis?)

She didn't know, and didn't think it mattered. What had been happening was just as deadly either way. She looked at Danny and thought

(God grant he lie still)

that if he was undisturbed, he might sleep the rest of the night through. Whatever talent he had, he was still a small boy and he needed his rest.

It was Jack she had begun to worry about.

She grimaced with sudden pain, took her hand away from her mouth, and saw she had torn off one of her fingernails. And her nails were one thing she'd always tried to keep nice. They weren't long enough to be called hooks, but still nicely shaped and

(and what are you worrying about your fingernails for?)

She laughed a little, but it was a shaky sound, without amusement.

First Jack had stopped howling and battering at the door. Then the party had begun again

(or did it ever stop? did it sometimes just drift into a slightly different angle of time where they weren't meant to hear it?)

counterpointed by the crashing, banging elevator. Then that had stopped. In that new silence, as Danny had been falling asleep, she had fancied she heard low, conspiratorial voices coming from the kitchen almost directly below them. At first she had dismissed it as the wind, which could mimic many different human vocal ranges, from a papery deathbed whisper around the doors and window frames to a full-out scream around the eaves . . . the sound of a woman fleeing a murderer in a cheap melodrama. Yet, sitting stiffly beside Danny, the idea that it was indeed voices became more and more convincing.

Jack and someone else, discussing his escape from the pantry.

Discussing the murder of his wife and son.

It would be nothing new inside these walls; murder had been done here before.

She had gone to the heating vent and had placed her ear against it, but at that exact moment the furnace had come on, and any sound was lost in the rush of warm air coming up from the basement. When the furnace had kicked off again, five minutes ago, the place was completely silent except for the wind, the gritty spatter of snow against the building, and the occasional groan of a board.

She looked down at her ripped fingernail. Small beads of blood were oozing up from beneath it.

(Jack's gotten out.)

(Don't talk nonsense.)

(Yes, he's out. He's gotten a knife from the kitchen or maybe the meat cleaver. He's on his way up here right now, walking along the sides of the risers so the stairs won't creak.)

(! You're insane!)

Her lips were trembling, and for a moment it seemed that she must have cried the words out loud. But the silence held.

She felt watched.

She whirled around and stared at the night-blackened window, and a hideous white face with circles of darkness for eyes was gibbering in at her, the face of a monstrous lunatic that had been hiding in these groaning walls all along—

It was only a pattern of frost on the outside of the glass.

She let her breath out in a long, susurrating whisper of fear, and it seemed to her that she heard, quite clearly this time, amused titters from somewhere.

(You're jumping at shadows. It's bad enough without that. By tomorrow morning, you'll be ready for the rubber room.)

There was only one way to allay those fears and she knew what it was.

She would have to go down and make sure Jack was still in the pantry.

Very simple. Go downstairs. Have a peek. Come back up. Oh, by the way, stop and grab the tray on the registration counter. The omelet would be a washout, but the soup could be reheated on the hotplate by Jack's typewriter.

(Oh yes and don't get killed if he's down there with a knife.)

She walked to the dresser, trying to shake off the mantle of fear that lay on her. Scattered across the dresser's top was a pile of change, a stack of gasoline chits for the hotel truck, the two pipes Jack brought with him everywhere but rarely smoked . . . and his key ring.

She picked it up, held it in her hand for a moment, and then put it back down. The idea of locking the bedroom door behind her had occurred, but it just didn't appeal. Danny was asleep. Vague thoughts of fire passed through her mind, and something else nibbled more strongly, but she let it go.

Wendy crossed the room, stood indecisively by the door for a moment, then took the knife from the pocket of her robe and curled her right hand around the wooden haft.

She pulled the door open.

The short corridor leading to their quarters was bare. The electric wall flambeaux all shone brightly at their regular intervals, showing off the rug's blue background and sinuous, weaving pattern.

(See? No boogies here.)

(No, of course not. They want you out. They want you to do something silly and womanish, and that is exactly what you are doing.)

She hesitated again, miserably caught, not wanting to leave Danny and the safety of the apartment and at the same time needing badly to reassure herself that Jack *was* still . . . safely packed away.

(Of course he is.)

(But the voices)

(There were no voices. It was your imagination. It was the wind.)

"It wasn't the wind."

The sound of her own voice made her jump. But the deadly certainty in it made her go forward. The knife swung by her side, catching angles of light and throwing them on the silk wallpaper. Her slippers whispered against the carpet's nap. Her nerves were singing like wires.

She reached the corner of the main corridor and peered around, her mind stiffened for whatever she might see there.

There was nothing to see.

After a moment's hesitation she rounded the corner and began down the main corridor. Each step toward the shadowy stairwell increased her dread and made her aware that she was leaving her sleeping son behind, alone and unprotected. The sound of her slippers against the carpet seemed louder and louder in her ears; twice she looked back over her shoulder to convince herself that someone wasn't creeping up behind her.

She reached the stairwell and put her hand on the cold newel post at the top of the railing. There were nineteen wide steps down to the lobby. She had counted them enough times to know. Nineteen carpeted stair risers, and nary a Jack crouching on any one of them. Of course not. Jack was locked in the pantry behind a hefty steel bolt and a thick wooden door.

But the lobby was dark and oh so full of shadows.

Her pulse thudded steadily and deeply in her throat.

Ahead and slightly to the left, the brass yaw of the elevator stood mockingly open, inviting her to step in and take the ride of her life.

(No thank you)

The inside of the car had been draped with pink and white crepe streamers. Confetti had burst from two tubular party favors. Lying in the rear left corner was an empty bottle of champagne.

She sensed movement above her and wheeled to look up the nineteen steps leading to the dark second-floor landing and saw nothing; yet there was a disturbing corner-of-the-eye sensation that things

(things)

had leaped back into the deeper darkness of the hallway up there just before her eyes could register them.

She looked down the stairs again.

Her right hand was sweating against the wooden handle of the knife; she switched it to her left, wiped her right palm against the pink terrycloth of her robe, and switched the knife back. Almost unaware that her mind had given her body the command to go forward, she began down the stairs, left foot then right, left foot then right, her free hand trailing lightly on the banister.

(Where's the party? Don't let me scare you away, you bunch of moldy sheets! Not one scared woman with a knife! Let's have a little music around here! Let's have a little life!)

Ten steps down, a dozen, a baker's dozen.

The light from the first-floor hall filtered a dull yellow down here, and she remembered that she would have to turn on the lobby lights either beside the entrance to the dining room or inside the manager's office.

Yet there was light coming from somewhere else, white and muted.

The fluorescents, of course. In the kitchen.

She paused on the thirteenth step, trying to remember if she had turned them off or left them on when she and Danny left. She simply couldn't remember.

Below her, in the lobby, highbacked chairs hulked in pools of shadow. The glass in the lobby doors was pressed white with a uniform blanket of drifted snow. Brass studs in the sofa cushions gleamed faintly like cat's eyes. There were a hundred places to hide.

Her legs stilted with fear, she continued down.

Now seventeen, now eighteen, now nineteen.

(Lobby level, madam. Step out carefully.)

The ballroom doors were thrown wide, only blackness spilling out. From within came a steady ticking, like a bomb. She stiffened, then remembered the clock on the mantel, the clock under glass. Jack or Danny must have wound it . . . or maybe it had wound itself up, like everything else in the Overlook. She turned toward the reception desk, meaning to go through the gate and the manager's office and into the kitchen. Gleaming dull silver, she could see the intended lunch tray.

Then the clock began to strike, little tinkling notes.

Wendy stiffened, her tongue rising to the roof of her mouth. Then she relaxed. It was striking eight, that was all. Eight o'clock

. . . *five, six, seven* . . .

She counted the strokes. It suddenly seemed wrong to move again until the clock had stilled.

. . . *eight* . . . *nine* . . .

(?? Nine ??)

. . . *ten* . . . *eleven* . . .

Suddenly, belatedly, it came to her. She turned back clumsily for the stairs, knowing already she was too late. But how could she have known?

Twelve.

All the lights in the ballroom went on. There was a huge, shrieking

flourish of brass. Wendy screamed aloud, the sound of her cry insignificant against the blare issuing from those brazen lungs.

"Unmask!" the cry echoed. *"Unmask! Unmask!"*

Then they faded, as if down a long corridor of time, leaving her
alone again.

No, not alone.

She turned and he was coming for her.

It was Jack and yet not Jack. His eyes were lit with a vacant, murder-
ous glow; his familiar mouth now wore a quivering, joyless grin.

He had the roque mallet in one hand.

"Thought you'd lock me in? Is that what you thought you'd do?"

The mallet whistled through the air. She stepped backward, tripped
over a hassock, fell to the lobby rug.

"Jack—"

"You bitch," he whispered. "I know what you are."

The mallet came down again with whistling, deadly velocity and
buried itself in her soft stomach. She screamed, suddenly submerged in
an ocean of pain. Dimly she saw the mallet rebound. It came to her
with sudden numbing reality that he meant to beat her to death with
the mallet he held in his hands.

She tried to cry out to him again, to beg him to stop for Danny's
sake, but her breath had been knocked loose. She could only force out
a weak whimper, hardly a sound at all.

"Now. Now, by Christ," he said, grinning. He kicked the hassock out
of his way. "I guess you'll take your medicine now."

The mallet whickered down. Wendy rolled to her left, her robe tan-
gling above her knees. Jack's hold on the mallet was jarred loose when
it hit the floor. He had to stoop and pick it up, and while he did she
ran for the stairs, the breath at last sobbing back into her. Her stomach
was a bruise of throbbing pain.

"Bitch," he said through his grin, and began to come after her. "You
stinking bitch, I guess you'll get what's coming to you. I guess you will."

She heard the mallet whistle through the air and then agony
exploded on her right side as the mallet-head took her just below the

line of her breasts, breaking two ribs. She fell forward on the steps and new agony ripped her as she struck on the wounded side. Yet instinct made her roll over, roll away, and the mallet whizzed past the side of her face, missing by a naked inch. It struck the deep pile of the stair carpeting with a muffled thud. That was when she saw the knife, which had been jarred out of her hand by her fall. It lay glittering on the fourth stair riser.

"Bitch," he repeated. The mallet came down. She shoved herself upward and it landed just below her kneecap. Her lower leg was suddenly on fire. Blood began to trickle down her calf. And then the mallet was coming down again. She jerked her head away from it and it smashed into the stair riser in the hollow between her neck and shoulder, scraping away the flesh from her ear.

He brought the mallet down again and this time she rolled toward him, down the stairs, inside the arc of his swing. A shriek escaped her as her broken ribs thumped and grated. She struck his shins with her body while he was offbalance and he fell backward with a yell of anger and surprise, his feet jigging to keep their purchase on the stair riser. Then he thumped to the floor, the mallet flying from his hand. He sat up, staring at her for a moment with shocked eyes.

"I'll kill you for that," he said.

He rolled over and stretched out for the handle of the mallet. Wendy forced herself to her feet. Her left leg sent bolt after bolt of pain all the way up to her hip. Her face was ashy pale but set. She leaped onto his back as his hand closed over the shaft of the roque mallet.

"*Oh dear God!*" she screamed to the Overlook's shadowy lobby, and buried the kitchen knife in his lower back up to the handle.

He stiffened beneath her and then shrieked. She thought she had never heard such an awful sound in her whole life; it was as if the very boards and windows and doors of the hotel had screamed. It seemed to go on and on while he remained board-stiff beneath her weight. They were like a parlor charade of horse and rider. Except that the back of his red-and-black-checked flannel shirt was growing darker, sodden, with spreading blood.

Then he collapsed forward on his face, bucking her off on her hurt side, making her groan.

She lay breathing harshly for a time, unable to move. She was an excruciating throb of pain from one end to the other. Every time she inhaled, something stabbed viciously at her, and her neck was wet with blood from her grazed ear.

There was only the sound of her struggle to breathe, the wind, and the ticking clock in the ballroom.

At last she forced herself to her feet and hobbled across to the stairway. When she got there she clung to the newel post, head down, waves of faintness washing over her. When it had passed a little, she began to climb, using her unhurt leg and pulling with her arms on the banister. Once she looked up, expecting to see Danny there, but the stairway was empty.

(Thank God he slept through it thank God thank God)

Six steps up she had to rest, her head down, her blond hair coiled on and over the banister. Air whistled painfully through her throat, as if it had grown barbs. Her right side was a swollen, hot mass.

(Come on Wendy come on old girl get a locked door behind you and then look at the damage thirteen more to go not so bad. And when you get to the upstairs corridor you can crawl. I give my permission.)

She drew in as much breath as her broken ribs would allow and half-pulled, half-fell up another riser. And another.

She was on the ninth, almost halfway up, when Jack's voice came from behind and below her. He said thickly: "You bitch. You killed me."

Terror as black as midnight swept through her. She looked over her shoulder and saw Jack getting slowly to his feet.

His back was bowed over, and she could see the handle of the kitchen knife sticking out of it. His eyes seemed to have contracted, almost to have lost themselves in the pale, sagging folds of the skin around them. He was grasping the roque mallet loosely in his left hand. The end of it was bloody. A scrap of her pink terrycloth robe stuck almost in the center.

"I'll give you your medicine," he whispered, and began to stagger toward the stairs.

Whimpering with fear, she began to pull herself upward again, Ten steps, a dozen, a baker's dozen. But still the first-floor hallway looked as far above her as an unattainable mountain peak. She was panting now, her side shrieking in protest. Her hair swung wildly back and forth in front of her face. Sweat stung her eyes. The ticking of the domed clock in the ballroom seemed to fill her ears, and counterpointing it, Jack's panting, agonized gasps as he began to mount the stairs.

The Cask of Amontillado
by Edgar Allan Poe

This story by Edgar Allan Poe (1809–1849) is the best story most of us will ever read about revenge and its twisted appeal: the nature of the pleasure that we take from the suffering of the people we take for our enemies.

The thousand injuries of Fortunato I had borne as I best could; but when he ventured upon insult, I vowed revenge. You, who so well know the nature of my soul, will not suppose, however, that I gave utterance to a threat. *At length* I would be avenged; this was a point definitively settled—but the very definitiveness with which it was resolved, precluded the idea of risk. I must not only punish, but punish with impunity. A wrong is unredressed when retribution overtakes its redresser. It is equally unredressed when the avenger fails to make himself felt as such to him who has done the wrong.

It must be understood, that neither by word nor deed had I given Fortunato cause to doubt my good-will. I continued, as was my wont, to smile in his face, and he did not perceive that my smile *now* was at the thought of his immolation.

He had a weak point—this Fortunato—although in other regards he was a man to be respected and even feared. He prided himself on his connoisseurship in wine. Few Italians have the true virtuoso spirit. For the most part their enthusiasm is adopted to suit the time and opportunity—to practise imposture upon the British and Austrian *millionnaires*. In painting and gemmary Fortunato, like his countrymen, was a quack—but in the matter of old wines he was sincere. In this respect I did not differ from him materially: I was skilful in the Italian vintages myself, and bought largely whenever I could.

It was about dusk, one evening during the supreme madness of the carnival season, that I encountered my friend. He accosted me with excessive warmth, for he had been drinking much. The man wore motley. He had on a tight-fitting parti-striped dress, and his head was surmounted by the conical cap and bells. I was so pleased to see him, that I thought I should never have done wringing his hand.

I said to him: 'My dear Fortunato, you are luckily met. How remarkably well you are looking to-day! But I have received a pipe of what passes for Amontillado, and I have my doubts.'

'How?' said he. 'Amontillado? A pipe? Impossible! And in the middle of the carnival!'

'I have my doubts,' I replied; 'and I was silly enough to pay the full Amontillado price without consulting you in the matter. You were not to be found, and I was fearful of losing a bargain.'

'Amontillado!'

'I have my doubts.'

'Amontillado!'

'And I must satisfy them.'

'Amontillado!'

'As you are engaged, I am on my way to Luchesi. If any one has a critical turn, it is he. He will tell me—'

'Luchesi cannot tell Amontillado from Sherry.'

'And yet some fools will have it that his taste is a match for your own.'

'Come, let us go.'

'Whither?'

'To your vaults.'

'My friend, no; I will not impose upon your good nature. I perceive you have an engagement. Luchesi—'

'I have no engagement;—come.'

'My friend, no. It is not the engagement, but the severe cold with which I perceive you are afflicted. The vaults are insufferably damp. They are encrusted with nitre.'

'Let us go, nevertheless. The cold is merely nothing. Amontillado! You have been imposed upon. And as for Luchesi, he cannot distinguish Sherry from Amontillado.'

Thus speaking, Fortunato possessed himself of my arm. Putting on a mask of black silk, and drawing a *roquelaire* closely about my person, I suffered him to hurry me to my palazzo.

There were no attendants at home; they had absconded to make merry in honor of the time. I had told them that I should not return until the morning, and had given them explicit orders not to stir from the house. These orders were sufficient, I well knew, to insure their immediate disappearance, one and all, as soon as my back was turned.

I took from their sconces two flambeaux, and giving one to Fortunato, bowed him through several suites of rooms to the archway that led into the vaults. I passed down a long and winding staircase, requesting him to be cautious as he followed. We came at length to the foot of the descent, and stood together on the damp ground of the catacombs of the Montresors.

The gait of my friend was unsteady, and the bells upon his cap jingled as he strode.

'The pipe?' said he.

'It is farther on,' said I; 'but observe the white web-work which gleams from these cavern walls.'

He turned toward me, and looked into my eyes with two filmy orbs that distilled the rheum of intoxication.

'Nitre?' he asked, at length.

'Nitre,' I replied. 'How long have you had that cough?'

'Ugh! ugh! ugh!—ugh! ugh! ugh!—ugh! ugh! ugh!—ugh! ugh! ugh!—ugh! ugh! ugh!'

My poor friend found it impossible to reply for many minutes.

'It is nothing,' he said, at last.

'Come,' I said, with decision, 'we will go back; your health is precious. You are rich, respected, admired, beloved; you are happy, as once I was. You are a man to be missed. For me it is no matter. We will go back; you will be ill, and I cannot be responsible. Besides, there is Luchesi—'

'Enough,' he said; 'the cough is a mere nothing; it will not kill me. I shall not die of a cough.'

'True—true,' I replied; 'and, indeed, I had no intention of alarming you unnecessarily; but you should use all proper caution. A draught of this Medoc will defend us from the damps.'

Here I knocked off the neck a bottle which I drew from a long row of its fellows that lay upon the mould.

'Drink,' I said, presenting him the wine.

He raised it to his lips with a leer. He paused and nodded to me familiarly, while his bells jingled.

'I drink,' he said, 'to the buried that repose around us.'

'And I to your long life.'

He again took my arm, and we proceeded.

'These vaults,' he said, 'are extensive.'

'The Montresors,' I replied, 'were a great and numerous family.'

'I forget your arms.'

'A huge human foot d'or, in a field azure; the foot crushes a serpent rampant whose fangs are imbedded in the heel.'

'And the motto?'

'*Nemo me impune lacessit.*'

'Good!' he said.

The wine sparkled in his eyes and the bells jingled. My own fancy grew warm with the Medoc. We had passed through walls of piled bones, with casks and puncheons intermingling, into the inmost recesses of the catacombs. I paused again, and this time I made bold to seize Fortunato by an arm above the elbow.

'The nitre!' I said; 'see, it increases. It hangs like moss upon the vaults. We are below the river's bed. The drops of moisture trickle among the bones. Come, we will go back ere it is too late. Your cough—'

'It is nothing,' he said; 'let us go on. But first, another draught of the Medoc.'

I broke and reached him a flagon of De Grâve. He emptied it at a breath. His eyes flashed with a fierce light. He laughed and threw the bottle upward with a gesticulation I did not understand.

I looked at him in surprise. He repeated the movement—a grotesque one.

'You do not comprehend?' he said.

'Not I,' I replied.

'Then you are not of the brotherhood.'

'How?'

'You are not of the masons.'

'Yes, yes,' I said; 'yes, yes.'

'You? Impossible! A mason?'

'A mason,' I replied.

'A sign,' he said.

'It is this,' I answered, producing a trowel from beneath the folds of my *roquelaure*.

'You jest,' he exclaimed, recoiling a few paces. 'But let us proceed to the Amontillado.'

'Be it so,' I said, replacing the tool beneath the cloak, and again offering him my arm. He leaned upon it heavily. We continued our route in search of the Amontillado. We passed through a range of low arches, descended, passed on, and descending again, arrived at a deep crypt, in which the foulness of the air caused our flambeaux rather to glow than flame.

At the most remote end of the crypt there appeared another less spacious. Its walls had been lined with human remains, piled to the vault overhead, in the fashion of the great catacombs of Paris. Three sides of this interior crypt were still ornamented in this manner. From the fourth the bones had been thrown down, and lay promiscuously upon the earth, forming at one point a mound of some size. Within the wall thus exposed by the displacing of the bones, we perceived a still interior recess, in depth about four feet, in width three, in height six or seven. It seemed to have been constructed for no especial use within itself, but formed merely the interval between two of the colossal supports of the roof of the catacombs, and was backed by one of their circumscribing walls of solid granite.

It was in vain that Fortunato, uplifting his dull torch, endeavored to pry into the depth of the recess. Its termination the feeble light did not enable us to see.

'Proceed,' I said; 'herein is the Amontillado. As for Luchesi—'

'He is an ignoramus,' interrupted my friend, as he stepped unsteadily forward, while I followed immediately at his heels. In an instant he had reached the extremity of the niche, and finding his progress arrested by the rock, stood stupidly bewildered. A moment more and I had fettered him to the granite. In its surface were two iron staples, distant from each other about two feet, horizontally. From one of these depended a short chain, from the other a padlock. Throwing the links about his waist, it was but the work of a few seconds to secure it. He was too much astounded to resist. Withdrawing the key I stepped back from the recess.

'Pass your hand,' I said, 'over the wall; you cannot help feeling the nitre. Indeed it is *very* damp. Once more let me *implore* you to return. No? Then I must positively leave you. But I must first render you all the little attentions in my power.'

'The Amontillado!' ejaculated my friend, not yet recovered from his astonishment.

'True,' I replied; the 'Amontillado.'

As I said these words I busied myself among the pile of bones of which I have before spoken. Throwing them aside, I soon uncovered a quantity of building stone and mortar. With these materials and with the aid of my trowel, I began vigorously to wall up the entrance of the niche.

I hard scarcely laid the first tier of the masonry when I discovered that the intoxication of Fortunato had in a great measure worn off. The earliest indication I had of this was a low moaning cry from the depth of the recess. It was *not* the cry of a drunken man. There was then a long and obstinate silence. I laid the second tier, and the third, and the fourth; and then I heard the furious vibrations of the chain. The noise lasted for several minutes, during which, that I might hearken to it with the more satisfaction, I ceased my labors and sat down upon the bones. When at last the clanking subsided, I resumed the trowel, and finished without interruption the fifth, the sixth, and the seventh tier. The wall was now nearly upon a level with my breast. I again paused, and holding the flambeaux over the mason-work, threw a few feeble rays upon the figure within.

A succession of loud and shrill screams, bursting suddenly from the throat of the chained form, seemed to thrust me violently back. For a brief moment I hesitated—I trembled. Unsheathing my rapier, I began to grope with it about the recess; but the thought of an instant reassured me. I placed my hand upon the solid fabric of the catacombs, and felt satisfied. I reapproached the wall. I replied to the yells of him who clamored. I re-echoed—I aided—I surpassed them in volume and in strength. I did this, and the clamorer grew still.

It was now midnight, and my task was drawing to a close. I had completed the eighth, the ninth, and the tenth tier. I had finished a portion of the last and the eleventh; there remained but a single stone to be fitted and plastered in. I struggled with its weight; I placed it partially in its destined position. But now there came from out the niche a low laugh that erected the hairs upon my head. It was succeeded by a sad voice, which I had difficulty in recognizing as that of the noble Fortunato. The voice said—

'Ha! ha! ha!—he! he!—a very good joke indeed—an excellent jest. We will have many a rich laugh about it at the palazzo—he! he! he!—over our wine—he! he! he!'

'The Amontillado!' I said.

'He! he! he!—he! he! he!—yes, the Amontillado. But is it not getting late? Will not they be awaiting us at the palazzo, the Lady Fortunato and the rest? Let us be gone."

'Yes,' I said, 'let us be gone.'

'*For the love of God, Montresor!*'

'Yes,' I said, 'for the love of God!'

But to these words I hearkened in vain for a reply. I grew impatient. I called aloud:

'Fortunato!'

No answer. I called again:

'Fortunato!'

No answer still. I thrust a torch through the remaining aperture and let it fall within. There came forth in return only a jingling of the bells. My heart grew sick—on account of the dampness of the catacombs. I hastened to make an end of my labor. I forced the last stone into its position; I plastered it up. Against the new masonry I re-erected the old rampart of bones. For the half of a century no mortal has disturbed them. *In pace requiescat!*

A Good Man Is Hard to Find

by Flannery O'Connor

People behave very badly in stories by Flannery O'Connor (1925–1964), but somehow it's difficult to judge their behavior. This story reminds its readers that we can't properly judge what we don't understand. That leaves questions: What is a good man, and why should it be hard to find one? How do we arrive at a place that is without grace or mercy?

The grandmother didn't want to go to Florida. She wanted to visit some of her connections in east Tennessee and she was seizing at every chance to change Bailey's mind. Bailey was the son she lived with, her only boy. He was sitting on the edge of his chair at the table, bent over the orange sports section of the *Journal*. "Now look here, Bailey," she said, "see here, read this," and she stood with one hand on her thin hip and the other rattling the newspaper at his bald head. "Here this fellow that calls himself The Misfit is aloose from the Federal Pen and headed toward Florida and you read here what it says he did to these people. Just you read it. I wouldn't take my children in any direction with a criminal like that aloose in it. I couldn't answer to my conscience if I did."

Bailey didn't look up from his reading so she wheeled around then and faced the children's mother, a young woman in slacks, whose face was as broad and innocent as a cabbage and was tied around with a green head-kerchief that had two points on the top like rabbit's ears.

She was sitting on the sofa, feeding the baby his apricots out of a jar. "The children have been to Florida before," the old lady said. "You all ought to take them somewhere else for a change so they would see different parts of the world and be broad. They never have been to east Tennessee."

The children's mother didn't seem to hear her but the eight-year-old boy, John Wesley, a stocky child with glasses, said, "If you don't want to go to Florida, why dontcha stay at home?" He and the little girl, June Star, were reading the funny papers on the floor.

"She wouldn't stay at home to be queen for a day," June Star said without raising her yellow head.

"Yes and what would you do if this fellow, The Misfit, caught you?" the grandmother asked.

"I'd smack his face," John Wesley said.

"She wouldn't stay at home for a million bucks," June Star said. "Afraid she'd miss something. She has to go everywhere we go."

"All right, Miss," the grandmother said. "Just remember that the next time you want me to curl your hair."

June Star said her hair was naturally curly.

The next morning the grandmother was the first one in the car, ready to go. She had her big black valise that looked like the head of a hippopotamus in one corner, and underneath it she was hiding a basket with Pitty Sing, the cat, in it. She didn't intend for the cat to be left alone in the house for three days because he would miss her too much and she was afraid he might brush against one of the gas burners and accidentally asphyxiate himself. Her son, Bailey, didn't like to arrive at a motel with a cat.

She sat in the middle of the back seat with John Wesley and June Star on either side of her. Bailey and the children's mother and the baby sat in front and they left Atlanta at eight forty-five with the mileage on the car at 55890. The grandmother wrote this down because she thought it would be interesting to say how many miles they had been when they got back. It took them twenty minutes to reach the outskirts of the city.

The old lady settled herself comfortably, removing her white cotton gloves and putting them up with her purse on the shelf in front of the back window. The children's mother still had on slacks and still had her head tied up in a green kerchief, but the grandmother had on a navy blue straw sailor hat with a bunch of white violets on the brim and a navy blue dress with a small white dot in the print. Her collars and cuffs were white organdy trimmed with lace and at her neckline she had pinned a purple spray of cloth violets containing a sachet. In case of an accident, anyone seeing her dead on the highway would know at once that she was a lady.

She said she thought it was going to be a good day for driving, neither too hot nor too cold, and she cautioned Bailey that the speed limit was fifty-five miles an hour and that the patrolmen hid themselves behind billboards and small clumps of trees and sped out after you before you had a chance to slow down. She pointed out interesting details of the scenery: Stone Mountain; the blue granite that in some places came up to both sides of the highway; the brilliant red clay banks slightly streaked with purple; and the various crops that made rows of green lace-work on the ground. The trees were full of silver-white sunlight and the meanest of them sparkled. The children were reading comic magazines and their mother had gone back to sleep.

"Let's go through Georgia fast so we won't have to look at it much," John Wesley said.

"If I were a little boy," said the grandmother, "I wouldn't talk about my native state that way. Tennessee has the mountains and Georgia has the hills."

"Tennessee is just a hillbilly dumping ground," John Wesley said, "and Georgia is a lousy state too."

"You said it," June Star said.

"In my time," said the grandmother, folding her thin veined fingers, "children were more respectful of their native states and their parents and everything else. People did right then. Oh look at the cute little pickaninny!" she said and pointed to a Negro child standing in the door of a shack. "Wouldn't that make a picture, now?" she asked and they all turned and looked at the little Negro out of the back window. He waved.

"He didn't have any britches on," June Star said.

"He probably didn't have any," the grandmother explained. "Little niggers in the country don't have things like we do. If I could paint, I'd paint that picture," she said.

The children exchanged comic books.

The grandmother offered to hold the baby and the children's mother passed him over the front seat to her. She set him on her knee and bounced him and told him about the things they were passing. She rolled her eyes and screwed up her mouth and stuck her leathery thin face into his smooth bland one. Occasionally he gave her a faraway smile. They passed a large cotton field with five or six graves fenced in the middle of it, like a small island. "Look at the graveyard!" the grandmother said, pointing it out. "That was the old family burying ground. That belonged to the plantation."

"Where's the plantation?" John Wesley asked.

"Gone with the Wind," said the grandmother. "Ha. Ha."

When the children finished all the comic books they had brought, they opened the lunch and ate it. The grandmother ate a peanut butter sandwich and an olive and would not let the children throw the box and the paper napkins out the window. When there was nothing else to do they played a game by choosing a cloud and making the other two guess what shape it suggested. John Wesley took one the shape of a cow and June Star guessed a cow and John Wesley said, no, an automobile, and June Star said he didn't play fair, and they began to slap each other over the grandmother.

The grandmother said she would tell them a story if they would keep quiet. When she told a story, she rolled her eyes and waved her head and was very dramatic. She said once when she was a maiden lady she had been courted by a Mr. Edgar Atkins Teagarden from Jasper, Georgia. She said he was a very good-looking man and a gentleman and that he brought her a watermelon every Saturday afternoon with his initials cut in it, E. A. T. Well, one Saturday, she said, Mr. Teagarden brought the watermelon and there was nobody at home and he left it on the front porch and returned in his buggy to Jasper, but she never got the watermelon, she said, because a nigger boy ate it when he saw the initials, E. A. T.! This story tickled John Wesley's funny bone and he giggled and giggled but June Star didn't think it was any good. She said she wouldn't marry a man that just brought her a watermelon on Saturday. The grandmother said she would have done well to marry Mr. Teagarden because he was a gentleman and had bought Coca-Cola stock when it first came out and that he had died only a few years ago, a very wealthy man.

They stopped at The Tower for barbecued sandwiches. The Tower was a part stucco and part wood filling station and dance hall set in a clearing outside of Timothy. A fat man named Red Sammy Butts ran it and there were signs stuck here and there on the building and for miles up and down the highway saying, TRY RED SAMMY'S FAMOUS BARBECUE. NONE LIKE FAMOUS RED SAMMY'S! RED SAM! THE FAT BOY WITH THE HAPPY LAUGH. A VETERAN! RED SAMMY'S YOUR MAN!

Red Sammy was lying on the bare ground outside The Tower with his head under a truck while a gray monkey about a foot high, chained to a small chinaberry tree, chattered nearby. The monkey sprang back into the tree and got on the highest limb as soon as he saw the children jump out of the car and run toward him.

Inside, The Tower was a long dark room with a counter at one end and tables at the other and dancing space in the middle. They all sat down at a board table next to the nickelodeon and Red Sam's wife, a tall burnt-brown woman with hair and eyes lighter than her skin, came and took their order. The children's mother put a dime in the machine and played "The Tennessee Waltz," and the grandmother said that tune always made her want to dance. She asked Bailey if he would like to dance but he only glared at her. He didn't have a naturally sunny disposition like she did and trips made him nervous. The grandmother's brown eyes were very bright. She swayed her head from side to side and pretended she was dancing in her chair. June Star said play something she could tap to so the children's mother put in another dime and played a fast number and June Star stepped out onto the dance floor and did her tap routine.

"Ain't she cute?" Red Sam's wife said, leaning over the counter. "Would you like to come be my little girl?"

"No I certainly wouldn't," June Star said. "I wouldn't live in a broken-down place like this for a million bucks!" and she ran back to the table.

"Ain't she cute?" the woman repeated, stretching her mouth politely.

"Aren't you ashamed?" hissed the grandmother.

Red Sam came in and told his wife to quit lounging on the counter and hurry up with these people's order. His khaki trousers reached just to his hip bones and his stomach hung over them like a sack of meal swaying under his shirt. He came over and sat down at a table nearby and let out a combination sigh and yodel. "You can't win," he said. "You can't win," and he wiped his sweating red face off with a gray handkerchief. "These days you don't know who to trust," he said. "Ain't that the truth?"

"People are certainly not nice like they used to be," said the grandmother.

"Two fellers come in here last week," Red Sammy said, "driving a Chrysler. It was a old beat-up car but it was a good one and these boys looked all right to me. Said they worked at the mill and you know I let them fellers charge the gas they bought? Now why did I do that?"

"Because you're a good man!" the grandmother said at once.

"Yes'm, I suppose so," Red Sam said as if he were struck with this answer.

His wife brought the orders, carrying the five plates all at once without a tray, two in each hand and one balanced on her arm. "It isn't a soul in this green world of God's that you can trust," she said. "And I don't count nobody out of that, not nobody," she repeated, looking at Red Sammy.

"Did you read about that criminal, The Misfit, that's escaped?" asked the grandmother.

"I wouldn't be a bit surprised if he didn't attack this place right here," said the woman. "If he hears about it being here, I wouldn't be none surprised to see him. If he hears it's two cent in the cash register, I wouldn't be a tall surprised if he . . ."

"That'll do," Red Sam said. "Go bring these people their Co'-Colas," and the woman went off to get the rest of the order.

"A good man is hard to find," Red Sammy said. "Everything is getting terrible. I remember the day you could go off and leave your screen door unlatched. Not no more."

He and the grandmother discussed better times. The old lady said that in her opinion Europe was entirely to blame for the way things were now. She said the way Europe acted you would think we were made of money and Red Sam said it was no use talking about it, she was exactly right. The children ran outside into the white sunlight and looked at the monkey in the lacy chinaberry tree. He was busy catching fleas on himself and biting each one carefully between his teeth as if it were a delicacy.

They drove off again into the hot afternoon. The grandmother took cat naps and woke up every few minutes with her own snoring. Outside of Toombsboro she woke up and recalled an old plantation that she had visited in this neighborhood once when she was a young lady. She said the house had six white columns across the front and that there was an avenue of oaks leading up to it and two little wooden trellis arbors on either side in front where you sat down with your suitor after a stroll in the garden. She recalled exactly which road to turn off to get to it. She knew that Bailey would not be willing to lose any time looking at an old house, but the more she talked about it, the more she wanted to see it once again and find out if the little twin arbors were still standing. "There was a secret panel in this house," she said craftily, not telling the truth but wishing that she were, "and the story went that all the family silver was hidden in it when Sherman came through but it was never found . . ."

"Hey!" John Wesley said. "Let's go see it! We'll find it! We'll poke all the woodwork and find it! Who lives there? Where do you turn off at? Hey Pop, can't we turn off there?"

"We never have seen a house with a secret panel!" June Star

shrieked. "Let's go to the house with the secret panel! Hey Pop, can't we go see the house with the secret panel!"

"It's not far from here, I know," the grandmother said. "It wouldn't take over twenty minutes."

Bailey was looking straight ahead. His jaw was as rigid as a horse-shoe. "No," he said.

The children began to yell and scream that they wanted to see the house with the secret panel. John Wesley kicked the back of the front seat and June Star hung over her mother's shoulder and whined desperately into her ear that they never had any fun even on their vacation, that they could never do what THEY wanted to do. The baby began to scream and John Wesley kicked the back of the seat so hard that his father could feel the blows in his kidney.

"All right!" he shouted and drew the car to a stop at the side of the road. "Will you all shut up? Will you all just shut up for one second? If you don't shut up, we won't go anywhere."

"It would be very educational for them," the grandmother murmured.

"All right," Bailey said, "but get this: this is the only time we're going to stop for anything like this. This is the one and only time."

"The dirt road that you have to turn down is about a mile back," the grandmother directed. "I marked it when we passed."

"A dirt road," Bailey groaned.

After they had turned around and were headed toward the dirt road, the grandmother recalled other points about the house, the beautiful glass over the front doorway and the candle-lamp in the hall. John Wesley said that the secret panel was probably in the fireplace.

"You can't go inside this house," Bailey said. "You don't know who lives there."

"While you all talk to the people in front, I'll run around behind and get in a window," John Wesley suggested.

"We'll all stay in the car," his mother said.

They turned onto the dirt road and the car raced roughly along in a swirl of pink dust. The grandmother recalled the times when there were no paved roads and thirty miles was a day's journey. The dirt road was

hilly and there were sudden washes in it and sharp curves on dangerous embankments. All at once they would be on a hill, looking down
over the blue tops of trees for miles around, then the next minute, they
would be in a red depression with the dust-coated trees looking down
on them.

"This place had better turn up in a minute," Bailey said, "or I'm
going to turn around."

The road looked as if no one had traveled on it in months.

"It's not much farther," the grandmother said and just as she said it,
a horrible thought came to her. The thought was so embarrassing that
she turned red in the face and her eyes dilated and her feet jumped up,
upsetting her valise in the corner. The instant the valise moved, the
newspaper top she had over the basket under it rose with a snarl and
Pitty Sing, the cat, sprang onto Bailey's shoulder.

The children were thrown to the floor and their mother, clutching the
baby, was thrown out the door onto the ground; the old lady was
thrown into the front seat. The car turned over once and landed right-
side-up in a gulch off the side of the road. Bailey remained in the driver's
seat with the cat—gray—striped with a broad white face and an orange
nose—clinging to his neck like a caterpillar.

As soon as the children saw they could move their arms and legs,
they scrambled out of the car, shouting, "We've had an ACCIDENT!"
The grandmother was curled up under the dashboard, hoping she was
injured so that Bailey's wrath would not come down on her all at once.
The horrible thought she had had before the accident was that the
house she had remembered so vividly was not in Georgia but in
Tennessee.

Bailey removed the cat from his neck with both hands and flung it
out the window against the side of a pine tree. Then he got out of the
car and started looking for the children's mother. She was sitting
against the side of the red gutted ditch, holding the screaming baby,
but she only had a cut down her face and a broken shoulder. "We've
had an ACCIDENT!" the children screamed in a frenzy of delight.

"But nobody's killed," June Star said with disappointment as the grandmother limped out of the car, her hat still pinned to her head but the broken front brim standing up at a jaunty angle and the violet spray hanging off the side. They all sat down in the ditch, except the children, to recover from the shock. They were all shaking.

"Maybe a car will come along," said the children's mother hoarsely.

"I believe I have injured an organ," said the grandmother, pressing her side, but no one answered her. Bailey's teeth were clattering. He had on a yellow sport shirt with bright blue parrots designed in it and his face was as yellow as the shirt. The grandmother decided that she would not mention that the house was in Tennessee.

The road was about ten feet above and they could see only the tops of the trees on the other side of it. Behind the ditch they were sitting in there were more woods, tall and dark and deep. In a few minutes they saw a car some distance away on top of a hill, coming slowly as if the occupants were watching them. The grandmother stood up and waved both arms dramatically to attract their attention. The car continued to come on slowly, disappeared around a bend and appeared again, moving even slower, on top of the hill they had gone over. It was a big black battered hearse-like automobile. There were three men in it.

It came to a stop just over them and for some minutes, the driver looked down with a steady expressionless gaze to where they were sitting, and didn't speak. Then he turned his head and muttered something to the other two and they got out. One was a fat boy in black trousers and a red sweat shirt with a silver stallion embossed on the front of it. He moved around on the right side of them and stood staring, his mouth partly open in a kind of loose grin. The other had on khaki pants and a blue striped coat and a gray hat pulled down very low, hiding most of his face. He came around slowly on the left side. Neither spoke.

The driver got out of the car and stood by the side of it, looking down at them. He was an older man than the other two. His hair was just beginning to gray and he wore silver-rimmed spectacles that gave him a scholarly look. He had a long creased face and didn't have on any shirt or undershirt. He had on blue jeans that were too tight for him and was holding a black hat and a gun. The two boys also had guns.

"We've had an ACCIDENT!" the children screamed.

The grandmother had the peculiar feeling that the bespectacled man was someone she knew. His face was as familiar to her as if she had known him all her life but she could not recall who he was. He moved away from the car and began to come down the embankment, placing his feet carefully so that he wouldn't slip. He had on tan and white shoes and no socks, and his ankles were red and thin. "Good afternoon," he said. "I see you all had you a little spill."

"We turned over twice!" said the grandmother.

"Oncet," he corrected. "We seen it happen. Try their car and see will it run, Hiram," he said quietly to the boy with the gray hat.

"What you got that gun for?" John Wesley asked. "Whatcha gonna do with that gun?"

"Lady," the man said to the children's mother, "would you mind calling them children to sit down by you? Children make me nervous. I want all you all to sit down right together there where you're at."

"What are you telling US what to do for?" June Star asked.

Behind them the line of woods gaped like a dark open mouth. "Come here," said their mother.

"Look here now," Bailey began suddenly, "we're in a predicament! We're in . . ."

The grandmother shrieked. She scrambled to her feet and stood staring. "You're The Misfit!" she said. "I recognized you at once!"

"Yes'm," the man said, smiling slightly as if he were pleased in spite of himself to be known, "but it would have been better for all of you, lady, if you hadn't of reckernized me."

Bailey turned his head sharply and said something to his mother that shocked even the children. The old lady began to cry and The Misfit reddened.

"Lady," he said, "don't you get upset. Sometimes a man says things he don't mean. I don't reckon he meant to talk to you thataway."

"You wouldn't shoot a lady, would you?" the grandmother said and removed a clean handkerchief from her cuff and began to slap at her eyes with it.

The Misfit pointed the toe of his shoe into the ground and made a little hole and then covered it up again. "I would hate to have to," he said.

"Listen," the grandmother almost screamed, "I know you're a good man. You don't look a bit like you have common blood. I know you must come from nice people!"

"Yes mam," he said, "finest people in the world." When he smiled he showed a row of strong white teeth. "God never made a finer woman than my mother and my daddy's heart was pure gold," he said. The boy with the red sweat shirt had come around behind them and was standing with his gun at his hip. The Misfit squatted down on the ground. "Watch them children, Bobby Lee," he said. "You know they make me nervous." He looked at the six of them huddled together in front of him and he seemed to be embarrassed as if he couldn't think of anything to say. "Ain't a cloud in the sky," he remarked, looking up at it. "Don't see no sun but don't see no cloud neither."

"Yes, it's a beautiful day," said the grandmother. "Listen," she said, "you shouldn't call yourself The Misfit because I know you're a good man at heart. I can just look at you and tell."

"Hush!" Bailey yelled. "Hush! Everybody shut up and let me handle this!" He was squatting in the position of a runner about to sprint forward but he didn't move.

"I pre-chate that, lady," The Misfit said and drew a little circle in the ground with the butt of his gun.

"It'll take a half a hour to fix this here car," Hiram called, looking over the raised hood of it.

"Well, first you and Bobby Lee get him and that little boy to step over yonder with you," The Misfit said, pointing to Bailey and John Wesley. "The boys want to ast you something," he said to Bailey. "Would you mind stepping back in them woods there with them?"

"Listen," Bailey began, "we're in a terrible predicament! Nobody realizes what this is," and his voice cracked. His eyes were as blue and intense as the parrots in his shirt and he remained perfectly still.

The grandmother reached up to adjust her hat brim as if she were going to the woods with him but it came off in her hand. She stood staring at it and after a second she let it fall on the ground. Hiram pulled Bailey up by the arm as if he were assisting an old man. John Wesley caught hold of his father's hand and Bobby Lee followed. They went off toward the woods and just as they reached the dark edge, Bailey turned and supporting himself against a gray naked pine trunk, he shouted, "I'll be back in a minute, Mamma, wait on me!"

"Come back this instant!" his mother shrilled but they all disappeared into the woods.

"Bailey Boy!" the grandmother called in a tragic voice but she found she was looking at The Misfit squatting on the ground in front of her. "I just know you're a good man," she said desperately. "You're not a bit common!"

"Nome, I ain't a good man," The Misfit said after a second as if he had considered her statement carefully, "but I ain't the worst in the world neither. My daddy said I was a different breed of dog from my brothers and sisters. 'You know,' Daddy said, 'it's some that can live their whole life out without asking about it and it's others has to know why it is, and this boy is one of the latters. He's going to be into everything!'" He put on his black hat and looked up suddenly and then away deep into the woods as if he were embarrassed again. "I'm sorry I don't have on a shirt before you ladies," he said, hunching his shoulders slightly. "We buried our clothes that we had on when we escaped and we're just making do until we can get better. We borrowed these from some folks we met," he explained.

"That's perfectly all right," the grandmother said. "Maybe Bailey has an extra shirt in his suitcase."

"I'll look and see terrectly," The Misfit said.

"Where are they taking him?" the children's mother screamed.

"Daddy was a card himself," The Misfit said. "You couldn't put anything over on him. He never got in trouble with the Authorities though. Just had the knack of handling them."

"You could be honest too if you'd only try," said the grandmother. "Think how wonderful it would be to settle down and live a comfortable life and not have to think about somebody chasing you all the time."

The Misfit kept scratching in the ground with the butt of his gun as if he were thinking about it. "Yes'm, somebody is always after you," he murmured.

The grandmother noticed how thin his shoulder blades were just behind his hat because she was standing up looking down on him. "Do you ever pray?" she asked.

He shook his head. All she saw was the black hat wiggle between his shoulder blades. "Nome," he said.

There was a pistol shot from the woods, followed closely by another. Then silence. The old lady's head jerked around. She could hear the wind move through the tree tops like a long satisfied insuck of breath. "Bailey Boy!" she called.

"I was a gospel singer for a while," The Misfit said. "I been most everything. Been in the arm service, both land and sea, at home and abroad, been twict married, been an undertaker, been with the rail-roads, plowed Mother Earth, been in a tornado, seen a man burnt alive oncet," and he looked up at the children's mother and the little girl who were sitting close together, their faces white and their eyes glassy; "I even seen a woman flogged," he said.

"Pray, pray," the grandmother began, "pray, pray . . ."

"I never was a bad boy that I remember of," The Misfit said in an almost dreamy voice, "but somewheres along the line I done some-thing wrong and got sent to the penitentiary. I was buried alive," and he looked up and held her attention to him by a steady stare.

"That's when you should have started to pray," she said. "What did you do to get sent to the penitentiary that first time?"

"Turn to the right, it was a wall," The Misfit said, looking up again at the cloudless sky. "Turn to the left, it was a wall. Look up it was a ceiling, look down it was a floor. I forget what I done, lady. I set there and set there, trying to remember what it was I done and I ain't recalled it to this day. Oncet in a while, I would think it was coming to me, but it never come."

"Maybe they put you in by mistake," the old lady said vaguely.

"Nome," he said. "It wasn't no mistake. They had the papers on me."

"You must have stolen something," she said.

The Misfit sneered slightly. "Nobody had nothing I wanted," he said. "It was a head-doctor at the penitentiary said what I had done was kill my daddy but I known that for a lie. My daddy died in nineteen ought nineteen of the epidemic flu and I never had a thing to do with it. He was buried in the Mount Hopewell Baptist churchyard and you can go there and see for yourself."

"If you would pray," the old lady said, "Jesus would help you."

"That's right," The Misfit said.

"Well then, why don't you pray?" she asked trembling with delight suddenly.

"I don't want no hep," he said. "I'm doing all right by myself."

Bobby Lee and Hiram came ambling back from the woods. Bobby Lee was dragging a yellow shirt with bright blue parrots in it.

"Thow me that shirt, Bobby Lee," The Misfit said. The shirt came flying at him and landed on his shoulder and he put it on. The grand-mother couldn't name what the shirt reminded her of. "No, lady," The Misfit said while he was buttoning it up, "I found out the crime don't matter. You can do one thing or you can do another, kill a man or take a tire off his car, because sooner or later you're going to forget what it was you done and just be punished for it."

The children's mother had begun to make heaving noises as if she couldn't get her breath. "Lady," he asked, "would you and that little girl like to step off yonder with Bobby Lee and Hiram and join your husband?"

"Yes, thank you," the mother said faintly. Her left arm dangled helplessly and she was holding the baby, who had gone to sleep, in the other. "Hep that lady up, Hiram," The Misfit said as she struggled to climb out of the ditch, "and Bobby Lee, you hold onto that little girl's hand."

"I don't want to hold hands with him," June Star said. "He reminds me of a pig."

The fat boy blushed and laughed and caught her by the arm and pulled her off into the woods after Hiram and her mother.

Alone with The Misfit, the grandmother found that she had lost her voice. There was not a cloud in the sky nor any sun. There was nothing around her but woods. She wanted to tell him that he must pray. She opened and closed her mouth several times before anything came out. Finally she found herself saying, "Jesus. Jesus," meaning, Jesus will help you, but the way she was saying it, it sounded as if she might be cursing.

"Yes'm," The Misfit said as if he agreed. "Jesus thown everything off balance. It was the same case with Him as with me except He hadn't committed any crime and they could prove I had committed one because they had the papers on me. Of course," he said, "they never shown me my papers. That's why I sign myself now. I said long ago, you get you a signature and sign everything you do and keep a copy of it. Then you'll know what you done and you can hold up the crime to the punishment and see do they match and in the end you'll have something to prove you ain't been treated right. I call myself The Misfit," he said, "because I can't make what all I done wrong fit what all I gone through in punishment."

There was a piercing scream from the woods, followed closely by a pistol report. "Does it seem right to you, lady, that one is punished a heap and another ain't punished at all?"

"Jesus!" the old lady cried. "You've got good blood! I know you wouldn't shoot a lady! I know you come from nice people! Pray! Jesus, you ought not to shoot a lady. I'll give you all the money I've got!"

"Lady," The Misfit said, looking beyond her far into the woods, "there never was a body that give the undertaker a tip."

There were two more pistol reports and the grandmother raised her head like a parched old turkey hen crying for water and called, "Bailey Boy, Bailey Boy!" as if her heart would break.

"Jesus was the only One that ever raised the dead," The Misfit continued, "and He shouldn't have done it. He thown everything off balance. If He did what He said, then it's nothing for you to do but thow away everything and follow Him, and if He didn't, then it's nothing for you to do but enjoy the few minutes you got left the best way you can—by killing somebody or burning down his house or doing some other meanness to him. No pleasure but meanness," he said and his voice had become almost a snarl.

"Maybe He didn't raise the dead," the old lady mumbled, not knowing what she was saying and feeling so dizzy that she sank down in the ditch with her legs twisted under her.

"I wasn't there so I can't say He didn't," The Misfit said. "I wisht I had of been there," he said, hitting the ground with his fist. "It ain't right I wasn't there because if I had of been there I would of known. Listen lady," he said in a high voice, "if I had of been there I would of known and I wouldn't be like I am now." His voice seemed about to crack and the grandmother's head cleared for an instant. She saw the man's face twisted close to her own as if he were going to cry and she murmured, "Why you're one of my babies. You're one of my own children!" She reached out and touched him on the shoulder. The Misfit sprang back as if a snake had bitten him and shot her three times through the chest. Then he put his gun down on the ground and took off his glasses and began to clean them.

Hiram and Bobby Lee returned from the woods and stood over the ditch, looking down at the grandmother who half sat and half lay in a puddle of blood with her legs crossed under her like a child's and her face smiling up at the cloudless sky.

Without his glasses, The Misfit's eyes were red-rimmed and pale and defenseless-looking. "Take her off and thow her where you thown the others," he said, picking up the cat that was rubbing itself against his leg.

"She was a talker, wasn't she?" Bobby Lee said, sliding down the ditch with a yodel.

"She would of been a good woman," The Misfit said, "if it had been somebody there to shoot her every minute of her life."

"Some fun!" Bobby Lee said.

"Shut up, Bobby Lee," The Misfit said. "It's no real pleasure in life."

The Beckoning Fair One

by Oliver Onions

Oliver Onions (1872–1961) wrote love stories,

murder mysteries and historical fiction, but is

remembered for ghost stories—in particular

this one, which juxtaposes the quaint mores of

Edwardian England with other elements that

are ... less quaint.

The three or four "To Let" boards had stood within the low paling as long as the inhabitants of the little triangular "Square" could remember, and if they had ever been vertical it was a very long time ago. They now overhung the palings each at its own angle, and resembled nothing so much as a row of wooden choppers, ever in the act of falling upon some passer-by, yet never cutting off a tenant for the old house from the stream of his fellows. Not that there was ever any great "stream" through the square; the stream passed a furlong and more away, beyond the intricacy of tenements and alleys and byways that had sprung up since the old house had been built, hemming it in completely; and probably the house itself was only suffered to stand pending the falling-in of a lease or two, when doubtless a clearance would be made of the whole neighborhood.

It was of bloomy old red brick, and built into its walls were the crowns and clasped hands and other insignia of insurance companies long since defunct. The children of the secluded square had swung upon the low gate at the end of the entrance alley until little more than the solid top bar of it remained, and the alley itself ran past boarded basement windows on which tramps had chalked their cryptic marks. The path was washed and worn uneven by the spilling of water from the eaves of the encroaching next house, and cats and dogs had made the approach their own. The chances of a tenant did not seem such as to warrant the keeping of the "To Let" boards in a state of legibility and repair, and as a matter of fact they were not so kept.

For six months Oleron had passed the old place twice a day or oftener, on his way from his lodgings to the room, ten minutes' walk away, he had taken to work in; and for six months no hatchet-like notice-board had fallen across his path. This might have been due to the fact that he usually took the other side of the square. But he chanced one morning to take the side that ran past the broken gate and the rain-worn entrance alley, and to pause before one of the inclined boards. The board bore, beside the agent's name, the announcement, written apparently about the time of Oleron's own early youth, that the key was to be had at Number Six.

Now Oleron was already paying, for his separate bedroom and workroom, more than an author who, without private means, habitually disregards his public, can afford; and he was paying in addition a small rent for the storage of the greater part of his grandmother's furniture. Moreover, it invariably happened that the book he wished to read in bed was at his working-quarters half a mile or more away, while the note or letter he had sudden need of during the day was as likely as not to be in the pocket of another coat hanging behind his bedroom door. And there were other inconveniences in having a divided domicile. Therefore Oleron, brought suddenly up by the hatchet-like notice-board, looked first down through some scanty privet-bushes at the boarded basement windows, then up at the blank and grimy windows of the first floor, and so up to the second floor and the flat stone coping of the leads. He stood for a minute thumbing his lean and shaven jaw; then, with another glance at the board, he walked slowly across the square to Number Six.

He knocked, and waited for two or three minutes, but, although the door stood open, received no answer. He was knocking again when a long-nosed man in shirt-sleeves appeared.

"I was arsking a blessing on our food," he said in a severe explanation.

Oleron asked if he might have the key of the old house; and the long-nosed man withdrew again.

Oleron waited for another five minutes on the step; then the man, appearing again and masticating some of the food of which he had spoken, announced that the key was lost.

"But you won't want it," he said. "The entrance door isn't closed, and a push'll open any of the others. I'm a agent for it, if you're thinking of taking it——"

Oleron recrossed the square, descended the two steps at the broken gate, passed along the alley, and turned in at the old wide doorway. To the right, immediately within the door, steps descended to the roomy cellars, and the staircase before him had a carved rail, and was broad and handsome and filthy. Oleron ascended it, avoiding contact with the rail and wall, and stopped at the first landing. A door facing him had been boarded up, but he pushed at that on his right hand, and an insecure bolt or staple yielded. He entered the empty first floor.

He spent a quarter of an hour in the place, and then came out again. Without mounting higher, he descended and recrossed the square to the house of the man who had lost the key.

"Can you tell me how much the rent is?" he asked.

The man mentioned a figure, the comparative lowness of which seemed accounted for by the character of the neighborhood and the abominable state of unrepair of the place.

"Would it be possible to rent a single floor?"

The long-nosed man did not know; they might . . . .

"Who are they?"

The man gave Oleron the name of a firm of lawyers in Lincoln's Inn.

"You might mention my name—Barrett," he added.

Pressure of work prevented Oleron from going down to Lincoln's Inn that afternoon, but he went on the morrow, and was instantly offered the whole house as a purchase for fifty pounds down, the remainder of the purchase-money to remain on mortgage. It took him half an hour to disabuse the lawyer's mind of the idea that he wished anything more of the place than to rent a single floor of it. This made certain hums and haws of a difference, and the lawyer was by no means certain that it lay within his power to do as Oleron suggested; but it was finally extracted from him that, provided the notice-boards were allowed to remain up, and that, provided it was agreed that in the event of the whole house letting, the arrangement should terminate automatically without further notice, something might be done. That the old place should suddenly let over his head seemed to Oleron the slightest of risks to take, and he promised a decision within a week. On the morrow he visited the house again, went through it from top to bottom, and then went home to his lodgings to take a bath.

He was immensely taken with that portion of the house he had already determined should be his own. Scraped clean and repainted, and with that old furniture of Oleron's grandmother's, it ought to be entirely charming. He went to the storage warehouse to refresh his memory of his half-forgotten belongings, and to take the measurements; and thence he went to a decorator's. He was very busy with his regular work, and could have wished that the notice-board had caught his attention either a few months earlier or else later in the year; but the quickest way would be to suspend work entirely until after his removal . . . .

A fortnight later his first floor was painted throughout in a tender, elder-flower white, the paint was dry, and Oleron was in the middle of his installation. He was animated, delighted; and he rubbed his hands as he polished and made disposals of his grandmother's effects—the tall lattice-paned china cupboard with its Derby and Mason and Spode, the large folding Sheraton table, the long, low bookshelves (he had had two of them "copied"), the chairs, the Sheffield candlesticks, the riveted rose-bowls. These things he set against his newly painted elder-white walls—walls of wood paneled in the happiest proportions, and molded and coffered to the low-seated window-recesses in a mood of gaiety and rest that the builders of rooms no longer know. The ceilings were lofty, and faintly painted with an old pattern of stars; even the tapering moldings of his iron fireplace were as delicately designed as jewelry; and Oleron walked about rubbing his hands, frequently stopping for the mere pleasure of the glimpses from white room to white room . . . .

"Charming, charming!' he said to himself. "I wonder what Elsie Bengough will think of this!"

He bought a bolt and a Yale lock for his door, and shut off his quarters from the rest of the house. If he now wanted to read in bed, his book could be had for stepping into the next room. All the time, he thought how exceedingly lucky he was to get the place. He put up a hat-rack in the little square hall, and hung up his hats and caps and coats; and passers through the small triangular square late at night, looking up over the little serried row of wooden "To Let" hatchets, could see the light within Oleron's red blinds, or else the sudden darkening of one blind and the illumination of another, as Oleron, candlestick in hand, passed from room to room, making final settlings of his furniture, or preparing to resume the work that his removal had interrupted.

As far as the chief business of his life—his writing—was concerned, Paul Oleron treated the world a good deal better than he was treated by it; but he seldom took the trouble to strike a balance, or to compute how far, at forty-four years of age, he was behind his points on the handicap. To have done so wouldn't have altered matters, and it might have depressed Oleron. He had chosen his path, and was committed to it beyond possibility of withdrawal. Perhaps he had chosen it in the days when he had been easily swayed by something a little disinterested, a little generous, a little noble; and had he ever thought of questioning himself he would still have held to it that a life without nobility and generosity and disinterestedness was no life for him. Only quite recently, and rarely, had he even vaguely suspected that there was more in it than this; but it was no good anticipating the day when, he supposed, he would reach that maximum point of his powers beyond which he must inevitably decline, and be left face to face with the question whether it would not have profited him better to have ruled his life by less exigent ideals.

In the meantime, his removal into the old house with the insurance marks built into its brick merely interrupted *Romilly Bishop* at the fifteenth chapter.

As this tall man with the lean, ascetic face moved about his new abode, arranging, changing, altering, hardly yet into his working stride again, he gave the impression of almost spinster-like precision and nicety. For twenty years past, in a score of lodgings, garrets, flats, and rooms furnished and unfurnished, he had been accustomed to do many things for himself, and he had discovered that it saves time and temper to be methodical. He had arranged with the wife of the long-nosed Barrett, a stout Welsh woman with a falsetto voice, the Merionethshire accent of which long residence in London had not perceptibly modified, to come across the square each morning to prepare his breakfast and also to "turn the place out" on Saturday mornings; and for the rest, he even welcomed a little housework as a relaxation from the strain of writing.

His kitchen, together with the adjoining strip of an apartment into which a modern bath had been fitted, overlooked the alley at the side of the house; and at one end of it was a large closet with a door, and a square sliding hatch in the upper part of the door. This had been a powder-closet, and through the hatch the elaborately dressed head had been thrust to receive the click and puff of the powder-pistol. Oleron puzzled a little over this closet; then, as its use occurred to him, he smiled faintly, a little moved, he knew not by what . . . . He would have to put it to a very different purpose from its original one; it would probably have to serve as a larder . . . . It was in this closet that he made a discovery. The back of it was shelved, and, rummaging on an upper shelf that ran deeply into the wall, Oleron found a couple of mushroom-shaped old wooden wig-stands. He did not know how they had come to be there. Doubtless the painters had turned them up somewhere or other, and had put them there. But his five rooms, as a whole, were short of cupboard and closetroom; and it was only by the exercise of some ingenuity that he was able to find places for the bestowal of his household linen, his boxes, and his seldom-used but not-to-be-destroyed accumulation of papers.

It was early spring that Oleron entered on his tenancy, and he was anxious to have *Romilly* ready for publication in the coming autumn. Nevertheless, he did not intend to force its production. Should it demand longer in the doing, so much the worse; he realized its importance, its crucial importance, in his artistic development, and it must have its own length and time. In the workroom he had recently left he had been making excellent progress; *Romilly* had begun, as the saying is, to speak and act of herself; and he did not doubt she would continue to do so the moment the distraction of his removal was over. This distraction was almost over; he told himself it was time he pulled himself together again; and on a March morning he went out and returned again with two great bunches of yellow daffodils, placed one bunch on his mantelpiece between the Sheffield sticks and the other on the table before him, and took out the half-completed manuscript of *Romilly Bishop.*

But before beginning work he went to a small rosewood cabinet and took from a drawer his check-book and pass-book. He totted them up, and his monk-like face grew thoughtful. His installation had cost him more than he had intended it should, and his balance was rather less than fifty pounds, with no immediate prospect of more.

"Hm! I'd forgotten rugs and chintz curtains and so forth mounted up so," said Oleron. "But it would have been a pity to spoil the place for the want of ten pounds or so .... Well, *Romilly* simply *must* be out for the autumn, that's all. So here goes——"

He drew his papers toward him.

But he worked badly; or, rather, he did not work at all. The square outside had its own noises, frequent and new, and Oleron could only hope that he would speedily become accustomed to these. First came hawkers, with their carts and cries; at midday the children, returning from school, trooped into the square and swung on Oleron's gate; and when the children had departed again for afternoon school, an itinerant musician with a mandoline posted himself beneath Oleron's window and began to strum. This was a not unpleasant distraction, and Oleron, pushing up his window, threw the man a penny. Then he returned to his table again . . . .

But it was no good. He came to himself, at long intervals, to find that he had been looking about his room and wondering how it had formerly been furnished—whether a settee in buttercup or petunia satin had stood under the farther window, whether from the center molding of the light lofty ceiling had depended a glimmering crystal chandelier, or where the tambour-frame or the piquet-table had stood . . . . No, it was no good; he had far better be frankly doing nothing than getting fruitlessly tired; and he decided that he would take a walk, but, chancing to sit down for a moment, dozed in his chair instead.

"This won't do," he yawned when he awoke at half-past four in the afternoon; "I must do better than this tomorrow——"

And he felt so deliciously lazy that for some minutes he even contemplated the breach of an appointment he had for the evening.

The next morning he sat down to work without even permitting himself to answer one of his three letters—two of them tradesman's accounts, the third a note from Miss Bengough, forwarded from his old address. It was a jolly day of white and blue, with a gay noisy wind and a subtle turn in the color of growing things; and over and over again, once or twice a minute, his room became suddenly light and then subdued again, as the shining white cloud rolled northeastward over the square. The soft fitful illumination was reflected in the polished surface of the table and even in the footworn old floor; and the morning noises had begun again.

Oleron made a pattern of dots on the paper before him, and then broke off to move the jar of daffodils exactly opposite the center of a creamy panel. Then he wrote a sentence that ran continuously for a couple of lines, after which it broke off into notes and jottings. For a time he succeeded in persuading himself that in making these memoranda he was really working; then he rose and began to pace his room. As he did so, he was struck by an idea. It was that the place might possibly be a little better for more positive color. It was, perhaps, a thought *too* pale—mild and sweet as a kind old face, but a little devitalized, even wan . . . . Yes, decidedly it would bear a robuster note—more and richer flowers, and possibly some warm and gay stuff for cushions for the window-seats . . . .

"Of course, I really can't afford it," he muttered, as he went for a two-foot and began to measure the width of the window recesses . . . .

In stooping to measure a recess, his attitude suddenly changed to one of interest and attention. Presently he rose again, rubbing his hands with gentle glee.

"Oho, oho! " he said. "These look to me very much like window-boxes, nailed up. We must look into this! Yes, those are boxes, or I'm . . . oho, this is an adventure!"

On that wall of his sitting room there were two windows (the third was in another corner), and, beyond the open bedroom door, on the same wall, was another. The seats of all had been painted, repainted, and painted again; and Oleron's investigating finger had barely detected the old nailheads beneath the paint. Under the ledge over which he stooped an old keyhole also had been puttied up. Oleron took out his penknife.

He worked carefully for five minutes, and then went into the kitchen for a hammer and chisel. Driving the chisel cautiously under the seat, he started the whole lid slightly. Again using the penknife, he cut along the hinged edge and outward along the ends; and then he fetched a wedge and a wooden mallet.

"Now for our little mystery——" he said.

The sound of the mallet on the wedge seemed, in that sweet and pale apartment, somehow a little brutal—nay, even shocking. The paneling rang and rattled and vibrated to the blows like a sounding-board. The whole house seemed to echo; from the roomy cellarage to the garrets above a flock of echoes seemed to awake; and the sound got a little on Oleron's nerve. All at once he paused, fetched a duster, and muffled the mallet . . . . When the edge was sufficiently raised he put his fingers under it and lifted. The paint flaked and starred a little; the rusty old nails squeaked and grunted; and the lid came up, laying open the box beneath. Oleron looked into it. Save for a couple of inches of scurf and mold and old cobwebs it was empty.

"No treasure there," said Oleron, a little amused that he should have fancied there might have been. "*Romilly* will still have to be out by the autumn. Let's have a look at the others."

He turned to the second window.

The raising of the two remaining seats occupied him until well into the afternoon. That of the bedroom, like the first, was empty; but from the second seat of his sitting room he drew out something yielding and folded and furred over an inch thick with dust. He carried the object into the kitchen, and having swept it over a bucket, took a duster to it.

It was some sort of a large bag, of an ancient frieze-like material, and when unfolded it occupied the greater part of the small kitchen floor. In shape it was an irregular, a very irregular, triangle, and it had a couple of wide flaps, with the remains of straps and buckles. The patch that had been uppermost in the folding was of a faded yellowish brown; but the rest of it was of shades of crimson that varied according to the exposure of the parts of it.

"Now whatever can that have been?" Oleron mused as he stood surveying it . . . . "I give it up. Whatever it is, it's settled my work for today, I'm afraid——"

He folded the object up carelessly and thrust it into a corner of the kitchen; then, taking pans and brushes and an old knife, he returned to the sitting room and began to scrape and to wash and to line with paper, his newly discovered receptacles. When he had finished, he put his spare boots and books and papers into them; and he closed the lids again, amused with this little adventure, but also a little anxious for the hour to come when he should settle fairly down to his work again.

It piqued Oleron a little that his friend, Miss Bengough, should dismiss with a glance the place he himself had found so singularly winning. Indeed she scarcely lifted her eyes to it. But then she had always been more or less like that—a little indifferent to the graces of life, careless of appearances, and perhaps a shade more herself when she ate biscuits from a paper bag than when she dined with greater observance of the convenances. She was an unattached journalist of thirty-four, large, showy, fair as butter, pink as a dogrose, reminding one of a florist's picked specimen bloom, and given to sudden and ample movements and moist and explosive utterances. She "pulled a better living out of the pool" (as she expressed it) than Oleron did; and by cunningly disguised puffs of drapers and haberdashers she "pulled" also the greater part of her very varied wardrobe. She left small whirlwinds of air behind her when she moved, in which her veils and scarves fluttered and spun.

Oleron heard the flurry of her skirts on his staircase and her single loud knock at his door when he had been a month in his new abode. Her garments brought in the outer air, and she flung a bundle of ladies' journals down on a chair.

"Don't knock off for me," she said across a mouthful of large-headed hatpins as she removed her hat and veil. "I didn't know whether you were straight yet, so I've brought some sandwiches for lunch. You've got coffee, I suppose? No, don't get up—I'll find the kitchen——"

"Oh, that's all right, I'll clear these things away. To tell the truth, I'm rather glad to be interrupted," said Oleron.

He gathered his work together and put it way. She was already in the kitchen; he heard the running of water into the kettle. He joined her, and ten minutes later followed her back to the sitting room with the coffee and sandwiches on a tray. They sat down, with the tray on a small table between them.

"Well, what do you think of the new place?" Oleron asked as she poured out coffee.

"Hm! . . . Anybody'd think you were going to get married, Paul."

He laughed.

"Oh no. But it's an improvement on some of them, isn't it?"

"Is it? I suppose it is; I don't know. I liked the last place, in spite of the black ceiling and no watertap. How's *Romilly*?"

Oleron thumbed his chin.

"Hm! I'm rather ashamed to tell you. The fact is, I've not got on very well with it. But it will be all right on the night, as you used to say."

"Stuck?"

"Rather stuck."

"Got any of it you care to read to me? . . ."

Oleron had long been in the habit of reading portions of his work to Miss Bengough occasionally. Her comments were always quick and practical, sometimes directly useful, sometimes indirectly suggestive. She, in return for his confidence, always kept all mention of her own work sedulously from him. His, she said, was "real work"; hers merely filled space, not always even grammatically.

"I'm afraid there isn't," Oleron replied, still meditatively dry-shaving his chin. Then he added, with a little burst of candor, "The fact is, Elsie, I've not written—not actually written—very much more of it—*any* more of it, in fact. But, of course, that doesn't mean I haven't progressed. I've progressed, in one sense, rather alarmingly. I'm now thinking of reconstructing the whole thing."

Miss Bengough gave a gasp. "Reconstructing!"

"Making Romilly herself a different type of woman. Somehow, I've begun to feel that I'm not getting the most out of her. As she stands, I've certainly lost interest in her to some extent."

"But—but——" Miss Bengough protested, "you had her so real, so *living*, Paul!"

Oleron smiled faintly. He had been quite prepared for Miss Bengough's disapproval. He wasn't surprised that she liked Romilly as she at present existed; she would. Whether she realized it or not, there was much of herself in his fictitious creation. Naturally Romilly would seem "real," "living," to her . . . .

"But are you really serious, Paul?" Miss Bengough asked presently, with a round-eyed stare.

"Quite serious."

"You're really going to scrap those fifteen chapters?"

"I didn't exactly say that."

"That fine, rich love-scene?"

"I should only do it reluctantly, and for the sake of something I thought better."

"And that beautiful, *beau*tiful description of Romilly on the shore?"

"It wouldn't necessarily be wasted," he said a little uneasily.

But Miss Bengough made a large and windy gesture, and then let him have it.

"Really, you are *too* trying!" she broke out. "I do wish sometimes you'd remember you're human, and live in a world! You know I'd be the *last* to wish you to lower your standard one inch, but it wouldn't be lowering it to bring it within human comprehension. Oh, you're sometimes altogether too godlike! . . . Why, it would be a wicked, criminal waste of your powers to destroy those fifteen chapters! Look at it reasonably, now. You've been working for nearly twenty years; you've now got what you've been working for almost within your grasp; your affairs are at a most critical stage (oh, don't tell me; I know you're about at the end of your money); and here you are, deliberately proposing to withdraw a thing that will probably make your name, and to substitute for it something that ten to one nobody on earth will ever want to read—and small blame to them! Really, you try my patience!"

Oleron had shaken his head slowly as she had talked. It was an old story between them. The noisy, able practical journalist was an admirable friend—up to a certain point; beyond that . . . well, each of us knows that point beyond which we stand alone. Elsie Bengough sometimes said that had she had one-tenth part of Oleron's genius there were few things she could not have done—thus making that genius a quantitatively divisible thing, a sort of ingredient, to be added to or to be subtracted from in the admixture of his work. That it was a qualitative thing, essential, indivisible, informing, passed her comprehension. Their spirits parted company at that point. Oleron knew it. She did not appear to know it.

"Yes, yes, yes," he said a little wearily, by-and-by, "practically you're quite right, entirely right, and I haven't a word to say. If I could only turn *Romilly* over to you you'd make an enormous success of her. But that can't be, and I, for my part, am seriously doubting whether she's worth my while. You know what that means."

"What does it mean?" she demanded bluntly.

"Well," he said, smiling wanly, "what *does* it mean when you're convinced a thing isn't worth doing? You simply don't do it."

Miss Bengough's eyes swept the ceiling for assistance against this impossible man.

"What utter rubbish!" she broke out at last. "Why, when I saw you last you were simply oozing *Romilly*; you were turning her off at the rate of four chapters a week; if you hadn't moved you'd have had her three parts done by now. What on earth possessed you to move right in the middle of your most important work?"

Oleron tried to put her off with a recital of inconveniences, but she wouldn't have it. Perhaps in her heart she partly suspected the reason. He was simply mortally weary of the narrow circumstances of his life. He had had twenty years of it—twenty years of garrets and roof-chambers and dingy flats and shabby lodgings, and he was tired of dinginess and shabbiness. The reward was as far off as ever—or if it was not, he no longer cared as once he would have cared to put out his hand and take it. It is all very well to tell a man who is at the point of exhaustion that only another effort is required of him; if he cannot make it he is as far off as ever . . . .

"Anyway," Oleron summed up, "I'm happier here than I've been for a long time. That's some sort of a justification."

"And doing no work," said Miss Bengough pointedly.

At that a trifling petulance that had been gathering in Oleron came to a head.

"And why should I do nothing but work?" he demanded. "How much happier am I for it? I don't say I don't love my work—when it's done; but I hate doing it. Sometimes it's an intolerable burden that I simply long to be rid of. Once in many weeks it has a moment, one moment, of glow and thrill for me; I remember the days when it was all glow and thrill; and now I'm forty-four, and it's becoming drudgery. Nobody wants it; I'm ceasing to want it myself; and if any ordinary sensible man were to ask me whether I didn't think I was a fool to go on, I think I should agree that I was."

Miss Bengough's comely pink face was serious.

"But you knew all that, many, many years ago, Paul—and still you chose it," she said in a low voice.

"Well, and how should I have known?" he demanded. "I didn't know. I was told so. My heart, if you like, told me so, and I thought I knew. Youth always thinks it knows; then, one day it discovers that it is nearly fifty——"

"Forty-four, Paul——"

"—forty-four, then—and it finds that the glamour isn't in front, but behind. Yes, I knew and chose, if *that's* knowing and choosing . . . but it's a costly choice we're called on to make when we're young!"

Miss Bengough's eyes were on the floor. Without moving them she said: "You're not regretting it, Paul?"

"Am I not?" he took her up. "Upon my word, I've lately thought I am! What *do* I get in return for it all?"

"You know what you get," she replied.

He might have known from her tone what else he could have had for the holding up of a finger—herself. She knew, but could not tell him, that he could have done no better thing for himself. Had he, any time these ten years, asked her to marry him, she would have replied quietly, "Very well, when?" He had never thought of it . . . .

"Yours is the real work," she continued quietly. "Without you we jackals couldn't exist. You and a few like you hold everything upon your shoulders."

For a minute there was a silence. Then it occurred to Oleron that this was common vulgar grumbling. It was not his habit. Suddenly he rose and began to stack cups and plates on the tray.

"Sorry you catch me like this, Elsie," he said, with a little laugh . . . . "No, I'll take them out; then we'll go for a walk, if you like . . . ."

He carried out the tray, and then began to show Miss Bengough round his flat. She made few comments. In the kitchen she asked what an old faded square of reddish frieze was, that Mrs. Barrett used as a cushion for her wooden chair.

"That? I should be glad if you could tell *me* what it is," Oleron replied as he unfolded the bag and related the story of its finding in the window-seat.

"I think I know what it is," said Miss Bengough. "It's been used to wrap up a harp before putting it into its case."

"By Jove, that's probably just what it was," said Oleron. "I could make neither head nor tail of it . . . ."

They finished the tour of the flat, and returned to the sitting room.

"And who lives in the rest of the house?" Miss Bengough asked.

"I dare say a tramp sleeps in the cellar occasionally. Nobody else."

"Hm! . . . Well, I'll tell you what I think about it, if you like."

"I should like."

"You'll never work here."

"Oh?" said Oleron quickly. "Why not?"

"You'll never finish *Romilly* here. Why, I don't know, but you won't. I know it. You'll have to leave before you get on with that book."

He mused for a moment, and then said:

"Isn't that a little—prejudiced, Elsie?"

"Perfectly ridiculous. As an argument it hasn't a leg to stand on. But there it is," she replied, her mouth once more full of the large-headed hat pins.

Oleron was reaching down his hat and coat. He laughed.

"I can only hope you're entirely wrong," he said, "for I shall be in a serious mess if *Romilly* isn't out in the autumn."

As Oleron sat by his fire that evening, pondering Miss Bengough's prognostication that difficulties awaited him in his work, he came to the conclusion that it would have been far better had she kept her beliefs to herself. No man does a thing better for having his confidence damped at the outset, and to speak of difficulties is in a sense to make them. Speech itself becomes a deterrent act, to which other discouragements accrete until the very event of which warning is given is as likely as not to come to pass. He heartily confounded her. An influence hostile to the completion of *Romilly* had been born.

And in some illogical, dogmatic way women seem to have, she had attached this antagonistic influence to his new abode. Was ever anything so absurd! "You'll never finish *Romilly* here." . . . Why not? Was this her idea of the luxury that saps the spring of action and brings a man down to indolence and dropping out of the race? The place was well enough—it was entirely charming, for that matter—but it was not so demoralizing as all that! No; Elsie had missed the mark that time . . . .

He moved his chair to look round the room that smiled, positively smiled, in the firelight. He too smiled, as if pity was to be entertained for a maligned apartment. Even that slight lack of robust color he had remarked was not noticeable in the soft glow. The drawn chintz curtains—they had a flowered and trellised pattern, with baskets and oaten pipes—fell in long quiet folds to the window-seats; the rows of bindings in old bookcases took the light richly; the last trace of sallowness had gone with the daylight; and, if the truth must be told, it had been Elsie herself who had seemed a little out of the picture.

That reflection struck him a little, and presently he returned to it. Yes, the room had, quite accidentally, done Miss Bengough a disservice that afternoon. It had, in some subtle but unmistakable way, placed her, marked a contrast of qualities. Assuming for the sake of argument the slightly ridiculous proposition that the room in which Oleron sat *was* characterized by a certain sparsity and lack of vigor; so much the worse for Miss Bengough; she certainly erred on the side of redundancy and general muchness. And if one must contrast abstract qualities, Oleron inclined to the austere in taste . . . .

Yes, here Oleron had made a distinct discovery; he wondered he had not made it before. He pictured Miss Bengough again as she had appeared that afternoon—large, showy, mostly pink, with that quality of the prize bloom exuding, as it were, from her; and instantly she suffered in his thought. He even recognized now that he had noticed something odd at the time, and that unconsciously his attitude, even while she had been there, had been one of criticism. The mechanism of her was a little obvious; her melting humidity was the result of analyzable processes; and behind her there had seemed to lurk some dim shape emblematic of mortality. He had never, during the ten years of their intimacy, dreamed for a moment of asking her to marry him; nonetheless, he now felt for the first time a thankfulness that he had not done so . . . .

Then, suddenly and swiftly, his face flamed that he should be thinking thus of his friend. What! Elsie Bengough, with whom he had spent weeks and weeks of afternoons—she, the good chum, on whose help he would have counted had all the rest of the world failed him—she, whose loyalty to him would not, he knew, swerve as long as there was breath in her—Elsie to be even in thought dissected thus! He was an ingrate and a cad . . . .

Had she been there in that moment he would have abased himself before her.

For ten minutes and more he sat, still gazing into the fire, with that humiliating red fading slowly from his cheeks. All was still within and without, save for a tiny musical tinkling that came from his kitchen— the dripping of water from an imperfectly turned-off tap into the vessel beneath it. Mechanically he began to beat with his fingers to the faintly heard falling of the drops; the tiny regular movement seemed to hasten that shameful withdrawal from his face. He grew cool once more; and when he resumed his meditation he was all unconscious that he took it up again at the same point . . . .

It was not only her florid superfluity of build that he had approached in the attitude of criticism; he was conscious also of the wide differences between her mind and his own. He felt no thankfulness that up to a certain point their natures had ever run companionably side by side; he was now full of questions beyond that point. Their intellects diverged; there was no denying it; and, looking back, he was inclined to doubt whether there had been any real coincidence. True, he had read his writings to her and she had appeared to speak comprehendingly and to the point; but what can a man do who, having assumed that another sees as he does, is suddenly brought up sharp by something that falsifies and discredits all that has gone before? He doubted all now . . . . It did for a moment occur to him that the man who demands of a friend more than can be given to him is in danger of losing that friend, but he put the thought aside.

Again he ceased to think, and again moved his finger to the distant dripping of the tap . . . .

And now (he resumed by-and-by), if these things were true of Elsie Bengough, they were also true of the creation of which she was the prototype—Romilly Bishop. And since he could say of Romilly what for very shame he could not say of Elsie, he gave his thoughts rein. He did so in that smiling, fire-lighted room, to the accompaniment of the faintly heard tap.

There was no longer any doubt about it; he hated the central character of his novel. Even as he had described her physically she overpowered the senses; she was coarse-fibered, overcolored, rank. It became true the moment he formulated his thought; Gulliver had described the Brobdingnagian maids-of-honor thus: and mentally and spiritually she corresponded—was unsensitive, limited, common. The model (he closed his eyes for a moment)—the model stuck out through fifteen vulgar and blatant chapters to such a pitch that, without seeing the reason, he had been unable to begin the sixteenth. He marveled that it had only just dawned upon him.

And *this* was to have been his Beatrice, his vision! As Elsie she was to have gone into the furnace of his art, and she was to have come out the Woman all men desire! Her thoughts were to have been culled from his own finest, her form from his dearest dreams, and her setting wherever he could find one fit for her worth. He had brooded long before making the attempt; then one day he had felt her stir within him as a mother feels a quickening, and he had begun to write; and so he had added chapter to chapter . . . .

And those fifteen sodden chapters were what he had produced!

Again he sat, softly moving his finger . . . .

Then he bestirred himself.

She must go, all fifteen chapters of her. That was settled. For what was to take her place his mind was a blank; but one thing at a time; a man is not excused from taking the wrong course because the right one is not immediately revealed to him. Better would come if it was to come; in the meantime——

He rose, fetched the fifteen chapters, and read them over before he should drop them into the fire.

But instead of putting them into the fire he let them fall from his hand. He became conscious of the dripping of the tap again. It had a tinkling gamut of four or five notes, on which it rang irregular changes, and it was foolishly sweet and dulcimer-like. In his mind Oleron could see the gathering of each drop, its little tremble on the lip of the tap, and the tiny percussion of its fall "Plink—plunk," minimized almost to inaudibility. Following the lowest note there seemed to be a brief phrase, irregularly repeated; and presently Oleron found himself waiting for the recurrence of this phrase. It was quite pretty . . . .

But it did not conduce to wakefulness, and Oleron dozed over his fire.

When he awoke again the fire had burned low and the flames of the candles were licking the rims of the Sheffield sticks. Sluggishly he rose, yawned, went his nightly round of door-locks, and window-fastenings, and passed into his bedroom. Soon, he slept soundly.

But a curious little sequel followed on the morrow. Mrs. Barrett usually tapped, not at his door, but at the wooden wall beyond which lay Oleron's bed; and then Oleron rose, put on his dressing-gown, and admitted her. He was not conscious that as he did so that morning he hummed an air; but Mrs. Barrett lingered with her hand on the door-knob and her face a little averted and smiling.

"De-ar me!" her soft falsetto rose. "But that will be a very o-ald tune, Mr. Oleron! I will not have heard it this for-ty years!"

"What tune?" Oleron asked.

"The tune, indeed, that you was humming, sir."

Oleron had his thumb in the flap of a letter. It remained there.

"*I* was humming? . . . Sing it, Mrs. Barrett."

Mrs. Barrett prut-prutted.

"I have no voice for singing, Mr. Oleron; it was Ann Pugh was the singer of our family; but the tune will be very o-ald, and it is called 'The Beckoning Fair One.'"

"Try to sing it," said Oleron, his thumb still in the envelope; and Mrs. Barrett, with much dimpling and confusion, hummed the air.

"They do say it was sung to a harp, Mr. Oleron, and it will be very o-ald," she concluded.

"And *I* was singing that?"

"Indeed you was. I would not be likely to tell you lies."

With a "Very well—let me have breakfast," Oleron opened his letter; but the trifling circumstance struck him as more odd than he would have admitted to himself. The phrase he had hummed had been that which he had associated with the falling from the tap on the evening before.

Even more curious than that the commonplace dripping of an ordinary water-tap should have tallied so closely with an actually existing air was another result it had, namely, that is awakened, or seemed to awaken, in Oleron an abnormal sensitiveness to other noises of the old house. It has been remarked that silence obtains its fullest and most impressive quality when it is broken by some minute sound; and, truth to tell, the place was never still. Perhaps the mildness of the spring air operated on its torpid old timbers; perhaps Oleron's fires caused it to stretch its old anatomy; and certainly a whole world of insect life bored and burrowed in its baulks and joists. At any rate Oleron had only to sit quiet in his chair and to wait for a minute or two in order to become aware of such a change in the auditory scale as comes upon a man who, conceiving the midsummer woods to be motionless and still, all at once finds his ear sharpened to the crepitation of a myriad insects.

And he smiled to think of man's arbitrary distinction between that which has life and that which has not. Here, quite apart from such recognizable sounds as the scampering of mice, the falling of plaster behind his paneling, and the popping of purses or coffins from his fire, was a whole house talking to him had he but known its language. Beams settled with a tired sigh into their old mortises; creatures ticked in the walls; joists cracked, boards complained; with no palpable stirring of the air window-sashes changed their positions with a soft knock in their frames. And whether the place had life in this sense or not, it had at all events a winsome personality. It needed but an hour of musing for Oleron to conceive the idea that, as his own body stood in friendly relation to his soul, so, by an extension and an attenuation, his habitation might fantastically be supposed to stand in some relation to himself. He even amused himself with the far-fetched fancy that he might so identify himself with the place that some future tenant, taking possession, might regard it as in a sense haunted. It would be rather a joke if he, a perfectly harmless author, with nothing on his mind worse than a novel he had discovered he must begin again, should turn out to be laying the foundation of a future ghost! . . .

In proportion, however, as he felt this growing attachment to the fabric of his abode, Elsie Bengough, from being merely unattracted, began to show a dislike of the place that was more and more marked. And she did not scruple to speak of her aversion.

"It doesn't belong to today at all, and for you especially it's bad," she said with decision. "You're only too ready to let go your hold on actual things and to slip into apathy; *you* ought to be in a place with concrete floors and a patent gas-meter and a tradesman's lift. And it would do you all the good in the world if you had a job that made you scramble and rub elbows with your fellow-men. Now, if I could get you a job, for, say, two or three days a week, one that would allow you heaps of time for your proper work—would you take it?"

Somehow, Oleron resented a little being diagnosed like this. He thanked Miss Bengough, but without a smile.

"Thank you, but I don't think so. After all each of us has his own life to live," he could not refrain from adding.

"His own life to live! . . . How long is it since you were out, Paul?"

"About two hours."

"I don't mean to buy stamps or to post a letter. How long is it since you had anything like a stretch?"

"Oh, some little time perhaps. I don't know."

"Since I was here last?"

"I haven't been out much."

"And has *Romilly* progressed much better for your being cooped up?"

"I think she has. I'm laying the foundations of her. I shall begin the actual writing presently."

It seemed as if Miss Bengough had forgotten their tussle about the first *Romilly*. She frowned, turned half away, and then quickly turned again.

"Ah! . . . So you've still got that ridiculous idea in your head?"

"If you mean," said Oleron slowly, "that I've discarded the old *Romilly*, and am at work on a new one, you're right. I have still got that idea in my head."

Something uncordial in his tone struck her; but she was a fighter. His own absurd sensitiveness hardened her. She gave a "Pshaw!" of impatience.

"Where is the old one?" she demanded abruptly.

"Why?" asked Oleron.

"I want to see it. I want to show some of it to you. I want, if you're not wool-gathering entirely, to bring you back to your senses."

This time it was he who turned his back. But when he turned round again he spoke more gently.

"It's no good, Elsie. I'm responsible for the way I go, and you must allow me to go it—even if it should seem wrong to you. Believe me, I am giving thought to it . . . . The manuscript, I was on the point of burning it, but I didn't. It's in that window-seat, if you must see it."

Miss Bengough crossed quickly to the window-seat, and lifted the lid. Suddenly she gave a little exclamation, and put the back of her hand to her mouth. She spoke over her shoulder:

"You ought to knock those nails in, Paul," she said.

He strode to her side.

"What? What is it? What's the matter?" he asked. "I did knock them in—or, rather pulled them out."

"You left enough to scratch with," she replied, showing her hand. From the upper wrist to the knuckle of the little finger a welling red wound showed.

"Good gracious!" Oleron ejaculated . . . . "Here, come to the bathroom and bathe it quickly——"

He hurried her to the bathroom, turned on warm water, and bathed and cleansed the bad gash. Then, still holding the hand, he turned cold water on it, uttering broken phrases of astonishment and concern.

"Good Lord, how did that happen! As far as I knew I'd . . . is this water too cold? Does that hurt? I can't imagine how on earth . . . there; that'll do——"

"No—one moment longer—I can bear it," she murmured, her eyes closed . . . .

Presently he led her back to the sitting room and bound the hand in one of his handkerchiefs; but his face did not lose its expression of perplexity. He had spent half a day in opening and making serviceable the three window-boxes, and he could not conceive how he had come to leave an inch and a half of rusty nail standing in the wood. He himself had opened the lids of each of them a dozen times and had not noticed any nail; but there it was . . . .

"It shall come out now, at all events," he muttered, as he went for a pair of pincers. And he made no mistake about it that time.

Elsie Bengough had sunk into a chair, and her face was rather white; but in her hand was the manuscript of *Romilly*. She had not finished with *Romilly* yet. Presently she returned to the charge.

"Oh, Paul, it will he the greatest mistake you ever, *ever* made if you do not publish this!" she said.

He hung his head, genuinely distressed. He couldn't get that incident of the nail out of his head, and *Romilly* occupied a second place in his thoughts for the moment. But still she insisted; and when presently he spoke it was almost as if he asked her pardon for something.

"What can I say, Elsie? I can only hope that when you see the new version, you'll see how right I am. And if in spite of all you *don't* like her, well . . ." he made a hopeless gesture. "Don't you see that I *must* be guided by my own lights?"

She was silent.

"Come, Elsie," he said gently. "We've got along well so far; don't let us split on this."

The last words had hardly passed his lips before he regretted them.

She had been nursing her injured hand, with her eyes once more closed; but her lips and lids quivered simultaneously. Her voice shook as she spoke.

"I can't help saying it, Paul, but you are so greatly changed."

"Hush, Elsie," he murmured soothingly; "you've had a shock; rest for a while. How could I change?"

"I don't know, but you are. You've not been yourself ever since you came here. I wish you'd never seen the place. It's stopped your work, it's making you into a person I hardly know, and it's made me horribly anxious about you . . . . Oh, how my hand is beginning to throb!"

"Poor child!" he murmured. "Will you let me take you to a doctor and have it properly dressed?"

"No—I shall be all right presently—I'll keep it raised——"

She put her elbow on the back of her chair, and the bandaged hand rested lightly on his shoulder.

At that touch an entirely new anxiety stirred suddenly within him. Hundreds of times previously, on their jaunts and excursions, she had slipped her hand within his arm as she might have slipped it into the arm of a brother, and he had accepted the little affectionate gesture as a brother might have accepted it. But now, for the first time, there rushed into his mind a hundred startling questions. Her eyes were still closed, and her head had fallen pathetically back; and there was a lost and ineffable smile on her parted lips. The truth broke in upon him. Good God! . . . And he had never divined it!

And stranger than all was that, now that he did see that she was lost in love of him, there came to him, not sorrow and humility and abasement, but something else that he struggled in vain against—something entirely strange and new, that, had he analyzed it, he would have found to be petulance and irritation and resentment and ungentleness. The sudden selfish prompting mastered him before he was aware. He all but gave it words. What was she doing there at all? Why was she not getting on with her own work? Why was she here interfering with his? Who had given her this guardianship over him that lately she had put forward so assertively? "Changed?" It was she, not himself, who had changed . . . .

But by the time she had opened her eyes again he had overcome his resentment sufficiently to speak gently, albeit with reserve.

"I wish you would let me take you to a doctor."

She rose.

"No, thank you, Paul," she said. "I'll go now. If I need a dressing I'll get one; take the other hand, please. Goodbye——"

He did not attempt to detain her. He walked with her to the foot of the stairs. Halfway along the narrow alley she turned.

"It would be a long way to come if you happened not to be in," she said. "I'll send you a postcard the next time."

At the gate she turned again.

"Leave here, Paul," she said, with a mournful look. "Everything's wrong with this house."

Then she was gone.

Oleron returned to his room. He crossed straight to the window-box. He opened the lid and stood long looking at it. Then he closed it again and turned away.

"That's rather frightening," he muttered. "It's simply not possible that I should not have removed that nail . . . ."

Oleron knew very well what Elsie had meant when she had said that her next visit would be preceded by a postcard. She, too, had realized that at last, at last he knew—knew, and didn't want her. It gave him a miserable, pitiful pang, therefore, when she came again within a week, knocking at the door unannounced. She spoke from the landing, she did not intend to stay, she said; and he had to press her before she would so much as enter.

Her excuse for calling was that she had heard of an inquiry for short stories that he might be wise to follow up. He thanked her. Then, her business over, she seemed anxious to get away again. Oleron did not seek to detain her; even he saw through the pretext of the stories; and he accompanied her down the stairs.

But Elsie Bengough had no luck whatever in that house. A second accident befell her. Halfway down the staircase there was the sharp sound of splintering wood, and she checked a loud cry. Oleron knew the woodwork to be old, but he himself had ascended and descended frequently enough without mishap . . . .

Elsie had put her foot through one of the stairs.

He sprang to her side in alarm.

"Oh, I say! My poor girl!"

She laughed hysterically.

"It's my weight—I know I'm getting fat——"

"Keep still—let me clear these splinters away," he muttered between his teeth.

She continued to laugh and sob that it was her weight—she was getting fat——

He thrust downward at the broken boards. The extrication was no easy matter, and her torn boot showed him how badly the foot and ankle within it must be abraded.

"Good God—good God!" he muttered over and over again.

"I shall be too heavy for anything soon," she sobbed and laughed.

But she refused to reascend and to examine her hurt.

"No, let me go quickly—let me go quickly," she repeated.

"But it's a frightful gash!"

"No—not so bad—let me get away quickly—I'm—I'm not wanted."

At her words, that she was not wanted, his head dropped as if she had given him a buffet.

"Elsie!" he choked, brokenly and shocked.

But she too made a quick gesture, as if she put something violently aside.

"Oh, Paul, not *that*—not *you*—of course I do mean that too in a sense—oh, you know what I mean! . . . But if the other can't be, spare me this now! I—I wouldn't have come, but—but oh, I did, I *did* try to keep away!"

It was intolerable, heartbreaking; but what could he do—what could he say? He did not love her . . . .

"Let me go—I'm not wanted—let me take away what's left of me——"

"Dear Elsie—you are very dear to me——"

But again she made the gesture, as of putting something violently aside.

"No, not that—not anything less—don't offer me anything less—
leave me a little pride——"

"Let me get my hat and coat—let me take you to a doctor," he
muttered.

But she refused. She refused even the support of his arm. She gave
another unsteady laugh.

"I'm sorry I broke your stairs, Paul . . . . You will go and see about
the short stories, won't you?"

He groaned.

"Then if you won't see a doctor, will you go across the square and
let Mrs. Barrett look at you? Look, there's Barrett passing now——"

The long-nosed Barrett was looking curiously down the alley, but as
Oleron was about to call him he made off without a word. Elsie
seemed anxious for nothing so much as to be clear of the place, and
finally promised to go straight to a doctor, but insisted on going alone.

"Good-bye," she said.

And Oleron watched her until she was past the hatchet-like "To Let"'
boards, as if he feared that even they might fall upon her and maim her.

That night Oleron did not dine. He had far too much on his mind.
He walked from room to room of his flat, as if he could have walked
away from Elsie Bengough's haunting cry that still rang in his ears. "I'm
not wanted—don't offer me anything less—let me take away what's left
of me——"

Oh, if he could only have persuaded himself that he loved her!

He walked until twilight fell, then, without lighting candles, he
stirred up the fire and flung himself into a chair.

Poor, poor Elsie! . . .

But even while his heart ached for her, it was out of the question. If
only he had known! If only he had used common observation! But
those walks, those sisterly takings of the arm—what a fool he had
been! . . . Well, it was too late now. It was she, not he, who must now
act—act by keeping away. He would help her all he could. He himself

would not sit in her presence. If she came, he would hurry her out again as fast as he could . . . . Poor, poor Elsie!

His room grew dark; the fire burned dead; and he continued to sit, wincing from time to time as a fresh tortured phrase rang again in his ears.

Then suddenly, he knew not why, he found himself anxious for her in a new sense—uneasy about her personal safety. A horrible fancy that even then she might be looking over an embankment down into dark water, that she might even now be glancing up at the hook on the door, took him. Women had been known to do those things . . . . Then there would be an inquest, and he himself would be called upon to identify her, and would be asked how she had come by an ill-healed wound on the hand and a bad abrasion of the ankle. Barrett would say that he had seen her leaving his house . . . .

Then he recognized that his thoughts were morbid. By an effort of will he put them aside, and sat for a while listening to the faint creakings and tickings and rappings within his paneling . . . .

If only he could have married her! . . . But he couldn't. Her face had risen before him again as he had seen it on the stairs, drawn with pain and ugly and swollen with tears. Ugly—yes, positively blubbered; if tears were women's weapons, as they were said to be, such tears were weapons turning against themselves . . . suicide again . . . .

Then all at once he found himself attentively considering her two accidents.

Extraordinary they had been, both of them. He *could not* have left that old nail standing in the wood; why, he had fetched tools specially from the kitchen; and he was convinced that that step that had broken beneath her weight had been as sound as the others. It was inexplicable. If these things could happen, anything could happen. There was not a beam nor a jamb in the place that might not fall without warning, not a plank that might not crash inward, not a nail that might not become a dagger. The whole place was full of life even now; as he sat there in the dark he heard its crowds of noises as if the house had been one great microphone . . . .

Only half conscious that he did so, he had been sitting for some time identifying these noises, attributing to each crack or creak or knock its material cause; but there was one noise which, again not fully conscious of the omission, he had not sought to account for. It had last come some minutes ago; it came again now—a sort of soft sweeping rustle that seemed to hold an almost inaudible minute crackling. For half a minute or so it had Oleron's attention; then his heavy thoughts were of Elsie Bengough again.

He was nearer to loving her in that moment than he had ever been. He thought how to some men their loved ones were but the dearer for those poor mortal blemishes that tell us we are but sojourners on earth, with a common fate not far distant that makes it hardly worth while to do anything but love for the time remaining. Strangling sobs, blearing tears, bodies buffeted by sickness, hearts and minds callous and hard with the rubs of the world—how little love there would be were these things a barrier to love! In that sense he did love Elsie Bengough. What her happiness had never moved in him her sorrow almost woke . . . .

Suddenly his meditation went. His ear had once more become conscious of that soft and repeated noise—the long sweep with the almost inaudible crackle in it. Again and again it came, with a curious insistence, and urgency. It quickened a little as he became increasingly attentive . . . it seemed to Oleron that it grew louder . . . .

All at once he started bolt upright in his chair, tense and listening. The silky rustle came again; he was trying to attach it to something . . . .

The next moment he had leapt to his feet, unnerved and terrified. His chair hung poised for a moment, and then went over, setting the fire-irons clattering as it fell. There was only one noise in the world like that which had caused him to spring thus to his feet . . . .

The next time it came Oleron felt behind him at the empty air with his hand, and backed slowly until be found himself against the wall.

"God in Heaven!" The ejaculation broke from Oleron's lips. The sound had ceased.

The next moment he had given a high cry.

"What is it? What's there? *Who's* there?"

A sound of scuttling caused his knees to bend under him for a moment; but that, he knew, was a mouse. That was not something that his stomach turned sick and his mind reeled to entertain. That other sound, the like of which was not in the world, had now entirely ceased; and again he called . . . .

He called and continued to call; and then another terror, a terror of the sound of his own voice, seized him. He did not dare to call again. His shaking hand went to his pocket for a match, but found none. He thought there might be matches on the mantelpiece——

He worked his way to the mantelpiece round a little recess, without for a moment leaving the wall. Then his hand encountered the mantelpiece, and groped along it. A box of matches fell to the hearth. He could just see them in the firelight, but his hand could not pick them up until he had cornered them inside the fender.

Then he rose and struck a light.

The room was as usual. He struck a second match. A candle stood on the table. He lighted it, and the flame sank for a moment and then burned up clear. Again he looked round.

There was nothing.

There was nothing; but there had been something, and might still be something. Formerly, Oleron had smiled at the fantastic thought that, by a merging and interplay of identities between himself and his beautiful room, he might be preparing a ghost for the future; it had not occurred to him *that there might have been a similar merging and coalescence in the past.* Yet with this staggering impossibility he was now face to face. Something did persist in the house; it had a tenant other than himself; and that tenant, whatsoever or whosoever, had appalled Oleron's soul by producing the sound of a woman brushing her hair.

Without quite knowing how he came to be there Oleron found himself striding over the loose board he had temporarily placed on the step broken by Miss Bengough. He was hatless and descending the stairs. Not until later did there return to him a hazy memory that he had left the candle burning on the table, had opened the door no wider than was necessary to allow the passage of his body, and had sidled out, closing the door softly behind him. At the foot of the stairs another shock awaited him. Something dashed with a flurry up from the disused cellars and disappeared out of the door. It was only a cat, but Oleron gave a childish sob.

He passed out of the gate, and stood for a moment under the "To Let" boards, plucking foolishly at his lip and looking up at the glimmer of light behind one of his red blinds. Then, still looking over his shoulder, he moved stumblingly up the square. There was a small public-house round the corner; Oleron had never entered it; but he entered it now, and put down a shilling that missed the counter by inches.

"B—b—bran—brandy," he said, and then stooped to look for the shilling.

He had the little sawdusted bar to himself; what company there was—carters and laborers and the small tradesmen of the neighborhood—was gathered in the farther compartment, beyond the space where the white-haired landlady moved among her taps and bottles. Oleron sat down on a hardwood settee with a perforated seat, drank half his brandy, and then, thinking he might as well drink it as spill it, finished it.

Then he fell to wondering which of the men whose voices he heard across the public-house would undertake the removal of his effects on the morrow.

In the meantime he ordered more brandy.

For he did not intend to go back to that room where he had left the candle burning. Oh no! He couldn't have faced even the entry and the staircase with the broken step—certainly not that pith-white, fascinating room. He would go back for the present to his old arrangement, of workroom and separate sleeping-quarters; he would go to his old landlady at once—presently—when he had finished his brandy—and see if she could put him up for the night. His glass was empty now . . . .

He rose, had it refilled, and sat down again.

And if anybody asked his reason for removing again? Oh, he had reason enough—reason enough! Nails that put themselves back into wood again and gashed people's hands, steps that broke when you trod on them, and women who came into a man's place and brushed their hair in the dark, were reasons enough! He was querulous and injured about it all. He had taken the place for himself, not for invisible women to brush their hair in; that lawyer fellow in Lincoln's Inn should be told so, too, before many hours were out; it was outrageous, letting people in for agreements like that!

A cut-glass partition divided the compartment where Oleron sat from the space where the white-haired landlady moved; but it stopped seven or eight inches above the level of the counter. There was no partition at the further bar. Presently Oleron, raising his eyes, saw that faces were watching him through the aperture. The faces disappeared when he looked at them.

He moved to a corner where he could not be seen from the other bar; but this brought him into line with the white-haired landlady.

She knew him by sight—had doubtless seen him passing and repassing, and presently she made a remark on the weather. Oleron did not know what he replied, but it sufficed to call forth the further remark that the winter had been a bad one for influenza, but that the spring weather seemed to be coming at last . . . . Even this slight contact with the commonplace steadied Oleron a little; an idle, nascent wonder whether the landlady brushed her hair every night, and, if so, whether it gave out those little electric cracklings, was shut down with a snap; and Oleron was better . . . .

With his next glass of brandy he was all for going back to his flat. Not go back? Indeed, he would go back! They should very soon see whether he was to be turned out of his place like that! He began to wonder why he was doing the rather unusual thing he was doing at that moment, unusual for him—sitting hatless, drinking brandy, in a public-house. Suppose he were to tell the white-haired landlady all about it—to tell her that a caller had scratched her hand on a nail, had later had the bad luck to put her foot through a rotten stair, and that he himself, in an old house full of squeaks and creaks and whispers, had heard a minute noise and had bolted from it in fright—what

would she think of him? That he was mad, of course . . . . Pshaw! The
real truth of the matter was that he hadn't been doing enough work to
occupy him. He had been dreaming his days away, filling his head with
a lot of moonshine about a new *Romilly* (as if the old one was not good
enough), and now he was surprised that the devil should enter an
empty head!

Yes, he would go back. He would take a walk in the air first—he
hadn't walked enough lately—and then he would take himself in hand,
settle the hash of that sixteenth chapter of *Romilly* (fancy, he had actually
been fool enough to think of destroying fifteen chapters!) and thenceforward he would remember that he had obligations to his fellow men
and work to do in the world. There was the matter in a nutshell.

He finished his brandy and went out.

He had walked for some time before any other bearing of the matter than that on himself occurred to him. At first, the fresh air had
increased the heady effect of the brandy he had drunk; but afterwards
his mind grew clearer than it had been since morning. And the clearer
it grew, the less final did his boastful self-assurances become, and the
firmer his conviction that, when all explanations had been made, there
remained something that could not be explained. His hysteria of an
hour before had passed; he grew steadily calmer; but the disquieting
conviction remained. A deep fear took possession of him. It was a fear
for Elsie.

For something in his place was inimical to her safety. Of themselves,
her two accidents might not have persuaded him of this; but she herself had said it. *"I'm not wanted here . . . ."* And she had declared that
there was something wrong with the place. She had seen it before he
had. Well and good. One thing stood out clearly: namely, that if this
was so, she must be kept away for quite another reason than that which
had so confounded and humiliated Oleron. Luckily she had expressed
her intention of staying away; she must be held to that intention. He
must see to it.

And he must see to it all the more that he now saw his first example, never to set foot in the place again, was absurd. People did not do

that kind of thing. With Elsie made secure, he could not with any respect to himself suffer himself to be turned out by a shadow, nor even by a danger merely because it was a danger. He had to live somewhere, and he would live there. He must return.

He mastered the faint chill of fear that came with the decision, and turned in his walk abruptly. Should fear grow on him again he would, perhaps, take one more glass of brandy . . . .

But by the time he reached the short street that led to the square he was too late for more brandy. The little public-house was still lighted, but closed, and one or two men were standing talking on the curb. Oleron noticed that a sudden silence fell on them as he passed, and he noticed further that the long-nosed Barrett, whom he passed a little lower down, did not return his good-night. He turned in at the broken gate, hesitated merely an instant in the alley, and then mounted his stairs again.

Only an inch of candle remained in the Sheffield stick, and Oleron did not light another one. Deliberately he forced himself to take it up and to make the tour of his five rooms before retiring. It was as he returned from the kitchen across his little hall that he noticed that a letter lay on the floor. He carried it into his sitting room, and glanced at the envelope before opening it.

It was unstamped, and had been put into the door by hand. Its handwriting was clumsy, and it ran from beginning to end without comma or period. Oleron read the first line, turned to the signature, and then finished the letter.

It was from the man Barrett, and it informed Oleron that he, Barrett, would be obliged if Mr. Oleron would make other arrangements for the preparing of his breakfasts and the cleaning out of his place. The sting lay in the tail, that is to say, the postscript. This consisted of a text of Scripture. It embodied an allusion that could only be to Elsie Bengough . . . .

A seldom-seen frown had cut deeply into Oleron's brow. So! That was it! Very well; they would see about that on the morrow . . . . For the rest, this seemed merely another reason why Elsie should keep away . . . .

Then his suppressed rage broke out . . . .

The foul-minded lot! The devil himself could not have given a leer at anything that had ever passed between Paul Oleron and Elsie Bengough, yet this nosing rascal must be prying and talking! . . .

Oleron crumpled the paper up, held it in the candle flame, and then ground the ashes under his heel.

One useful purpose, however, the letter had served: it had created in Oleron a wrathful blaze that effectually banished pale shadows. Nevertheless, one other puzzling circumstance was to close the day. As he undressed, he chanced to glance at his bed. The coverlets bore an impress as if somebody had lain on them. Oleron could not remember that he himself had lain down during the day—off-handed, he would have said that certainly he had not; but after all he could not be positive. His indignation for Elsie, acting possibly with the residue of the brandy in him, excluded all other considerations; and he put out his candle, lay down, and passed immediately into a deep and dreamless sleep, which, in the absence of Mrs. Barrett's morning call, lasted almost once round the clock.

To the man who pays heed to that voice within him which warns him that twilight and danger are settling over his soul, terror is apt to appear an absolute thing, against which his heart must be safeguarded in a twink unless there is to take place an alteration in the whole range and scale of his nature. Mercifully, he has never far to look for safeguards. Of the immediate and small and common and momentary things of life, of usages and observances and modes and conventions, he builds up fortifications against the powers of darkness. He is even content that, not terror only, but joy also, should for working purposes be placed in the category of the absolute things; and the last treason he will commit will he that breaking down of terms and limits that strikes, not at one man, but at the welfare of the souls of all.

In his own person, Oleron began to commit this treason. He began to commit it by admitting the inexplicable and horrible to an increasing familiarity. He did it insensibly, unconsciously, by a neglect of the things that he now regarded it as an impertinence in Elsie Bengough to have prescribed. Two months before, the words "a haunted house," applied to his lovely bemusing dwelling, would have chilled his marrow; now his scale of sensation becoming depressed, he could ask "Haunted by what?" and remain unconscious that horror, when it can be proved to be relative, by so much loses its proper quality. He was setting aside the landmarks. Mists and confusion had begun to enwrap him.

And he was conscious of nothing so much as of a voracious inquisitiveness. He wanted to *know.* He was resolved to know. Nothing but the knowledge would satisfy him; and craftily he cast about for means whereby he might attain it.

He might have spared his craft. The matter was the easiest imaginable. As in time past he had known, in his writing, moments when his thoughts had seemed to rise of themselves and to embody themselves in words not to be altered afterwards, so now the questions he put himself seemed to be answered even in the moment of their asking. There was exhilaration in the swift, easy processes. He had known no such joy in his own power since the days when his writing had been a daily freshness and a delight to him. It was almost as if the course he must pursue was being dictated to him.

And the first thing he must do, of course, was to define the problem. He defined it in terms of mathematics. Granted that he had not the place to himself; granted that the old house had inexpressibly caught and engaged his spirit; granted that, by virtue of the common denominator of the place, this unknown co-tenant stood in some relation to himself: what next? Clearly, the nature of the other numerator must be ascertained.

And how? Ordinarily this would not have seemed simple, but to Oleron it was now pellucidly clear. The key, *of course,* lay in his half-written novel—or rather, in both *Romillys,* the old and the proposed new one.

A little while before Oleron would have thought himself mad to have embraced such an opinion; now he accepted the dizzying hypothesis without a quiver.

He began to examine the first and second *Romillys*.

From the moment of his doing so the thing advanced by leaps and bounds. Swiftly he reviewed the history of the *Romilly* of the fifteen chapters. He remembered clearly now that he had found her insufficient on the very first morning on which he had sat down to work in his new place. Other instances of his aversion leaped up to confirm his obscure investigation. There had come the night when he had hardly forborne to throw the whole thing into the fire; and the next morning he had begun the planning of the new *Romilly*. It had been on that morning that Mrs. Barrett, overhearing him humming a brief phrase that the dripping of a tap the night before had suggested, had informed him that he was singing some air he had never in his life heard before, called "The Beckoning Fair One.". . .

The Beckoning Fair One! . . .

With scarcely a pause in thought he continued:

The first *Romilly* having been definitely thrown over, the second had instantly fastened herself upon him, clamoring for birth in his brain. He even fancied now, looking back, that there had been something like passion, hate almost, in the supplanting, and that more than once a stray thought given to his discarded creation had—(it was astonishing how credible Oleron found the almost unthinkable idea)—had offended the supplanter.

Yet that a malignancy almost homicidal should be extended to his fiction's poor mortal prototype . . . .

In spite of his inuring to a scale in which the horrible was now a thing to be fingered and turned this way and that, a "Good God!" broke from Oleron.

This intrusion of the first *Romilly's* prototype into his thought again was a factor that for the moment brought his inquiry into the nature of his problem to a termination; the mere thought of Elsie was fatal to anything abstract. For another thing, he could not yet think of that letter of Barrett's, nor of a little scene that had followed it, without a mounting of color and a quick contraction of the brow. For, wisely or not, he had had that argument out at once. Striding across the square on the following morning, he had bearded Barrett on his own doorstep. Coming back again a few minutes later, he had been strongly of opinion that he had only made matters worse. The man had been vagueness itself. He had not been able to be either challenged or browbeaten into anything more definite than a muttered farrago in which the words "Certain things . . . Mrs. Barrett . . . respectable house . . . if the cap fits . . . proceedings that shall be nameless," had been constantly repeated.

"Not that I make any charge——" he had concluded.

"Charge!" Oleron had cried.

"I 'ave my idears of things, as I don't doubt you 'ave yours——"

"Ideas—mine!" Oleron had cried wrathfully, immediately dropping his voice as heads had appeared at windows of the square. "Look you here, my man; you've an unwholesome mind, which probably you can't help, but a tongue which you can help, and shall! If there is a breath of this repeated . . . ."

"I'll not be talked to on my own doorstep like this by anybody . . ." Barrett had blustered . . . .

"You shall, and I'm doing it . . ."

"Don't you forget there's a Gawd above all, Who 'as said . . ."

"You're a low scandalmonger! . . . "

And so forth, continuing badly what was already badly begun. Oleron had returned wrathfully to his own house and thenceforward, looking out of his windows, had seen Barrett's face at odd times, lifting blinds or peering round curtains, as if he sought to put himself in possession of Heaven knew what evidence, in case it should be required of him.

The unfortunate occurrence made certain minor differences in Oleron's domestic arrangements. Barrett's tongue, he gathered, had already been busy; he was looked at askance by the dwellers of the square; and he judged it better, until he should be able to obtain other help, to make his purchases of provisions a little farther afield rather than at the small shops of the immediate neighborhood. For the rest, housekeeping was no new thing to him, and he would resume his old bachelor habits . . . .

Besides, he was deep in certain rather abstruse investigations, in which it was better that he should not be disturbed. He was looking out of his window one midday rather tired, not very well, and glad that it was not very likely he would have to stir out of doors, when he saw Elsie Bengough crossing the square towards his house. The weather had broken; it was a raw and gusty day; and she had to force her way against the wind that set her ample skirts bellying about her opulent figure and her veil spinning and streaming behind her.

Oleron acted swiftly and instinctively. Seizing his hat, he sprang to the door and descended the stairs at a run. A sort of panic had seized him. She must be prevented from setting foot in the place. As he ran along the alley he was conscious that his eyes went up to the eaves as if something drew them. He did not know that a slate might not accidentally fall . . . .

He met her at the gate, and spoke with curious volubleness.

"This is really too bad, Elsie! Just as I'm urgently called away! I'm afraid it can't be helped though, and that you'll have to think me an inhospitable beast." He poured it out just as it came into his head.

She asked if he was going to town.

"Yes, yes—to town," he replied. "I've got to call on—on Chambers. You know Chambers, don't you? No, I remember you don't; a big man you once saw me with . . . . I ought to have gone yesterday, and"—this he felt to be a brilliant effort—"and he's going out of town this afternoon. To Brighton. I had a letter from him this morning."

He took her arm and led her up the square. She had to remind him that his way to town lay in the other direction.

"Of course—how stupid of me!" he said, with a little loud laugh. "I'm so used to going the other way with you—of course; it's the other way to the bus. Will you come along with me? I am so awfully sorry it's happened like this . . . ."

They took the street to the bus terminus.

This time Elsie bore no signs of having gone through interior struggles. If she detected anything unusual in his manner she made no comment, and he, seeing her calm, began to talk less recklessly through silences. By the time they reached the bus terminus, nobody, seeing the pallid-faced man without an overcoat and the large ample-skirted girl at his side, would have supposed that one of them was ready to sink on his knees for thankfulness that he had, as he believed, saved the other from a wildly unthinkable danger.

They mounted to the top of the bus, Oleron protesting that he should not miss his overcoat, and that he found the day, if anything, rather oppressively hot. They sat down on a front seat.

Now that this meeting was forced upon him, he had something else to say that would make demands upon his tact. It had been on his mind for some time, and was, indeed, peculiarly difficult to put. He revolved it for some minutes, and then, remembering the success of his story of a sudden call to town, cut the knot of his difficulty with another lie.

"I'm thinking of going away for a little while, Elsie," he said.

She merely said: "Oh?"

"Somewhere for a change. I need a change. I think I shall go tomorrow, or the day after. Yes, tomorrow, I think."

"Yes," she replied.

"I don't quite know how long I shall be," he continued. "I shall have to let you know when I am back."

"Yes, let me know," she replied in an even tone.

The tone was, for her, suspiciously even. He was a little uneasy.

"You don't ask me where I'm going," he said, with a little cumbrous effort to rally her.

She was looking straight before her, past the bus driver.

"I know," she said.

He was startled. "How, you know?"

"You're not going anywhere," she replied.

He found not a word to say. It was a minute or so before she continued, in the same controlled voice she had employed from the start.

"You're not going anywhere. You weren't going out this morning. You only came out because I appeared; don't behave as if we were strangers, Paul."

A flush of pink had mounted to his cheeks. He noticed that the wind had given her the pink of early rhubarb. Still he found nothing to say.

"Of course, you ought to go away," she continued. "I don't know whether you look at yourself often in the glass, but you're rather noticeable. Several people have turned to look at you this morning. So, of course, you ought to go away. But you won't, and I know why."

He shivered, coughed a little, and then broke silence.

"Then if you know, there's no use in continuing this discussion," he said curtly.

"Not for me, perhaps, but there is for you," she replied "Shall I tell you what I know?"

"No," he said in a voice slightly raised.

"No?" she asked, her round eyes earnestly on him.

"No."

Again he was getting out of patience with her; again he was conscious of the strain. Her devotion and fidelity and love plagued him; she was only humiliating both herself and him. It would have been bad enough had he ever, by word or deed, given her cause for thus fastening herself on him . . . but there; that was the worst of that kind of life for a woman. Women such as she, business women, in and out of offices all the time, always, whether they realized it or not, made comradeship a cover for something else. They accepted the unconventional status, came and went freely, as men did, were honestly taken by men at their own valuation—and then it turned out to be the other thing after all, and they went and fell in love. No wonder there was gossip in shops and squares and public-houses! In a sense the gossipers were in the right of it. Independent, yet not efficient; with some of womanhood's graces foregone, and yet with all the woman's hunger and need; half sophisticated yet not wise; Oleron was tired of it all . . . .

And it was time he told her so.

"I suppose," he said tremblingly, looking down between his knees, "I suppose the real trouble is in the life women who earn their own living are obliged to lead."

He could not tell in what sense she took the lame generality; she merely replied: "I suppose so."

"It can't be helped," he continued, "but you do sacrifice a good deal."

She agreed: a good deal; and then she added after a moment: "What, for instance?"

"You may or may not be gradually attaining a new status, but you're in a false position today."

It was very likely, she said; she hadn't thought of it much in that light——

"And," he continued desperately, "you're bound to suffer. Your most innocent acts are misunderstood; motives you never dreamed of are attributed to you; and in the end it comes to"—he hesitated a moment and then took the plunge—"to the sidelong look and the leer."

She took his meaning with perfect ease. She merely shivered a little as she pronounced the name.

"Barrett?"

His silence told her the rest.

Anything further that was to be said must come from her. It came as the bus stopped at a stage and fresh passengers mounted the stairs.

"You'd better get down here and go back, Paul," she said. "I understand perfectly—perfectly. It isn't Barrett. You'd be able to deal with Barrett. It's merely convenient for you to say it's Barrett. I know what it is . . . but you said I wasn't to tell you that. Very well. But before you go let me tell you why I came up this morning."

In a dull tone he asked her why. Again she looked straight before her as she replied:

"I came to force your hand. Things couldn't go on as they have been going, you know; and now that's all over."

"All over," he repeated stupidly.

"All over. I want you now to consider yourself, as far as I'm concerned, perfectly free. I make only one reservation."

He hardly had the spirit to ask her what that was.

"If I merely need you," she said, "please don't give that a thought; that's nothing; I shan't come near for that. But," she dropped her voice, "if *you're* in need of *me*, Paul—I shall know if you are, *and you will be*—then I shall come at no matter what cost. You understand that?"

He could only groan.

"So that's understood," she concluded. "And I think that's all. Now go back. I should advise you to walk back, for you're shivering—good-bye——"

She gave him a cold hand, and he descended. He turned on the edge of the curb as the bus started again. For the first time in all the years he had known her she parted from him with no smile and no wave of her long arm.

He stood on the curb plunged in misery, looking after her as long as she remained in sight; but almost instantly with her disappearance he felt the heaviness lift a little from his spirit. She had given him his liberty; true, there was a sense in which he had never parted with it, but now was no time for splitting hairs; he was free to act, and all was clear ahead. Swiftly the sense of lightness grew on him: it became a positive rejoicing in his liberty; and before he was halfway home he had decided what must be done next.

The vicar of the parish in which his dwelling was situated lived within ten minutes of the square. To his house Oleron turned his steps. It was necessary that he should have all the information he could get about this old house with the insurance marks and the sloping "To Let" boards, and the vicar was the person most likely to be able to furnish it. This last preliminary out of the way, and—aha! Oleron chuckled—things might be expected to happen!

But he gained less information than he had hoped for. The house, the vicar said, was old—but there needed no vicar to tell Oleron that; it was reputed (Oleron pricked up his ears) to be haunted—but there were few old houses about which some such rumor did not circulate among the ignorant; and the deplorable lack of Faith of the modern world, the vicar thought, did not tend to dissipate these superstitions. For the rest, his manner was the soothing manner of one who prefers not to make statements without knowing how they will be taken by his hearer. Oleron smiled as he perceived this.

"You may leave my nerves out of the question," he said. "How long has the place been empty?"

"A dozen years, I should say," the vicar replied.

"And the last tenant—did you know him—or her?" Oleron was conscious of a tingling of his nerves as he offered the vicar the alternative of sex.

"Him," said the vicar. "A man. If I remember rightly, his name was Madley; an artist. He was a great recluse; seldom went out of the place, and"—the vicar hesitated and then broke into a little gush of candor—"and since you appear to have come for this information, and since it is better that the truth should be told than that garbled versions should get about, I don't mind saying that this man Madley died there, under somewhat unusual circumstances. It was ascertained at the post-mortem that there was not a particle of food in his stomach, although he was found to be not without money. And his frame was simply worn out. Suicide was spoken of, but you'll agree with me that deliberate starvation is, to say the least, an uncommon form of suicide. An open verdict was returned."

"Ah! " said Oleron . . . . "Does there happen to be any comprehensive history of this parish?"

"No; partial ones only. I myself am not guiltless of having made a number of notes on its purely ecclesiastical history, its registers and so forth, which I shall be happy to show you if you would care to see them; but it is a large parish, I have only one curate, and my leisure, as you will readily understand . . . ."

The extent of the parish and the scantiness of the vicar's leisure occupied the remainder of the interview, and Oleron thanked the vicar, took his leave, and walked slowly home.

He walked slowly for a reason, twice turning away from the house within a stone's throw of the gate and taking another turn of twenty minutes or so. He had a very ticklish piece of work now before him; it required the greatest mental concentration; it was nothing less than to bring his mind, if he might, into such a state of unpreoccupation and receptivity that he should see the place as he had seen it on that morn-

ing when, his removal accomplished, he had sat down to begin the sixteenth chapter of the first *Romilly*.

For, could he recapture that first impression, he now hoped for far
more from it. Formerly, he had carried no end of mental lumber.
Before the influence of the place had been able to find him out at all,
it had had the inertia of those dreary chapters to overcome. No results
had shown. The process had been one of slow saturation, charging, filling up to a brim. But now he was light, unburdened, rid at last both of
that *Romilly* and of her prototype. Now for the new unknown, coy, jealous, bewitching Beckoning Fair! . . .

At half-past two of the afternoon he put his key into the Yale lock,
entered, and closed the door behind him . . . .

His fantastic attempt was instantly and astonishingly successful. He
could have shouted with triumph as he entered the room; it was as if he
had *escaped* into it. Once more, as in the days when his writing had had a
daily freshness and wonder and promise for him, he was conscious of
that new ease and mastery and exhilaration and release. The air of the
place seemed to hold more oxygen; as if his own specific gravity had
changed, his very tread seemed less ponderable. The flowers in the bowls,
the fair proportions of the meadowsweet-colored panels and moldings,
the polished floor, and the lofty and faintly starred ceiling, fairly laughed
their welcome, Oleron actually laughed back, and spoke aloud.

"Oh, you're pretty, pretty!" he flattered it.

Then he lay down on his couch.

He spent that afternoon as a convalescent who expected a dear visitor might have spent it—in a delicious vacancy, smiling now and then
as if in his sleep, and ever lifting drowsy and contented eyes to his
alluring surroundings. He lay thus until darkness came, and, with darkness, the nocturnal noises of the old house . . . .

But if he waited for any specific happening, he waited in vain.

He waited similarly in vain on the morrow, maintaining, though
with less ease, that sensitized lake-like condition of his mind. Nothing
occurred to give it an impression. Whatever it was which he so
patiently wooed, it seemed to be both shy and exacting.

Then on the third day he thought he understood. A look of gentle drollery and cunning came into his eyes, and he chuckled.

"Oho, oho . . . Well, if the wind sits in *that* quarter we must see what else there is to be done. What is there, now? . . . No, I won't send for Elsie; we don't need a wheel to break the butterfly on; we won't go to those lengths, my butterfly . . . ."

He was standing musing, thumbing his lean jaw, looking aslant; suddenly he crossed to his hall, took down his hat, and went out.

"My lady is coquettish, is she? Well, we'll see what a little neglect will do," he chuckled as he went down the stairs.

He sought a railway station, got into a train, and spent the rest of the day in the country. Oh, yes: Oleron thought *he* was the man to deal with Fair Ones who beckoned, and invited, and then took refuge in shyness and hanging back!

He did not return until after eleven that night.

"*Now*, my Fair Beckoner!" he murmured as he walked along the alley and felt in his pocket for his keys . . . .

Inside his flat, he was perfectly composed, perfectly deliberate, exceedingly careful not to give himself away. As if to intimate that he intended to retire immediately, he lighted only a single candle; and as he set out with it on his nightly round he affected to yawn. He went first into his kitchen. There was a full moon, and a lozenge of moonlight, almost peacock-blue by contrast with his candle-flame, lay on the floor. The window was uncurtained, and he could see the reflection of the candle, and, faintly, that of his own face, as he moved about. The door of the powder-closet stood a little ajar, and he closed it before sitting down to remove his boots on the chair with the cushion made of the folded harp-bag. From the kitchen he passed to the bathroom. There, another slant of blue moonlight cut the window-sill and lay across the pipes on the wall. He visited his seldom-used study, and stood for a moment gazing at the silvered roofs across the square. Then, walking straight through his sitting room, his stockinged feet making no noise, he entered his bedroom and put the candle on the chest of drawers. His face all this time wore no expression save that of tiredness. He had never been wilier nor more alert.

His small bedroom fireplace was opposite the chest of drawers on which the mirror stood, and his bed and the window occupied the remaining sides of the room. Oleron drew down his blind, took off his coat, and then stooped to get his slippers from under the bed.

He could have given no reason for the conviction, but that the manifestation that for two days had been withheld was close at hand he never for an instant doubted. Nor, though he could not form the faintest guess of the shape it might take, did he experience fear. Startling or surprising it might be; he was prepared for that; but that was all; his scale of sensation had become depressed. His hand moved this way and that under the bed in search of his slippers . . . .

But for all his caution and method and preparedness, his heart all at once gave a leap and a pause that was almost horrid. His hand had found the slippers, but he was still on his knees; save for this circumstance he would have fallen. The bed was a low one; the groping for the slippers accounted for the turn of his head to one side; and he was careful to keep the attitude until he had partly recovered his self-possession. When presently he rose there was a drop of blood on his lower lip where he had caught at it with his teeth, and his watch had jerked out of the pocket of his waistcoat and was dangling at the end of its short leather guard . . . .

Then, before the watch had ceased its little oscillation, he was himself again.

In the middle of his mantelpiece there stood a picture, a portrait of his grandmother; he placed himself before this picture, so that he could see in the glass of it the steady flame of the candle that burned behind him on the chest of drawers. He could see also in the picture-glass the little glancings of light from the bevels and facets of the objects about the mirror and candle. But he could see more. These twinklings and reflections and re-reflections did not change their position; but there was one gleam that had motion. It was fainter than the rest, and it moved up and down through the air. It was the reflection of the candle on Oleron's black vulcanite comb, and each of its downward movements was accompanied by a silky and crackling rustle.

Oleron, watching what went on in the glass of his grandmother's portrait, continued to play his part. He felt for his dangling watch and began slowly to wind it up. Then, for a moment ceasing to watch, he began to empty his trousers' pockets and to place methodically in a little row on the mantelpiece the pennies and halfpennies he took from them. The sweeping, minutely electric noise filled the whole bedroom, and had Oleron altered his point of observation he could have brought the dim gleam of the moving comb so into position that it would almost have outlined his grandmother's head.

Any other head of which it might have been following the outline was invisible.

Oleron finished the emptying of his pockets; then, under cover of another simulated yawn, not so much summoning his resolution as overmastered by an exorbitant curiosity, he swung suddenly round. That which was being combed was still not to be seen, but the comb did not stop. It had altered its angle a little, and had moved a little to the left. It was passing, in fairly regular sweeps, from a point rather more than five feet from the ground, in a direction roughly vertical, to another point a few inches below the level of the chest of drawers.

Oleron continued to act to admiration. He walked to his little washstand in the corner, poured out water, and began to wash his hands. He removed his waistcoat, and continued his preparations for bed. The combing did not cease, and he stood for a moment in thought. Again his eyes twinkled. The next was very cunning——

"Hm! . . . *I think I'll read for a quarter of an hour,*" he said aloud . . . .

He passed out of the room.

He was away a couple of minutes; when he returned again the room was suddenly quiet. He glanced at the chest of drawers; the comb lay still, between the collar he had removed and a pair of gloves. Without hesitation Oleron put out his hand and picked it up. It was an ordinary eighteen-penny comb, taken from a card in a chemist's shop, of a substance of a definite specific gravity, and no more capable of rebellion against the Laws by which it existed than are the worlds that keep their orbits through the void. Oleron put it down again; then he glanced at the bundle of papers he held in his hand. What he had gone to fetch had been the fifteen chapters of the original *Romilly*.

"Hm!" he muttered as he threw the manuscript into a chair . . . . "As I thought . . . . She's just blindly, ragingly, murderously jealous."

On the night after that, and on the following night, and for many nights and days, so many that he began to be uncertain about the count of them, Oleron, courting, cajoling, neglecting, threatening, beseeching, eaten out with unappeased curiosity and regardless that his life was becoming one consuming passion and desire, continued his search for the unknown co-numerator of his abode.

As time went on, it came to pass that few except the postman mounted Oleron's stairs; and since men who do not write letters receive few, even the postman's tread became so infrequent that it was not heard more than once or twice a week. There came a letter from Oleron's publishers, asking when they might expect to receive the manuscript of his new book; he delayed for some days to answer it, and finally forgot it. A second letter came, which also he failed to answer. He received no third.

The weather grew bright and warm. The privet bushes among the chopper-like notice-boards flowered, and in the streets where Oleron did his shopping the baskets of flower-women lined the curbs. Oleron purchased flowers daily; his room clamored for flowers, fresh and continually renewed; and Oleron did not stint its demands. Nevertheless, the necessity for going out to buy them began to irk him more and more, and it was with a greater and ever greater sense of relief that he returned home again. He began to be conscious that again his scale of sensation had suffered a subtle change—a change that was not restoration to its former capacity, but an extension and enlarging that once more included terror. It admitted it in an entirely new form. *Lux orco, tenebræ Jovi*. The name of this terror was agoraphobia. Oleron had begun to dread air and space and the horror that might pounce upon the unguarded back.

Presently he so contrived it that his food and flowers were delivered daily at his door. He rubbed his hands when he had hit upon this expedient. That was better! Now he could please himself whether he went out or not . . . .

Quickly he was confirmed in his choice. It became his pleasure to remain immured.

But he was not happy—or, if he was, his happiness took an extraordinary turn. He fretted discontentedly, could sometimes have wept for mere weakness and misery; and yet he was dimly conscious that he would not have exchanged his sadness for all the noisy mirth of the world outside. And speaking of noise: noise, much noise, now caused him the acutest discomfort. It was hardly more to be endured than that new-born fear that kept him, on the increasingly rare occasions when he did go out, sidling close to walls and feeling friendly railings with his hand. He moved from room to room softly and in slippers, and sometimes stood for many seconds closing a door so gently that not a sound broke the stillness that was in itself a delight. Sunday now became an intolerable day to him, for, since the coming of the fine weather, there had begun to assemble in the square under his windows each Sunday morning certain members of the sect to which the long-nosed Barrett adhered. These came with a great drum and large brass-bellied instruments; men and women uplifted anguished voices, struggling with their God; and Barrett himself, with upraised face and closed eyes and working brows, prayed that the sound of his voice might penetrate the ears of all unbelievers—as it certainly did Oleron's. One day, in the middle of one of these rhapsodies, Oleron sprang to his blind and pulled it down, and heard, as he did so, his own name made the object of a fresh torrent of outpouring.

And sometimes, but not as expecting a reply, Oleron stood still and called softly. Once or twice he called "*Romilly!*" and then waited; but more often his whispering did not take the shape of a name.

There was one spot in particular of his abode that he began to haunt with increasing persistency. This was just within the opening of his bedroom door. He had discovered one day that by opening every door in his place (always excepting the outer one, which he only opened unwillingly) and by placing himself on this particular spot, he could actually see to a greater or less extent into each of his five rooms without changing his position. He could see the whole of his sitting room, all of his bedroom except the part hidden by the open door, and glimpses of his kitchen, bathroom, and of his rarely used study. He was often in this place, breathless and with his finger on his lip. One day, as he stood there, he suddenly found himself wondering whether this Madley, of whom the vicar had spoken, had ever discovered the strategic importance of the bedroom entry.

Light, moreover, now caused him greater disquietude than did darkness. Direct sunlight, of which as the sun passed daily round the house, each of his rooms had now its share, was like a flame in his brain; and even diffused light was a dull and numbing ache. He began, at successive hours of the day, one after another, to lower his crimson blinds. He made short and daring excursions in order to do this; but he was ever careful to leave his retreat open, in case he should have sudden need of it. Presently this lowering of the blinds had become a daily methodical exercise, and his rooms, when he had been his round, had the blood-red half-light of a photographer's darkroom.

One day, as he drew down the blind of his little study and backed in good order out of the room again, he broke into a soft laugh.

"*That* bilks Mr. Barrett!" he said; and the baffling of Barrett continued to afford him mirth for an hour.

But on another day, soon after, he had a fright that left him trembling also for an hour. He had seized the cord to darken the window over the seat in which he had found the harp-bag, and was standing with his back well protected in the embrasure, when he thought he saw the tail of a black-and-white check skirt disappear round the corner of the house. He could not be sure—had he run to the window of the other wall, which was blinded, the skirt must have been already past—but he was *almost* sure that it was Elsie. He listened in an agony of suspense for her tread on the stairs . . . .

But no tread came, and after three or four minutes he drew a long, breath of relief.

"By Jove, but that would have compromised me horribly!" he muttered . . . .

And he continued to mutter from time to time: "Horribly compromising . . . *no* woman would stand that . . . not *any* kind of woman . . . oh, compromising in the extreme!"

Yet he was not happy. He could not have assigned the cause of the fits of quiet weeping which took him sometimes; they came and went, like the fitful illumination of the clouds that traveled over the square; and perhaps, after all, if he was not happy, he was not unhappy. Before he could be unhappy something must have been withdrawn, and nothing had been granted. He was waiting for that granting, in that flower-laden, frightfully enticing apartment of his, with the pith-white walls tinged and subdued by the crimson blinds to a blood-like gloom.

He paid no heed to it that his stock of money was running perilously low, nor that he had ceased to work. Ceased to work? He had not ceased to work. They knew very little about it who supposed that Oleron had ceased to work! He was in truth only now beginning to work. He was preparing such a work . . . such a work . . . such a Mistress was a-making in the gestation of his Art . . . let him but get this period of probation and poignant waiting over and men should see . . . . How should men know her, this Fair One of Oleron's, until Oleron himself knew her? Lovely radiant creations are not thrown off like How-d'ye-do's. The men to whom it is committed to father them must weep wretched tears, as Oleron did, must swell with vain presumptuous hopes, as Oleron did, must pursue, as Oleron pursued, the capricious, fair, mocking, slippery, eager Spirit that, ever eluding, ever sees to it that the chase does not slacken. Let Oleron but hunt this Huntress a little longer . . . he would have her sparkling and panting in his arms yet . . . . Oh, no: they were very far from the truth who supposed that Oleron had ceased to work!

And if all else was falling away from Oleron, gladly he was letting it go. So do we all when our Fair Ones beckon. Quite at the beginning we wink, and promise ourselves that we will put Her Ladyship through her paces, neglect her for a day, turn her own jealous wiles against her, flout and ignore her when she comes wheedling; perhaps there lurks within us all the time a heartless sprite who is never fooled; but in the end all falls away. She beckons, beckons, and all goes . . . .

And so Oleron kept his strategic post within the frame of his bedroom door, and watched, and waited, and smiled, with his finger on his lips . . . . It was his duteous service, his worship, his troth-plighting, all that he had ever known of Love. And when he found himself, as he now and then did, hating the dead man Madley, and wishing that he had never lived, he felt that that, too, was an acceptable service . . . .

But, as he thus prepared himself, as it were, for a Marriage, and moped and chafed more and more that the Bride made no sign, he made a discovery that he ought to have made weeks before.

It was through a thought of the dead Madley that he made it. Since that night when he had thought in his greenness that a little studied neglect would bring the lovely Beckoner to her knees, and had made use of her own jealousy to banish her, he had not set eyes on those fifteen discarded chapters of *Romilly*. He had thrown them back into the window seat, forgotten their very existence. But his own jealousy of Madley put him in mind of hers, of her jilted rival of flesh and blood, and he remembered them . . . . Fool that he had been! Had he, then, expected his Desire to manifest herself while there still existed the evidence of his divided allegiance? What, and she with a passion so fierce and centered that it had not hesitated at the destruction, twice attempted, of her rival? Fool that he had been! . . .

But if *that* was all the pledge and sacrifice she required she should have it—ah, yes, and quickly!

He took the manuscript from the window-seat, and brought it to the fire.

He kept his fire always burning now; the warmth brought out the last vestige of odor of the flowers with which his room was banked. He did not know what time it was; long since he had allowed his clock to run down—it had seemed a foolish measurer of time in regard to the stupendous things that were happening to Oleron; but he knew it was late. He took the *Romilly* manuscript and knelt before the fire.

But he had not finished removing the fastening that held the sheets together before he suddenly gave a start, turned his head over his shoulder, and listened intently. The sound he had heard had not been loud—it had been, indeed, no more than a tap, twice or thrice repeated—but it had filled Oleron with alarm. His face grew dark as it came again.

He heard a voice outside on his landing.

"Paul! . . . Paul! . . . "

It was Elsie's voice.

"Paul! . . . I know you're in . . . I want to see you . . . ."

He cursed her under his breath, but kept perfectly still. He did not intend to admit her.

"Paul! . . . You're in trouble . . . . I believe you're in danger . . . at least come to the door! . . ."

Oleron smothered a low laugh. It somehow amused him that she, in such danger herself, should talk to him of *his* danger! . . . Well, if she was, serve her right; she knew, or said she knew, all about it . . . .

"Paul! . . . Paul! . . ."

"Paul! . . . Paul! . . ." He mimicked her under his breath.

"Oh, Paul, it's *horrible!* . . ."

Horrible was it? thought Oleron. Then let her get away. . . .

"I only want to help you, Paul . . . . I didn't promise not to come if you needed me. . . ."

He was impervious to the pitiful sob that interrupted the low cry. The devil take the woman! Should he shout to her to go away and not come back? No: let her call and knock and sob. She had a gift for sobbing; she mustn't think her sobs would move him. They irritated him, so that he set his teeth and shook his fist at her, but that was all. Let her sob.

"Paul! . . . Paul! . . ."

With his teeth hard set, he dropped the first page of *Romilly* into the fire. Then he began to drop the rest in, sheet by sheet.

For many minutes the calling behind his door continued; then suddenly it ceased. He heard the sound of feet slowly descending the stairs.

He listened for the noise of a fall or a cry or the crash of a piece of the handrail of the upper landing; but none of these things came. She was spared. Apparently her rival suffered her to crawl abject and beaten away. Oleron heard the passing of her steps under his window; then she was gone.

He dropped the last page into the fire, and then, with a low laugh, rose. He looked fondly round his room.

"Lucky to get away like that," he remarked. "She wouldn't have got away if I'd given her as much as a word or a look! What devils these women are! . . . But no; I oughtn't to say that; one of 'em showed forbearance . . . ."

Who showed forbearance? And what was forborne? Ah, Oleron knew! . . . Contempt, no doubt, had been at the bottom of it, but that didn't matter: the pestering creature had been allowed to go unharmed. Yes, she was lucky; Oleron hoped she knew it . . . .

And now, now, now for his reward!

Oleron crossed the room. All his doors were open; his eyes shone as he placed himself within that of his bedroom.

Fool that he had been, not to think of destroying the manuscript sooner! . . .

How, in a houseful of shadows, should he know his own Shadow? How, in a houseful of noises, distinguish the summons he felt to be at hand? Ah, trust him! He would know! The place was full of a jugglery of dim lights. The blind at his elbow that allowed the light of a street lamp to struggle vaguely through—the glimpse of greeny blue moonlight seen through the distant kitchen door—the sulky glow of the fire under the black ashes of the burnt manuscript—the glimmering of the tulips and the moon-daisies and narcissi in the bowls and jugs and jars—these did not so trick and bewilder his eyes that he would not know his Own! It was he, not she, who had been delaying the shadowy Bridal; he hung his head for a moment in mute acknowledgment; then he bent his eyes on the deceiving, puzzling gloom again. He would have called her name had he known it—but now he would not ask her to share even a name with the other . . . .

His own face, within the frame of the door, glimmered white as the narcissi in the darkness . . . .

A shadow, light as fleece, seemed to take shape in the kitchen (the time had been when Oleron would have said that a cloud had passed over the unseen moon). The low illumination on the blind at his elbow grew dimmer (the time had been when Oleron would have concluded that the lamplighter going his rounds had turned low the flame of the lamp). The fire settled, letting down the black and charred papers; a flower fell from a bowl, and lay indistinct upon the floor; all was still; and then a stray draught moved through the old house, passing before Oleron's face . . . .

Suddenly, inclining his head, he withdrew a little from the doorjamb. The wandering draught caused the door to move a little on its hinges. Oleron trembled violently, stood for a moment longer, and then, putting his hand out to the knob, softly drew the door to, sat down on the nearest chair, and waited, as a man might await the calling of his name that should summon him to some weighty, high and privy Audience . . . .

One knows not whether there can be human compassion for anæmia of the soul. When the pitch of Life is dropped, and the spirit is so put over and reversed that that only is horrible which before was sweet and worldly and of the day, the human relation disappears. The sane soul turns appalled away, lest not merely itself, but sanity should suffer. We are not gods. We cannot drive out devils. We must see selfishly to it that devils do not enter into ourselves.

And this we must do even though Love so transfuse us that we may well deem our nature to be half divine. We shall but speak of honor and duty in vain. The letter dropped within the dark door will lie unregarded, or, if regarded for a brief instant between two unspeakable lapses, left and forgotten again. The telegram will be undelivered, nor will the whistling messenger (wiselier guided than he knows to whistle) be conscious as he walks away of the drawn blind that is pushed aside an inch by a finger and then fearfully replaced again. No: let the miserable wrestle with his own shadows; let him, if indeed he be so mad, clip and strain and enfold and crouch the succubus; but let him do so in a house into which not an air of Heaven penetrates, nor a bright finger of the sun pierces the filthy twilight. The lost must remain lost. Humanity has other business to attend to.

For the handwriting of the two letters that Oleron, stealing noiselessly one June day into his kitchen to rid his sitting room of an armful of fetid and decaying flowers, had seen on the floor within his door, had had no more meaning for him than if it had belonged to some dim and far-away dream. And at the beating of the telegraph-boy upon the door, within a few feet of the bed where he lay, he had gnashed his teeth and stopped his ears. He had pictured the lad standing there, just beyond his partition, among packets of provisions and bundles of dead and dying flowers. For his outer landing was littered with these. Oleron had feared to open his door to take them in. After a week, the errand lads had reported that there must be some mistake about the order, and had left no more. Inside, in the red twilight, the old flowers turned brown and fell and decayed where they lay.

Gradually his power was draining away. The Abominaton fastened on Oleron's power. The steady sapping sometimes left him for many hours of prostration gazing vacantly up at his red-tinged ceiling, idly suffering such fancies as came of themselves to have their way with him. Even the strongest of his memories had no more than a precarious hold upon his attention. Sometimes a flitting half-memory, of a novel to be written, a novel it was important that he should write, tantalized him for a space before vanishing again; and sometimes whole novels, perfect, splendid, established to endure, rose magically before him. And sometimes the memories were absurdly remote and trivial, of garrets he had inhabited and lodgings that had sheltered him, and so forth. Oleron had known a good deal about such things in his time, but all that was now past. He had at last found a place which he did not intend to leave until they fetched him out—a place that some might have thought a little on the green-sick side, that others might have considered to be a little too redolent of long-dead and morbid

things for a living man to be mewed up in, but ah, so irresistible, with
such an authority of its own, with such an associate of its own, and a
place of such delights when once a man had ceased to struggle against
its inexorable will! A novel? Somebody ought to write a novel about a
place like that! There must be lots to write about in a place like that if
one could but get to the bottom of it! It had probably already been
painted, by a man called Madley who had lived there . . . but Oleron
had not known this Madley—had a strong feeling that he wouldn't
have liked him—would rather he had lived somewhere else—really
couldn't stand the fellow—hated him, Madley, in fact. (Aha! That was
a joke!) He seriously doubted whether the man had led the life he
ought; Oleron was in two minds sometimes whether he wouldn't tell
that long-nosed guardian of the public morals across the way about
him; but probably he knew, and had made his praying hullabaloos for
him also. That was his line. Why, Oleron himself had had a dust-up
with him about something or other . . . some girl or other . . . Elsie
Bengough her name was, he remembered . . . .

Oleron had moments of deep uneasiness about this Elsie Bengough.
Or rather, he was not so much uneasy about her as restless about the
things she did. Chief of these was the way in which she persisted in
thrusting herself into his thoughts; and, whenever he was quick
enough, he sent her packing the moment she made her appearance
there. The truth was that she was not merely a bore; she had always
been that; it had now come to the pitch when her very presence in his
fancy was inimical to the full enjoyment of certain experiences . . . . She
had no tact; really ought to have known that people are not at home to
the thoughts of everybody all the time; ought in mere politeness to
have allowed him certain seasons quite to himself; and was monstrously ignorant of things if she did not know, as she appeared not to
know, that there were certain special hours when a man's veins ran
with fire and daring and power, in which . . . well, in which he had a
reasonable right to treat folk as he had treated that prying Barrett—to
shut them out completely . . . . But no, up she popped: the thought of
her, and ruined all. Bright towering fabrics, by the side of which even

those perfect, magical novels of which he dreamed were dun and gray, vanished utterly at her intrusion. It was as if a fog should suddenly quench some fair-beaming star, as if at the threshold of some golden portal prepared for Oleron a pit should suddenly gape, as if a bat-like shadow should turn the growing dawn to murk and darkness again . . . . Therefore, Oleron strove to stifle even the nascent thought of her.

Nevertheless, there came an occasion on which this woman Bengough absolutely refused to be suppressed. Oleron could not have told exactly when this happened; he only knew by the glimmer of the street lamp on his blind that it was some time during the night, and that for some time she had not presented herself.

He had no warning, none, of her coming; she just came—was there. Strive as he would, he could not shake off the thought of her nor the image of her face. She haunted him.

But for her to come at *that* moment of all moments! . . . Really, it was past belief! How *she* could endure it, Oleron could not conceive! Actually, to look on, as it were, at the triumph of a Rival . . . . Good God! It was monstrous! tact—reticence—he had never credited her with an overwhelming amount of either; but he had never attributed mere—oh, there was no word for it! Monstrous—monstrous! Did she intend thenceforward . . . . Good God! To look on! . . .

Oleron felt the blood rush up to the roots of his hair with anger against her.

"Damnation take her!" he choked . . . .

But the next moment his heat and resentment had changed to a cold sweat of cowering fear. Panic-stricken, he strove to comprehend what he had done. For though he knew not what, he knew he had done something, something fatal, irreparable, blasting. Anger he had felt, but not *this* blaze of ire that suddenly flooded the twilight of his consciousness with a white infernal light. *That* appalling flash was not his—not his *that* open rift of bright and searing Hell—not his, not his! His had been the hand of a child, preparing a puny blow; but what was *this other* horrific hand that was drawn back to strike in the same place? Had *he* set that in motion? Had *he* provided the spark that had touched off the whole accumulated power of that formidable and relentless place? He did not know. He only knew that that poor igniting particle in himself was blown out, that——Oh, impossible!—a clinging kiss (how else to express it?) had changed on his very lips to a gnashing and a removal, and that for very pity of the awful odds he must cry out to her against whom he had lately ranged to guard herself . . . guard herself . . . .

"Look out!" he shrieked aloud . . . .

The revulsion was instant. As if a cold slow billow had broken over him, he came to find that he was lying in his bed, that the mist and horror that had for so long enwrapped him had departed, that he was Paul Oleron, and that he was sick, naked, helpless, and unutterably abandoned and alone. His faculties, though weak, answered at last to his calls upon them; and he knew that it must have been a hideous nightmare that had left him sweating and shaking thus.

Yes, he was himself, Paul Oleron, a tired novelist, already past the summit of his best work, and slipping downhill again empty-handed from it all. He had struck short in his life's aim. He had tried too much, had overestimated his strength, and was a failure, a failure . . . .

It all came to him in the single word, enwrapped and complete; it needed no sequential thought; he was a failure. He had missed . . . .

And he had missed not one happiness, but two. He had missed the ease of this world, which men love, and he had missed also that other shining prize for which men forego ease, the snatching and holding and triumphant bearing up aloft of which is the only justification of the mad adventurer who hazards the enterprise. And there was no second attempt. Fate has no morrow. Oleron's morrow must be to sit down to profitless, ill-done, unrequired work again, and so on the morrow after that, and the morrow after that, and as many morrows as there might be . . . .

He lay there, weakly yet sanely considering it . . . .

And since the whole attempt had failed, it was hardly worth while to consider whether a little might not be saved from the general wreck. No good would ever come out of that half-finished novel. He had intended that it should appear in the autumn; was under contract that it should appear; no matter; it was better to pay forfeit to his publishers than to waste what days were left. He was spent; age was not far off; and paths of wisdom and sadness were the properest for the remainder of the journey . . . .

If only he had chosen the wife, the child, the faithful friend at the fireside, and let them follow an *ignis fatuus* that list! . . .

In the meantime it began to puzzle him exceedingly why he should be so weak, that his room should smell so overpoweringly of decaying vegetable matter, and that his hand, chancing to tray to his face in the darkness, should encounter a beard.

"Most extraordinary!" he began to mutter to himself. "Have I been ill? Am I ill now? And if so, why have they left me alone? . . . Extraordinary! . . ."

He thought he heard a sound from the kitchen or bathroom. He rose a little on his pillow, and listened . . . . Ah! He was not alone, then! It certainly would have been extraordinary if they had left him ill and alone——Alone? Oh, no. He would be looked after. He wouldn't be left, ill, to shift for himself. If everybody else had forsaken him, he could trust Elsie Bengough, the dearest chum he had, for that . . . bless her faithful heart!

But suddenly a short, stifled, spluttering cry rang sharply out:

"*Paul!*"

It came from the kitchen.

And in the same moment it flashed upon Oleron, he knew not how, that two, three, five, he knew not how many minutes before, another sound, unmarked at the time, but suddenly transfixing his attention now, had striven to reach his intelligence. This sound had been the slight touch of metal on metal—just such a sound as Oleron made when he put his key into the lock.

"Hallo! . . . Who's that?" he called sharply from his bed.

He had no answer.

He called again. "Hallo! . . . Who's there? . . . Who is it?"

This time he was sure he heard noises, soft and heavy, in the kitchen.

"This is a queer thing altogether," he muttered. "By Jove, I'm as weak as a kitten, too . . . . Hallo, there! Somebody called, didn't they? . . . Elsie! Is that you? . . ."

Then he began to knock with his hand on the wall at the side of his bed.

"Elsie! . . . Elsie! . . . You called, didn't you? . . . Please come here, whoever it is! . . ."

There was a sound as of a closing door, and then silence. Oleron began to get rather alarmed.

"It may be a nurse," he muttered: "Elsie'd have to get me a nurse, of course. She'd sit with me as long as she could spare the time, brave lass, and she'd get a nurse for the rest . . . . But it was awfully like her voice . . . . Elsie, or whoever it is! . . . I can't make this out at all. I must go and see what's the matter . . . ."

He put one leg out of bed. Feeling its feebleness, he reached with his hand for the additional support of the wall . . . .

But before putting out the other leg he stopped and considered, picking at his new-found beard. He was suddenly wondering whether he *dared* go into the kitchen. It was such a frightfully long way; no man knew what horror might not leap and huddle on his shoulders if he went so far; when a man has an overmastering impulse to get back into bed he ought to take heed of the warning and obey it. Besides, why should he go? What was there to go for? If it was that Bengough creature again, let her look after herself; Oleron was not going to have things cramp themselves on his defenseless back for the sake of such a spoil-sport as *she*! . . . If she was in, let her let herself out again, and the sooner the better for her! Oleron simply couldn't be bothered. He had his work to do. On the morrow, he must set about the writing of a novel with a heroine so winsome, capricious, adorable, jealous, wicked, beautiful, inflaming, and altogether evil, that men should stand amazed. She was coming over him now; he knew by the alteration of the very air of the room when she was near him; and that soft thrill of bliss that had begun to stir in him never came unless she was beckoning, beckoning . . . .

He let go the wall and fell back into bed again as—oh, unthinkable!—the other half of that kiss that a gnash had interrupted was placed (how else convey it?) on his lips, robbing him of very breath . . . .

In the bright June sunlight a crowd filled the square, and looked up at the windows of the old house with the antique insurance marks on its walls of red brick and the agents' notice-boards hanging like wooden choppers over the paling. Two constables stood at the broken gate of the narrow entrance alley, keeping folk back. The women kept to the outskirts of the throng, moving now and then as if to see the drawn red blinds of the old house from a new angle, and talking in whispers. The children were in the houses, behind closed doors.

A long-nosed man had a little group about him, and he was telling some story over and over again; and another man, little and fat and wide-eyed, sought to capture the long-nosed man's audience with some relation in which a key figured.

". . . and it was revealed to me that there'd been something that very afternoon," the long-nosed man was saying. "I was standing there, where Constable Saunders is—or rather, I was passing about my business, when they came out. There was no deceiving me, oh, no deceiving *me*! I saw her face . . . .

"What was it like, Mr. Barrett?" a man asked.

"It was like hers whom our Lord said to, 'Woman, doth any man accuse thee?'—white as paper, and no mistake! Don't tell *me*! . . . And so I walks straight across to Mrs. Barrett, and 'Jane,' I says, 'this must stop, and stop at once; we are commanded to avoid evil,' I says, 'and it must come to an end now; let him get help elsewhere.' And she says to me, 'John,' she says, 'it's four-and-sixpence a week'—them was her words. 'Jane,' I says, 'if it was forty-six thousand pounds it should stop' . . . and from that day to this she hasn't set foot inside that gate." There was a short silence: then:

"Did Mrs. Barrett ever . . . *see* anything, like?" somebody vaguely inquired.

Barrett turned austerely on the speaker.

"What Mrs. Barrett saw and Mrs. Barrett didn't see shall not pass these lips; even as it is written, keep thy tongue from speaking evil," he said.

Another man spoke.

"He was pretty near canned up in the *Wagon and Horses* that night, weren't he, Jim?

"Yes, 'e 'adn't 'alf copped it . . ."

"Not standing treat much, neither; he was in the bar, all on his own . . . ."

"So 'e was; we talked about it . . ."

The fat, scared-eyed man made another attempt.

"She got the key off of me—she 'ad the number of it—she came into my shop of a Tuesday evening . . . ."

Nobody heeded him.

"Shut your heads," a heavy laborer commented gruffly, "she hasn't been found yet. 'Ere's the inspectors; we shall know more in a bit."

Two inspectors had come up and were talking to the constables who guarded the gate. The little fat man ran eagerly forward, saying that she had bought the key of him. "I remember the number, because of its being three ones and three threes—111333!" he exclaimed excitedly.

An inspector put him aside.

"Nobody's been in?" he asked of one of the constables.

"No, sir."

"Then you, Brackley, come with us; you, Smith, keep the gate. There's a squad on its way."

The two inspectors and the constable passed down the alley and entered the house. They mounted the wide carved staircase.

"This don't look as if he'd been out much lately," one of the inspectors muttered as he kicked aside a litter of dead leaves and paper that lay outside Oleron's door. "I don't think we need knock—break a pane, Brackley."

The door had two glazed panels; there was a sound of shattered glass; and Brackley put his hand through the hole his elbow had made and drew back the latch.

"Faugh!" . . . choked one of the inspectors as they entered. "Let some light and air in, quick. It stinks like a hearse——"

The assembly out in the square saw the red blinds go up and the windows of the old house flung open.

"That's better," said one of the inspectors, putting his head out of a window and drawing a deep breath . . . . "That seems to be the bedroom in there; will you go in, Simms, while I go over the rest? . . ."

They had drawn up the bedroom blind also, and the waxy-white, emaciated man on the bed had made a blinker of his hand against the torturing flood of brightness. Nor could he believe that his hearing was not playing tricks with him, for there were two policemen in his room, bending over him and asking where "she" was. He shook his head.

"This woman Bengough . . . goes by the name of Miss Elsie Bengough . . . d'ye hear? Where is she? . . . No good, Brackley; get him up; be careful with him; I'll just shove *my* head out of the window, I think . . . ."

The other inspector had been through Oleron's study and had found nothing, and was now in the kitchen, kicking aside an ankle-deep mass of vegetable refuse that cumbered the floor. The kitchen window had no blind, and was overshadowed by the blank end of the house across the alley. The kitchen appeared to be empty.

But the inspector, kicking aside the dead flowers, noticed that a shuffling track that was not of his making had been swept to a cupboard in the corner. In the upper part of the door of the cupboard was a square panel that looked as if it slid on runners. The door itself was closed.

The inspector advanced, put out his hand to the little knob, and slid the hatch along its groove.

Then he took an involuntary step back again.

Framed in the aperture, and falling forward a little before it jammed again in its frame, was something that resembled a large lumpy pudding, done up in a pudding-bag of faded browny red frieze.

"Ah!" said the inspector.

To close the hatch again he would have had to thrust that pudding back with his hand; and somehow he did not quite like the idea of touching it. Instead, he turned the handle of the cupboard itself. There was weight behind it, so much weight that, after opening the door three or four inches and peering inside, he had to put his shoulder to it in order to close it again. In closing it he left sticking out, a few inches from the floor, a triangle of black and white check skirt.

He went into the small hall.

"All right!" he called.

They had got Oleron into his clothes. He still used his hands as blinkers, and his brain was very confused. A number of things were happening that he couldn't understand. He couldn't understand the extraordinary mess of dead flowers there seemed to be everywhere; he couldn't understand why there should be police officers in his room; he couldn't understand why one of these should be sent for a four-wheeler and a stretcher; and he couldn't understand what heavy article they seemed to be moving about in the kitchen—his kitchen. . . .

"What's the matter?" he muttered sleepily . . . .

Then he heard a murmur in the square, and the stopping of a four-wheeler outside. A police officer was at his elbow again, and Oleron wondered why, when he whispered something to him, he should run off a string of words—something about "used in evidence against you." They had lifted him to his feet, and were assisting him towards the door . . . .

No, Oleron couldn't understand it at all,

They got him down the stairs and along the alley. Oleron was aware of confused angry shoutings; he gathered that a number of people wanted to lynch somebody or other. Then his attention became fixed on a little fat frightened-eyed man who appeared to be making a statement that an officer was taking down in a notebook.

"I'd seen her with him . . . they was often together . . . she came into my shop and said it was for him . . . I thought it was all right . . . 111333 the number was," the man was saying.

The people seemed to be very angry; many police were keeping them back; but one of the inspectors had a voice that Oleron thought quite kind and friendly. He was telling somebody to get somebody else into the cab before something or other was brought out; and Oleron noticed that a four-wheeler was drawn up at the gate. It appeared that it was himself who was to be put into it; and as they lifted him up he saw that the inspector tried to stand between him and something that stood behind the cab, but was not quick enough to prevent Oleron seeing that this something was a hooded stretcher. The angry voices sounded like a sea, something hard, like a stone, hit the back of the cab; and the inspector followed Oleron in and stood with his back to the window nearer the side where the people were. The door they had put Oleron in at remained open, apparently till the other inspector should come; and through the opening Oleron had a glimpse of the hatchet-like "To Let" boards among the privet-trees. One of them said that the key was at Number Six. . . .

Suddenly the raging of voices was hushed. Along the entrance alley shuffling steps were heard, and the other inspector appeared at the cab door.

"Right away," he said to the driver.

He entered, fastened the door after him, and blocked up the second window with his back. Between the two inspectors Oleron slept peacefully. The cab moved down the square, the other vehicle went up the hill. The mortuary lay that way.

They

by Blue Balliett

Blue Balliett (born 1955) has collected dozens of first-hand accounts of encounters with ghosts on the island of Nantucket. She does not adorn these accounts with speculation or hyperbole, which helps to account for their power. Stories like this one do not prove that ghosts exist on Nantucket or anywhere else—but they feel true enough to disconcert the average skeptic.

I was twenty-one when Mrs. Deauville hired me. I cleaned her house for one full season, from early May to late September, and then I quit. I couldn't stand it any more. I was really frightened.

"I was born on Nantucket, and I'm one of those people who's sensitive to anything strange lingering in an old house. I know the moment I walk in the door. As a child, I lived with a visible ghost in a house on the east end of the island, and so the whole idea of spirits has never seemed that odd. I don't welcome that kind of experience, but it has a way of happening to me.

"Mrs. Deauville hired me to clean every week, whether she was there or not. Most of the time the house was empty while I was working. Sometimes she had guests for the weekend, so I'd prepare the house for them and then clean up after they were gone. But she is a meticulous sort of person, and she wanted me to go around and dust and vacuum even if no one had been in the house since the last time I was there.

"On my first day at work, I brought my dog with me. He hopped out of the truck, ran up to the front door, and then wouldn't set foot inside. In all the time I worked there, he would always wait for me in the truck. I tried coaxing him in the front door, and then I tried the back; it was as if there were an invisible line that he wouldn't cross. I couldn't pull him, push him, or carry him inside. He's never done that at any other house.

"When I first stepped in the front door, I remember feeling the hair go up on the back of my neck. I thought to myself, Oh, no. Here we go. There's something here.

"At first they started by doing insignificant, annoying things. They? Yes, I guess I always thought of the source of these goings-on as 'they.' It felt like a group of presences in the house; it never seemed, at least to me, like a single spirit. At any rate, I'd be cleaning, and I'd hear the bleeping signal a phone makes when it's been taken off the hook. I'd put down my dust rag and go downstairs to find that the telephone receiver had been lifted off and laid on its side on the table. I'd hang it back up. Okay, I'd say to myself, I can deal with it.

"I'd be vacuuming, and sometimes I'd hear talking and laughter, the sound of a group of people. I'd shut off the vacuum, and the house would be dead quiet. I'd turn it on, and the voices would start up again. It wasn't an irregular sound in the vacuum motor or anything like that, it was definitely the sound of people conversing, the low and high tones of men and women talking.

"After a few weeks the level of activity began to pick up. I'd be upstairs, and I'd hear furniture being dragged across the floor downstairs. I'd gallop down the stairs and find that a chair had been pulled to the other side of the room or a table dragged into the middle of the floor. I'd say something like, 'Look, I know you don't like me being here, but can you please put up with me for a little while longer? I'm just trying to do my job.' Now, these disturbances only occurred when I was in the house alone, when Mrs. Deauville and her family and guests were nowhere near the place.

"Things got worse. I'd hear the sofa or a sea chest, something really big and heavy, scraping across the floor in the living room, and so I'd hurry down. At first I really wanted to catch them, to see who was doing it and whose voices I was hearing. I wanted, at least, to actually see the furniture being moved. I'd get downstairs, and I'd hear the muffled *thwack! whump!* sound of scatter rugs from upstairs being thrown over the railing behind me. I never did witness these things being done; I'd hear it happening in another part of the house, and find, when I got there, that the objects *had* been moved, but when I arrived at the scene everything was always as still as could be. At that point it was more irritating than frightening; I was trying to straighten out and clean, and they were messing things up as fast as I was putting them in order.

"The house would be worse on some days than on others. I figured I could put up with it as long as it was just silly, bothersome stuff. And I began talking to them the instant they acted up. 'Now stop!' I'd say. 'You're making things awfully difficult for me. This is something I'm being paid to do, you know, and I need to get this done.' It didn't seem to do much good, but it made *me* feel better.

"One day I went up to the attic, where I'd been cleaning the previous week, and found a really lovely picture right smack in the middle of the floor. It had most definitely not been there before. It was an old photograph of a little girl. She was all dressed up in what looked like her Sunday best. She had long hair in ringlets, a big bow, high ankle shoes that buttoned up the side, and a lovely frilly dress. The picture was in a gorgeous mahogany frame. I'd say it dated back to the early 1900s, maybe the late 1800s.

"I picked up the picture and wondered who the little girl was. I put it on top of one of the boxes in the corner of the attic. I remembered Mrs. Deauville telling me that the house had had quite a bit of family stuff in it when she bought it. She had liked the old furniture and kept most of it around, putting away in the attic the things she didn't care for.

"The next time I came to clean, the picture of the little girl was downstairs on the telephone table. The house had been empty all week. This happened four or five times; I found the picture in the dining room and then in the bedroom. *They* obviously wanted me to see they had moved it.

"When I saw Mrs. Deauville, I mentioned the photograph, just asking her if she knew who the little girl was. She didn't know what I was talking about. I described it in detail. She gave me a strange look, for apparently she had never even seen the photograph. It disappeared shortly after that, again during a week when the house was empty, and I never ran across it again.

"I didn't tell Mrs. Deauville about my crazier experiences in the house; I didn't feel it was my place to tell her that stuff unless she brought it up. And she never did.

"I'd feel more comfortable in some areas of the house than in others. Certain rooms just seemed to have specific things attached to them. When I was in the downstairs bedroom, I sometimes heard the sound of a horse and carriage coming up the driveway, clear as could be. I think the driveway may have been paving stones at one time, because I'd hear the horses' hoofs, the sounds of their harness creaking and clinking, the grinding of wheels rolling over rock. I'd look out the window as soon as I heard the carriage, but I never saw a thing.

"That downstairs room had a very old-looking mahogany bed. It was short and narrow; perhaps it was a child's bed. It had been in the house when she bought it, Mrs. Deauville told me, and she seemed to feel it was quite valuable. I remember she told me to take special care of it.

"One day I was vacuuming under that bed, and something grabbed the end of my vacuum hose *and held onto it.* I pulled hard, and then the end of the vacuum, the attachment, came right off. It wasn't stuck on anything; I had only been running the vacuum over the bare floorboards. And when I had pulled, it felt like someone was holding on to the other end—you know, there was a slight give to it. When I finally got up my courage to peek under that bed, it all looked as quiet and normal as could be. There was nothing the vacuum could've gotten stuck on, no exposed springs or fabric or anything. It was a good bit later before I dared to reach under there and get the attachment.

"My husband fixed some plumbing in the house, and he noticed a funny thing. He'd take the hoses off the back of the washing machine, during the time it wasn't in use, and put them in the sink. They'd be thrown right out of the sink and onto the floor. This happened over and over. He also felt that same back-of-the-neck prickly sensation I had in the house, and he felt the cold spots. You could walk right into freezing cold areas in any given room; the change in temperature was hard to ignore.

"I mowed the lawn for Mrs. Deauville during the summer. I used a hand mower, and it took quite a long time because there's a good big field out behind the house. I always knew that I was being watched from one of the windows, watched by somebody inside the house. I could *feel* it. I'd glance up quickly, really expecting to see a face, but I only saw the flat, blank reflection of daylight on glass.

"It was when I started going in twice a week, for shorter periods of time, that it got really bad. I had thought it might be easier to stop in and do three hours at a time instead of staying for a full six.

"It got so that I would unlock the front door and get the strangest feeling. I felt as though the house was *too* quiet when I stepped inside; it seemed like the place was full of people holding their breath. I got the impression that all sorts of things had been going on and that when I opened the door everyone fell silent.

"Trying to jolly myself out of the feeling, I'd say, 'Hello! I'm here! I'll be as quick as I can!' I didn't have much success.

"Things began to get nasty. The furniture-moving started happening behind my back every ten or twenty minutes. When I was upstairs, I'd hear it happening downstairs, and when I was downstairs I'd hear it happening up. All kinds of things scraped and bumped along over the floor. Objects were never carried, they were always dragged. I remember I ran downstairs once, after an especially noisy session, and found all of the chairs arranged in a tight little circle in the middle of the living room. Another time, while I was in the kitchen, all of the chairs in the outer room were piled up against the back of the kitchen door. Of course I tripped over the chairs and knocked them all over in trying to get out. It was almost like naughty children, but it was also premeditated, deliberate-feeling, and increasingly sinister. Something in the house was trying to get rid of me.

"One day pictures started coming down off the walls. A stack of dishes was moved with a noisy clatter in the kitchen. A rug flew through the air and hit me in the back, and I got whacked by some sofa pillows that zipped half-way across the room on their own. Finally a chair was thrown at me. It missed me and I wasn't hurt, but that did it. I was afraid, really afraid I was going to get injured. My husband urged me to quit, and I did. It was such a relief. They wanted me out of there, and, Lord knows, I was happy to go."

The Crown Derby Plate
by Marjorie Bowen

Marjorie Bowen (1886–1952) knew unhappiness firsthand. She was born Gabrielle Margaret Vere Long, to a depressed and abusive mother and an alcoholic father. Bowen grew up to be a prolific writer of—no surprise—rather dark fiction. Her best work includes this story.

Martha Pym said that she had never seen a ghost and that she would very much like to do so, "particularly at Christmas, for you can laugh as you like, that is the correct time to see a ghost."

"I don't suppose you ever will," replied her cousin Mabel comfortably, while her cousin Clara shuddered and said that she hoped they would change the subject for she disliked even to think of such things.

The three elderly, cheerful women sat round a big fire, cozy and content after a day of pleasant activities; Martha was the guest of the other two, who owned the handsome, convenient country house; she always came to spend her Christmas with the Wyntons and found the leisurely country life delightful after the bustling round of London, for Martha managed an antique shop of the better sort and worked extremely hard. She was, however, still full of zest for work or pleasure, though sixty years old, and looked backwards and forwards to a succession of delightful days.

The other two, Mabel and Clara, led quieter but nonetheless agreeable lives; they had more money and fewer interests, but nevertheless enjoyed themselves very well.

"Talking of ghosts," said Mabel, "I wonder how that old woman at 'Hartleys' is getting on, for 'Hartleys,' you know, is supposed to be haunted."

"Yes, I know," smiled Miss Pym, "but all the years that we have known of the place we have never heard anything definite, have we?"

"No," put in Clara, "but there *is* that persistent rumor that the house is uncanny, and for myself, *nothing* would induce me to live there!"

"It is certainly very lonely and dreary down there on the marshes," conceded Mabel. "But as for the ghost—you never hear *what* it is supposed to be even."

"Who has taken it?" asked Miss Pym, remembering "Hartleys" as very desolate indeed, and long shut up.

"A Miss Lefain, an eccentric old creature—I think you met her here once, two years ago—"

"I believe that I did, but I don't recall her at all."

"We have not seen her since, 'Hartleys' is so un-get-at-able and she didn't seem to want visitors. She collects china, Martha, so really you ought to go and see her and talk 'shop.'"

With the word "china" some curious associations came into the mind of Martha Pym; she was silent while she strove to put them together, and after a second or two they all fitted together into a very clear picture.

She remembered that thirty years ago—yes, it must be thirty years ago, when, as a young woman, she had put all her capital into the antique business, and had been staying with her cousins (her aunt had then been alive) that she had driven across the marsh to "Hartleys," where there was an auction sale; all the details of this she had completely forgotten, but she could recall quite clearly purchasing a set of gorgeous china which was still one of her proud delights, a perfect set of Crown Derby save that one plate was missing.

"How odd," she remarked, "that this Miss Lefain should collect china too, for it was at 'Hartleys' that I purchased my dear old Derby service—I've never been able to match that plate—"

"A plate was missing? I seem to remember," said Clara. "Didn't they say that it must be in the house somewhere and that it should be looked for?"

"I believe they did, but of course I never heard any more and that missing plate has annoyed me ever since. Who had 'Hartleys'?"

"An old connoisseur, Sir James Sewell; I believe he was some relation to this Miss Lefain, but I don't know—"

"I wonder if she has found the plate," mused Miss Pym. "I expect she has turned out and ransacked the whole place—"

"Why not trot over and ask?" suggested Mabel. "It's not much use to her, if she has found it, one odd plate."

"Don't be silly," said Clara. "Fancy going over the marshes, this weather, to ask about a plate missed all those years ago. I'm sure Martha wouldn't think of it—"

But Martha did think of it; she was rather fascinated by the idea; how queer and pleasant it would be if, after all these years, nearly a lifetime, she should find the Crown Derby plate, the loss of which had always irked her! And this hope did not seem so altogether fantastical, it was quite likely that old Miss Lefain, poking about in the ancient house, had found the missing piece.

And, of course, if she had, being a fellow-collector, she would be quite willing to part with it to complete the set.

Her cousin endeavored to dissuade her; Miss Lefain, she declared, was a recluse, an odd creature who might greatly resent such a visit and such a request.

"Well, if she does I can but come away again," smiled Miss Pym. "I suppose she can't bite my head off, and I rather like meeting these curious types—we've got a love for old china in common, anyhow."

"It seems so silly to think of it—after all these years—a plate!"

"A Crown Derby plate," corrected Miss Pym. "It is certainly strange that I didn't think of it before, but now that I have got it into my head I can't get it out. Besides," she added hopefully, "I might see the ghost."

So full, however, were the days with pleasant local engagements that Miss Pym had no immediate chance of putting her scheme into practice; but she did not relinquish it, and she asked several different people what they knew about "Hartleys" and Miss Lefain.

And no one knew anything save that the house was supposed to be haunted and the owner "cracky."

"Is there a story?" asked Miss Pym, who associated ghosts with neat tales into which they fitted as exactly as nuts into shells.

But she was always told: "Oh, no, there isn't a story, no one knows anything about the place, don't know how the idea got about; old Sewell was half-crazy, I believe, he was buried in the garden and that gives a house a nasty name—"

"Very unpleasant," said Martha Pym, undisturbed.

This ghost seemed too elusive for her to track down; she would have to be content if she could recover the Crown Derby plate; for that at least she was determined to make a try and also to satisfy that faint tingling of curiosity roused in her by this talk about "Hartleys" and the remembrance of that day, so long ago, when she had gone to the auction sale at the lonely old house.

So the first free afternoon, while Mabel and Clara were comfortably taking their afternoon repose, Martha Pym, who was of a more lively habit, got out her little governess cart and dashed away across the Essex flats.

She had taken minute directions with her, but she had soon lost her way.

Under the wintry sky, which looked as gray and hard as metal, the marshes stretched bleakly to the horizon, the olive-brown broken reeds were harsh as scars on the saffron-tinted bogs, where the sluggish waters that rose so high in winter were filmed over with the first stillness of a frost; the air was cold but not keen, everything was damp; faintest of mists bluffed the black outlines of trees that rose stark from the ridges above the stagnant dykes; the flooded fields were haunted by black birds and white birds, gulls and crows, whining above the long ditch grass and wintry wastes.

Miss Pym stopped the little horse and surveyed this spectral scene, which had a certain relish about it to one sure to return to a homely village, a cheerful house and good company.

A withered and bleached old man, in color like the dun landscape, came along the road between the sparse alders.

Miss Pym, buttoning up her coat, asked the way to "Hartley," as he passed her; he told her, straight on, and she proceeded, straight indeed across the road that went with undeviating length across the marshes.

"Of course," thought Miss Pym, "if you live in a place like this, you are bound to invent ghosts."

The house sprang up suddenly on a knoll ringed with rotting trees, encompassed by an old brick wall that the perpetual damp had overrun with lichen, blue, green, white colors of decay.

"Hartleys," no doubt, there was no other residence of human being in sight in all the wide expanse; besides, she could remember it, surely, after all this time, the sharp rising out of the marsh, the colony of tall trees, but then fields and trees had been green and bright—there had been no water on the flats, it had been summertime.

"She certainly," thought Miss Pym, "must be crazy to live here. And I rather doubt if I shall get my plate."

She fastened up the good little horse by the garden gate which stood negligently ajar and entered; the garden itself was so neglected that it was quite surprising to see a trim appearance in the house, curtains at the window and a polish on the brass door knocker, which must have been recently rubbed there, considering the taint in the sea damp which rusted and rotted everything.

It was a square-built, substantial house with "nothing wrong with it but the situation," Miss Pym decided, though it was not very attractive, being built of that drab plastered stone so popular a hundred years ago, with flat windows and door, while one side was gloomily shaded by a large evergreen tree of the cypress variety which gave a blackish tinge to that portion of the garden.

There was no pretense at flowerbeds nor any manner of cultivation in this garden where a few rank weeds and straggling bushes matted together above the dead grass; on the enclosing wall which appeared to have been built high as protection against the ceaseless winds that swung along the flats were the remains of fruit trees; their crucified branches, rotting under the great nails that held them up, looked like the skeletons of those who had died in torment.

Miss Pym took in these noxious details as she knocked firmly at the door, they did not depress her; she merely felt extremely sorry for anyone who could live in such a place.

She noticed, at the far end of the garden, in the corner of the wall, a headstone showing above the sodden colorless grass, and remembered what she had been told about the old antiquary being buried there, in the grounds of "Hartleys."

As the knock had no effect she stepped back and looked at the house; it was certainly inhabited—with those neat windows, white curtains and drab blinds all pulled to precisely the same level.

And when she brought her glance back to the door she saw that it had been opened and that someone, considerably obscured by the darkness of the passage, was looking at her intently.

"Good afternoon," said Miss Pym cheerfully. "I just thought that I would call to see Miss Lefain—it is Miss Lefain, isn't it?"

"It's my house," was the querulous reply.

Martha Pym had hardly expected to find any servants here, though the old lady must, she thought, work pretty hard to keep the house so clean and tidy as it appeared to be.

"Of course," she replied. "May I come in? I'm Martha Pym, staying with the Wyntons, I met you there—"

"Do come in," was the faint reply. "I get so few people to visit me, I'm really very lonely."

"I don't wonder," thought Miss Pym; but she had resolved to take no notice of any eccentricity on the part of her hostess, and so she entered the house with her usual agreeable candor and courtesy.

The passage was badly lit, but she was able to get a fair idea of Miss Lefain; her first impression was that this poor creature was most dreadfully old, older than any human being had the right to be, why, she felt young in comparison—so faded, feeble, and pallid was Miss Lefain.

She was also monstrously fat; her gross, flaccid figure was shapeless and she wore a badly cut, full dress of no color at all, but stained with earth and damp where Miss Pym supposed she had been doing futile gardening; this gown was doubtless designed to disguise her stoutness, but had been so carelessly pulled about that it only added to it, being rucked and rolled "all over the place" as Miss Pym put it to herself.

Another ridiculous touch about the appearance of the poor old lady was her short hair; decrepit as she was, and lonely as she lived she had actually had her scanty relics of white hair cropped round her shaking head.

"Dear me, dear me," she said in her thin treble voice. "How very kind of you to come. I suppose you prefer the parlor? I generally sit in the garden."

"The garden? But not in this weather?"

"I get used to the weather. You've no idea how used one gets to the weather."

"I suppose so," conceded Miss Pym doubtfully. "You don't live here quite alone, do you?"

"Quite alone, lately. I had a little company, but she was taken away, I'm sure I don't know where. I haven't been able to find a trace of her anywhere," replied the old lady peevishly.

"Some wretched companion that couldn't stick it, I suppose," thought Miss Pym. "Well, I don't wonder—but someone ought to be here to look after her."

They went into the parlor, which, the visitor was dismayed to see, was without a fire but otherwise well kept.

And there, on dozens of shelves was a choice array of china at which Martha Pym's eyes glistened.

"Aha!" cried Miss Lefain. "I see you've noticed my treasures! Don't you envy me? Don't you wish that you had some of those pieces?"

Martha Pym certainly did and she looked eagerly and greedily round the walls, tables, and cabinets while the old woman followed her with little thin squeals of pleasure.

It was a beautiful little collection, most choicely and elegantly arranged, and Martha thought it marvelous that this feeble ancient creature should be able to keep it in such precise order as well as doing her own housework.

"Do you really do everything yourself here and live quite alone?" she asked, and she shivered even in her thick coat and wished that Miss Lefain's energy had risen to a fire, but then probably she lived in the kitchen, as these lonely eccentrics often did.

"There was someone," answered Miss Lefain cunningly, "but I had to send her away. I told you she's gone, I can't find her, and I am so glad. Of course," she added wistfully, "it leaves me very lonely, but then I couldn't stand her impertinence any longer. She used to say that it was *her* house and her collection of china! Would you believe it? She used to try to chase me away from looking at my own things!"

"How very disagreeable," said Miss Pym, wondering which of the two women had been crazy. "But hadn't you better get someone else."

"Oh, no," was the jealous answer. "I would rather be alone with my things, I daren't leave the house for fear someone takes them away—there was a dreadful time once when an auction sale was held here—"

"Were you here then?" asked Miss Pym; but indeed she looked old enough to have been anywhere.

"Yes, of course," Miss Lefain replied rather peevishly and Miss Pym decided that she must be a relation of old Sir James Sewell. Clara and Mabel had been very foggy about it all. "I was very busy hiding all the china—but one set they got—a Crown Derby tea service—"

"With one plate missing!" cried Martha Pym. "I bought it, and do you know, I was wondering if you'd found it—"

"I hid it," piped Miss Lefain.

"Oh, you did, did you? Well, that's rather funny behavior. Why did you hide the stuff away instead of buying it?"

"How could I buy what was mine?"

"Old Sir James left it to you, then?" asked Martha Pym, feeling very muddled.

"*She* bought a lot more," squeaked Miss Lefain, but Martha Pym tried to keep her to the point.

"If you've got the plate," she insisted, "you might let me have it—I'll pay quite handsomely, it would be so pleasant to have it after all these years."

"Money is no use to me," said Miss Lefain mournfully. "Not a bit of use. I can't leave the house or the garden."

"Well, you have to live, I suppose," replied Martha Pym cheerfully. "And, do you know, I'm afraid you are getting rather morbid and dull, living here all alone—you really ought to have a fire—why, it's just on Christmas and very damp."

"I haven't felt the cold for a long time," replied the other; she seated herself with a sigh on one of the horsehair chairs and Miss Pym noticed with a start that her feet were covered only by a pair of white stockings; "one of those nasty health fiends," thought Miss Pym, "but she doesn't look too well for an that."

"So you don't think that you could let me have the plate?" she asked briskly, walking up and down, for the dark, neat, clean parlor was very cold indeed, and she thought that she couldn't stand this much longer; as there seemed no sign of tea or anything pleasant and comfortable she had really better go.

"I might let you have it," sighed Miss Lefain, "since you've been so kind as to pay me a visit. After all, one plate isn't much use, is it?"

"Of course not, I wonder you troubled to hide it—"

"I couldn't *bear*," wailed the other, "to see the things going out of the house!"

Martha Pym couldn't stop to go into all this; it was quite clear that the old lady was very eccentric indeed and that nothing very much could be done with her; no wonder that she had "dropped out" of everything and that no one ever saw her or knew anything about her, though Miss Pym felt that some effort ought really to be made to save her from herself.

"Wouldn't you like a run in my little governess cart?" she suggested. "We might go to tea with the Wyntons on the way back, they'd be delighted to see you, and I really think that you do want taking out of yourself."

"I was taken out of myself some time ago," replied Miss Lefain. "I really was, and I couldn't leave my things—though," she added with pathetic gratitude, "it is very, very kind of you—"

"Your things would be quite safe, I'm sure," said Martha Pym, humoring her. "Who ever would come up here, this hour of a winter's day?"

"They do, oh, they do! And *she* might come back, prying and nosing and saying that it was all hers, all my beautiful china, hers!"

Miss Lefain squealed in her agitation and rising up, ran round the wall fingering with flaccid yellow hands the brilliant glossy pieces on the shelves.

"Well, then, I'm afraid that I must go, they'll be expecting me, and it's quite a long ride; perhaps some other time you'll come and see us?"

"Oh, must you go?" quavered Miss Lefain dolefully. "I do like a little company now and then and I trusted you from the first—the others, when they do come, are always after my things and I have to frighten them away!"

"Frighten them away!" replied Martha Pym. "However do you do that?"

"It doesn't seem difficult, people are so easily frightened, aren't they?"

Miss Pym suddenly remembered that "Hartleys" had the reputation of being haunted—perhaps the queer old thing played on that; the lonely house with the grave in the garden was dreary enough around which to create a legend.

"I suppose you've never seen a ghost?" she asked pleasantly. "I'd rather like to see one, you know—"

"There is no one here but myself," said Miss Lefain.

"So you've never seen anything? I thought it must be all nonsense. Still, I do think it rather melancholy for you to live here all alone—"

Miss Lefain sighed:

"Yes, it's very lonely. Do stay and talk to me a little longer." Her whistling voice dropped cunningly. "And I'll give you the Crown Derby plate!"

"Are you sure you've really got it?" Miss Pym asked.

"I'll show you."

Fat and waddling as she was, she seemed to move very lightly as she slipped in front of Miss Pym and conducted her from the room, going slowly up the stairs—such a gross odd figure in that clumsy dress with the fringe of white hair hanging on to her shoulders.

The upstairs of the house was as neat as the parlor, everything well in its place, but there was no sign of occupancy; the beds were covered with dust sheets, there were no lamps or fires set ready. "I suppose," said Miss Pym to herself, "she doesn't care to show me where she really lives."

But as they passed from one room to another, she could not help saying:

"Where *do* you live, Miss Lefain?"

"Mostly in the garden," said the other.

Miss Pym thought of those horrible health huts that some people indulged in.

"Well, sooner you than I," she replied cheerfully.

In the most distant room of all, a dark, tiny closet, Miss Lefain opened a deep cupboard and brought out a Crown Derby plate which her guest received with a spasm of joy, for it was actually that missing from her cherished set.

"It's very good of you," she said in delight. "Won't you take something for it, or let me do something for you?"

"You might come and see me again," replied Miss Lefain wistfully.

"Oh, yes, of course I should like to come and see you again—"

But now that she had got what she had really come for, the plate, Martha Pym wanted to be gone; it was really very dismal and depressing in the house and she began to notice a fearful smell—the place had been shut up too long, there was something damp rotting somewhere, in this horrid little dark closet no doubt.

"I really must be going," she said hurriedly.

Miss Lefain turned as if to cling to her, but Martha Pym moved quickly away.

"Dear me," wailed the old lady. "Why are you in such haste?"

"There's—a smell," murmured Miss Pym rather faintly.

She found herself hastening down the stairs, with Miss Lefain complaining behind her.

"How peculiar people are—*she* used to talk of a smell—"

"Well, you must notice it yourself."

Miss Pym was in the hall; the old woman had not followed her, but stood in the semidarkness at the head of the stairs, a pale shapeless figure.

Martha Pym hated to be rude and ungrateful but she could not stay another moment; she hurried away and was in her cart in a moment—really—that smell—

"Good-bye!" she called out with false cheerfulness, "and thank you *so* much!"

There was no answer from the house.

Miss Pym drove on; she was rather upset and took another way than that by which she had come, a way that led past a little house raised above the marsh; she was glad to think that the poor old creature at "Hartleys" had such near neighbors, and she reined up the horse, dubious as to whether she should call someone and tell them that poor old Miss Lefain really wanted a little looking after, alone in a house like that, and plainly not quite right in her head.

A young woman, attracted by the sound of the governess cart, came to the door of the house and seeing Miss Pym called out, asking if she wanted the keys of the house?

"What house?" asked Miss Pym.

"'Hartleys,' mum, they don't put a board out, as no one is likely to pass, but it's to be sold. Miss Lefain wants to sell or let it—"

"I've just been up to see her—"

"Oh, no, mum—she's been away a year, abroad somewhere, couldn't stand the place, it's been empty since then, I just run in every day and keep things tidy—"

Loquacious and curious the young woman had come to the fence; Miss Pym had stopped her horse.

"Miss Lefain is there now," she said. "She must have just come back—"

"She wasn't there this morning, mum, 'tisn't likely she'd come, either—fair scared she was, mum, fair chased away, didn't dare move her china. Can't say I've noticed anything myself, but I never stay long—and there's a smell—"

"Yes," murmured Martha Pym faintly, "there's a smell. What—what—chased her away?"

The young woman, even in that lonely place, lowered her voice.

"Well, as you aren't thinking of taking the place, she got an idea in her head that old Sir James—well, he couldn't bear to leave 'Hartleys,' mum, he's buried in the garden, and she thought he was after her, chasing round them bits of china—"

"Oh!" cried Miss Pym.

"Some of it used to be his, she found a lot stuffed away, he said they were to be left in 'Hartleys,' but Miss Lefain would have the things sold, I believe—that's years ago—"

"Yes, yes," said Miss Pym with a sick look. "You don't know what he was like, do you?"

"No, mum—but I've heard tell he was very stout and very old—I wonder who it was you saw up at 'Hartleys'?"

Miss Pym took a Crown Derby plate from her bag.

"You might take that back when you go," she whispered. "I shan't want it, after all—"

Before the astonished young woman could answer Miss Pym had darted off across the marsh; that short hair, that earth-stained robe, the white socks, "I generally live in the garden—"

Miss Pym drove away, breakneck speed, frantically resolving to mention to no one that she had paid a visit to "Hartleys," nor lightly again to bring up the subject of ghosts.

She shook and shuddered in the damp, trying to get out of her clothes and her nostrils—that indescribable smell.

The Cafeteria

by Isaac Bashevis Singer

Issac Bashevis Singer (1904–1991) drew upon the tumult and richness of Jewish life in Eastern Europe and elsewhere to create the immensely sophisticated novels and stories that won him the 1978 Nobel Prize in literature. Singer's characters often are cynical mystics—the kind of people who inhabit a world plagued by disaster and visited by miracles.

Even though I have reached the point where a great part of my earnings is given away in taxes, I still have the habit of eating in cafeterias when I am by myself. I like to take a tray with a tin knife, fork, spoon, and paper napkin and to choose at the counter the food I enjoy. Besides, I meet there the *landsleit* from Poland, as well as all kinds of literary beginners and readers who know Yiddish. The moment I sit down at a table, they come over. "Hello, Aaron!" they greet me, and we talk about Yiddish literature, the Holocaust, the state of Israel, and often about acquaintances who were eating rice pudding or stewed prunes the last time I was here and are already in their graves. Since I seldom read a paper, I learn this news only later. Each time, I am startled, but at my age one has to be ready for such tidings. The food sticks in the throat; we look at one another in confusion, and our eyes ask mutely, Whose turn is next? Soon we begin to chew again. I am often reminded of a scene in a film about Africa. A lion attacks a herd of zebras and kills one. The frightened zebras run for a while and then they stop and start to graze again. Do they have a choice?

I cannot spend too long with these Yiddishists, because I am always busy. I am writing a novel, a story, an article. I have to lecture today or tomorrow; my datebook is crowded with all kinds of appointments for weeks and months in advance. It can happen that an hour after I leave the cafeteria I am on a train to Chicago or flying to California. But meanwhile we converse in the mother language and I hear of intrigues and pettiness about which, from a moral point of view, it would be better not to be informed. Everyone tries in his own way with all his means to grab as many honors and as much money and prestige as he can. None of us learns from all these deaths. Old age does not cleanse us. We don't repent at the gate of hell.

I have been moving around in this neighborhood for over thirty years—as long as I lived in Poland. I know each block, each house. There has been little building here on uptown Broadway in the last decades, and I have the illusion of having put down roots here. I have spoken in most of the synagogues. They know me in some of the stores and in the vegetarian restaurants. Women with whom I have had affairs live on the side streets. Even the pigeons know me; the moment I come out with a bag of feed, they begin to fly toward me from blocks away. It is an area that stretches from Ninety-sixth Street to Seventy-second Street and from Central Park to Riverside Drive. Almost every day on my walk after lunch, I pass the funeral parlor that waits for us and all our ambitions and illusions. Sometimes I imagine that the funeral parlor is also a kind of cafeteria where one gets a quick eulogy or Kaddish on the way to eternity.

The cafeteria people I meet are mostly men: old bachelors like myself, would-be writers, retired teachers, some with dubious doctorate titles, a rabbi without a congregation, a painter of Jewish themes, a few translators—all immigrants from Poland or Russia. I seldom know their names. One of them disappears and I think he is already in the next world; suddenly he reappears and he tells me that he has tried to settle in Tel Aviv or Los Angeles. Again he eats his rice pudding, sweetens his coffee with saccharin. He has a few more wrinkles, but he tells the same stories and makes the same gestures. It may happen that he takes a paper from his pocket and reads me a poem he has written.

It was in the fifties that a woman appeared in the group who looked younger than the rest of us. She must have been in her early thirties; she was short, slim, with a girlish face, brown hair that she wore in a bun, a short nose, and dimples in her cheeks. Her eyes were hazel—actually, of an indefinite color. She dressed in a modest European way. She spoke Polish, Russian, and an idiomatic Yiddish. She always carried Yiddish newspapers and magazines. She had been in a prison camp in Russia and had spent some time in the camps in Germany before she obtained a visa for the United States. The men all hovered around her. They didn't let her pay the check. They gallantly brought her coffee and cheese cake. They listened to her talk and jokes. She had returned from the devastation still gay. She was introduced to me. Her name was Esther. I didn't know if she was unmarried, a widow, a divorcée. She told me she was working in a factory, where she sorted buttons. This fresh young woman did not fit into the group of elderly has-beens. It was also hard to understand why she couldn't find a better job than sorting buttons in New Jersey. But I didn't ask too many questions. She told me that she had read my writing while still in Poland, and later in the camps in Germany after the war. She said to me, "You are my writer."

The moment she uttered those words I imagined I was in love with her. We were sitting alone (the other man at our table had gone to make a telephone call), and I said, "For such words I must kiss you."

"Well, what are you waiting for?"

She gave me both a kiss and a bite.

I said, "You are a ball of fire."

"Yes, fire from Gehenna."

A few days later, she invited me to her home. She lived on a street between Broadway and Riverside Drive with her father, who had no legs and sat in a wheelchair. His legs had been frozen in Siberia. He had tried to run away from one of Stalin's slave camps in the winter of 1944. He looked like a strong man, had a head of thick white hair, a ruddy face, and eyes full of energy. He spoke in a swaggering fashion, with boyish boastfulness and a cheerful laugh. In an hour, he told me his story. He was born in White Russia but he had lived long years in Warsaw, Lodz, and Vilna. In the beginning of the thirties, he became a Communist and soon afterward a functionary in the Party. In 1939 he escaped to Russia with his daughter. His wife and the other children remained in Nazi-occupied Warsaw. In Russia, somebody denounced him as a Trotskyite and he was sent to mine gold in the north. The G.P.U. sent people there to die. Even the strongest could not survive the cold and hunger for more than a year. They were exiled without a sentence. They died together: Zionists, Bundists, members of the Polish Socialist Party, Ukrainian Nationalists, and just refugees, all caught because of the labor shortage. They often died of scurvy or beriberi. Boris Merkin, Esther's father, spoke about this as if it were a big joke. He called the Stalinists outcasts, bandits, sycophants. He assured me that had it not been for the United States Hitler would have overrun all of Russia. He told how prisoners tricked the guards to get an extra piece of bread or a double portion of watery soup, and what methods were used in picking lice.

Esther called out, "Father, enough!"

"What's the matter—am I lying?"

"One can have enough even of kreplaech."

"Daughter, you did it yourself."

When Esther went to the kitchen to make tea, I learned from her father that she had had a husband in Russia—a Polish Jew who had volunteered in the Red Army and perished in the war. Here in New York she was courted by a refugee, a former smuggler in Germany who had opened a bookbinding factory and become rich. "Persuade her to marry him," Boris Merkin said to me. "It would be good for me, too."

"Maybe she doesn't love him."

"There is no such thing as love. Give me a cigarette. In the camp, people climbed on one another like worms."

I had invited Esther to supper, but she called to say she had the grippe and must remain in bed. Then in a few days' time a situation arose that made me leave for Israel. On the way back, I stopped over in London and Paris. I wanted to write to Esther, but I had lost her address. When I returned to New York, I tried to call her, but there was no telephone listing for Boris Merkin or Esther Merkin—father and daughter must have been boarders in somebody else's apartment. Weeks passed and she did not show up in the cafeteria. I asked the group about her; nobody knew where she was. "She has most probably married that bookbinder," I said to myself. One evening, I went to the cafeteria with the premonition that I would find Esther there. I saw a black wall and boarded windows—the cafeteria had burned. The old bachelors were no doubt meeting in another cafeteria, or an Automat. But where? To search is not in my nature. I had plenty of complications without Esther.

The summer passed; it was winter. Late one day, I walked by the cafeteria and again saw lights, a counter, guests. The owners had rebuilt. I entered, took a check, and saw Esther sitting alone at a table reading a Yiddish newspaper. She did not notice me, and I observed her for a while. She wore a man's fur fez and a jacket trimmed with a faded fur collar. She looked pale, as though recuperating from a sickness. Could that grippe have been the start of a serious illness? I went over to her table and asked, "What's new in buttons?"

She started and smiled. Then she called out, "Miracles do happen!"

"Where have you been?"

"Where did you disappear to?" she replied. "I thought you were still abroad."

"Where are our cafeterianiks?"

"They now go to the cafeteria on Fifty-seventh Street and Eighth Avenue. They only reopened this place yesterday."

"May I bring you a cup of coffee?"

"I drink too much coffee. All right."

I went to get her coffee and a large egg cookie. While I stood at the counter, I turned my head and looked at her. Esther had taken off her mannish fur hat and smoothed her hair. She folded the newspaper, which meant that she was ready to talk. She got up and tilted the

other chair against the table as a sign that the seat was taken. When I
sat down, Esther said, "You left without saying goodbye, and there I
was about to knock at the pearly gates of heaven."

"What happened?"

"Oh, the grippe became pneumonia. They gave me penicillin, and I
am one of those who cannot take it. I got a rash all over my body. My
father, too, is not well."

"What's the matter with your father?"

"High blood pressure. He had a kind of stroke and his mouth
became all crooked."

"Oh, I'm sorry. Do you still work with buttons?"

"Yes, with buttons. At least I don't have to use my head, only my
hands. I can think my own thoughts."

"What do you think about?"

"What not. The other workers are all Puerto Ricans. They rattle away
in Spanish from morning to night."

"Who takes care of your father?"

"Who? Nobody. I come home in the evening to make supper. He
has one desire—to marry me off for my own good and, perhaps, for his
comfort, but I can't marry a man I don't love."

"What is love?"

"You ask me! You write novels about it. But you're a man—I assume
you really don't know what it is. A woman is a piece of merchandise to
you. To me a man who talks nonsense or smiles like an idiot is repulsive.
I would rather die than live with him. And a man who goes from one
woman to another is not for me. I don't want to share with anybody."

"I'm afraid a time is coming when everybody will."

"That is not for me."

"What kind of person was your husband?"

"How did you know I had a husband? My father, I suppose. The
minute I leave the room, he prattles. My husband believed in things
and was ready to die for them. He was not exactly my type but I
respected him and loved him, too. He wanted to die and he died like
a hero. What else can I say?"

"And the others?"

"There were no others. Men were after me. The way people behaved in the war—you will never know. They lost all shame. On the bunks near me one time, a mother lay with one man and her daughter with another. People were like beasts—worse than beasts. In the middle of it all, I dreamed about love. Now I have even stopped dreaming. The men who come here are terrible bores. Most of them are half mad, too. One of them tried to read me a forty-page poem. I almost fainted."

"I wouldn't read you anything I'd written."

"I've been told how you behave—no!"

"No is no. Drink your coffee."

"You don't even try to persuade me. Most men around here plague you and you can't get rid of them. In Russia people suffered, but I have never met as many maniacs there as in New York City. The building where I live is a madhouse. My neighbors are lunatics. They accuse each other of all kinds of things. They sing, cry, break dishes. One of them jumped out of the window and killed herself. She was having an affair with a boy twenty years younger. In Russia the problem was to escape the lice; here you're surrounded by insanity."

We drank coffee and shared the egg cookie. Esther put down her cup. "I can't believe that I'm sitting with you at this table. I read all your articles under all your pen names. You tell so much about yourself I have the feeling I've known you for years. Still, you are a riddle to me."

"Men and women can never understand one another."

"No—I cannot understand my own father. Sometimes he is a complete stranger to me. He won't live long."

"Is he so sick?"

"It's everything together. He's lost the will to live. Why live without legs, without friends, without a family? They have all perished. He sits and reads the newspapers all day long. He acts as though he were interested in what's going on in the world. His ideals are gone, but he still hopes for a just revolution. How can a revolution help him? I myself never put my hopes in any movement or party. How can we hope when everything ends in death?"

"Hope in itself is a proof that there is no death."

"Yes, I know you often write about this. For me, death is the only comfort. What do the dead do? They continue to drink coffee and eat egg cookies? They still read newspapers? A life after death would be nothing but a joke."

Some of the cafeterianiks came back to the rebuilt cafeteria. New people appeared—all of them Europeans. They launched into long discussions in Yiddish, Polish, Russian, even Hebrew. Some of those who came from Hungary mixed German, Hungarian, Yiddish-German— then all of a sudden they began to speak plain Galician Yiddish. They asked to have their coffee in glasses, and held lumps of sugar between their teeth when they drank. Many of them were my readers. They introduced themselves and reproached me for all kinds of literary errors: I contradicted myself, went too far in descriptions of sex, described Jews in such a way that anti-Semites could use it for propaganda. They told me their experiences in the ghettos, in the Nazi concentration camps, in Russia. They pointed out one another. "Do you see that fellow—in Russia he immediately became a Stalinist. He denounced his own friends. Here in America he has switched to anti-Bolshevism." The one who was spoken about seemed to sense that he was being maligned, because the moment my informant left he took his cup of coffee and his rice pudding, sat down at my table, and said, "Don't believe a word of what you are told. They invent all kinds of lies. What could you do in a country where the rope was always around your neck? You had to adjust yourself if you wanted to live and not die somewhere in Kazakhstan. To get a bowl of soup or a place to stay you had to sell your soul."

There was a table with a group of refugees who ignored me. They were not interested in literature and journalism but strictly in business. In Germany they had been smugglers. They seemed to be doing shady business here, too; they whispered to one another and winked, counted their money, wrote long lists of numbers. Somebody pointed out one of them. "He had a store in Auschwitz."

"What do you mean, a store?"

"God help us. He kept his merchandise in the straw where he slept —a rotten potato, sometimes a piece of soap, a tin spoon, a little fat. Still, he did business. Later, in Germany, he became such a big smuggler they once took forty thousand dollars away from him."

Sometimes months passed between my visits to the cafeteria. A year or two had gone by (perhaps three or four; I lost count), and Esther did not show up. I asked about her a few times. Someone said that she was going to the cafeteria on Forty-second Street; another had heard that she was married. I learned that some of the cafeterianiks had died. They were beginning to settle down in the United States, had remarried, opened businesses, workshops, even had children again. Then came cancer or a heart attack. The result of the Hitler and Stalin years, it was said.

One day, I entered the cafeteria and saw Esther. She was sitting alone at a table. It was the same Esther. She was even wearing the same fur hat, but a strand of gray hair fell over her forehead. How strange—the fur hat, too, seemed to have grayed. The other cafeterianiks did not appear to be interested in her any more, or they did not know her. Her face told of the time that had passed. There were shadows under her eyes. Her gaze was no longer so clear. Around her mouth was an expression that could be called bitterness, disenchantment. I greeted her. She smiled, but her smile immediately faded away. I asked, "What happened to you?"

"Oh, I'm still alive."

"May I sit down?"

"Please—certainly."

"May I bring you a cup of coffee?"

"No. Well, if you insist."

I noticed that she was smoking, and also that she was reading not the newspaper to which I contribute but a competition paper. She had gone over to the enemy. I brought her coffee and for myself stewed prunes—a remedy for constipation. I sat down. "Where were you all this time? I have asked for you."

"Really? Thank you."

"What happened?"

"Nothing good." She looked at me. I knew that she saw in me what I saw in her: the slow wilting of the flesh. She said, "You have no hair but you are white."

For a while we were silent. Then I said, "Your father—" and as I said it I knew that her father was not alive.

Esther said, "He has been dead for almost a year."

"Do you still sort buttons?"

"No, I became an operator in a dress shop."

"What happened to you personally, may I ask?"

"Oh nothing—absolutely nothing. You will not believe it, but I was sitting here thinking about you. I have fallen into some kind of trap. I don't know what to call it. I thought perhaps you could advise me. Do you still have the patience to listen to the troubles of little people like me? No, I didn't mean to insult you. I even doubted you would remember me. To make it short, I work but work is growing more difficult for me. I suffer from arthritis. I feel as if my bones would crack. I wake up in the morning and can't sit up. One doctor tells me that it's a disc in my back, others try to cure my nerves. One took X-rays and says that I have a tumor. He wanted me to go to the hospital for a few weeks, but I'm in no hurry for an operation. Suddenly a little lawyer showed up. He is a refugee himself and is connected with the German government. You know they're now giving reparation money. It's true that I escaped to Russia, but I'm a victim of the Nazis just the same. Besides, they don't know my biography so exactly. I could get a pension plus a few thousand dollars, but my dislocated disc is no good for the purpose because I got it later—after the camps. This lawyer says my only chance is to convince them that I am ruined psychically. It's the bitter truth, but how can you prove it? The German doctors, the neurologists, the psychiatrists require proof. Everything has to be according to the textbooks—just so and no different. The lawyer wants me to play insane. Naturally, he gets twenty percent of the reparation money—maybe more. Why he needs so much money I don't understand. He's already in his seventies, an old bachelor. He tried to make love to me and whatnot. He's half meshugga himself.

But how can I play insane when actually I *am* insane? The whole thing revolts me and I'm afraid it will really drive me crazy. I hate swindle. But this shyster pursues me. I don't sleep. When the alarm rings in the morning, I wake up as shattered as I used to be in Russia when I had to walk to the forest and saw logs at four in the morning. Naturally, I take sleeping pills—if I didn't, I couldn't sleep at all. That is more or less the situation."

"Why don't you get married? You are still a good-looking woman."

"Well, the old question—there is nobody. It's too late. If you knew how I felt, you wouldn't ask such a question."

A few weeks passed. Snow had been falling. After the snow came rain, then frost. I stood at my window and looked out at Broadway. The passers-by half walked, half slipped. Cars moved slowly. The sky above the roofs shone violet, without a moon, without stars, and even though it was eight o'clock in the evening the light and the emptiness reminded me of dawn. The stores were deserted. For a moment, I had the feeling I was in Warsaw. The telephone rang and I rushed to answer it as I did ten, twenty, thirty years ago—still expecting the good tidings that a telephone call was about to bring me. I said hello, but there was no answer and I was seized by the fear that some evil power was trying to keep back the good news at the last minute. Then I heard a stammering. A woman's voice muttered my name.

"Yes, it is I."

"Excuse me for disturbing you. My name is Esther. We met a few weeks ago in the cafeteria—"

"Esther!" I exclaimed.

"I don't know how I got the courage to phone you. I need to talk to you about something. Naturally, if you have the time and—please forgive my presumption."

"No presumption. Would you like to come to my apartment?"

"If I will not be interrupting. It's difficult to talk in the cafeteria. It's noisy and there are eavesdroppers. What I want to tell you is a secret I wouldn't trust to anyone else."

"Please, come up."

I gave Esther directions. Then I tried to make order in my apartment, but I soon realized this was impossible. Letters, manuscripts lay around on tables and chairs. In the corners books and magazines were piled high. I opened the closets and threw inside whatever was under my hand: jackets, pants, shirts, shoes, slippers. I picked up an envelope and to my amazement saw that it had never been opened. I tore it open and found a check. "What's the matter with me—have I lost my mind?" I said out loud. I tried to read the letter that came with the check, but I had misplaced my glasses; my fountain pen was gone, too. Well—and where were my keys? I heard a bell ring and I didn't know whether it was the door or the telephone. I opened the door and saw Esther. It must have been snowing again, because her hat and the shoulders of her coat were trimmed with white. I asked her in, and my neighbor, the divorcée, who spied on me openly with no shame—and, God knows, with no sense of purpose—opened her door and stared at my guest.

Esther removed her boots and I took her coat and put it on the case of the Encyclopaedia Britannica. I shoved a few manuscripts off the sofa so she could sit down. I said, "In my house there is sheer chaos."

"It doesn't matter."

I sat in an armchair strewn with socks and handkerchiefs. For a while we spoke about the weather, about the danger of being out in New York at night—even early in the evening. Then Esther said, "Do you remember the time I spoke to you about my lawyer—that I had to go to a psychiatrist because of the reparation money?"

"Yes, I remember."

"I didn't tell you everything. It was too wild. It still seems unbelievable, even to me. Don't interrupt me, I implore you. I'm not completely healthy—I may even say that I'm sick—but I know the difference between fact and illusion. I haven't slept for nights, and I kept wondering whether I should call you or not. I decided not to—but this evening it occurred to me that if I couldn't trust you with a thing like this, then there is no one I could talk to. I read you and I know that you have a sense of the great mysteries—" Esther said all this stammering and with pauses. For a moment her eyes smiled, and then they became sad and wavering.

I said, "You can tell me everything."

"I am afraid that you'll think me insane."

"I swear I will not."

Esther bit her lower lip. "I want you to know that I saw Hitler," she said.

Even though I was prepared for something unusual, my throat constricted. "When—where?"

"You see, you are frightened already. It happened three years ago—almost four. I saw him here on Broadway."

"On the street?"

"In the cafeteria."

I tried to swallow the lump in my throat. "Most probably someone resembling him," I said finally.

"I knew you would say that. But remember, you've promised to listen. You recall the fire in the cafeteria?"

"Yes, certainly."

"The fire has to do with it. Since you don't believe me anyhow, why draw it out? It happened this way. That night I didn't sleep. Usually when I can't sleep, I get up and make tea, or I try to read a book, but this time some power commanded me to get dressed and go out. I can't explain to you how I dared walk on Broadway at that late hour. It must have been two or three o'clock. I reached the cafeteria, thinking perhaps it stays open all night. I tried to look in, but the large window was covered by a curtain. There was a pale glow inside. I tried the revolving door and it turned. I went in and saw a scene I will not forget to the last day of my life. The tables were shoved together and around them sat men in white robes, like doctors or orderlies, all with swastikas on their sleeves. At the head sat Hitler. I beg you to hear me out—even a deranged person sometimes deserves to be listened to. They all spoke German. They didn't see me. They were busy with the Führer. It grew quiet and he started to talk. That abominable voice—I heard it many times on the radio. I didn't make out exactly what he said. I was too terrified to take it in. Suddenly one of his henchmen looked back at me and jumped up from his chair. How I came out alive I will never know. I ran with all my strength, and I was trembling all over. When I got home, I said to myself, 'Esther, you are not right in the head.' I still don't know how I lived through that night. The next morning, I didn't go straight to work but walked to the cafeteria to see if it was really there. Such an experience makes a person doubt his own senses. When I arrived, I found the place had burned down. When I saw this, I knew it had to do with what I had seen. Those who were there wanted all traces erased. These are the plain facts. I have no reason to fabricate such queer things."

We were both silent. Then I said, "You had a vision."

"What do you mean, a vision?"

"The past is not lost. An image from years ago remained present somewhere in the fourth dimension and it reached you just at that moment."

"As far as I know, Hitler never wore a long white robe."

"Perhaps he did."

"Why did the cafeteria burn down just that night?" Esther asked.

"It could be that the fire evoked the vision."

"There was no fire then. Somehow I foresaw that you would give me this kind of explanation. If this was a vision, my sitting here with you is also a vision."

"It couldn't have been anything else. Even if Hitler is living and is hiding out in the United States, he is not likely to meet his cronies at a cafeteria on Broadway. Besides, the cafeteria belongs to a Jew."

"I saw him as I am seeing you now."

"You had a glimpse back in time."

"Well, let it be so. But since then I have had no rest. I keep thinking about it. If I am destined to lose my mind, this will drive me to it."

The telephone rang and I jumped up with a start. It was a wrong number. I sat down again. "What about the psychiatrist your lawyer sent you to? Tell it to him and you'll get full compensation."

Esther looked at me sidewise and unfriendly. "I know what you mean. I haven't fallen that low yet."

• • •

I was afraid that Esther would continue to call me. I even planned to change my telephone number. But weeks and months passed and I never heard from her or saw her. I didn't go to the cafeteria. But I often thought about her. How can the brain produce such nightmares? What goes on in that little marrow behind the skull? And what guarantee do I have that the same sort of thing will not happen to me? And how do we know that the human species will not end like this? I have played with the idea that all of humanity suffers from schizophrenia. Along with the atom, the personality of Homo sapiens has been splitting. When it comes to technology, the brain still functions, but in everything else degeneration has begun. They are all insane: the Communists, the Fascists, the preachers of democracy, the writers, the painters, the clergy, the atheists. Soon technology, too, will disintegrate. Buildings will collapse, power plants will stop generating electricity. Generals will drop atomic bombs on their own populations. Mad revolutionaries will run in the streets, crying fantastic slogans. I have often thought that it would begin in New York. This metropolis has all the symptoms of a mind gone berserk.

But since insanity has not yet taken over altogether, one has to act as though there were still order—according to Vaihinger's principle of "as if." I continued with my scribbling. I delivered manuscripts to the publisher. I lectured. Four times a year, I sent checks to the federal government, the state. What was left after my expenses I put in the savings bank. A teller entered some numbers in my bankbook and this meant that I was provided for. Somebody printed a few lines in a magazine or newspaper, and this signified that my value as a writer had gone up. I saw with amazement that all my efforts turned into paper. My apartment was one big wastepaper basket. From day to day, all this paper was getting drier and more parched. I woke up at night fearful that it would ignite. There was not an hour when I did not hear the sirens of fire engines.

A year after I had last seen Esther, I was going to Toronto to read a paper about Yiddish in the second half of the nineteenth century. I put a few shirts in my valise as well as papers of all kinds, among them one that made me a citizen of the United States. I had enough paper money in my pocket to pay for a taxi to Grand Central. But the taxis seemed to be taken. Those that were not refused to stop. Didn't the drivers see me? Had I suddenly become one of those who see and are not seen? I decided to take the subway. On my way, I saw Esther. She was not alone but with someone I had known years ago, soon after I arrived in the United States. He was a frequenter of a cafeteria on East Broadway. He used to sit at a table, express opinions, criticize, grumble. He was a small man, with sunken cheeks the color of brick, and bulging eyes. He was angry at the new writers. He belittled the old ones. He rolled his own cigarettes and dropped ashes into the plates from which we ate. Almost two decades had passed since I had last seen him. Suddenly he appears with Esther. He was even holding her arm. I had never seen Esther look so well. She was wearing a new coat, a new hat. She smiled at me and nodded. I wanted to stop her, but my watch showed that it was late. I barely managed to catch the train. In my bedroom, the bed was already made. I undressed and went to sleep.

In the middle of the night, I awoke. My car was being switched, and I almost fell out of bed. I could not sleep any more and I tried to remember the name of the little man I had seen with Esther. But I was unable to. The thing I did remember was that even thirty years ago he had been far from young. He had come to the United States in 1905 after the revolution in Russia. In Europe, he had a reputation as a speaker and public figure. How old must he be now? According to my calculations, he had to be in the late eighties—perhaps even ninety. Is it possible that Esther could be intimate with such an old man? But this evening he had not looked old. The longer I brooded about it in the darkness, the stranger the encounter seemed to me. I even imagined that somewhere in a newspaper I had read that he had died. Do corpses walk around on Broadway? This would mean that Esther, too, was not living. I raised the window shade and sat up and looked out into the night—black, impenetrable, without a moon. A few stars ran along with the train for a while and then they disappeared. A lighted factory emerged; I saw machines but no operators. Then it was swallowed in the darkness and another group of stars began to follow the train. I was turning with the earth on its axis. I was circling with it around the sun and moving in the direction of a constellation whose name I had forgotten. Is there no death? Or is there no life?

I thought about what Esther had told me of seeing Hitler in the cafeteria. It had seemed utter nonsense, but now I began to reappraise the idea. If time and space are nothing more than forms of perception, as Kant argues, and quality, quantity, causality are only categories of thinking, why shouldn't Hitler confer with his Nazis in a cafeteria on Broadway? Esther didn't sound insane. She had seen a piece of reality that the heavenly censorship prohibits as a rule. She had caught a glimpse behind the curtain of the phenomena. I regretted that I had not asked for more details.

In Toronto, I had little time to ponder these matters, but when I returned to New York I went to the cafeteria for some private investigation. I met only one man I knew: a rabbi who had become an agnostic and given up his job. I asked him about Esther. He said, "The pretty little woman who used to come here?"

"Yes."

"I heard that she committed suicide."

"When—how?"

"I don't know. Perhaps we are not speaking about the same person."

No matter how many questions I asked and how much I described Esther, everything remained vague. Some young woman who used to come here had turned on the gas and made an end of herself—that was all the ex-rabbi could tell me.

I decided not to rest until I knew for certain what had happened to Esther and also to that half writer, half politician I remembered from East Broadway. But I grew busier from day to day. The cafeteria closed. The neighborhood changed. Years have passed and I have never seen Esther again. Yes, corpses do walk on Broadway. But why did Esther choose that particular corpse? She could have got a better bargain even in this world.

a c k n o w l e d g m e n t s

Many people made this anthology.

At Thunder's Mouth Press and Avalon Publishing Group:
Neil Ortenberg and Susan Reich offered vital support and expertise.
Dan O'Connor and Ghadah Alrawi also were indispensable.

At Balliett & Fitzgerald Inc.:
Tom Dyja suggested several of the selections, and with f-stop
Fitzgerald lent critical intellectual and moral support. Sue Canavan created the book's look. Maria Fernandez oversaw production with help
from Mike Walters and Paul Paddock.

At the Writing Company:
Nate Hardcastle played a vital role in finding and choosing the selections for this book. Nat May and John Bishop provided research assistance. Taylor Smith, Mark Klimek and Deborah Satter also helped with
the book, and took up slack on other projects.

At the Thomas Memorial Library in Cape Elizabeth, Maine:
Susan Sandberg and other librarians cheerfully worked to locate and
borrow books from across the country.

At Shawneric.com:
Shawneric Hachey handled permissions with his usual aplomb and
found exactly the right photograph for each selection; he also scanned
copy.

At various publishing companies and literary agencies:
Many people helped. Thanks especially to Peter London at Harper
Collins for some last-minute fast footwork.

Among friends and family:
My father read and told me ghost stories a long time ago.
Jennifer Schwamm Willis lent me her judgement—again.
Will Balliett, my collaborator, made it a pleasure—again.

Finally, I am very grateful to the writers whose work appears in this
book.

We gratefully acknowledge all those who gave permission for written material to appear in this book. We have made every effort to trace and contact copyright holders. If an error or omission is brought to our notice we will be pleased to remedy the situation in future editions of this book. For further information, please contact the publisher.

Excerpt from *Asylum* by Patrick McGrath. Copyright © 1997 by Patrick McGrath. Reprinted by permission of Random House, Inc. ✤ Excerpt from *The Haunting of Hill House* by Shirley Jackson. Copyright © 1959 by Shirley Jackson, renewed © 1987 by Laurence Hyman, Barry Hyman, Sarah Webster, Joanne Schnurer. Used by permission of Viking Penguin, a division of Penguin Putnam, Inc. and the Linda Allen Literary Agency, San Francisco. ✤ Excerpt from *The Wasp Factory* by Iain Banks. Reprinted by permission of Scribner, a Division of Simon & Schuster. Copyright © 1984 by Iain Banks. ✤ "Seaton's Aunt", excerpted from *The Riddle* by Walter de la Mare. Used by permission of The Society of Authors, London. ✤ "Zombies" from *Tell My Horse* by Zora Neale Hurston. Copyright © 1990 by The Estate of Zora Neale Hurston. Used by permission of Harper Collins Publishers, New York. ✤ "A Distant Episode" from *A Distant Episode: The Selected Stories* by Paul Bowles. Copyright © 1988 by Paul Bowles. Used by permission of William Morris Agency, New York, and Peter Owen Publishers, London. ✤ Excerpt from *My Idea of Fun* by Will Self. Copyright © 1993 by Will Self. Used by permission of Grove/Atlantic, Inc. ✤ "The Cicerones" by Robert Aickman. Copyright © 2000 by The Estate of Robert Aickman c/o Artellus Limited, 30 Dorset House, Gloucester Place, London, NW15AD. ✤ Excerpt from *Communion: A True Story* by Whitley Strieber. Copyright © 1987 by Whitley Strieber. Used by permission of William Morrow & Company, a division of Harper Collins Publishers, New York. ✤ Excerpt from *The Shining* by Stephen King. Copyright © 1977 by Stephen King. Used by permission of Doubleday, a division of Random House, Inc., and Hodder & Stoughton, London. ✤ "A Good Man is Hard to Find" from *A Good Man is Hard to Find and Other Stories*

379

b i b l i o g r a p h y

The selections used in this anthology were taken from the editions listed below. In some cases, other editions may be easier to find. Hard to find or out-of-print titles often can be acquired through inter-library loan services. Internet booksellers also may be able to locate these books.

Balliett, Blue. *Nantucket Hauntings*. Camden, Maine: Down East Books, 1990.

Banks, Iain. *The Wasp Factory: A Novel*. New York: Simon & Schuster, 1988.

Black Water: The Book of Fantastic Literature. Edited by Alberto Manguel. New York: Clarkson Potter, 1983 (for "Seaton's Aunt" by Walter de la Mare.)

Christmas Ghosts. Edited by Kathryn Cramer and David G. Hartwell. New York: Dell Publishing, 1988. (For "The Crown Derby Plate" by Marjorie Bowen)

Famous Ghost Stories. New York: Random House, 1944. (For "The Monkey's Paw" by W.W. Jacobs.)

Frost, Robert. *Robert Frost*. New York: Borzoi Books, 1997.

Hurston, Zora Neale. *Folklore, Memoirs, and Other Writings*. New York: The Library of America, 1995.

Jackson, Shirley. *The Haunting of Hill House*. New York: Viking, 1959.

King, Stephen. *The Shining*. New York: Signet Books, 1978.

Kipling, Rudyard. *Traffics and Discoveries*. New York: Penguin Classics, 1987.

McGrath, Patrick. *Asylum*. New York: Vintage Contemporaries, 1998.

Norton Book of Ghost Stories, The. Edited by Brad Leithauser. New York: W.W. Norton & Company, 1994. (For "The Beckoning Fair One" by Oliver Onions.)

O'Connor, Flannery. *A Good Man Is Hard to Find and Other Stories*. Orlando, FL: Harcourt, Brace & Company, 1955.

Oxford Book of American Short Stories, The. Edited by Joyce Carol Oates. New York: Oxford University Press, 1992. (For "A Distant Episode" by Paul Bowles.)

Oxford Book of English Ghost Stories, The. Chosen by Michael Cox and R.A. Gilbert. New York: Oxford University Press, 1989. (For "The Yellow Wallpaper" by Charlotte Perkins Gilman and "Smee" by A.M. Burrage.)

Poe, Edgar Allen. *The Complete Stories*. New York: Borzoi Books, 1992.

Self, Will. *My Idea of Fun*. New York: Atlantic Monthly Press, 1993.

Singer, Isaac Bashevis. *The Collected Stories of Isaac Bashevis Singer.* New York: Farrar, Straus & Giroux, 1982.

Strieber, Whitley. *Communion: A True Story.* New York: Avon Books, 1995.

Sub Rosa. London: Victor Gollancz, 1968 (for "The Cicerones" by Robert Aickman.)

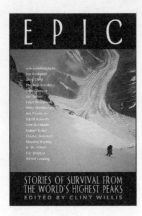

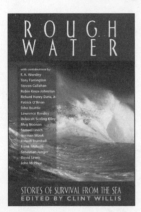

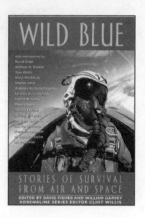